P9-ELO-073

THE HEALING

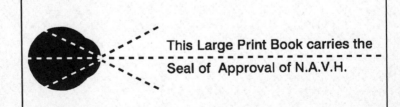

This Large Print Book carries the
Seal of Approval of N.A.V.H.

THE HEALING

JONATHAN ODELL

WHEELER PUBLISHING
A part of Gale, Cengage Learning

Detroit • New York • San Francisco • New Haven, Conn • Waterville, Maine • London

GALE
CENGAGE Learning

LIBRARY OF CONGRESS CATALOGING-IN-PUBLICATION DATA

Odell, Jonathan, 1951–
   The healing / by Jonathan Odell.
     pages ; cm
     ISBN-13: 978-1-4104-4783-8 (hardcover)
     ISBN-10: 1-4104-4783-9 (hardcover)
     1. Healing—Fiction. 2. Catatonia—Fiction. 3. Loss (Psychology)—Fiction.
4. Mississippi—Fiction. 5. Large type books. I. Title.
PS3615.D454H43 2012
813'.6—dc23   2011052841

Published in 2012 by arrangement with Nan A. Talese, an imprint of Knopf Doubleday Publishing Group, a division of Random House, Inc.

To Jim
We promised to make up as we go.
It's been a great trip.

"The world is not imperfect or slowly evolving along a long path to perfection. No, it is perfect at every moment; every sin already carries grace within it."

— HERMANN HESSE, *Siddhartha*

CHAPTER 1

1933

The winter dampness crept through the kitchen door, chilling Gran Gran through her worn, flour-sack shift. The little girl standing in the doorway had not moved since she first appeared, her gaze fixed on the cot across the room where her mother lay.

The room, the kitchen of an old plantation, was immense, and the fire from a claw-footed stove in a far corner cast flickering shadows against walls stained and slick with a century's worth of wood smoke and bacon grease. Dividing the room was a roughly hewn pine table longer than a ship's gangplank, big enough to seat a dozen people and heaped with baskets and gourds, clay pots, syrup buckets. One wall was taken up by a massive fireplace, boarded over.

Through the open door the old woman heard the Buick spin its tires furiously in the mud, finally gain traction, and power off in the direction from which it had come, Memphis the man had said, his load lighter now by one dead woman and her child.

"Good news never comes in bad weather," she had predicted when the white man had driven up less than half an hour ago in his fancy car. She had been right about that.

Again Gran Gran noticed the dark stains on the girl's baby-blue dress. Violet, they said her name was, just before they had abandoned the girl to her care. With nothing but the clothes on the child's back. She couldn't be more than seven. Her skin the same honey-brown as her mother's. The same color-shifting eyes.

The old woman released a heavy breath. "You don't need to be seeing this." She walked over to a shelf to retrieve a ragged patchwork quilt.

"Nobody got no respect for the healing no more," she tried explaining as she covered the body. "Can't take things into your own hands. You got to pay respect."

Violet showed no sign of hearing Gran Gran's complaint, but the old woman continued regardless. "Why?" she demanded angrily. "Why did she do that? I explained it to her careful. Teaspoon in the morning. For nine days. It ain't my fault.

And only early on. Never this late. Never after the quickening. I told her that, too. I told her it would kill her and the child both. They had no right to bring her to me like this."

The old woman shook her head sadly at Violet. "It ain't my fault, little girl. She went against the healing!"

The girl was motionless, except for the almost imperceptible ticking of her head from side to side, as if marking time to some faint melody. The old woman carefully reached behind Violet to shut the door against the cold. "Might as well get yourself over by the fire."

Gran Gran reached down for the girl, but Violet jerked her hand away and swung it protectively behind her back.

"Suit yourself." She gripped the girl firmly by the shoulders and steered her to the stove. Violet didn't resist, but all the time she kept her eyes on the covered body, her head ticking ever so slightly to the secret rhythm.

The old woman bent down to study the girl's face in the light of the cookstove, venturing a look into her eyes. They seemed to peer right through her. The girl's pupils were tiny pinpricks.

"You ain't heard a word I said, have you?"

Gran Gran let out a tired breath. "You ain't having none of it. I can tell that much." She touched the child gently on the cheek with the back of her weathered hand. "A shadow been put across your face. You walking with the spirits now."

Violet's shivering grew more violent. The old woman led the girl to the pantry, many years ago a bedroom for the plantation cook. It contained another cot and shelves which were lined with bottles and jars and sacks tied off at the neck. All were marked with what appeared to be a child's attempt at lettering. After carefully removing the girl's stained dress and then covering her with quilts, Gran Gran selected a paper sack and went back into the kitchen. She returned shortly with a chipped cup held closely between her palms.

Steadying the murky contents, she sat down on the edge of the bed beside the girl. Violet did not move, but the old woman could see that her eyes were open, staring through the dark. She lifted the back of the girl's head and put the china cup to her mouth, and slowly, sip by sip, Violet emptied it.

While the girl lay silent, her eyes now closed, Gran Gran studied her, looking for some sign that would tell her what to do.

She carefully placed the heel of her palm against the girl's forehead, and closed her own eyes tightly, trying to enter the child's dreams.

"I can't see nothing," she said finally. "A darkness been put between me and you."

Then the old woman shook her head, and sighed. "Who I trying to fool? I can't see nothing no more. God's put a darkness between me and His whole damned world."

She should have known better. The woman had come to Gran Gran months ago for a remedy. She said her name was Lucy. That's all. No family name. She wanted Gran Gran to unfix an early pregnancy. She had told Gran Gran that if she didn't help her, the white man she worked for would get his butcher to do it. She never mentioned she already had one child.

White men, Gran Gran thought, forever trying to be master over a black woman's body. Always been that way. And according to Lucy, still was.

Why had she waited so long? Had she planned on keeping it, then changed her mind, deciding to drink the whole bottle and kill herself along with her unborn child?

They used to say Gran Gran had the sight. No more. There was nothing but darkness.

The old woman returned to her bed in

13

the kitchen, not bothering to undress or even to pull up a cover. She only slept for a few moments when she was startled awake by a wordless murmuring. She lay there, eyes open, exhausted, trying to decipher the hushed whispers, the shadowed faces. But there was nothing that remained of her dream but the shapeless foreboding.

When she was a young girl, she believed that the Old Ones would forever show her the way. She herself had heard their words, as distinct and reassuring as church bells.

Nor was she the only one who heard. In those earlier times, voices seemed to travel on a river of breath and memory through the lives of all the people, looking out for their children, stirring eddies and currents to catch their eye, faithfully giving up signs to help them along the way. All a person had to do was stop and listen to those who came before.

But it was not that way anymore.

The voices came only at night now, when she was asleep in her bed, but she could not make out the words, just their anger. Each night their cries grew more piercing, the current colder, freezing the breath in her lungs and forcing her to awaken gasping for air.

Sometimes she believed the current car-

14

ried death. Or perhaps her sins, dislodged from the past, circling and reaching for her with icy fingers.

Whatever it was, it had exhausted her. She hoped it would finally arrive and do with her what it would.

Not yet dawn, the sound of muffled voices woke Violet. At first she believed she was still in the car. "Reach back here and touch your momma's hand," her mother's friend said. It was raining. The only sound, other than her mother's soft moans, were the wipers, beating back the rain. "Violet," the woman said, "pet your momma's hand. She needs you to. She loves you so." Then silence again. Except for the beat of the wipers. Loud, steady, incessant.

After a moment, Violet knew that she was not in the car but in a strange bed. She strained to peer into the kitchen. Across the cavernous room another door stood open, faintly lit. There were shadows moving about, and she made a motion to rise but was not able to fend off the drugged sleep. Later, even the tap-tap-tapping of the hammer and the loud scuffle of men's boots didn't serve to keep her awake long. The tea had been strong and was doing its work.

It was only much later, when she heard

her mother calling out to her, that she wrestled herself from beneath the covers.

Violet struggled into her dress. When she entered the kitchen, lit now by a weak light, she saw that her mother was no longer on the cot. The front door was ajar, and through the crack she heard her mother's voice again, sounding farther away. With her legs woozy beneath her, Violet trudged toward the dim light that bled through the doorway.

From the porch she saw small clusters of people gathered in the road across the field. She tried to find her mother's face among them. Then she saw what the others watched. Up the track, veiled by the morning mist, a pair of mules strained to draw a wagon through the mud. Two identical black-clad figures sat upon the buckboard, one snapping the reins and the other straight-backed, facing ahead. In the bed of the buckboard was something the size of a large trunk, draped by the same quilt she'd seen the night before. Violet, even in her fogginess, understood. Her mother was leaving without her.

She meant to scream out, but the only sound she made was a thick, strangled cry not audible to the people standing in the road, yet almost as one, they turned to see the girl in a bloodstained dress. They watched as her legs collapsed beneath her and she fell into the arms of the old woman.

Gran Gran struggled mightily to get Violet back to the cot, gripping her tightly under her arms, dragging her through the kitchen and into the pantry where she finally hoisted the limp body onto the striped tick. After she buried the girl once more in quilts, she went back to the open door. People were returning to their homes now, still casting glances in the direction of the house.

"Go ahead and get an eyeful," she scolded in a tired voice. "No telling what you can make out of it by supper if you get right to it."

She shut the door on them and returned to the pantry, finding the girl sleeping, her breathing labored. The woman slumped into her rocker by the side of the bed.

The girl didn't belong here. Gran Gran was too old to be taking in swap-dog kin. Anyway, an orphan appearing out of nowhere would stir up trouble she was too worn out to handle. She was done with fighting trouble.

And what if she died?

A colored prostitute was bad enough. It was only luck that the Choctaw twins who kept Gran Gran stocked with provisions had seen her lantern hanging out on the porch. They came as soon as they saw her signal for trouble, in time to get the dead woman up to the burying ground with no questions asked.

But if a child were to die in Gran Gran's hands? That would surely get these self-respecting colored folks up in arms. They'd put her under the jail for sure.

The old woman's hands trembled with fatigue.

With strained eyes she watched the girl for signs, hoping she would give up anything that would tell her what to do, to unfix this mess she didn't ask for, until weariness finally overwhelmed her. She dropped her chin to her chest and fell into a dark, dreamless sleep, the only kind she had known for years.

Midmorning found the girl tossing restless in the bed, her loud muttering waking the old woman with a start. She tried to decipher the sounds.

"Listen to this now," she said to nobody. "Can't make heads or tails out of what she saying."

Gran Gran fogged her glasses with her breath and then wiped them on her apron.

18

Leaning over the girl, she carefully considered Violet's changing expressions, the muscles in her face, how they tensed, grimaced, relaxed, and then contorted again. How the head shook off each expression.

"How am I going to fix her," the old woman asked aloud, "when I don't even know what her misery is?"

She pulled back from Violet and drew in a deep breath. Then the old woman closed her eyes, trying to summon the thing that ailed the girl. But the shadows would not yield their names. She lingered within the girl's darkness, seeing no face nor hearing any voice.

"I can't see, little girl," she said at last. "Used to could. I could look into a person's eyes and divine their spirit. Now when I look into somebody's eyes, it's just the ancient dead looking back at me." She shook her head grimly. "And they ain't speaking."

The girl called out in her delirium, her panicked voice now loud enough to carry through the windows.

Gran Gran had to get the girl quiet.

A mixture of sweet-gum bark fortified with a strong dose of whiskey eventually settled her down, but even after Violet had calmed, Gran Gran became aware of a peculiar thing, the movement of the girl's head. It was only a slight rhythmic gesture, a steady pulse. But upon noticing it, she remembered that it was that same repetitive motion the girl brought with her.

Gran Gran began to keep exact time with the patting of her foot, trying to enter the rhythm. Was it the throb of a heartbeat she was sounding out? Was she measuring in-breaths and out-breaths? When Gran Gran tried to decipher the sign, she could not get past the darkness that clung to the girl like a shroud.

The old woman rose up straining from her chair. She drew back the tattered red-checked curtain to let what little light the watery sky would allow into the room. The sun had been stingy with its rays all day, the gray expanse broken only by the white furls of smoke from cookstoves down in the quarter.

For a long while she gazed out upon the only stretch of earth she had known her entire life. This was all that was left of her childhood days, the great house in ruin, the foundation being eaten away by the creek, and across the field, the double row of slave cabins, fixed up now by the grandchildren and great-grandchildren of house slaves, the ones who had stayed on after Freedom. They acted as white as the God they worshipped. That's what they were, all right. They were all soul sick.

A weak shaft of sunlight broke through the heavy, blanketed sky and dimly lit the room. Gran Gran turned from the window. A ray illuminated Violet's face.

"And what you going to think when you remember tonight?" she asked the sleeping girl. "Turn on me like the rest of them done, I reckon."

She leaned over and placed her mouth near the child's ear. "I want you to know, girl, I listened to your momma's cries. She was hurting real bad inside. I listened to the deepest parts of her. I believed I understood. I surely did. But I swear to you, I didn't know what she'd end up doing."

The sleeping girl was unmoved by Gran Gran's defense.

"Sometimes, when you look at a person, all you see is the tangle and you miss the weave."

Gran Gran breathed a heavy sigh and then straightened back up. "Never you mind," she said. "No matter what I tell you, I figure it'll be a long time before you ever see nothing but the tangle in all this mess."

Gran Gran took a rag from the pan of

21

water and wrung it out, to cool Violet's forehead. She knew that a person needed to make sense out of calamity, no matter how old they were. If not, the soul, frustrated at abiding within a vessel of shattered mirrors, takes flight.

"I hope what happened to my mistress ain't happening to you, girl. Her body healed, but her spirit roamed homeless through the world. Creation is filled with soul-sick folks, colored and white, never knowing where they belong. They tangle everybody else up in their grief."

The old woman began to suspect that this was the battle the girl was fighting. If that were so, she was beyond the reach of any medicine Gran Gran knew of. She had spent her life tending to the flesh and to the bone, leaving the rest to the preachers and superstition.

"But that's what it is all right," the woman muttered. "She's knitting and a'patching. Patching and a'knitting. This girl is piecing together a tale. Trying to put some sense behind what all she seen." Gran Gran laid her hand on the girl's face. "And God only knows what tale she's going to tell on me."

Violet's skin burned to the touch. She stammered more syllables, fervent but jumbled, and then shook off the old woman's hand with a fierce toss of her head.

Gran Gran smiled grimly. "But that's all right, little girl. I lost my momma, too. Don't remember it to this day. And all they gave me was bits and pieces, here and there. But I done the best I could. Sometimes it takes a whole lifetime to get the story right. I'm still working on it." She laughed. "Some memories don't come store-bought and readymade."

Gran Gran stood and walked over to the window. "They told me I wasn't born in this house. I was born over there across the yard in Shinetown. Course it wasn't called that then. Back then it was called the slave quarters." Her sigh was heavy, as if weighted by a century of memory. "That's what they told me anyway. When you quilting up a life, you sometimes got to start with any piece you can get your hands on."

As she spoke, the sleeping girl calmed a bit, as if the words themselves were smoothing out the rough weather inside.

Gran Gran walked over to her. "That what you telling me, Violet? You need to be talked to for a while? Now, if that's the case, I can sure do that. I can always give you a heavy dose of words."

The old woman sat back in her chair and laced her fingers in her lap. "What was I saying?"

After a moment she remembered.

"They tell me my momma's name was Ella," she began.

CHAPTER 2

1847

Ella was awake when she heard the first timid knock at the cabin door. Her husband, who lay beside her on the corn-shuck mattress, snored undisturbed. She kept still as well, not wanting to wake the newborn that slept in the crook of her arm. The baby had cried most of the night and had only just settled into a fitful sleep. Ella couldn't blame the girl for being miserable. The room was intolerably hot.

Like everybody else in the quarter, Ella believed the cholera was carried by foul nocturnal vapors arising from the surrounding swamp, so she and Thomas kept their shutters and doors closed tight against the night air, doing their best to protect their daughter from the killing disease that had already taken so many.

The rapping on the door became more insistent. Ella pushed against Thomas with her foot. On the second shove he awoke with a snort.

"Thomas! See to the door," she whispered, "and mind Yewande."

Wearing only a pair of cotton trousers, Thomas eased himself from the bed and crossed the room. He lifted the bar and pulled open the door, but his broad, muscled back blocked the visitors' faces. From the flickering glare cast around her husband, Ella could tell one of the callers held a lantern.

"Thomas," came the familiar voice, "get Ella up."

Ella started at the words. It was Sylvie, the master's cook. The woman lived all the way up at the mansion and would have no good reason to be out this time of night unless it was something bad.

"Now?" Thomas whispered. "She's sleeping."

"She needs to carry her baby up to the master's house," Sylvie said. "Ella got to make haste on it. Mistress Amanda is waiting on her."

"What she wanting with my woman and child in the dead of night?" Ella heard the alarm rising in her husband's voice.

"Thomas, you know it ain't neither night nor day for Mistress Amanda. She ain't slept a wink since the funeral. And she's grieving particular bad tonight. Her medicine don't calm her down no more. She ain't in no mood to be trifled with."

"Old Silas," Thomas pled to another unseen caller, "you tell the mistress that Ella will come by tomorrow, early in the morning." Then he dropped his voice to a hush. "You know the mistress ain't right in her head."

Old Silas had more pull than anybody with the master, but from the lack of response, Ella imagined Silas's gray head, weathered skin stretched tight over his skull, shaking solemnly.

Thomas let go a deep breath and then turned back to his wife. Behind him, Ella could hear the talk as it continued between the couple outside.

"You know good and well she didn't say to fetch Ella," Old Silas whispered harshly to his wife. "Just the baby, she said. What's in your head?"

"Shush!" Aunt Sylvie fussed. "You didn't see what I seen. I know what I'm doing."

Ella met them at the door holding the swaddled infant. Not yet fourteen, Ella wore a ripped cotton shift cut low for nursing, and even in the heat of the cabin, she trembled. The yellow light lit the faces of

27

the cook and her husband.

"What she want with Yewande?" Ella whimpered. "What she going to do to my baby?"

"Ella, she ain't going to hurt your baby," Sylvie assured. "Mistress wouldn't do that for the world."

"But why —"

Old Silas reached out and laid a gentle hand on Ella's shoulder. "I expect she wants to name your girl, is all." His voice was firm but comforting. He spoke more like the master than any slave. "That right, Sylvie?"

"Of course!" Sylvie said, as if hearing the explanation for the first time. "I expect that's all it is. Mistress Amanda wants to name your girl."

"But Master Ben names the children," Ella argued.

"You heard what the master said," Sylvie fussed. "Things got to change. We all got to mind her wishes until she comes through this thing. No use fighting it."

Silas's tone was kinder. "Mistress has taken an interest in your child from the start," he explained. "Her Becky passed the very hour your girl was born. I suppose their souls might have touched, one coming and the other leaving. No doubt that's why the mistress thinks your child so special. Every time the mistress hears your baby cry, she asks after Yewande's health."

Ella pulled the child closer to her breast and set her mouth to protest.

"Ella, don't make a fuss," Sylvie said impatiently. "Just do what she says tonight. Anything in the world to calm her down. Nobody getting any rest until she do. Let her name your baby if she has a mind. She been taking so much medicine, she'll forget her own name by morning."

Ella saw the resoluteness in the faces of the couple. She finally gave a trembling nod.

As the three walked down the lane of cabins, they passed smoldering heaps of pine and cypress, attempts by the inhabitants to purify the air and keep the mosquitoes at bay. The acrid, suffocating smoke seemed to travel with the little group, enveloping them in a cloud that seared the lungs. Up in the distance, the lights in the great house came into view. No words were spoken as Sylvie, ever crisp and efficient, walked beside Ella while Silas lit the path.

It was Old Silas whom the master had first sent down to the quarters days ago with the news of Miss Becky's death. Ella remembered how odd Silas's little speech had been.

"Miss Becky has passed of a summer

fever," he said, "*not* the cholera, understand? If any of those who come to pay respects should ask you, that is what you are to say. It was a summer fever that took Miss Becky. Don't say a word more."

Someone had asked Silas why they had to lie. It was known to everyone on the plantation that the girl had come down with the same sickness that had killed nearly two dozen of his field hands. Sylvie had already let it be known that she had watched Miss Becky suffering in her four-poster bed, halfway to heaven on her feather mattress. Sylvie had witnessed the sudden nausea and the involuntary discharges that didn't let up through the entire night. She had seen the girl's eyes, once the color of new violets, go dim and sink deep into their sockets, her face looking more like that of an ancient woman exhausted by life than a twelve-year-old girl. From what Sylvie had said, Miss Becky's dying had been no different than their own children's.

Before answering the question, Silas jawed the chaw of tobacco to his other cheek. "He's doing it to protect Miss Becky's good name. Master says the cholera is not a quality disease. The highborn don't come down with such. Especially no innocent twelve-year-old white girl." Silas put two fingers up

30

to his mouth and let go a stream of brown juice.

A dark laughter rippled through the survivors who stood there, all of whom had lost family or friends. What Silas wouldn't say, Sylvie made sure the others knew She said the master was so afraid of what his neighbors thought he had refused to send to Delphi for the doctor lest the news get out that Miss Becky had caught a sickness so foul that it was reserved for Negroes and the Irish. He had stood there and watched while the girl's breathing became so faint it didn't even disturb the fine linen sheet that covered her. He ranted about how Rubina, Becky's constant companion and the daughter of a house slave, was healthy as a colt. "There is no way," he swore, "the cholera would pass over a slave and strike down my own daughter!"

Sylvie remembered the mistress's face when her husband had said that. The cook had never seen that much agony in a white person's eyes.

When all hope was lost, the master finally turned his back on his wife and daughter and home, leaving Becky to lie motionless, shrouded by the embroidered canopy of pink-and-white roses; Mistress Amanda to witness alone the inevitable end; and little

31

Rubina to sob outside her dying playmate's room. He rounded up a work gang and several bottles of whiskey, saddled his horse, and hightailed it out to the swamps to burn more Delta acreage.

"I guess that's the white man's way," Sylvie had told them all, disgusted. "Lose a child, sire more land."

That's when the mistress's mind finally broke. At first she wanted to have little Rubina whipped and her wounds salted, sure the girl had given her daughter the disease. But soon enough she relented. It was clear that she couldn't hurt Becky's friend. Mistress Amanda's crazed search for blame finally settled on her husband. She cursed him night and day and threw china dishes against the wall. When Master Ben sent for some medicine to calm her, she swallowed all she could get her hands on. Anyway, that's what those who worked in the house said.

Sylvie reached her arm around the young mother's shoulder. Ella felt sure it was as much to keep her from bolting as it was to comfort her. Not that Ella hadn't thought about running off with her baby into the darkness and hiding in the swamps, waiting out the mistress's memory. But nobody had ever survived for more than two days out in the swamps.

Even if she did make it past two days, it was no guarantee the mistress would come to her senses. Since the day of the funeral, the mistress's silhouette could be seen through her bedroom window at all times of night, her arms animated, her fists shaking accusingly at nobody.

Ella didn't know what happened first, Sylvie's grip tightening to a bruising clench or the gunshot that seemed to crack right over her head. The small procession halted and they all gazed up at the house.

"Lord, what she done now?" Sylvie said.

While they watched, Master Ben came storming down the back steps from the upstairs gallery in his nightshirt and bare feet, dragging his bed linen behind him.

"It's about time y'all got here. She's about to hunt you down and she's got her daddy's derringer."

The group stepped aside to let him pass. "My advice," he grumbled without looking back, "is to hurry up before she reloads."

"God be great," Sylvie said under her breath. "I wish she would go ahead and shoot the man so we could all get some peace."

At the water stand on the back gallery, Aunt

Sylvie emptied the cedar bucket into the basin. "Now wash your baby," she commanded. "Mistress say make sure she's clean before bringing her inside the house."

With trembling hands, Ella bathed Yewande under the light of Silas's lantern. When Ella finished, Sylvie held out one of the mistress's fine towels. Next the cook produced a tiny white gown and bonnet made of lace. Ella had never touched anything as delicate.

Perhaps it was true, she thought, that the mistress had been taken with her girl. The house servants weren't dressed this fine. Not even little Rubina, who was almost white herself and had slept at the foot of Miss Becky's bed! Maybe when Yewande got older, she could get a job in the house like Rubina, instead of draining swamps. Maybe Yewande wasn't too dark for housework after all!

"These really for my girl?" Ella asked.

Sylvie nodded carefully, but said nothing.

Old Silas seemed surprised as well. "When did the mistress give you these, Sylvie?"

"Before I come to get you," Sylvie said, almost under her breath. Silas kept his gaze on her until she finally dropped her eyes. "They Miss Becky's christening gown when she was a baby."

"She handed you her dead daughter's dress?" Silas blurted. "Does the master know?"

"I ain't asking no questions, Silas!" Sylvie answered defensively. "You seen him. High-tailing it out of his own house dragging his bedsheets behind him. If her own husband done give up on her, nothing I can say to talk any sense into the woman. Right now he's going to do anything she asks, just to keep her from writing her daddy. We got to do the same or we all might be sold off again."

"Aunt Sylvie," Ella stammered, "I don't understand . . ."

Sylvie turned to Ella. "Understand?" the cook scoffed. "You got to listen to me, girl. You ain't never worked in a white man's house. When you walk through them doors, say 'goodbye' to understanding and 'how do you do' to madness. Remember, half the things you going to see tonight ain't real. The way to survive it is to play dumb, stay out of the way, and pray for the half that does make sense to show up quick. Hear me? Just keep quiet and tuck your head down low."

Silas led the way into the back of the darkened great house. The smells were sweet and delicious, and the carpeted floors as soft and cool as moss under Ella's bare feet. This was the first time Ella had passed through the threshold, and the foreignness of the finery only ratcheted up her fear. Through the dark she heard the soft weeping of a young girl and at first thought Miss Becky's spirit had yet to leave the house. It was then that Silas's lantern threw its light across an immense dining-room table, illuminating the crying girl, her head of fine curly hair slumped facedown on her arms. It was Rubina, still mourning the death of her friend.

Sylvie reached down and stroked Rubina's hair once gently but said nothing, and continued to lead Ella through the cavernous downstairs and up the winding staircase.

Silas held back at the top of the stairs while Ella and Sylvie proceeded down the hallway to the mistress's room. Outside the door stood Lizzie, the mistress's maid and Rubina's mother.

When they approached, Lizzie grabbed Sylvie by the arm. The maid's fretful stare pierced the dark. "You got to help Rubina!" Lizzie pleaded urgently, talking rapidly, as if trying to get everything said before Sylvie turned away. "With Miss Becky dead, the master been after my little Rubina. And her not older than his own girl was! I seen the way he looks at her, Sylvie. And so has the mistress. She say she don't want to lay eyes on Rubina no more! Don't want her in the house! Says it breaks her heart every time she looks at my girl. What's going to happen to her, Sylvie? They going to send her to the fields? What if they sell her off? Sylvie," she said slowing down and dropping her whisper so that Ella could barely make out the words, "you know what the white men do with the pretty, light-skinned ones. You got to do something, Sylvie! She ain't —"

Sylvie halted Lizzie's desperate plea by pulling Ella forward with a jerk, almost thrusting her into Lizzie's face. For the first time Lizzie seemed to notice Ella and then she looked down at the dark child in Ella's arms, dressed in fine lace.

"Can't you see I got my hands full right now, Lizzie?" Sylvie whispered harshly. "I'll do what I can for Rubina. But I can only save one child at a time! Now move aside, Lizzie, and go tend to your girl."

By the time Sylvie pushed back the mistress's door, Ella had seen enough. Sylvie had been right. They had set foot in the house only moments ago and already the world had become a hellish puzzlement.

How could the death of one little white girl set loose so much trouble?

But the most fearsome thing had yet to come. When Sylvie led Ella, breathless, into the bedroom, she got her first up-close look at Mistress Amanda.

The woman sat unmoving in the big stuffed chair, her long raven hair knotted tight behind her head. Fine white fingers gripping the brocaded arms like she was expecting at any minute to be bucked off. She had the features of a child herself and stared back at Ella vacantly, saying nothing.

At last Mistress Amanda turned her empty gaze to Sylvie and spoke so faintly, Ella could barely make out the words: "Aunt Sylvie," she said, "bring the baby to me like I asked you to."

Ella glanced fearfully at Sylvie. The cook's expression had gone to one of befuddlement. "What's that you say, Mistress?" Sylvie asked. "I fetched the baby to your room just like you said to."

"No, I meant bring the child *to me*."

Ella stood frozen, her baby clasped tightly in her arms.

"Sylvie, why are you doing this?" The mistress paused, as if to collect herself. Then she caught Ella's eye. "You, girl. You bring me that baby." The mistress offered a pitiful smile. "Let me show you how to hold it."

Ella hesitated, and then looked back to Sylvie. Now Sylvie would not even return her gaze. The cook was silent, shaking her head, like she couldn't figure out what it was the mistress wanted.

The suffocating silence took Ella's breath away. The baby began to fidget in her arms.

"Didn't you hear me, girl!" the mistress cried. "You must do what I tell you!"

Ella turned her shoulder to Mistress Amanda, as if shielding the baby from an advancing gale. She dared to shake her head in protest.

Mistress Amanda gave a pleading look at the cook. "Bring the baby here, Sylvie."

Sylvie gave a short nod, but instead of reaching for the child, she gripped Ella by the arm and drew the girl to where the mistress sat. The baby began to cry and her feet kicked at the skirt of the gown.

"Now, see? Y'all upset her." The mistress held her arms out before her. "Give her here."

Ella took a step back with the bawling child. "No, Mistress! Don't!" Ella tugged against Sylvie's grip, trying to make it to the door, but the cook's hold was tight.

The mistress got herself unsteadily to her feet. Then she reached out for the child as

39

Ella struggled vainly to loose herself. When the mistress got a two-handed grip and began tugging roughly on the infant, Ella finally released Yewande with a heaving sob.

Cradling the child in her emaciated arms, Mistress Amanda gazed into the baby's face.

"Isn't she precious? And look at that expression!" She giggled, now childlike. "Like an angry black fist. I'm sure she's hungry. You see, I know all about babies."

"No, ma'am," Ella cried. "She ain't hungry. She scared."

"What did the master name her?" Mistress Amanda asked airily.

"Master ain't said yet. I been calling her Yewande. After my granny."

"No, no," the mistress said, speaking to the baby. "That's not right at all, is it, my little ebony doll? That's a name for a baboon or an orangutan." She laughed and then lifted the girl up in the air. "I'll think of a name. One that favors you."

The baby calmed with the mistress's attention, which seemed to delight her to no end. She smiled almost appreciatively at the child.

"Why, your face is like an inky daub in that field of Spanish lace," Mistress Amanda mused, walking the baby toward the open window. "What was it Daddy always said?

40

Ah, I remember! 'Black as a Moor.' "

Then she exclaimed, "That's it! We'll name you after their city." She giggled, as if delighted with her cleverness. "I christen you Granada, Queen of the Mississippi Moors."

The mistress's laughter grew manic as she rocked the baby roughly in her arms. She lurched about the room on unsteady feet.

Ella struggled to break Sylvie's grip. "Mistress, please. Can I take Yewande back now? She —"

The mistress put a finger to her pale lips to shush Ella. "See? She's resting so quietly now" — and then abruptly turned her back to the weeping mother. "It's time for all of you to go, before you upset Granada again."

"Mistress!" Ella cried. "She's *my* baby! Yewande! Please —"

"Aunt Sylvie, you all have got to leave now," the mistress said over her shoulder. "This girl is upsetting the child. She's not good for Granada."

Ella began screaming for her child, fighting Sylvie to get away.

"Silas!" Sylvie shouted. "Get in here!"

It took both Silas and Sylvie to drag the hysterical girl from the room, down the stairs, and out of the house. By the time they made it into the yard, Ella had ceased

41

fighting. She stood forlornly on the bare ground, clutching empty arms to her chest, gazing up at the mistress's window.

Sylvie pulled Ella to her and let the girl sob inconsolably in her beefy arms.

"Sylvie," Old Silas said, "it would be best if you got her back to her cabin. The mistress's window is wide open."

"I know it hurts, Ella," Sylvie soothed. "You go ahead and cry your eyes out. Loud as you want to. I got you."

"Sylvie!" Silas fussed. "What in the world you doing?"

"What I *can,* Silas!" she said, patting Ella on the back. "I might have to do what mistress says, but I don't have to make it easy on her. I'm going to remind that fish-blooded woman what it's like for a momma to lose her child. Maybe she'll remember. If I have to, I might get Lizzie out here, too, crying for Rubina. It ain't much, but it's what I can do. We'll be out here every night if we have to, every one of us, wailing up a storm." Sylvie shot her husband a hard look. "Now what *you* going to do, Silas?"

"All right, Sylvie," he said with a sigh. "I'll talk with Master Ben."

"About both of them? Yewande and Rubina?"

Silas nodded.

Ella quieted her sobbing to look up at the old man, finding a glimmer of hope. Silas was smart and knew the master better than anyone. They say he as good as raised the master. Surely he could get her baby back!

"I should have told him a long time ago, I reckon," Silas said. "He brought her down too soon. Should have told him to bring her daddy's money and his slaves, but leave that girl in Kentucky. She's not the kind you bring at the beginning of things, when there's nothing but wilderness and sickness. She's lost one baby after the next and ain't nothing but a pampered child herself. Broke her spirit. He needs to send her back home before she brings everything down around our ears."

Aunt Sylvie took Ella by the shoulders and beamed into her face. "Ain't my man something?" she said. "He'll get this mess straightened out by breakfast time."

CHAPTER 3

Violet slept soundly.

Gran Gran eased back in her chair, the old memories rising in her like smoke. Thinking about the dead, she figured, must be akin to breath on a dying ember. As the memory smoldered, she wondered if any of her words had penetrated the girl's darkness.

"Don't know what got into me, Violet," the woman said, "talking to you about folks long passed. Telling you things that might not even be true. But that's all I got. One day you'll be telling somebody about all this. You'll be telling about this old woman who you'd like to strangle in her sleep. I won't blame you one whit. If that's what gets you on your feet."

Through the rest of the day Gran Gran sat watch by the bedside, placing her hands on the girl, forcing broths and potions for the fever, rubbing horse-hoof salve into her chest. But by evening the girl became agitated again. She threw her head from one side of the pillow to the other, as if a heated battle raged in her brain. Her eyes worked determinedly beneath the lids, sketching out pictures the old lady could not read.

The girl's incessant babbling grew more hysterical until it turned into a terrible shrieking, sending the woman to the window to see if the awful racket had attracted trouble yet.

"Folks going to think I'm up in here murdering you," she laughed bleakly. "They'll sic the law on me sure as the world." She looked at the girl. "I'm sorry, child, but I got to get you quieted down."

Gran Gran turned to go back to the kitchen to fix a narcotic of jimsonweed, but she stopped short of the door. She glanced back once more at Violet as she lay whimpering in the bed, her face dark and desolate, tormented by some nightmare Gran Gran could not even imagine. It looked as if that child was taking on all the demons of hell single-handedly.

I could drug her, the woman thought, again remembering the mistress, but what about her soul? Probably wind up broken and lost, wandering from pillar to post, like too many others.

"Calming ain't curing, is it, girl?" the woman asked aloud, shaking her head wearily. "Keeping you hushed might keep me out of jail, but sure as the world, calming ain't curing."

Gran Gran watched the girl as she struggled. "And I'd hate to see somebody with so much scrap lose the battle. You a fighter, that's what you are," she said, half smiling.

The old woman heaved a long breath. "Lord, help us both." She returned to her chair by the bed where the girl was kicking at the covers.

"This is your battle, Violet. I can't fight it for you. Like somebody told me when I was a girl, I can chew your food, but you got to swallow for yourself." The old woman smiled, thinking how mad it had made her when Polly Shine had told her that. Gran Gran reached to take hold of Violet's hand.

The girl yelped as if seared by a hot poker and yanked back her arm. The scare threw Gran Gran backward into her chair.

Violet bolted upright. Her face contorted into an expression at once of terror and grief, and then she let out a gut-wrenching shriek. It was like nothing human Gran Gran had heard before.

The girl's eyes were opened wide and

fixed, staring off into some region beyond the old woman. Her skin was afire with fever, and she desperately tried to get free of the covers that held her back. The screams continued, piercing the watchful quiet of the quarter.

The old woman drew Violet to her, stifling the screams in her chest. The girl beat her fists fiercely against Gran Gran's humped back and clawed her neck, but the old woman continued to hold her tight, unflinching, until the struggling died out and Violet went limp in Gran Gran's arms.

When she gently lowered the girl's head to the pillow, her eyes were still open, darting wildly around the room but settling on no one thing. Her breathing was panicked and uncertain.

It was not over yet.

There was nothing Gran Gran understood to do. If the girl had a broken body, that was easy. But this, this was not what she knew. Afraid for both of them now, she did the only thing she could think of. She lay down beside the girl and drew the frail, spent body close, nestling Violet into the protective hollow of herself. She then began to whisper into the girl's ear the words she had learned long ago, hoping they might seep into Violet's dreams.

She chanted softly, rhythmically, "In the beginning God created in the beginning God created in the beginning . . ."

It was late into the night when Violet's breathing finally took hold of the easy rhythm of the words and evened out.

Through the flickering light of the lamp, Gran Gran could see that the girl's eyes were still open, but they had calmed. They seemed to have settled intently on the face of the old woman. The look was sad and wanting, but for now, the terror was gone.

The old woman rose from the cramped little cot and when she looked down on the girl, the panic seemed to rise up in her face again.

"No, I ain't going to leave you, Violet. I'm going to sit right here. And we'll have us a chat. I'm not sleepy, neither. Don't sleep much anymore. Older you get, the more sleep seems like practice for dying. What you want to talk about?"

Gran Gran's eyes fell on the girl's shoes where they lay on the floor. Even covered in mud, they looked expensive. The woman drew one to her with her cane and picked it up. She wet a finger to clear a window to the leather grain below. The white man said he would send the rest of the girl's clothes later. Gran Gran wondered if they were all this fine.

Gran Gran recalled the bloodstained dress she had taken off the girl. It was made of blue silk muslin and finely embroidered, stitched by somebody who knew what they were doing. She hated having to toss the ruined garment into the stove. The smell had sickened her. Since she was a girl, she had never forgotten the odor of beautiful things set afire. Such a waste!

She looked upon Violet where she lay watching. "I guess somebody sure loved you to fit you up in these first-class clothes. I know finery when I see it. Right there, you and me got a lot in common."

Gran Gran ran her hands over the lap of her feed-sack dress, washed so many times she had forgotten what the print pattern used to be.

"I sure loved to wear fancy frocks," she mused. "Some folks said I had a pretty face. I couldn't see it. But, oh my! When I put on them dresses, I believed I was the best-looking little thing south of Memphis. I reckon you could say pretty clothes was my downfall."

CHAPTER 4

1860

"What sort a dress you reckon she'll bring me?" Granada asked for the third time that morning.

It was early dawn and the plantation kitchen was chilly, Granada having neglected the coals in the hearth during the night. The only thing she wore was her rough homespun shimmy. The close-plank floor was cold to her bare feet, but she was too excited to care.

"That dead girl sure got some pretty frocks, don't she?" Granada asked. "Silk's my favorite, I reckon."

When the cook still didn't respond, Granada called out louder, "Aunt Sylvie! What *color* you reckon?"

Not bothering to look at Granada, the cook wiped the flour from her hands with the hem of her starched white apron. Sylvie was sturdily built and didn't stand much

50

taller than the twelve-year-old who presently was doing everything she could think of to get her attention.

"I'm not going to abide no more of this kind of talk in my kitchen," the cook pronounced, "especially coming from a child as coal black as any swamp slave." Aunt Sylvie, whose skin was the light color of an underdone biscuit, still hadn't turned her face from her dough. "You get this way every Preaching Sunday, Granada. Near about wears me out. Please, light somewhere and quiet down."

Granada wasn't discouraged. Her mind stayed on the dress and the shoes and the hair ribbons that would be delivered any minute now.

Sylvie clomped to the door in her loose-fitting brogans to peer out across the darkened yard. "Old Silas ain't even lit a lantern yet," she grumbled. "I sent that fool Chester over to Silas's cabin ages ago. He's going to make my breakfast late sure as the world."

Though husband and wife, Sylvie and Silas didn't stay together. Sylvie slept in a room behind the kitchen and Silas stayed alone in his cabin. They both seemed to like it that way. Silas was nearly twice Sylvie's age, and she said old folks are easier to care

51

for from a distance.

Sylvie turned away from the door and got back to her biscuit dough. "If Silas don't show pretty soon with some firewood, Granada, I'm going to send you out to the yard and gather some kindling chips. That might work off some of your sass."

"Aunt Sylvie —"

The cook waved her off. "Baby, stop running your mouth and dip me a cup of sweet milk from the crock. You got me so flustered I done made my dough crumbly."

Granada stomped her foot at Sylvie, but then did as she was told, with a few groans thrown in for good measure.

She handed the cup to Aunt Sylvie with a dramatic sigh.

"Life must be hard on you Christian martyrs," Aunt Sylvie said, but Granada saw the smile.

After pouring the milk into her great hickory bowl, Sylvie worked the batter vigorously with her short, blunt fingers. "Thank the Lord Preaching Sunday don't come every week," she muttered, lifting her shoulder to wipe her face on the checked gingham dress.

Granada couldn't understand why the cook didn't look forward to Preaching Sundays. Everybody else did. Several times a year, the master's slaves were herded in from miles around, from every settlement the master had built, spread across his four thousand acres of plantation land. Hundreds of black bodies flooded into the yard like a dark, slow-moving river. These were all-day affairs, called by the master when conditions warranted sending for Bishop Kerry to give everybody a good preaching-to. Master Ben invited his white friends from town and neighboring plantations to join him high up on the gallery where they listened to the bishop give the sermon. And Granada got to be at the very center of it all.

Sylvie finally looked down at Granada and shook her head sadly. "You mind your manners today. I don't think you know how lucky you are not to be out working in them swamps. You come mighty close. Don't you forget it! If you don't act right, the mistress can always send you back where she found you, like you know who!"

Granada stuck out her tongue. Aunt Sylvie was always threatening to send Granada to one of the settlements where the field slaves lived. Supposedly that's where Granada's mother was moved off to after the cholera. And Sylvie often tried to scare Granada by telling her the story of Lizzie's little girl with skin the color of cream and eyes like the mistress's emeralds, all proper and house-raised, now working the swamps like a common field slave. "If it can happen to an almost white girl, it can sure happen to you!"

Granada forced that possibility from her mind. The mistress would never allow it, she told herself. And if that woman who was supposed to be Granada's mother ever tried to lay claim, the girl would fight tooth and nail. She wanted no mother but the mistress.

Sylvie turned toward the cold fireplace, but Granada again stepped into her path, determined Sylvie would not ignore her this time.

"You think it's going to be silk this time, Aunt Sylvie?" she asked, her ink-black eyes wide and unblinking.

"Listen at you, a kitchen girl talking like she knows something about silk." She took Granada by the shoulders and swung her aside like a garden gate. "Don't matter if it's made out of corn silk. You best learn now, white folks don't look at you. They only look at what you toting on your back or carrying in your hands. That don't change because the wrapping is pretty,

Granada. Just don't bring attention to yourself."

Sylvie shook her head. "What am I saying? The second they see you dressed up like a white girl, they always bust a gut." She looked at Granada sadly. "Baby, I hope you know they ain't flattering you. You the mistress's little joke on the master."

"I ain't funny," Granada said.

"White folks seem to think so. I heard a lawyer tell his wife that coming to Master Ben's was better than going to the circus. With a trained monkey and a black girl acting like a midget queen, all presided over by a wild-eyed opium fiend."

The girl had tired of hearing this long ago. Let them laugh if they wanted to. Sometimes Sylvie told Granada how pretty she was, despite her dark skin. But Granada never believed it. After all, the mistress never noticed her without the beautiful clothes. The clothes made her more than beautiful. They made her visible.

Granada sat down at the table and cradled her head in her hands. "Last time, the mistress brought me pretty red satin bows for my hair. Same color as that dress," she mused, remembering the gown of pale rose gauze trimmed with silver lace. "Remember that, Aunt Sylvie? How pretty I looked fixed up with red bows?" She patted herself on the side of her head.

"I'm telling you, Granada," Aunt Sylvie said, "tying a scrap of red on a straw broom don't make it no Christmas tree."

As she was still talking, a tall, lanky man stepped lightly into the kitchen with an arm-load of wood.

"Chester, where's Old Silas?" Aunt Sylvie asked, scowling at the plantation coachman, a handsome, fine-featured fellow who seemed to forever sport a grin that warned of tomfoolery.

"Your man is fussing about his swolled-up feet. Said his dropsy was acting up. I told him he ought to stay in bed. Wants you to bring him a hot pan of water to soak in."

Sylvie liked to brag how her man Silas was once the topmost man on the plantation, right next to the master. Granada found that hard to believe. Now all Silas did was odd jobs for Sylvie around the kitchen and complain about his feet.

Chester dropped the wood on the hearth with a racket. "Aunt Sylvie, if you'll be real sweet to me, I'll fix your fire this morning."

"Hop to it then," Sylvie snapped. "Sooner I got a fire, sooner I can get y'all fed. When the house wakes up, y'all have to root, hog, or die on your own. I won't have time to fool with you. And you tell Silas to get his own water."

Chester winked at Granada. "I reckon she didn't hear me say that piece about being sweet."

Granada tried winking back, but the best she could do was blink.

The coachman knelt down before the hearth and began stacking the wood for the breakfast fire. The pile he made looked like matchsticks in the man-tall fireplace. But by midmorning it would be aglow with the coals from a forest of logs, and the kitchen would be sweltering hot, chock-full with the aromas of roasting meats, bubbling stews, and baking pies, abuzz with the chatter of serving girls. They would keep the master's guests fed like this for days.

"The house ain't up yet?" Chester asked. He rose from the fire and brushed bits of bark off his blue wool coat with gleaming brass buttons. The mistress would be furious if she caught him with tarnished buttons. He polished them in the kitchen with ashes every evening.

Aunt Sylvie stood at the smooth oak biscuit block, rolling out the dough. "I sent Lizzie to see about getting the mistress dressed. She usually up pacing the floor about this time. Master still be sleeping."

57

"I reckon so!" Chester chuckled. "Master Ben was mighty drunk when I brought him and the bishop home last night. Singing hymns and laughing and carrying on. Should have seen me toting him up the stairs like a sack of oats."

"Bishop Kerry seen him like that?" Aunt Sylvie asked, acting scandalized.

"Seen him? I had to tote the bishop up next. And he so big, it took me two trips!"

Granada slapped her hand over her mouth and snorted through her fingers. Chester didn't crack a smile. Sometimes when Granada got tickled over something he said, she had to check twice to see if he was fooling or not. That man lived to prank folks.

Aunt Sylvie shook her head. "Man of God doing that way."

"The bishop might be a man of God this Sunday morning," Chester said, "but he sure took a whipping from the devil Saturday night."

Granada walked up to the cook and tugged on her apron. "Aunt Sylvie, when you going to grease my hair? Mistress be down anytime with my new clothes."

Aunt Sylvie swatted Granada's hand away. "Listen to this girl! Talking 'bout *her* new clothes!"

Chester winked at Granada again and

said, "Now let her be, Aunt Sylvie. Ain't every day she gets to throw off her head rag and play the white girl. Anyway, she as pretty as any white girl I ever seen."

Sylvie ignored him. "Them clothes *ain't* new and they *ain't* yours," she reminded Granada. "Them's Miss Becky's clothes."

Granada had heard all this before, but it meant nothing to her. To Aunt Sylvie, Miss Becky was the beautiful little white girl who looked down sweetly from a gilded frame over the mantel, sitting in a tree swing and cradling a raven-haired doll. But to Granada she wasn't a person at all. To Granada, Rebecca Satterfield was only a name that signified a pair of locked mahogany wardrobes in an unoccupied bedroom in the great house, both of them crammed full of elegant garments, ribbons, and rare perfumes. When Aunt Sylvie spoke of Miss Becky, she made her sound like somebody the bishop preached about in one of his sermons, all teary eyed and crackly voiced. One of those snowy white angels in heaven.

"Chester, why you still here?" Sylvie fussed. "You ain't doing nothing but getting in the way. Get on back to the stables. I imagine your brother Mister Mule is missing you about now. Don't come back until you smell the meat frying."

"And miss the big spectacle? This is better than a corn shucking."

"You ought to be ashamed! Making light of Mistress Amanda and Miss Becky. One mad and the other one dead. Rest her soul."

"Aunt Sylvie —" Granada began again.

"I swear, girl, if you ask me one more question about that dress, I'll switch your legs!"

Granada raised her foot, but Sylvie warned, "And don't you go stomping the floor at me, neither. Don't know where you get that from. I taught you better. Act like you was reared in one of Chester's mule stalls." She shook her head with disdain. "And you supposed to be a house girl, hand-raised."

Chester slapped his thigh. "Come over here, Granada, and get out of that woman's reach."

Granada ran to Chester and put her arm around his neck.

"How about one of Chester's riddles?" he asked.

Granada nodded eagerly. "I bet I get it this time."

"Chester, you ain't happy until you get somebody to guessing some fool thing," Aunt Sylvie said, greasing an iron skillet.

Chester waved Sylvie off and then turned

back to Granada. "All right," he said, looking around the kitchen, scratching his freshly shaved chin. "I got one. What's slick as a mole, black as coal, got a great long tail like a fishing pole?"

Granada repeated the riddle and then frowned. "The master's big black horse?" she said without conviction.

"You always guessing that horse. You way off."

"I done heard it," Aunt Sylvie blurted. "It's an iron skillet. I win. Now give out the prize and get out of my kitchen!"

Before Granada could fuss at Sylvie for spoiling the riddle, the door that led to the great house swung open and in strode a woman as pale as death, her long hair undone, cascading in gray-black ribbons over her dressing gown. Her eyes had the look of someone permanently startled. On her shoulder sat her pet, a tufted capuchin monkey, his little black hands clutching a rope of her hair.

Chester nearly knocked Granada over when he scrambled to his feet to give the mistress a little bow. The girl quickly found her balance and caught the skirt of her shimmy with her thumb and forefinger, curtsying like she had seen white women do. But all the time she kept an eye on the

61

delicate, blue satin gown draped over the mistress's rail-thin arm.

Mistress Amanda's maid, Lizzie, followed shortly, holding out before her a pair of dainty slippers, one in each hand. She pulled up beside her mistress and the kitchen became dead quiet. Even the monkey sat motionless on his mistress's shoulder.

The sight of Lizzie always troubled Granada. The woman had aged into a sullen, yellow-toned creature with one dead, milk-white eye, the other constantly circling the room until it lit on Granada, and there it would stay for long moments at a time. The girl got the distinct feeling that Lizzie was warning her.

It was the monkey that broke the horrible silence. He began to sniff noisily at the cooking smells and made sharp smacking noises with his mouth. Then he dropped from Mistress Amanda's shoulder, scampered across the table, and leaped into Chester's arms.

Sometimes Granada was plain jealous of that monkey. Daniel Webster was an anniversary gift from Master Ben and slept in a wrought-iron cage right in the mistress's bedroom. Sylvie swore the master had to have been drunk to have paid that New

Orleans street vendor good money for the dirty beast. But Mistress Amanda loved that monkey. Even though she had a son a few years younger than Granada, it was obvious to everyone the mistress favored the monkey over poor Little Lord.

The monkey was now grinning childlike at Chester and began plucking at the shiny buttons on his coat. When the mistress turned her forlorn gaze to Sylvie, Chester swatted at the monkey's paws. The beast responded with a high-pitched shriek.

"Take this gown, Aunt Sylvie," the mistress said, her small voice rustling like dead leaves.

To Granada the mistress seemed to grow more fragile every day, her features more gaunt, and the circles beneath her delicate blue eyes were now dark as old bruises that never healed. The mistress glanced about the kitchen nervously, but never once did her eyes light upon the girl.

Granada knew she would not exist for the mistress until she had changed into the dress, and then only as a shadow, like the silhouette portraits of Miss Becky that were displayed in nearly every room of the house. The mistress hardly ever touched Granada anymore, not since she was a very small child and the mistress would go to sleep holding Granada in her arms. Today she was to wear the dress, remain silent, and stand close, never to leave the mistress's side when company was around.

"And remember, launder the gown and return it by tomorrow night. You bring it to me yourself."

Aunt Sylvie brusquely took the dress from the mistress and then coolly studied Miss Becky's lace cuffs going to yellow.

"You know how Becky was about her things. She wouldn't abide a wrinkle or —"

"I know what to do, Mistress Amanda," Aunt Sylvie cut in.

Next the mistress took the shiny leather shoes from Lizzie, who kept her head down, as if not to remind the mistress of her dead eye the color of a porcelain cup. She presented the shoes to Aunt Sylvie, as though she was entrusting her with the most fragile of treasures. "And the slippers —"

"Yes, ma'am. I know," Sylvie muttered, taking the shoes from the mistress with much less reverence than they were given. "I'll dust them out good with lime after the girl wears them."

"Nobody else, Aunt Sylvie. You do it, you hear? Nobody else touches Becky's things. She never could abide —"

"I know that, Mistress Amanda."

"If Becky knew that anybody else —"

"Yes, ma'am!" Sylvie broke in again. "I'll take good care like I always do," she said bluntly. "I best get busy, then."

The mistress didn't make a move to leave. She was searching Aunt Sylvie's face. After long moments of leaden silence, she released the expression of vague helplessness, and her cold, lifeless eyes lit up with a fiery flash.

Granada tensed.

Lizzie hunched her shoulders and squinched her face, as if she were expecting the mistress to flare up and slap her other eye blind.

But today Mistress Amanda hit no one. She abruptly swung about and tromped from the kitchen, uttering not a word. Chester released Daniel Webster, who went scurrying after her. Lizzie's good eye circled the room once. She breathed deeply and then sped off, hurrying to catch up.

Everyone held their tongues until the hollow sounds of heels clopping down the covered walkway connecting the kitchen to the great house died away.

"She worse ever day," Aunt Sylvie said, making no effort to hide her disapproval. "Just ain't right. Acting like she don't remember she got a little boy still alive and breathing. No, the only one she thinks about is the dead one. I reckon Little Lord looks too much like his daddy to suit her."

Little Lord was Granada's best friend, and it pained her to hear Sylvie say he was never noticed, either.

Sylvie gently stroked the satiny softness of the gown draped over her arm. "I remember the first time Miss Becky wore this frock. It was for a children's tea party up in the bluffs at Delphi. Bless her baby-doll soul. One day Master Ben is going to put a stop to this mess."

Granada pulled at one of the velvet ribbons dangling from the cook's fingers. She touched the soft fabric to her lips, kissing it gently. "Put it on me, Aunt Sylvie," Granada pleaded.

"You keep wearing a dead girl's clothes," Aunt Sylvie warned, "and you'll get her haint after you."

Granada shrugged. She didn't believe in ghosts. "The mistress likes me to wear them. And Little Lord said I looked pretty all dressed up."

Aunt Sylvie planted her fists on her broad hips. "Just because Mistress Amanda is mad enough to parade you around in her dead baby's frocks don't make it right. And they don't make you white and they don't make anybody love you any more. Little Lord likes you just fine in your kitchen dress." Aunt Sylvie slapped her hands together. "Look at me, girl, while I'm talking!"

Granada crossed her arms over her chest and gave Sylvie a look of pure exasperation.

"Mark my words. Just as sure as Judgment Day, they going to come a time when the mistress reaches inside that wardrobe for another pretty costume and come up empty-handed. Only one left to wear be the one I put on Miss Becky before I laid her in her grave box. Then what you going to do? Go dig it up?"

Before Granada could think to protest, Sylvie had already drawn her hand back. "And if I see you raising up that stomping foot, I swear to merciful God I'll —"

Chester laughed at the cook's outburst. "Sylvie, you think that white girl was the Jesus child." He turned to Granada with kind eyes. "Them dresses look just as fine on you as they did Miss Becky. And she didn't have those pretty licorice-drop eyes and skin as fine as the mistress's best velvet. You just listen to old Chester here. Go on and have yourself a big time. Don't pay Sylvie no mind."

"Ain't no danger in this girl paying me no nevermind," Sylvie groused, stooping over to pick up the bowl of tallow that had been warming by the fire. "One day, girl, you going to learn that every fine road comes to a stopping place. Better be careful, one day your momma is going to show up and drag you off to them swamps. Then what you going to do? I'll tell you. You'll be sad you didn't pay Aunt Sylvie no heed."

Aunt Sylvie drew a chair from the table and sat down. "If you can tear yourself away from Chester and his foolishness, come on over to me, baby," Sylvie said warmly. "I'll grease your hair."

This was the Sylvie that the girl loved — the nice one who wasn't shouting orders and fussing about her kitchen. The one who called Granada "baby." She hurried to Aunt Sylvie and plopped herself on the floor, wedging between the cook's knees.

"I don't know how to explain it where you ain't going to get hurt," Sylvie said, dipping two fingers into the bowl. "You too young to understand, I guess. Like I told your momma when she was about your age, half the things you see in any white man's house ain't real. But in this particular house, real done took a holiday."

Before applying the dab of tallow, Sylvie leaned over and kissed Granada on the top of her head. "My pretty baby don't even know her own momma. Worse, you don'

68

care. Don't think I can never forgive the mistress for doing that to you. One day you going to see how all your life, you been tangled up in somebody else's grief."

Sylvie sighed. "I reckon it takes age to understand the kind of devilry that even the littlest death can give birth to."

CHAPTER 5

Granada knew that the first of the guests were in sight when she heard the distant sound of carriage wheels slicing into the carefully graded drive of crushed shells.

While the master was giving last-minute instructions to the servants, Granada ran out onto the gallery off the upstairs parlor to watch the guests arrive. The driver of the fancy brougham coach was elegant and fine-boned, outfitted in a black greatcoat and opera hat. He was expertly managing two high-stepping bays up the drive of gleaming white shells that had been hauled all the way from New Orleans and were replenished each year after the winter floods washed them away.

Granada tried to imagine the mansion as the passengers were seeing it — majestically columned and galleried on three sides, upstairs and down, and surmounted with a copper-domed observatory from which they would soon be invited to survey the master's swamp kingdom.

When Granada saw Chester, his buttons gleaming, march onto the drive to meet the carriage, she raced back inside the parlor and proudly claimed her place by the chair where the mistress sat. For it was here, by the mistress's side, more than any other place in all the master's glimmering universe, that Granada desired to be.

The mistress, on the other hand, didn't seem to be aware of where she was at the moment. The woman had doubled up on her laudanum in preparation for her guests, nearly sixty drops according to Granada's count. It took both Granada and Lizzie to lead the mistress down the hall to her chair in the parlor, each gripping an elbow.

Except for the embarrassed looks from the master, nobody ever seemed to mind. That was because Master Ben carefully managed his visitors' impressions so that little attention ever fell upon his unpredictable wife. The guests, even longtime callers, were so awed by the workings of the place that the mistress's condition could be easily overlooked.

Even now Granada could hear them chattering, throwing out words like "stunning" and "breathtaking" as they took in the floors

71

laid with marble, the crystal chandeliers, the floating double staircase with the polished mahogany banisters.

Granada stiffened and mentally rehearsed her first curtsy. Above the gleam and glitter of the mansion, the thing she wanted them all to remember from the day was *her.*

In strode Pomp, the butler, grandly dressed in one of his master's splendid old claw-hammer coats with its narrow tails down past his knees. To complement the polished banisters, the master made sure that Pomp's yellow skin glistened and gleamed by insisting he rub his face amply with tallow. As Pomp solemnly led the party into the room, Granada immediately recognized the two planters and their elegantly dressed wives. They had come all the way from the town of Delphi up in the bluffs.

Benjamin Satterfield, looking tall and lean and very much in charge, heartily greeted his visitors as they crossed the threshold. His fair skin seemed to pink up with enthusiasm.

The mistress remained seated in her massive chair with brocade the color of dried blood. Daniel Webster crouched a few inches to the left of her bonneted head, perched on the back of the chair.

But as Granada had hoped, it was her all eyes found first. She stood beaming at the mistress's side, bedecked in the elegant blue satin gown and creamy patent-leather shoes, her hair greased, combed, and ribboned. The intoxicating scents of Miss Becky's powders and perfumes rose off her skin.

Mistress Amanda acknowledged her guests with a single nod and a vacant smile, while Granada competed by showing off her curtsy. To make sure no one doubted her abilities, she bowed with exaggerated flourish, thrusting her right foot forward and drawing back the left, at the same time dramatically plucking her skirt upward on either side like turkey wings. Her spare fingers stuck out stiff and straight.

While she held the pose for the speechless guests, the monkey chittered frantically, scampering across the back of the chair, as if he were jealous of the attention. Granada remained outstretched in midcurtsy, while the manic monkey leaped off the chair onto the girl's back, causing her to totter. She struggled desperately, staggering about, flapping her arms to regain her balance.

With mayhem erupting about her, Mistress Amanda sat rigidly erect, her eyes staring blankly before her, like a queen bored with her court jesters. Her only movement was a quick jerk of her head when she caught herself listing too far in one direction.

Granada valiantly attempted to hold her curtsy, even with Daniel Webster bounding up and down on her shoulder, tugging on one of her plaits, and causing her to tilt considerably to one side. The girl peeked to note the reactions of the guests.

The women had dropped their eyes to the floor, looking red-faced, as if they had been slapped in church, and the bald-headed man with a high stomach and eyebrows like furry caterpillars hid his mouth behind his hand and coughed loudly. Granada thought he might be strangling, but then she noticed his eyes. They danced with a wicked merriment. When she looked at the master, she saw that his cheeks were ablaze, and he was now talking rapidly to his guests, shunting them as best he could toward the pastries on the sideboard.

Granada didn't mind. They could be as mean and as jealous as they cared to, just like Aunt Sylvie. The girl was used to it. All Granada knew was that the immense gold-framed mirror on the wall before her proved a kindlier presence. It did not avert its gaze nor did it scorn her. It did not exclude Granada because her skin was darker than all the rest. In spite of the creature on her shoulder, the reflection showed Granada to be as beautiful as anybody in the room, and the mistress loved her best for it.

Pomp broke the tension by lifting a tray of goblets from the sideboard and moving among the guests. "Drink, Master? Drink, Mistress?" he asked all around, proffering the silver tray.

As the guests chitchatted, and Daniel Webster quit Granada's shoulder for a higher perch on the marble mantel below Miss Becky's smiling portrait, the girl knew that she had become invisible again. She took the opportunity to shift her weight from one foot to the other. The dead girl's feet were too small and the shoes pinched Granada's toes. When she first saw them earlier that morning, they had gleamed so, her heart nearly stopped. But now she would much prefer to have on the soft silvery slippers studded with tiny glass beads that she wore when Senator Davis came calling.

Granada knew she was supposed to avert her eyes, but she couldn't help stealing glances as more white folks entered the room and then stood about with their company manners, all stiff and formal, performing half bows, with their stifled laughs that sounded like coughs.

More interesting than their words were the spaces they left between, the gaps of silence separating the speakers. They talked the way they danced at their fancy balls, holding each other at considerable distance. Nobody ever crowded in on top of another. They reminded Granada of cold pots in the fireplace. Not like Chester or Aunt Sylvie and Pomp when they got to carrying on in the kitchen. They came to full boil, sloshed over the sides, and didn't care who noticed.

"It's a grand day for preaching to the nigras, isn't it, Bishop?" the bald-headed man called out, removing a toddy from Pomp's tray.

"Now leave the good bishop alone, Charles," his wife teased.

The fat bishop smiled, as if pleased to be noticed. "The day was made for it, Mr. Stogner," he said, "as is every Sabbath, rain or shine."

Their words were ponderous but dead, and Granada imagined them falling at her feet like wet leaves after a winter rain. Aunt Sylvie fussed that white folks only talked about four things: "Slaves and cotton and cotton and slaves." Then she would add: "And they don't know a damn thing about none of them."

It was then Granada heard someone whisper her name.

The girl cut her eyes to the doorway where stood a child several years younger than she with corn-silk hair.

"Hey, Granada!" he called again.

It was Little Lord, the master's son, peering at her from around the doorframe. The boy smiled at her in pure delight and then waved. He was about to say something else before milky-eyed Lizzie came up behind him and grabbed his arm, hauling him back to his room.

The boy's reaction was all Granada needed to reaffirm her earlier estimation of herself. Little Lord had probably never seen a white girl looking this splendid. Including that dead sister of his.

"What's your game, Bishop Kerry?" the bald man was saying. "You trying to get a job preaching to all our nigras?"

"I just sow the seeds, Mr. Stogner. They fall where they may and take root where they can." He drained his goblet and nodded his head with a little quiver of chins to Pomp for another drink. "I sow liberally," he chirped. "The rest is up to God."

"Bishop, you can sow until you're blue in the face, but it won't change the fact of the matter."

Granada noticed that the bald-headed man was becoming animated, those caterpillar eyebrows rising higher and higher like they were trying to crawl up his slick-as-an-egg noggin. "Admit it, Bishop," he said, "everybody knows that the nigra doesn't have a soul."

Granada shifted about uncomfortably in her shoes and then stifled a yawn, wishing Little Lord would sneak away again. Which Negroes was he talking about not having souls? she wondered.

"Charles, please," the man's pretty wife said, not at all unpleasantly. "We know what you're going to say before you say it. How will Amanda ever forgive us for spoiling this fine gathering?"

Perhaps hearing her name, or maybe sensing a twinge of tension among her guests, Mistress Amanda smiled instinctively, doing the minimum of what was required of her as a hostess. But just as quickly her face fell back to cloudy dullness.

The bishop bowed politely. "I don't mind the jousting. Not in the least." Then he turned to the bald man. "All I tell them is what the Scripture tells them. Obedience here on earth is a qualification for life eternal."

"You talking about *nigras* in heaven?" the

man scoffed, glancing over at Granada and scrunching his eyebrows together so that the two caterpillars merged to become one enormous bug. "Ha! Only if God raises cotton!"

Granada's cheeks burned with fury. She raised her foot to stomp, but then thought better of it. What she wanted to do was kick this bald-headed man in the shins. Of course she was going to heaven. The mistress would make sure of it, writing Granada a pass if she needed one. Anyway, he was probably talking about those Negroes who lived out in the far-flung settlements. "Swamp slaves" was what Aunt Sylvie called them. They probably didn't have a white person to recommend them to heaven like Granada did.

As the guests resumed talking in their mechanical fashion, Granada detected the growing sound of chatter in the plantation yard. The slave families from out in the swamps were arriving! Now there were loud calls of recognition followed by outbursts of hooting and sturdy laughter. Soon it would be time for the preaching.

She checked her reflection in the mirror and touched Miss Becky's pearl necklace. Her stomach tingled, anticipating all the admiring looks that would be cast her way when the preaching commenced.

The bishop had begun to weave a little on his feet. "All I'm saying is religion, sensibly dispensed, only bolsters the proper order of things. That's what the planter desires above all things, isn't it? Order?"

"Well, you can preach to Satterfield's nigras as much as you want. But leave mine alone," the man said, now sounding like a bully. "I never knew a slave with religion to fetch one dollar more on the block than one without." He turned to Master Ben. "But of course the slave market doesn't concern you, does it, Ben? You neither buy nor sell off your place. Breed your own and keep them close. That's your motto."

"Why buy trouble?" another guest said. "Isn't that what you say, Ben?"

"I know when I'm being played the fool," Master Ben said, his cheeks blazing. "But you've got to admit the logic of it. It's not like the old days of the saltwater Negro, when you could ship your cargo straight from Africa uninfected with the abolitionist's poison. No, now the domestic market is full up with other planters' troublesome slaves. Our only salvation is to scientifically breed a stable order of docile Negro. I've come up with three tenets: Isolation. Religion. Family.

80

"First of all," he began what sounded like the start of a long speech, "keep your stock quarantined from dangerous notions. This Mississippi Delta wilderness is ideal. Most of my young ones have never heard of a free black, much less seen one."

The men nodded.

"And there are ways to employ both family and religious instincts to instill loyalty. I've done experiments on my own stock."

Granada was becoming impatient. She wondered how long the master was going to lecture his guests. He was typically excited about some new "experiment" he was running and would often produce one of the elegantly bound journals he was always writing in. Sylvie said he had begun a book on every slave, all three hundred of them, keeping track of what they ate, what they weighed, how well they bred, and how much cotton they picked. Sylvie said that after his wife began acting so daft, Master Ben started one on her, too. Last Preaching Sunday the master had read to his guests about how feeding the girls milk from an early age would get them to menstruating two to three years early. He figured he had increased his stock ten percent by that method alone. Granada had asked Sylvie what menstruating was, but all she would say was, "When it happens, let me know. I'll tell you then."

"You've done more experiments than the mad scientist," said the bald-headed man. "What's his name? You remember. The one that woman writes about."

"Frankenstein!" someone called out and laughed.

But the laughter only made Master Ben even more shrill. "If Lincoln wins this election and tries to free my slaves, not a one of them will take to the road. They are with me, in slavery or emancipation." He then said with particular emphasis, "One day soon, mark my words, the slaves are going to have their freedom. The best strategy for us planters is to make sure when they get it, they have no use for it."

The bald-headed man glanced over at Granada again, catching her in the act of surveying the guests. He smiled and the glint in his eye made her quiver with dread. Then he raised his eyebrows, smirking. "No, I expect you would have to chase off some of your slaves with a stick to get them to leave."

She quickly dropped her eyes. Daniel Webster reached down from the mantel and pulled at the ribbon in her hair, but the weight of the man's gaze kept her chin pushed into her chest.

He laughed. "If you ask me, it's the gators, cottonmouths, and a million acres of swamp that keep your slaves from running off."

Then he took a drink and his face darkened. "I'll make you a wager, Ben," he said, solemn now. "I predict that before this scourge of the blacktongue is through decimating your stock, you'll be rushing to the market with the rest of us. I buried a dozen of mine already."

The man's talk of blacktongue sent a shiver down Granada's spine. All the servants had been abuzz with rumors about the disfiguring disease. It made your tongue swell up and your fingers and toes fall off. It was said those out in the swamps had been dropping like flies. Again Granada comforted herself with the fact that so far it was only felling the swamp Negroes. The house and yard slaves seemed to be immune.

"Charles, you are disrespecting our host," his wife admonished again. "This is Benjamin's home. As long as we are accepting his gracious hospitality, we should respect his customs."

The man seemed ready to argue, but then reconsidered. "My wife's right, as always," he said and then performed a slight bow to his host. "Sorry, Ben. I know you've got your Kentucky ways, and I wouldn't ever want to place my welcome in jeopardy. The major benefit of these peculiar gatherings is always yours and Amanda's company. Not to mention Aunt Sylvie's cooking."

Master Ben responded with a stiff bow of his own. "Thank you, Charles."

"I guess we should be thankful this epidemic is playing out like the cholera," the man added, "another nigra disease." He raised his empty cup in a toast. "Nigras, or *Negroes,* as Benjamin calls them, can be replaced. Good friends can't. Again, please forgive me my boorishness."

Mistress Amanda stirred in her chair and looked around the room with an expression of puzzled concern.

"You honor us," the master said coldly, cutting his eyes toward his wife. "Isn't that so, Amanda?"

Mistress Amanda did not speak right away and seemed vaguely surprised that she had been addressed directly by her husband. When the guests looked to her anxiously for a response, they saw that her eyes, once dry and vacant, seemed to tear up.

As she always did when the mistress was troubled and her countenance softened,

Granada ached to soothe her, to burrow deep inside the woman's grief in hopes of locating a home for herself somewhere close to her mistress's heart. But she had been warned never to address the mistress directly, and as much as she wanted to comfort the mistress, Granada feared disobeying her more. She held her tongue.

"A Negro disease," Mistress Amanda muttered, her tone unaccountably sad. Then she sighed heavily and with such anguish that Granada thought the mistress was about to cry out in agony. She reached for Granada's hand, startling the girl, and gripped it tightly.

Everyone saw the gesture, but no one said a word. From out in the yard, the sound of three hundred congregating field slaves thundered loud against the silence in the room, but louder still was the throbbing of Granada's heart.

The mistress had reached out for her in front of these white people! Granada stood there with her hand in the mistress's, holding her breath lest that physical bond be broken. Then she dared to return the mistress's grip. They held to each other tight, the moment so welcome, yet so foreign, that tears welled up in the girl's eyes as well.

The guests did not notice. Their gaze was

still upon the two clutched hands, the girl's dark one and the nearly translucent blue-veined one.

Granada was proud that they were seeing it! She would not have released the mistress's hand now if an entire army of white people had shaken their heads in disgust. This moment belonged to her, not them.

"Amanda!" Master Ben said sternly, but his wife's eyes did not go to him. She had the look of a person in a dream, witnessing events beyond these four walls.

"I tell you what," the bald man chirped, drawing attention to himself and ending the awkward moment, "if it will get Aunt Sylvie and her roast lamb into heaven, I'll attend all the preaching the good bishop can serve up and pray mightily for her ascension! Negro or no Negro!"

"Now you're being sacrilegious, Charles," his wife said, but her tone was gentle. She took the goblet from his hand. "This is your last drink before the service. You better watch him, Bishop Kerry. He's likely to jostle you aside mid-sermon and deliver his own heretical theology."

They all laughed uncomfortably, and then to everyone's relief another guest was ushered into the parlor. The men gravitated toward the newly arrived banker, eagerly distancing themselves from Master Ben's wife and the awkward scene she was presently making. The women, though, hovered around Amanda, discreetly concealing her with their voluminous petticoats and close attention.

"Amanda, my poor dear," the bald-headed man's wife said tenderly. As she spoke she reached up to separate Amanda's hand from Granada's, artfully replacing the girl's with her own gloved one. She did not glance at Granada when she broke that link.

Yet that's all it took to make Granada once more invisible, aching for the touch of the mistress again.

"They spoke of death," Amanda said in great agitation. "Has anyone died? Please tell me," she demanded. "Who is it that's died?"

"No one, dear Amanda," said an old woman with a ruby on her finger. "No one has died."

"Slaves," said the woman who now held the mistress's hand, "only slaves," and this seemed to calm her.

When the last of the guests arrived, Master Ben led them all out onto the grand gallery and bade them sit in the chairs that Pomp had arranged earlier. Bishop Kerry strode up to the polished oak lectern, one that

Barnabas, the plantation carpenter, had built especially for these services. The red-faced bishop scanned his audience of black faces down below and then began to speak his big, puzzling words to the population of Satterfield Plantation — the only world that Granada knew existed.

Once she had heard the master say that he could look out from this gallery toward forever, and without lying claim he owned everything and everybody as far as a keen-sighted person could see — more than three hundred slaves housed in three separate settlements and four thousand acres spreading across the western half of Hopalachie County. It took him three days to ride his land. To Granada that had to be the whole world, plus some.

She looked across the sea of black bodies sitting in a yard enclosed by the stable, several barns, the smokehouse, the dairy, the ginhouse, the sawmill, Silas's cabin, and farther down the cabins for the dozens of family servants. Every plank and board on the place was whitewashed and gleaming in the sun. Beyond them were countless miles of levees and ditches and high ridges, alligator swamps and deep Delta forests.

It was indeed an immense world, a world in which she often felt alien. Like when the house servants laughed at her dark skin or taunted her for wearing a dead white girl's clothes. Or when Mistress Amanda let weeks pass without sending for Granada to sit with her in the darkened bedroom.

But this moment was different. Granada was as happy as she could ever hope to be. For *in this moment* she knew where she belonged. Hadn't the touch from the mistress's hand told her once and for all? She could still almost feel the warmth of it.

Sylvie had warned Granada what a fickle thing belonging was. Perhaps down below in the yard, among all the black faces, looking up at her with emerald-green eyes was a light-skinned woman with fine curly hair, who in another moment, one long ago, most likely stood where Granada stood today.

But Granada could not think of that. Nor could she think about what would happen when the last of Becky's dresses was drawn from the mahogany wardrobe. Instead Granada told herself: I belong in this dress, wearing these beautiful shoes, standing next to my mistress, warmed by the gentle sunshine of an early-spring afternoon. Why, she wondered, couldn't one perfect moment such as this be woven into a warm blanket against any chill winds that might come? Perhaps it would last, after all.

It was an immense world, and right now Granada felt that she stood at the very heart of it, and she told herself again: This is where I belong.

CHAPTER 6

Gran Gran awoke the next morning in her chair, her body stiff. She looked down at Violet who slept serenely on her cot and knew right away that something had settled within the girl. Sure enough, over the hours that followed there were no screams, and the odd movement of her head had stopped. There was only deep, hard sleep, as if the girl were nestled in some healing cocoon of calm.

At last Gran Gran felt she could leave Violet's side and lay herself down on the cot in the kitchen. She had barely shut her eyes when she fell into a black, dreamless sleep, and when she woke several hours later she realized that for the first time in ages the muttering voices had been absent. There was only the dark and the quiet, and she thought, if death were like this, then dying would not be so bad.

After another day, Gran Gran was able to

91

get the girl to rise from her bed. She even began to take her meals at the table. But Violet had yet to utter a single word.

The old woman was patient. She had seen enough to know a body had to work this out on its own schedule.

Violet was so quiet during the day there were moments Gran Gran forgot the girl was nearby, until she looked around and found her standing close, studying the woman with those color-shifting eyes, her stare so penetrating it filled Gran Gran with a cold unease.

The old woman would take the girl by the shoulders and gaze deep into those fearsome eyes. "I can see, Violet. You still patching and knitting. That's good. That's real good. You doing what you got to do."

Although Violet wouldn't let Gran Gran out of her sight, neither did the girl ever touch the woman, and she flinched when the old woman forgot and reached for the child's small, china-fine hands. In fact, Violet mostly kept them hidden — in a pocket, behind her back, or under the table.

She was giving off a second sign, Gran Gran figured, like the shaking of the head had been. Though the old woman could not get a feeling for the meaning, it wasn't hard to venture a guess.

The old woman predicted the girl's ailment would settle in her hands for a while before finally emptying out the tips of her fingers. When she had healed from the tribulation of her mother's death, she would again be able to touch and in turn be touched by another.

CHAPTER 7

Violet woke to the distant muttering of voices. This happened almost nightly since the day of her arrival, after the old lady had put out the light and gone to bed. As the girl did the other times, she carefully pushed back the covers and rose from her cot.

She had come to think that there might be other people living in this house, and at night they gathered in some room beyond the kitchen to talk with one another. Perhaps they knew the whereabouts of her mother.

She walked barefoot across the cold plank floor into the moon-drenched kitchen. The old woman lay snoring in the bed next to the boarded-over hearth. Too slight to call forth the creaking of the floorboards, Violet soundlessly crossed the room in the direction of the voices. They seemed to come from behind the far wall, where the tattered remnant of an old damask curtain hung. It was nailed up high and dropped nearly to the floor. On every other night, when she had gotten this far, the voices ceased. Tonight, they grew louder. Violet pulled back the drapery and there it was, the door that held back the sounds, shut tight.

The girl put her ear to a cold panel of white pine. From somewhere in the distance a dog belled out and others answered. Perhaps they were hearing what she heard.

Even standing on the tips of her toes, the latch was out of her reach. She quietly eased a chair over to the door. From its height, she lifted the little metal hook from its eye and then pushed, not reacting to the rusty creak. A fetid rush of air greeted her. It was the sharp, musty odor of things shut up for too long.

She climbed down from the chair and haltingly entered the unlit passageway. The planks beneath her feet were icy and the floor sloped downward, urging her forward through the narrow bricked hallway. Waiting for her at the end of the passageway was another door, this one open.

She entered a room as vast as nighttime, only there were no stars above her. She stood stock-still as her eyes adjusted to the light.

To her left was a succession of floor-to-ceiling windows, covered from the inside with immense slatted shutters, some partially covered with heavy drapes, identical to the damask panel that hung in the kitchen.

Directly before her was a seemingly endless table, extending into the inky blackness beyond. The whispering now was all around her. Hundreds of voices, some saying her name, some uttering sounds she did not know as words but could feel their meanings — happy, afraid, angry, sad.

Something on the table drew her attention. When she looked down and saw what it was, she let out a strangled cry.

A pair of glowing eyes peered back at her in a wide, petrified stare. Next two dark nostrils emerged from the void, and a large mouth smiled up at her.

The face remained frozen.

Violet found her breath and screamed, and kept screaming until she heard the sound of approaching footsteps, and a light bloomed from behind.

"Violet! What you doing in here?"

The girl turned and threw herself into the old woman's arms, shivering from the sight.

Violet's embrace caught Gran Gran off guard. It had been so long since anyone had sought her out with such fervor, with such desperate need.

"It's nothing to be a'scared of, Violet," Gran Gran said. "Look a'here."

She held the lantern over the face on the table. Violet peeked through the tiny slits between her lids. When she saw, she carefully reached out to touch it. The surface was smooth and cold and solid, not fleshy at all. It was clay! A face molded of clay and baked hard.

Gran Gran raised the lantern and threw the flickering light against the wall. "And here, Violet."

The girl gasped. All down the wall there were other faces, dozens of them, each different, some smiling, some frowning, some looked as if they were about to say something, others like they had been startled awake, others still asleep. Some had coarse, patchy heads of hair made from moss and string. Rows and rows of them. There were too many to count.

"Nothing to be scared of. Only dried mud," Gran Gran laughed, "just like me!"

The girl seemed calm now, but she still shivered.

"You ought be in bed," the old woman fussed. "You not well yet and you and me both in our naked feet."

The girl didn't respond, her eyes still taking in the wall of faces.

When Gran Gran took the girl by the shoulder to lead her to the kitchen, she drew back and then reached for the edge of the table. She was making a stand. Since the night she had arrived, this was the first thing the girl had shown an interest in.

"You want to stay? You want to study these faces?" Gran Gran ventured. "Maybe one of them favors somebody you remember?" she asked hopefully.

The girl's eyes scanned the wall, shifting from face to face.

After a long while, Gran Gran said, "I don't know what you want to hear about. But I'll just tell you what you looking at. How's that?"

The girl turned to Gran Gran, her expression expectant, like a child eager to be taken by a tale.

"Since I'm going to have to do the talking for both of us, let me see what's something a little girl might ask." She studied Violet, making out like she could read the girl.

"Now, if I was you, I might ask, 'Where all them silly faces come from?' And I would say back to the girl what asked, 'I made them every one with my own two hands. Dug the clay and fired them in that very fireplace in that very kitchen.'"

Gran Gran paused, waiting for the girl's

reaction. Her head tilted upward at the old woman, as if intent on hearing every word.

"And then you might ask, 'Are them real folks?' And I would say, 'Yes, they real people. Knew ever soul.' " Gran Gran smiled. "I'm nearly ninety years old. That's why I needed me a whole wall."

The girl nodded, almost imperceptibly.

Gran Gran continued. "You see, a long time ago I was thinking it might help cut down on my forgetting. I figured if I could get all their faces in one place, I could remember them better." Gran Gran shook her head at the silliness of the idea. "Like I said, mostly foolishness." She looked carefully at Violet. "Forgetting got its place, I reckon."

Gran Gran held the lantern over the table, illuminating a face sporting a wide grin and a set of perfect white teeth. "Now like this one. The one that scared you. This is Chester. He was the driver for Mistress Amanda. When I was a girl like you. Chester, now he loved to tell riddles. When he weren't telling riddles, he was polishing the brass buttons on his coachman's coat. He was proud of them buttons. Chester!" Gran Gran said, addressing the mask. "Like you to meet my friend Violet." Gran Gran nodded at the mask and waited, as if for a response. She turned to the girl. "Violet, Chester say he glad to make your acquaintance and to forgive him for putting a fright in you."

There it was! Gran Gran definitely discerned a smile on the girl's face. And the shivering had ceased.

Gran Gran carried the lantern over to the wall. "Now this giant of a man with a nose as big as a housecat, he called Big Dante." Gran Gran laughed at the memory of him. "Big Dante could pick six hundred pounds of cotton a day. Had fingers tough as hawks' feet. Most gentle man with children I ever seen.

"Next to him we got Aunt Sylvie. The cook." The face was plump and stern. "She helped lay the bricks for her own fireplace when this wasn't nothing but swamp. The very same one in the kitchen today. And she cooked up a storm back there. Nobody never made biscuits like Aunt Sylvie."

Gran Gran sniffed the air and then laughed in wonderment. "I could swear I smell them biscuits right this minute. Lord, ain't it strange how the memory can play tricks on you!"

The expression on Violet's face was rapt, even hungry. But for what? For her words? For the tales of folks long dead? Polly used to say that it was the people's story that kept

100

them bound one to another. Everybody holds their own thread.

"Stories!" Gran Gran laughed. "It's the stories you needing, ain't it? Well, you come to the right place. All these faces got a tale. Like this one!" She moved on to a mask that appeared to have a fresh coat of whitewash. "That be Mistress Amanda herself," Gran Gran said shaking her head. "She up there in the Satterfield burying ground. 'Long with her babies." Gran Gran chuckled. "Now she was a mess. She even got a vault for her monkey. He's buried right next to her. Her precious daughter on one side and that monkey on the other and her boy at her feet.

"Now if I was you, I wouldn't believe a word I just said. But I ain't lying!" Gran Gran exclaimed.

"Satterfield family burying ground is what you call exclusive. It just for white folks and monkeys." She laughed again. "Slaves, they buried by themselves. Neither one nothing but bramble now. Satterfields all dead and after Freedom, colored started burying at their churches. Nobody left to tend no graves."

Gran Gran breathed deeply and scanned the wall. Almost to herself she said, "I guess I'm the last one left to carry these tales. I used to come in here and study these folks. Even talk to them. But they never said nothing back. So I let them be. Let the dead bury the dead and dust to dust."

Violet pointed to the wall.

Gran Gran smiled. That was almost as good as a word. "Which one, baby? This one?"

The old woman carefully lifted a mask off the wall and for a moment studied the face with pointed cheekbones and eyes the color of sunlit amber. "This is the one I spent most of my time on. Trying to bring her back, I reckon."

Gran Gran had perfectly replicated the head scarf lined with the beaten disks of brass. She held it up to the light so the girl could see how the metal shone like yellow moons. "I used Chester's old coat buttons to make it."

The girl was smiling now, holding her hands out. Gran Gran gave it to Violet to hold.

"Yes, ma'am. You got good taste in people, Violet. You went straight to the biggest bug of them all. Polly Shine. But to really know her, you need to know how things were before she showed up to turn them all upside down."

CHAPTER 8

Granada was asleep on her thin pallet by the fireplace when Aunt Sylvie nudged the girl with the toe of her brogan. "Get up, now, baby," she said. "I got to get breakfast ready and you under my feet."

This morning Granada was just a regular house girl, only darker than the others. She would go back to performing her usual duties helping in the kitchen and watching over Little Lord for Lizzie. By the dim light of the new day, she donned her plain servant's dress, the beautiful gown and the pretty shoes and the velvet ribbons of yesterday a faraway dream.

"Granada," Aunt Sylvie said, "the best way to unburden the heart is to busy the hand."

"Yes, ma'am."

Soon Granada was helping with breakfast — stirring pots, tending the fire, and making trips out to the smokehouse, trying her

103

best to get over her great comedown.

The night before, after the household had gone to bed, she had begged Aunt Sylvie to allow her to wear the dress a little while longer. Granada promised that she would not even sit down and crush the fabric.

"Anyhow," she said, "Little Lord ain't got a good look at me all dressed up."

Aunt Sylvie scowled. "I told you to stay away from that boy unless you in my sight. He's only eight but one day he'll be your master. Not your playfriend."

Granada didn't think that would be such a bad thing, belonging to Little Lord. She liked being around him. And studying him. He was put together in such a curious way. His hair was as soft as Miss Becky's satins and silks. And his skin, so pale and thin, if she were to back him up to a lantern, the light would probably shine right through.

"Please, Aunt Sylvie, just a little while."

The cook would have none of it. "Scoot yourself out of those clothes," Sylvie had said. "Don't you know you tempting the devil wearing the raiments of the dead?"

When the cook saw the tears in Granada's eyes, she softened her tone. She drew Granada to her and held the satin-clad girl in her arms. Sylvie didn't seem to care anymore about wrinkling Miss Becky's dress.

"You and me both just too tired to fight no more," Sylvie whispered into the girl's ear. "I know it's hard on you, too. I don't know what Mistress Amanda expects you to make out of all this. Some days it makes me want to cry with you. And you a poor motherless girl."

After a few moments, Sylvie released Granada and said, "Enough of this talk. Let's get you undressed."

As she lifted the dress over Granada's head, Sylvie muttered, "I thought for sure one day the master would put an end to this silliness. But he didn't listen to Silas way back when. Brushed him aside like a fly. I reckon as long as the mistress's daddy got his name on the deed, the master won't go against her. One word from her, daft or not, her daddy could turn Master Ben into a regular Mr. Ben. He knows it and she knows it. They at a draw and you in the middle."

Sylvie had been right about busy hands. As the thick slabs of side meat began to sizzle, giving off its aroma, and the house servants, the only family Granada had ever known, ambled into the kitchen, taking their usual places around the big pine table, Granada's spirits began to rise.

By the time she returned from the cistern with a bucket of water, Chester had already made himself the center of attention. He caught Granada's eye and winked, like he was saying, Watch this!

Granada went about her work minding the pots and putting the food on platters, but she kept an eye on Chester so as not to miss his latest caper.

"Now just the other day I rode the master by the banker's house in Delphi. While I stayed back in the buggy, I heard the master tell that banker to draw out a draft for five thousand dollars."

"That ain't no big secret," Pomp groused as he sat down to join them at the table. "That banker keeps the master's money. To get his money, he naturally got to go where the money is kept."

"But what you ain't guessed is what that money is going to buy. See, I'm telling you I got some answers none of y'all can guess." Chester smiled and waited.

"Well, I suspect it's probably for some sheep or some cows," Aunt Sylvie ventured. "Nothing special about that."

"Maybe a new horse," Granada guessed, taken up in the show Chester was putting on.

"Listen to that girl," Chester laughed,

shaking his head. "Don't matter what the question is, she's all the time guessing the answer is a horse."

Aunt Sylvie frowned at Granada, letting her know this was her time to work, not to guess. Granada grabbed a kitchen rag and pulled a skillet of corn pone from the rack.

"Could be a boatload of near about anything," Pomp said. "Molasses, spirits, a hundred barrels full of brogan shoes. This don't sound like a big secret to me."

Satisfied he had stumped them, Chester leaned in over the table and whispered, "He says he was going to market and buy him a slave!"

"Naw!" snorted Pomp, the saddle of red freckles across his nose bunching up when he scowled. "Five thousand dollars for just one head? You bound to misheard. Ain't no slave costs that much. And the master don't buy slaves off the plantation no way. He was bragging about that yesterday to his company, how he can raise as many as he needs."

"I ain't lying!" Chester exclaimed. "And you should of been there to hear that pink-faced banker squeal! Sounded like a stuck pig." Chester squeaked in his highest register, imitating the banker. " 'Mr. Satterfield! That's enough for four good niggers or a wagonload of used-up ones. What's so special about this one?' "

Granada set out the tin plates. The talk about buying slaves was new to her. She believed everybody on the plantation was like her, born and raised on the place. She figured slaves were just something that came with the land, like trees and swamps and white-tailed deer.

But whatever the answer, Granada could tell that Chester was enjoying himself, savoring the fact that he knew something the others were dying to be let in on. The only person making any sound was half-blind Silas slurping hot coffee from his saucer.

Pomp, whose buttermilk cheeks were always the first to redden, finally blurted, "Go on and finish what you started, Chester. What did the master say? What so special about this one?"

Chester leaned in over the table again and whispered, "That was the queerest thing of all. Master Ben, he don't say *nothing* to explain himself. All he said was it'll be something like nobody in these parts has ever seen before. Then he told that banker to make a draft written out to a broker in North Carolina. Master just turned his back on that gape-mouthed banker and walked back to the buggy whistling to hisself."

Aunt Sylvie motioned for Granada to set the platter of fatback on the table and then turned to the coachman. "Hurry along this tale of yours, Chester, or I'm liable to be just as slow with your grub," she said. "What's so special about some slave from up the country?"

Chester shrugged coyly and then took a sip of coffee. "I tried to ease it out of the master on the way back from town," he said. "But drunk as he was, he still wouldn't say. And if he ain't telling me, he ain't telling nobody. Y'all know I'm the master's right-hand man."

"Biggity fool!" Aunt Sylvie said, dropping a corn pone on his plate. She cast a quick glance over at Old Silas. "Right-hand man" was a title that used to be Silas's. Everybody knew that a while back Old Silas was the one who carried the plantation keys for the master.

But if Silas had heard, he didn't show it. All his attention appeared to be on cutting his fatback into pieces he could easily gum.

Aunt Sylvie turned her ire back on Chester. "You so stuck on yourself you liable to break a sweat trying to get loose. You don't know nothing!"

Everybody laughed, including Chester. He seemed to like getting Aunt Sylvie's goat best of all.

"Don't get me mad or I won't tell you the rest of it," Chester bluffed. He looked around the table at his audience. They were growing impatient with his pranking so he decided against teasing them any longer.

"Well, yesterday after the preaching, the master told Barnabas to start up on a new cabin." Chester nodded toward the kitchen door. "It's going to be setting right out on the other side of the yard. Four big rooms and a brick fireplace big as Aunt Sylvie's over there. Told Barnabas to make sure it was finished when he got back from North Carolina. He catching a steamboat out of Port Gayoso next week."

Chester leaned in over the table. "Now don't y'all reckon him buying a new hand and building a new cabin at the identical same time has got something to do with one another? I figure them two mules is hitched to the same wagon."

Aunt Sylvie, having fixed her own plate, sat down at the table next to Old Silas. "Now ain't that curious?" she said. "You sure about that fireplace? Reckon he might be buying another cook and ain't told me about it?" she asked, her eyes anxious. "You smart with riddles, Chester, what you reckon it means?"

"Don't think it's no cook, Sylvie," he reassured. "What does he need with two cookhouses and two fine cooks all in the same yard?"

Sylvie straightened. "Of course that's right!"

"Way I figure," Chester continued, "that cabin is bound to be a stable he's building special for some ten-foot-tall stud slave, taller than Big Dante, somebody man enough to straddle three rows of cotton and plow two teams at once. Need two rooms jest to stretch out at night and another to wiggle his toes."

Granada giggled, but Aunt Sylvie seemed offended. "That ain't it," she snapped. "Master ain't going to have no common field slave staying here in the yard with us and the family. No matter how big a giant he is. They spread disease. That's why he moved them all out in the swamps after the cholera."

"Now look who's stuck on themselves," Chester chided. "Them folks are just like us. But they get treated like cattle is all. Only difference is we get treated like pet dogs. Don't make us any better. We just know more tricks."

"Y'all talking like it's got to be a 'him,' " Pomp grumbled, getting back to the subject at hand. He glanced toward the kitchen door and then lowered his voice. "Knowing the master, I suspect this new one is a high-yellow fancy gal. Somebody Master Ben will keep all to hisself in that big ol' cabin."

Aunt Sylvie huffed. "That cabin will be in sight of the great house. The mistress ain't going to allow any frolicking where Little Lord can see. No matter how much medicine she swallows, she ain't going to swallow that! He ain't going to misbehave right under her nose."

Pomp chuckled to himself. "Guess he'll have to keep hisself satisfied with that pretty green-eyed gal out at Burnt Tree quarter."

Aunt Sylvie scowled at Pomp, and then fussed in a violent whisper, "Shut your damn mouth, fool!" And without missing a beat she looked up at the doorway, acting surprised to see Lizzie standing there. "Good morning, Lizzie!" the cook sang out for all to hear. "Come on in here and get you something to eat. Granada, tend to Lizzie's plate."

Lizzie stepped into the room, her movements as leaden as her expression. If she had heard Pomp's remark about Rubina, she didn't show it.

Granada didn't stir a muscle, not able to take her eyes off Lizzie. Whenever talk o

Lizzie's poor daughter arose, Granada wanted to disappear. "Every fine road comes to a stopping place," Aunt Sylvie was always warning Granada. "Poor Rubina was green-eyed with soft curly hair and look what happened to her!" In Lizzie's scowl, Granada could sense the tragic and shifting nature of whims and preferences, and the ground became unsteady beneath her feet.

"How you doing, Lizzie?" Chester asked in his cheeriest voice.

Lizzie looked around the table with her good eye, and watched silently as Granada, with a shaky hand, put meat and bread on her plate. Then Lizzie looked up again. "I know what y'all sayin. Ain't no secret to it. Don't let me spoil your fun."

Everybody was now frowning at Pomp. The house servants had a soft spot for Rubina, especially after the mistress had exiled the girl to the swamps when Miss Becky died. Of course Sylvie always said it could have been a lot worse. If she hadn't pleaded with the master, Mistress Amanda would have sold the poor little girl to one of those houses down in New Orleans just to get her out of the master's reach. White men paid pockets full of gold to be with a young light-skinned girl like that, Sylvie said. Even though it was common knowledge that the master visited Rubina on occasion in her cabin, Sylvie insisted, "At least it's just the one. Thanks to me, it ain't a new caller every night."

It was Chester who broke the tension. With a straight face, he offered, "Maybe the master found him a first-rate breeder. One that only hatches triple-yolkers. And she needs all that room to nurse them babies like a queen bee."

There was an explosion of laughter, fueled by the relief everyone felt for Chester maneuvering the conversation away from Rubina. Even Old Silas, who hardly ever spoke up when the servants gathered to swap tales, cracked a toothless smile.

Seeing her man enjoying himself, Aunt Sylvie decided to push him into talking. "What you reckon, Silas?" she asked, reminding everybody he was still among the living. "What you figure that cabin's for?"

In the old days, before he got in crossways with the mistress, they said Silas was the first to know anything. He received his information mouth to ear from the master. And some said the master got his orders mouth to ear from Silas. Said Silas was the one who laid out the entire plantation, designing the complicated system of levees, dams, drainage ditches, and irrigatic canals. Silas was just as dark as Granada, though she had never heard anybody bringing it to *his* attention.

"Yeah, what you think, Old Silas?" Chester laughed. "You think the master going to get him a gal that's been bred from a setting hen?"

Old Silas looked around the table. His eyes were dark, the whites nearly yellowed. He seemed surprised he had been spoken to. He then nodded slowly and answered, his voice faint and trembling with age and memory, "That's what he needs most, I reckon."

Chester and Pomp laughed, probably thinking Silas was making a joke. Old Silas acted like he hadn't heard them and kept talking into his coffee cup. "He's lost many a head over the years to sickness. The yellow fever. The cholera. But he never bought from off the plantation unless things were awfully bad."

There was a nodding of heads. They all had stopped smirking and started listening.

"That blacktongue must be taking out more hands than we know about. It's been as bad as the cholera was," he continued and then gave a half grin. "Yep, maybe that's just what he needs now, Chester, a flock of first-rate breeders."

"Those were some terrible days," Sylvie remembered aloud. "We carried those poor souls out by the wagonful."

"Sure cut down on his breeding stock," Old Silas added. "But Master Ben never went off the place to buy. Doesn't believe in it. Doesn't like to buy bad habits."

"He's a stubborn man," Sylvie said. She leaned in and spoke just above a whisper, "Lost his own daughter because of that bull head of his. I could have told him. 'Now you listen to me, Master Ben, it was me who washed and shrouded her body. And don't you reckon I know? The Angel of Death that took Miss Becky was the exact same color as the one what took all the rest of them . . .' " Sylvie let her words trail off. "He still ain't admitted that the sickness made it past a white man's door."

"Now it's the blacktongue," Old Silas said. "Last I counted he got twenty-five hands out at Mott's quarter on their backs ready to up and die on him like they're doing ever place else in the county. Master Ben buried three himself."

"I hope the master learned his lesson," Aunt Sylvie said, and then closed her eyes. "Please, God, don't let it travel here to us. 'Death he is a little man, he go from door to door . . .' "

116

Chester, rarely serious, now seemed dispirited. "Don't know what he's going to do with them that's already down with it. I know he ain't going to ask me to fetch that Dr. Barbour. Calls him the killing doctor. I suspect he's right. I heard of one gal so scared of that man and his purgatives she let her baby die from the measles instead of turning the child over to that white doctor. That's sure what they call him. The killing doctor with his black bottle of medicine."

"Same all over," Pomp grumbled. "Everybody saying it's best to let it roll with God than tell your miseries to any white doctor. Puke and purge is all they know. Treat you like a field mule. Old Silas is right, it must be going to get a lot worse if the master is buying off the place."

"That what he needs all right," Silas said again, "a flock of powerful breeders."

Chester rose from the table and looked down upon the morose group. He laughed darkly. "I guess Old Silas answered my riddle. Master bought him some gal with hips as broad as an oxen yoke. A gal so fertile, the master won't never have to buy off of the plantation again."

He slapped his hands together at the thought. "It'll sure be a sight. I'm going to be right there in the yard watching when they tote in that gold goose and set her down on her nest."

CHAPTER 9

Aunt Sylvie hurried from the smokehouse, gripping a leg of mutton like an ax. She called out to Granada, "Master Ben going to be here most any minute, and he got that miracle slave with him! I seen the dust rising up along the levee. Bound to be them."

Granada was at that moment shooting marbles with Little Lord under the live oak. She was as curious as anybody to see what this slave from up the country looked like. It had been all anyone had talked about for weeks. But she wasn't curious enough to lose her precious marbles to the master's boy. The blond-headed cheater was at that moment positioning himself for his next shot.

As she passed under the tree, Sylvie fussed at Granada. "I told you to get that boy cleaned off! Master come home to Little Lord looking pig-dirty and you'll be the one to catch the feathers for sure."

Granada still didn't answer.

Sylvie huffed and then continued her lope toward the kitchen, calling out over her shoulder, "I ain't got time to fool with you, gal. Don't blame me when you get the strap."

That particular threat carried no weight with Granada. The mistress wouldn't allow Master Ben to harm her.

Granada kept both eyes glued to the red-clay marble in Little Lord's tight fist, watching him knuckle down for his shot. He was the worst marble-cheater in the world, and she could tell right then from the way his alabaster cheeks had reddened, his mind was clearly on just that.

"Look!" Little Lord shouted. "The bull got loose!"

Granada swung her gaze toward the barn, and as soon as she did, Little Lord reached over and dropped his marble into the duck hole instead of knuckle-shooting it like he was supposed to. But he had not been fast enough. Granada whacked the boy upside the head with the flat of her hand. His face clouded and then he took off running for the great house, threatening to tell his mother.

Granada was quick on his heels. "Master Little Lord, you better not tell on me or I'll yank a knot in your noggin for sure!"

She meant it. Granada knew she wasn't supposed to be nasty to the boy, but sometimes she didn't know what got into her. When he acted so full of the devil, she couldn't resist being mean. It did her spirits good to take a whack at him every once in a while. And sometimes that yellow-headed, blue-eyed boy was just too pretty for his own good.

Little Lord had made it up the stairs and onto the gallery when he stopped dead in his tracks. "Daddy's home!" he shouted, and then ran to the railing, pointing off in the distance. "And he's got the bought slave with him!"

This time he wasn't fooling. Granada looked in the direction the boy was pointing and saw a storm of dust rising off the Delphi road. The master was riding out ahead of the roiling cloud on his black horse. Granada sucked in her breath at the sight. She loved to see the master ride, switching his whip, making that big-blooded stallion fly, its muscles sleek and sweaty and pulsing, all shiny and beautiful and sassy. She wondered how the master managed to keep his seat with a horse so fast its hooves were nothing but a blur of motion and dust.

Coming up close behind was a speeding

wagon, driven by what she first took to be an old woman because of the two long black plaits of hair dangling from beneath a beat-up felt hat. Then Granada second-guessed herself. It couldn't be a woman. The driver handled the four-mule wagon like a man, spitting tobacco off the side of the wheels and popping the reins sharply. A Choctaw Indian maybe!

Little Lord took off down the steps and Granada took off after him. At the foot of the stairs Granada came to a stop, but Little Lord continued to race toward the galloping horse. Master Ben grasped the boy under the arm and hoisted him up into the saddle. From his perch between his father and the pommel, Little Lord found Granada's eyes and then stuck his tongue out at her. They both exploded into fits of giggles.

A spirit of hilarity hung over the entire plantation. For days servants had been in a state of high anticipation. Like Granada, the younger ones had never seen a bought Negro before, and the older ones thought they might never see one again, especially one from as far away as the Carolinas.

The whole yard came out to watch. Wash-women and spinners and weavers, dairy and stable hands, the children too young to work and the old ones too feeble, they all gathered in the yard. From inside the mansion, house slaves peeked out from French plate windows. Even Mistress Amanda stepped onto the upstairs gallery with Daniel Webster perched upon her shoulder and watched as the wagon rolled into the yard.

The driver jerked back on the reins and the horses pulled to a stop in front of the new four-room cabin while everybody stood there with chins nearly touching the ground.

It was a woman after all!

"Lord, she a sight!" Granada whispered to herself. She had never seen anything like her. The stranger was reddish brown with pointed cheekbones and amber eyes. Bird feathers stuck out of her braids this way and that, and around her neck she wore a ponderous necklace made of gleaming white shells. She was as skinny as a river bird, and draped over her shoulders was a mangy wrap made from the fur of some animal Granada imagined being too ugly to ever have lived.

Granada heard the whispers all around her.

"Got some Indian in her, that's for sure!"

"Mostly African, still."

"Exactly what kind of creature is it?" they asked one another.

She was too unsightly to be thought of as

frolic in bed for the master. She was too far past her childbearing years to multiply the stock. Though she seemed nimble enough, it was hard to imagine her being brought all the way from North Carolina for field work.

Granada surprised herself by laughing out loud with glee, but not only at the woman's outlandish manner of dress. It was the way the odd-looking stranger jerked back on the reins, tied them off, and then jumped down off the wagon, spry as a pullet chicken. Granada eased closer to get a better look.

She wasn't the only one.

Aunt Sylvie and the servant girls came out into the yard to inspect the odd sight, all of them gathering in a tight knot at the kitchen steps, unable to take their eyes off the gangly, yellow-eyed woman.

"She old as black pepper," Aunt Sylvie whispered. "Got wrinkles you could grow cotton in."

"But she can manage them mules like a crack hand," came Chester's reply.

People began to speculate aloud that there had to be somebody worth five thousand dollars hiding under the dusty tarpaulin in the back of the wagon. Maybe the master had bought him a bunch of children after all, and she was the used-up mammy thrown into the bargain.

But not a peep emerged from under the wagon's tarp.

All eyes went back to the woman, waiting for her to do something worth a pot of gold.

First thing she did was walk with a limber-jointed step across the yard right up to the new cabin with the huge brick chimney. She disappeared through the door and then emerged a few moments later with hands on her hips like she had taken ownership. She strode right over to where the master had reined his horse to a halt and was lowering Little Lord down from the saddle.

The master opened his mouth to speak, but before he could get a word out, she looked him square in the face and said, "I'll need me a couple of hands to unload the wagon and get everything moved in." Her voice was firm and clear-throated.

Master Ben commenced to turn as purple as bullis grape. He lifted himself up in his stirrups, clenching his jaw so that the muscles in his face bulged.

The servants watched the master's reaction with great apprehension. Though he was known to be slow to the whip, preferring to get rid of troublesome slaves rather than beat them, he surely couldn't stand for this. Granada didn't hear one person take a reath.

Master Ben finally swallowed hard and barked at two old yard hands to wait on the woman. There followed a wave of headshaking from the onlookers.

Next she took to bossing the pair of hands like she had Master Ben. With a voice that sounded curiously comfortable with authority, she told the old men to unload her wagon. They didn't argue and got right to it, unfastening the tarp and then whipping it off.

Not a child to be seen. Instead, the wagon was filled with all sizes of gourds and bulging burlap bags, intricately woven coiled-grass baskets and glazed pots of all sizes made out of clays of strange hues.

Granada whispered to Aunt Sylvie, "Did she bring her own grub to eat, too?," thinking she was some special kind of creature, like the mistress's pet monkey.

Aunt Sylvie shrugged. "Girl, I got no idea. But I'm going to tell you one thing I do know. Ain't none of it coming in my kitchen. That woman makes the hair crawl off my head."

They all watched silently as she walked toward her cabin, but when she got to the doorway she stopped and turned around. She stood for a moment with her chin lifted and her eyes closed.

What on earth was she doing? Granada wondered.

The woman took a long, deep breath and smacked her lips like she could taste the air. Nodding thoughtfully, she looked in the direction of the kitchen where the evening's meal was cooking — roast lamb. Then she threw back her head and exploded into a fit of high-pitched cackling that could be heard across the plantation yard.

The woman swung one last gaze over the yard full of dumbfounded spectators, and for the weightiest of moments her eyes settled on Granada, turning the girl's skin to chicken flesh.

No one had ever looked at her that way before, studying her so thoroughly. The old woman's all-consuming glare was nothing like the master's sharp glances. Or the look she got from the cold blue eyes of the mistress, momentarily glinting in icy recollection but then frosting over opaque.

No, the strange woman's eyes gripped her like two fists and held her tight. That stare was not one of questioning or of doubt, but one of rock-sure recognition. It gave Granada the eerie feeling that there was something she was supposed to yield up to the woman, and she had no idea what.

The woman nodded once to herself and

pulled the door closed behind her.

Granada remained where she stood. She could still feel the woman's eyes on her, peeling her back like the skin of an onion, reading her layer by layer. Not since she was a child, with troubling nightmares, had she felt this sense of foreboding. She would wake sweat-soaked from muddled dreams and random visions of people she knew, and those she didn't — yet somehow was supposed to. They all came seeking, wanting something from her desperately, and she would wake to a terrible silence haunted by their grasping.

This woman's evil gaze had cast exactly such a mood over Granada.

Aunt Sylvie was upset as well. "I got a bad feeling about this woman coming here," she said. "Yes, Lord, I got a bad feeling in my bones about her. I know she some kind of conjure woman."

"A conjure woman?" Granada gasped. Whatever it was, it sounded very bad.

"Uh-huh. Hoodoo woman. Got some Indian in her, too. They're bad to put a fix on folks. You saw them snapping yellow eyes of hers. Snapping at people's souls, she was. She's done put a fix on the master for sure. Running round here like she Queen Sheba."

Aunt Sylvie turned to the girl and waved

128

a cook spoon in her face. "Granada, that woman's going to bear watching. Whatever she's up to, the devil is surely grinning with delight."

CHAPTER 10

The next morning Granada was in the kitchen with Aunt Sylvie when they heard the sound of footsteps on the stairs off the gallery. It was first light and early for any of the family to be out, but from the heaviness of the steps, Granada figured it had to be the master's boots.

They spied on him through the kitchen window as he left the house and strode directly over to the old woman's cabin. The door was open and she stepped out to meet him. No word was exchanged.

"Well, I'll be," Aunt Sylvie said. "What nature of rag she got tied on her head?"

Indeed the old woman had lost the tattered hat and feathers she had worn the previous day and now her hair was covered with a head rag, tied turban style. As the woman followed the master closely, Granada noticed something peculiar about the scarf. From it hung a fringe of a shiny metal that lined the old woman's brow and glimmered in the early-morning light.

The two disappeared from sight as they walked in the direction of the quarter, the collection of cabins that sat on the plantation grounds. These were especially set aside for the slaves who worked closely with the family, those who did the ginning, weaving, blacksmithing, and the tending to the animals and vegetable gardens. The ones for whom Sylvie oversaw the cooking.

Aunt Sylvie shook her head worriedly. She was still suspicious as to why somebody should need a fireplace almost as big as hers. In spite of Chester's reassurances, she hadn't ruled out the possibility that the master had brought another cook to the plantation, especially when she spied all the supplies the woman had brought with her. Sylvie said maybe the woman knew secret recipes that made the slaves multiply faster. She said she had heard of such things. In fact, she herself had been told by Mistress Amanda to put cotton root in the food of the house servants with the lightest complexions to stop them from getting bigged-up with ever whiter children. "One day the mistress grew so flustered," Sylvie had once said to everybody at the kitchen table, "she told me, 'My God, Aunt Sylvie, can't he bring one Negro into this house that doesn't look like they dropped off the Satterfield family tree?' " Everybody had laughed then. But Sylvie wasn't laughing now.

"I wager there are things that work the other way around," Aunt Sylvie said. "Maybe that Chester wasn't far off the track when he was pranking about triple-yolkers. Maybe that witch can make a stew that causes a woman to drop a litter like a cat."

"You making me scared, Aunt Sylvie. I think she's got her eye on me."

"Well, I reckon you best go see what she up to."

Granada gasped. "What if she conjure me?"

"Then don't let her catch you looking! And mind your leavings. I hear they can take a hank of your hair or your toenails or even a shoelace and lay a curse on you."

Granada took a step back, but Sylvie grabbed the girl's arm. "Go on now. You come back here and tell me everything she does."

Granada steeled herself and then slipped quietly down the kitchen steps. As she crept like a cat across the yard and down toward the cluster of cabins, Granada wondered exactly what it was she was supposed to be looking for. Whatever the woman did, the girl thought, was bound to be strange. For all she knew, the woman had already put a hex on her. When she got near enough to the cabins to watch, she made sure that she was well hidden behind the large cottonwood.

That's when Granada got a better look at what the woman was wearing on her head. Unlike the sugar sacks or checked gingham or homespun cloth Granada had seen the other women wear for head scarves, this one was violently flowered and slightly faded. But that wasn't the thing that riveted her attention. From the turban dangled bright disks that looked like coins. Even in the dim morning light her wrinkled brow seemed to be lit in a soft glow.

The master pounded on the door of the first cabin. "Cassius! Get your family out here."

The cobbler, a long-faced, saddle-colored man, emerged from the cabin first. His woman, the milky-eyed Lizzie, followed him outside with his two little boys from his first wife. The children wiped the sleep from their eyes.

Lizzie and Cassius hadn't been together long. A few years after the jealous mistress got Lizzie's Rubina sent to the swamps,

Lizzie had lost her husband to malaria. Aunt Sylvie never got tired of telling the story. She said Lizzie hadn't wanted a man, swearing she would never have another child that could be snatched away so easily, but the master had insisted. That's why she had chosen a man with a readymade family. But just in case she got with child and needed to be unfixed, Lizzie kept a supply of Aunt Sylvie's cotton root hidden away.

Right there outside the front door, the old woman studied the eldest boy, rubbing his skin, peering into his eyes, and then caught his tongue with her fingers to get a closer look. She noisily sniffed his breath. She did the same with each member of the family. The only words she uttered were sharp commands to open a mouth or to roll an eyeball about in its socket. When she got to Lizzie and examined her milky eye, the one damaged by the excellent aim of the mistress, the old woman laid the palms of her withered hands against the luckless Lizzie's face. The look she gave old sour Lizzie was so full of tenderness, Granada found herself suddenly lost in that astonishing act. For a moment she was filled not with the usual foreboding about Lizzie but with an overpowering love. Granada felt the deep, unrelenting ache the woman had been carrying in her chest, that dark crevice of grief.

The girl had no idea how long it lasted, if it had been a fleeting moment or several minutes, only that during the spell she was aware of nothing but Lizzie. She came to her senses only when she found Polly Shine, her disks shimmering, staring hard in her direction, giving Granada a knowing look.

Granada tensed at having been found out, but the old woman smiled and turned away. She looked once more at Lizzie, and then cut her scalding gaze up toward the great house. As if pronouncing judgment, Polly Shine let go a hurtling stream of tobacco juice with so much fury the little disks that hung from her scarf commenced to jingle. Then, as if nothing had happened, she and the master went on to the next cabin, where she repeated her probing and prodding.

At the last cabin the old woman announced confidently, "Ain't nothing wrong with this batch. Least nothing your family can catch. You best take me out to them you say is dying."

That was it! The woman was looking for diseased slaves! Granada recalled all the frightened talk in the kitchen about the horrible sickness that had broken out among the slaves out at Mott's quarter.

But what could this witch want with

135

them? If the white doctor couldn't save them, she asked herself, what was this meddlesome slave woman going to do? Maybe she was looking to cull them out like sick biddies, Granada guessed.

When the master called for Chester to bring both the buggy and the stallion, Granada decided it was time to return to the great house and report what she had observed. She stepped carefully from behind the tree, trying not to draw attention to herself. Granada had only gone a few feet when she heard the woman's voice piercing the morning calm.

"Girl! You come with me."

Granada stopped in her tracks, her feet rooted in the ground by the woman's words. The girl waited, listening for the master's voice, hoping he would scold her for leaving the house and send her back to help Sylvie with breakfast.

"You heard her, Granada," he said from up on his horse. "You ride with Polly."

Before Granada could argue, he was off at a gallop.

Morning broke with a weak sun struggling to peek through a dirty smear of soot-colored clouds. The two rode side by side in the buggy, the woman called Polly Shine acting like she was more interested in the rumps of the mules than in Granada. Each time Polly flicked the reins, or the wheel found a deep rut throwing the buggy to one side, the little coins suspended from her scarf tinkled against one another like the crystal pendants in the mistress's chandelier.

When they were out of sight of the plantation grounds, Polly all at once reined the mules to a stop, right in the middle of a canebrake. There was no one else in sight. The old woman turned to Granada and demanded, "Hold out your hands."

"I ain't took nothing of yours!" Granada exclaimed.

"Hold out your hands," the old woman repeated in her bossy tone that didn't require a raised voice.

Granada did as she was told.

Polly grabbed both hands and turned them palm-side up. She examined them for a long moment, and while she did, Granada became alarmed by the heat intensifying in the old woman's grip. The woman's hands were on fire. She finally released Granada.

Polly shook her head and grumbled, "I ain't got no idea why the Lord chose somebody like you. Don't make any sense, giving you the gift."

"Chose me for what?" Granada asked.

"Who's giving me a gift?"

"And them hands," Polly mused to herself, "one day they be big as dinner plates. Big enough to choke a boar hog. How they going to be any use to nobody?"

Polly glared straight into Granada's eyes until the girl dropped her face. Polly snatched Granada roughly by the chin and lifted her head.

After a few moments of studying the girl, Polly's grip softened. "But the eyes don't lie, child," the woman said, now smiling at Granada. "I seen you back there. You don't know it, but you got the gift."

Polly was right. Granada didn't know what the old woman was getting at. The experience earlier at the quarters had been so foreign and fragile, it had already dissolved like sugar in tea.

Polly shook her head and laughed. "Lord save the people."

That was all she had to say. The woman clucked the mules once and trained her eyes straight ahead. Every now and then as they progressed through the wilds she would rear up and spit a stream of tobacco juice over the wheel, but paid no more attention to Granada.

Nevertheless the girl was certain she was still being studied. She couldn't shake the

138

feeling that some part of her was being prodded, pulled back, exposed, and it frightened her. She sat on her hands, as if that could keep the woman away from places she didn't belong.

A steady drizzle began to fall and steam rose from the heaving sides of the mules. The week had been cool and wet, so the road was mostly mud, and several times during the journey Polly had to get out and coax the mules across the log planking and cypress branches that work gangs had laid over the bottomless mud holes.

Soon the buggy rimmed the bank of a roadside slough. Rising out of the green-skimmed water was a grove of towering cypress, their bulging roots resembling the feet of trolls from Little Lord's volume of the Brothers Grimm. Past the slough came an expanse of newly cleared fields hazed with the smoke from massive smoldering trunks of oak and sycamore. Set farther back on the horizon was a line of more cypress emerging from yet another swamp, their tops feathered with new growth brushing against the clouded sky.

When they reached a rough track that edged rich black fields, Granada noticed they looked abandoned. It was the planting season, when entire slave families should be out in the newly broken fields spreading seed, but there was not a soul to be seen.

She discovered why after the buggy rounded another stand of cypress. Granada spied two rows of porchless, whitewashed cabins. In the wide lane between stood all the people missing from the fields. There had to be a hundred or more.

Granada sat up straight and rigid next to Polly. The skin quivered across the back of the girl's neck. Her legs tensed with the thought of jumping out of the buggy and fleeing down the road back to the mansion.

The darkest of the dark were kept here. Granada believed she could smell them already, their unwashed odor sharp to her nose. She began breathing in quick, shallow gulps. This is where Aunt Sylvie said the mistress would send Granada if she misbehaved. "Back to live with your *real* momma," Sylvie would scold, sending shivers of terror through the girl, who imagined a place worse than the bishop's hell. She had not been wrong.

As the buggy drew close, Granada's chest tightened and her temples pounded. She was no longer gazing down on these people safely from the upstairs gallery. She was at eye level and any one of them could reach out and drag her off. She quickly scanned their faces, looking for that one particular woman she had only seen in her darkest dreams. All she knew was her name: Ella.

Long ago Chester had told Granada about the woman, but the girl hadn't wanted to hear and had covered her ears. She refused to follow his finger when he pointed to the woman from up on the gallery one Preaching Sunday. Granada didn't want to know the woman's face.

Now she felt for sure, as she continued to skim the faces, this was where the woman stayed, the woman from whom the mistress had rescued Granada. She wished now she had looked when Chester had pointed. Then she could run and hide if she saw Ella coming.

A March wind, piercing and sodden with swamp dampness, swept across the settlement and Granada could almost feel the crowd shiver as one. The clothes they wore were filthy and in tatters, and they shuffled about in the yard wearily.

Granada dug her fingernails into the skin of her arms, hating the thing that linked her to them.

Polly jerked the mules to a halt, tied off the reins, and hoisted herself down over the wheel. Granada remained where she sat. She lowered her head to hide her face.

Through the tops of her eyes she saw the master sitting astride his horse beyond the throng of Negroes, talking to a white man on foot. Why was the master letting this happen to her? she wondered. Wait until the mistress found out she was missing!

The master turned his face toward Polly and motioned her over.

Polly grinned at Granada menacingly. "Get down, now," she commanded and then almost under her breath, she muttered, "we got to go see about *your* people."

A band of fear tightened around Granada's chest, making it hard for her to breathe. "My people?" Granada stammered. Again she frantically scanned the faces in the yard and then looked back at the old woman.

She knew!

I'm not one of them, Granada wanted to explain. She might look like them, but her insides were not the same. She had to let the woman know.

"I belong in the great house with the mistress," Granada whispered. "I'm a house-raised girl."

"I say, get down!" Polly ordered, her words set with an iron resolve.

Granada winced, and then did as she was told. As they walked over to where the master sat astride his horse, a cold blast of

142

wind swept through the yard, and the rain began falling in drops as big as pennies.

"Let me see them about to die first," Polly said to the master. "These here can wait."

Bridger, the overseer, scowled at Polly. He was a sinewy, weather-toughened man with a flint-sharp face who, along with a couple of white hands and several Negro drivers, managed the master's operations, including all three settlements. "Wait? I just now called them in from the fields," he fumed. "We wasting time and money here." He looked up at the master for confirmation.

Master Ben frowned. "Then we best get to it." He dismounted and handed the reins to one of the drivers.

Bridger went into a sulk. He spun on his heels and stomped off down the foot-worn track between the cabins. When the track played out, he led the group onto a weeded path that wound away from the cabins, through a recently burned-over field and finally to a long hutlike structure built on the edge of the woods. It was constructed from cut saplings set upright in the ground and had three walls and a roof laid with brush. On the open side stood a grizzle-bearded white man cradling a rifle, rain dripping from the crease in his hat. His mouth was stained with tobacco spit and he

143

glared at Polly with small menacing eyes.

"I raised up this here brush arbor to quarantine the sick ones," the master said. "Least until I know if it's catching or not." He didn't look at Polly, but the words were obviously for her benefit.

Polly grunted irritably at the tobacco-chewing man with the rifle. Again without acknowledging her directly, Master Ben said to nobody in particular, "He's got orders to shoot anybody that tries to get in or get out."

Master Ben entered first, followed by Polly and Bridger. After the girl took the first two hesitant steps, she held back. Peering into the gloom, Granada saw nothing but vague shapes. As she stood there waiting for her eyes to adjust, she heard the sounds of raspy breathing and strangled cries emerging from the bowels of the cavernous hovel. The putrid smell was overpowering, like dead animals left out to rot, forcing Granada to put her hand over her mouth and nose. As her eyes grew accustomed to the dark, she was able to make out silhouettes of bodies on thin pallets spread across the earthen floor. All around she heard the patter of rain dripping through the roof of interwoven branches onto cold, bare earth.

A woman's ragged scream penetrated the

darkness. "There she is!" she screeched in an unearthly voice. "There the witch that been riding me to hell!"

Granada's legs trembled beneath her.

"Quiet, you!" Bridger snapped. The screaming ceased, only to be replaced by deep sobbing.

"Some gone plum out their heads since you left," he said. "Hollering out to invisible spirits and such. Big Dante here run off down to the creek and tried to drown hisself. Took four of us to haul him back. I don't blame him one bit, neither," Bridger said with a rare inflection of pity, looking down on the man at his feet. "Them that died appear to be the lucky ones."

The master didn't respond. He was kneeling on the ground now, gazing into the face of the prostrate body. He removed his hat and leaned over the man.

"Big Dante, it's Master Ben," he said. Granada was surprised to hear what she took as tenderness in the master's voice. "I brought somebody to get you better."

The man bucked up from the middle at the master's words and began a frantic, thick-throated grunting. Master Ben reached out to hold him down. Granada saw that it was not a man the master had reached out to but a giant. Master Ben's hand appeared child-size on Big Dante's shoulder.

"No, not Dr. Barbour. Somebody else. I sent after one of your own kind. It's going to be all right, you hear, Big Dante?"

Again the man tried to talk but could only produce garbled sounds.

"I brung you safe all the way down from Daddy's place in Kentucky, didn't I?" the master said. "Goddamn if I won't get you through this, too!"

Big Dante stilled himself and the master nodded for Polly to come closer. When the master stood to make room for the old woman, Granada got a good look at Big Dante's face. His tongue was swelled up horribly, too big for his head, lolling out of his mouth. The organ was as black as ink and appeared to be cracking open like a ripe fig. Granada turned her face away lest she retch. She stood for a long while with her eyes closed and a hand over her mouth. She reminded herself that soon she would be back in Aunt Sylvie's kitchen where the smells would be pleasant and tempting, and where people kept themselves neat and clean.

Granada waited for her stomach to settle and then looked again. Polly was now nose to nose with the diseased man. The old woman was sniffing his horrible breath! Then Polly put her mouth to his ear and whispered something no one could hear. Granada thought she saw the muscles in that grotesque face relax. Polly smiled at the man like he might be her long-lost son. The entire sight had made the bile raise in the girl's throat.

Polly went on to do the same with every ailing man, woman, and child in the arbor. All of them, regardless of how contorted their faces or how badly their skin had ruptured, seemed more at peace after she whispered the secret words into their ears. Even the woman who had screamed that she was being ridden by a witch stilled herself in Polly's presence.

When she was done, Polly stepped out of the brush arbor. Without speaking a word she took off at an angry clip down the track toward the quarter. The master and Bridger scrambled after her. Granada was in no such hurry, thinking the woman had obviously left her gentleness and compassion back in the brush arbor.

They all caught up to her in the quarter where the families of the sick and dying were gathering around Polly, studying her face with worried expressions. The rain had stopped and there was a heavy silence all

147

around. No one was sure what to make of the woman, only that she was as much a slave as they and had been allowed to see their family and friends.

The master was breathing hard when he strode up to her. "You seen it before? Is it catching?" he asked her anxiously. "Do you have a remedy?"

That's when it occurred to Granada that the master was not simply sorting the sick from the healthy; he was expecting this woman to make them well. He was looking to a *slave woman* to heal them!

The silence grew more intense as they waited for the old woman's response. But the old witch still held her tongue.

"For all the money I paid," the master spat, "I expect you to have a ready remedy."

Polly still didn't answer Master Ben. She stood there glaring at him, looking as if she might be too angry to speak.

He shook his fist in her face. "I could maybe fix it for you to come down with the same thing. If you can't save them, I wager you can figure a way to save yourself."

The old woman finally spoke. "What you feeding them sick ones?" she asked.

"Corn and molasses," he said.

"No meat? No greens?"

"They on half rations until they get well.

148

That's my policy. It's scientific. A body don't need as much when they're sick," he said confidently. "And nobody's allowed to forage the woods for food. Can't eat nothing that I don't approve myself. Leastwise, no telling what they'd get into."

"You lucky they ain't all dead," Polly said, not bothering to hide her contempt. "Bring ever one up to my hospital."

"*Your* hosp . . ." the master stammered. Then he said emphatically, "No. Not these. These are to be kept here in quarantine. I'll not have them near the house. Nothing contagious is to be treated in the hospital."

"Yes, sir," she said, like they were in full agreement, "we could leave them here like you say. Without no proper roof over their heads. Sleeping on the sopping-wet ground. That way if the blacktongue don't kill them, the pneumonia will."

She spat on the ground and then put her fists on her bony hips. "Or we can get them gathered up in one place with sound walls, a raised-up floor, and a warming fire so I can keep an eye on this thing. I reckon that hospital you built for me is the only place you got stout enough. Except your own grand house."

The master stood stone-still with his jaw clenched. His blue eyes blazed with fury.

Granada figured Polly Shine had worn out her welcome for good. When the master turned against a slave, if he didn't have them whipped, he could do worse. He could sell them to labor on a sugarcane plantation down in Louisiana, a certain death sentence.

The woman wouldn't be rattled. "Master," she said with a certain bold sympathy in her voice, "I ain't going to let it carry to your family. I'll stop this thing in its tracks. Yes, sir. I got me a notion for a remedy, but I need to get them all under the same roof."

He looked away for a moment, and then turned back to her. "Swear it to me. Swear to me you can make them all well. You swear to it, and I'll do what you say."

She shook her head, setting the little brass disks to tinkling. "I can't swear to what God Hisself got to do."

"Damn it, woman! You better do more than pray over them. You better have some remedies in them pots and bottles and bushel baskets I hauled halfway across the country."

"I ain't got the remedy. You do."

"Me?" he snapped. "Then tell me what it is and I'll have some hands go collect it."

"Yes, sir," she said and then spat again. "Here's what I need. I need enough mutton to feed them all for three weeks and enough port wine to get ever last one of them drunk five times over."

A collective gasp emerged from all around, except from the overseer who burst out laughing. He quickly brought himself up short when he caught the stunned look on the master's face.

"What? What?" Master Ben began sputtering. "You trying to make a fool out of me? That ain't no remedy for no Negro! They all get a fair ration of cornmeal and fatback and molasses. That's all the African body craves. It's scientific. I've done *proved* it." He hit the word hard, like it was as unquestionable as one of God's "Thou shalt"s.

Granada wondered if the master was going to read to the old woman out of one of his journals.

"They don't even *like* lean meat," he continued. "Wouldn't eat it if they tried it."

Polly said nothing and while the master continued his rant, she looked up at the sun as it began to break through the cloud cover. The first rays caught the disks that framed her face, setting them to winking.

"Negroes eating like white folks," Master Ben was squawking. "I can't have it. What next, china plates?"

The woman pulled her gaze from the

heavens and looked the master straight in the eye, causing Granada to wonder if Polly Shine was putting another fix on him.

"Master, do like I advise and most be back in the fields after two weeks," she said, calm but firm. "But if you don't, the ones back there in your grass tepee hut are going to start dying off tomorrow. The first one to die will be that giant fellow you call Big Dante." She grinned showing off her tobacco-stained teeth. "Master, I reckon I won't be the last head of stock you'll have to buy at market, bad habits and all."

Nobody breathed. Granada saw that Bridger had a nasty smile on his face and a tight grasp on the stock of his cowhide whip, as if waiting to be summoned. There was no way a slave could get away with this.

Sure enough, the master called a very smug Bridger over to his side and then grumbled something into his ear. The smile dropped off Bridger's face and his eyes bugged out like he had swallowed a flopping catfish. That's when everybody knew it was true.

Somebody close to Granada whispered low, "Lord to God. Slaves eating like white folks."

Another mumbled, "Looks like what heals the slave might kill the master." There followed sounds of suppressed laughter rippling through the crowd.

When Bridger didn't hop to it, instead remaining where he stood with a white-knuckled grip on his whip, the bluster returned to the master's voice. "Load all the sick ones and bring them to the hospital. *My* hospital," he emphasized. "I sure paid for it. I might as well get my money's worth."

He held up a finger in Polly's face. "If a single one dies, I'll give you thirty lashes and then turn you over to the speculators." He stiffened. "That all?"

The crowd leaned in close. Granada strained to hear if this bought slave was crazy enough to ask for anything else. Even among these illiterate field hands, everybody could count up to two and that was how many licks she had already gotten off the master and it was still morning.

"Yes sir, that's all," she said in that exaggerated tone the white folks took as obedience but Granada knew to be sass. "You been generous. You a wise and good master. I couldn't think of asking no more."

"It's a damn good thing," he said, jerking his shoulders straight before mounting his horse.

But the girl doubted Polly Shine was tell-

ing the truth. Granada had the strong feeling that this woman had more licks saved
up.

CHAPTER 11

The mansion at last began to appear on the rise and Granada's insides settled with relief.

Polly drove the buggy up to the stable lot, but before she could bring the team to a full halt, Granada leaped over the wheel and took off in a dead run. She was more than ready to be done with this peculiar creature and get back to the kitchen.

There was so much to tell! Wait until Aunt Sylvie heard how brazen the woman had been to Master Ben. Tonight it would be Granada instead of Chester who would have the best story to tell at the kitchen table!

Granada had barely made it around the gate when, from behind her, she heard the old woman's voice. The girl thought she had understood the words, but prayed she had been mistaken. Yet in the pit of her stomach, she knew the old woman was talking about her. She could feel those sharp eyes digging into her back.

Granada quit her flight and turned to cast a worried look at the woman, who was still in the buggy. The master turned out his horse into the lot and was now walking in Polly's direction. The old woman's snapping eyes were set on Granada. The look made the girl's scalp creep.

Polly repeated the words Granada thought she had heard earlier. "She the one."

The one who did what? Granada wondered. She blurted, "What she saying I done?"

But it was clear Master Ben knew what Polly was talking about. He stood there in the yard shaking his head at the woman. "Can't have her," he said. "She's the mistress's pet."

Polly was undeterred. "She the one," she said a third time, stern as a preacher. Then she smiled. "I'll take her off your hands for nothing," she said, cackling crazily.

Granada sucked in her breath.

The master seemed to waver. Granada emboldened herself. She stuck out her tongue at the old woman, and then ran up to her master begging, "Please, Master! Tell her I belong in the great house with you and the mistress and Little Lord."

Master Ben cast an eye toward the house

and when Granada followed his gaze, she saw the mistress looking down upon them from the upstairs gallery. She gripped the iron grillwork with both hands like she was about to vault over the railing.

The master winced and turned his eyes to Granada again. This time he stared at her longer than any time she could remember. He neither smiled nor frowned, and those weak water-blue eyes gave nothing away. She could tell he was thinking things through carefully, giving it the same cold-blooded deliberation he gave every decision he encountered, whether it was to sell off a slave or to have a second glass of Madeira.

He let go a deep breath and then his face brightened a bit. "You're Polly's problem now," he said evenly. "Do what she tells you or I'll have your hide."

Granada saw Polly Shine smirk like she had won, so the girl put her hands on her hips as she had seen the old woman do. "I ain't going with you!" she screamed at Polly with a solid stomp of her foot.

Granada felt the knuckle side of Master Ben's hand crashing across her jaw. Her ears roared. She staggered backward several feet before catching herself.

"Benjamin!"

It was the mistress's piercing voice. This

was the first time he had ever raised a hand to Granada and the mistress had been there to see it. Now he was going to get it!

When Granada saw the master grimacing at his wife's shocked outburst, the girl regained her confidence. She pointed to Polly and stomped her foot again. "You only hitting me 'cause you too scared to hit her!"

He took a step toward her with his hand raised, aiming to strike her again, but before he could get into range, she took off running. She scurried across the dirt yard, under the live oak, and up the steps to the gallery where she dived behind the mistress and wrapped herself in the woman's skirts.

"Mistress!" she cried. "Don't let him give me to that old witch. Tell him I belong with you."

Granada didn't hear Mistress Amanda answer. She stood silent as the master tromped up the stairs cursing Granada's name.

Out of breath, he commanded, "Come with me, girl. We got business."

Finally the mistress reacted. "That old woman can have another, can't she?" she asked, barely above a whisper. "And Benjamin, you shouldn't treat Granada so roughly."

Granada grinned.

"She sassed me," he said. "That's another reason she's going."

Still holding tightly to Mistress Amanda's skirts, Granada could feel the woman's erratic sway. She hoped the mistress could keep on her feet long enough to win the argument. This was no time for one of her sinking spells. Granada peeked up at her.

The mistress had lifted her handkerchief to her face and was dabbing her lips, as if trying to locate precisely the right words. "Sometimes it seems you show more compassion to your Negroes than to your own family, Benjamin."

"Granada is not family," he said firmly.

She let out a startled laugh, as brief as a hiccup. "No, of course not!" she exclaimed, as if she were surprised at herself for inferring such a thing.

Once more she put the handkerchief to her mouth, as if to blot away her words. "That's not what I meant, of course," she said. The mistress ran a hand down her skirts like she was going after a stubborn wrinkle. "After all, you don't need to tell me who is and who isn't a member of this family, do you? I at least know that much. You do believe that I am aware of that, don't you? That I can tell one daughter from another."

159

He opened his mouth to answer, but she continued. "That's not what I meant, either," she said sadly. "I only had one daughter. Now I have no daughters. I know that as well. No daughters at all." She twisted the handkerchief in her hands. "What happened to our children, Benjamin? Where did they get off to?"

Granada hid her head behind the mistress's skirt again. The girl could tell Mistress Amanda was on the brink. She might do anything now.

The master must have known it as well, for when he spoke, his words were calm and measured. "Amanda," he said, "it's not my intention to upset you."

"I'm not upset. Why should I be? Granada is mine," she said. "She is not family, but she is mine. You gave her to me. See, I understand it all very well."

Granada trembled behind the mistress's skirts. "Please, Mistress, please!" she cried out, her voice muffled by satin and crinoline. To the girl, Polly was as fierce-looking as the witch in Little Lord's fairytale books. "Don't let him send me to that witch woman," Granada shouted. "She'll eat me up for supper like Hansel and Gretel. I know she will!"

"Amanda, she's nothing to you," Master

Ben said loud enough to be heard over the rumpus the girl was making. "A dress-up doll to send for when you're bored. Or when you need to take a slap at me. Admit it now, please. You don't care for her, not really. Do you?"

"You *told* that old woman to pick Granada, didn't you?" she blurted, as if the thought had just occurred to her. "You did, didn't you? You're using Granada to hurt me!"

"Like you use her to get at me? Listen to me, Amanda," he said, his voice strained. "To keep the peace, I've let you have your way with Granada. But all that's over with now. Granada is needed elsewhere. This is not personal. It's business."

The shrieks of Daniel Webster broke through the open windows. From the gallery Granada could see into the parlor and watched as Little Lord chased the monkey, trying to lasso him with a length of curtain rope. The animal jumped from the piano bench and onto the keyboard with a sudden explosion of discordant notes. All the time Lizzie stood by the window looking out upon her owners' dilemma and smiling, while her charge wreaked havoc behind her.

Through it all, the master kept his gaze fixed on his wife. He reached out and took her hand. She flinched at his touch.

161

"Amanda, I know you blame me for Becky," he said.

The mistress jerked her arm trying to free her hand, but he wouldn't let go.

"You blame me for . . . for many things. And God knows I've deserved your wrath, but I think I've paid my penance, don't you? After all," he continued, "I've spent twelve years with the blackest slave on the plantation grinning at my guests."

Again Granada felt the tug of the mistress's arm, but the master held fast to his wife's hand.

"The blackest Negro on the plantation standing at my table, Amanda. Looking up at me from Becky's leftovers. It's nearly killed me. People laugh at us behind our backs. I know that. But I've not said a word, have I?"

When she didn't answer, he pulled her toward him and repeated, *"Have I?"*

The mistress looked like she was pushing back on her heels, but she couldn't get away.

"Because I don't blame you, Amanda," he said, his voice quivering with an emotion like anger, but frailer. "I deserved it every bit. I admit it. You were upset that I wasn't there when you needed me. And I'm sorry for it."

"Sorry for it," she repeated evenly. "That's

162

what you have to say? You're *sorry* for it?"

"Yes, Amanda."

Granada could sense the intensity returning to the mistress's voice. To urge her on, the girl stuck her head out from behind the skirts again. "Please, Mistress Amanda, don't let him send me away to that old hoodoo woman. Save me, Mistress. I'll surely die."

With a sudden show of strength Mistress Amanda jerked her hand free from the master's grip. She said in a dry voice, crackling with rage, "It was *you* who said nothing bad could happen to her. It was *you* who said she couldn't get sick. Because *you* couldn't admit that the daughter of the great Benjamin Lord Satterfield could come down with a 'Negro disease.' Isn't that what you called it? We could have left in time. I pleaded with you to let us go back to civilization. Now you spend five thousand dollars *of my daddy's money* to doctor your slaves? When your own daughter went —"

"That's enough now, Amanda. Please, calm down," Master Ben said.

Granada was getting hopeful again. The mistress had him scrambling like somebody trying to plug a levee that had breached in three places.

"It's all in the past," he stammered. "Just

let it go." He reached for her hand again, but she was too quick. Granada saw that it was a fist now.

"No!" Mistress Amanda spat. "Becky knows the truth and she wants me to say it."

"That's insane talk, Amanda. This has nothing to do with Becky. We're talking about Granada. She's my property and, like I said, any decision I make about her is business. Let's not make it personal."

"Not personal," she repeated bitterly. "I want to ask you, Benjamin, is it business or personal when you go skulking down to the quarters at night? It's Lizzie's girl, Rubina, isn't it?"

The master opened his mouth to speak but not a sound emerged.

"Yes, I knew it. You think I'm not told things? You think I don't know about the pretty little love nest you've created for the two of you out in the swamps? How she works in the fields by day and whores for you by —"

The master found his voice. "That's enough, Amanda!"

"No, it's not enough! Our Becky played dolls with Rubina. They were raised up together. My God, Benjamin, that girl's got Satterfield blood in her veins." She was shouting now, loud enough for everyone in the yard to hear. When Granada looked again through the window, Lizzie's expression had changed to one murderous with hate.

"Tell me this," the mistress screamed, "if you can stand a Negro lying in your bed, why can't you abide one standing at your table?"

"Be quiet!" he shouted. "We're done with this nonsense."

"Benjamin Lord Satterfield!" She laughed hysterically. "*Lord!* How ridiculous! The fact that it's merely your middle name says it all. You're pathetic. My father was right. You don't deserve me or his money."

When he lunged, Mistress Amanda shrieked, "Don't you dare touch me!"

But it wasn't the mistress he was after. Before Granada could react, he had reached around the skirts and had her by the arm. He began dragging her toward the steps that led out to the yard.

The mistress found her legs and fled inside the house, shouting for all the outside world to hear. "You're a murderer and a thief, Benjamin Satterfield. And you're not going to get away with it."

A crowd had gathered below, looking up

from the yard at the spectacle on the gallery.

Master Ben had not yet made it to the steps when the mistress returned. As she sneaked up behind her husband, Granada fought him like a wild panther, screaming, scratching his hands, and kicking at his legs. Each time he tried loosening a hand to slap her, she would nearly break his hold and he would have to regain his two-fisted purchase.

Both Little Lord and the monkey had joined Lizzie at the window. The monkey and child stood quiet and wide-eyed, looking on with twin expressions of astonishment.

Then Little Lord shouted, "Look out, Daddy!"

Master Ben jerked his head to the side, just in time for the iron poker to clear his ear on the way to crashing into his shoulder. He yelped in pain, bringing the rest of the house servants to the doors and windows. The master released Granada and clutched his injured shoulder.

Granada took advantage of the moment and raced for the gallery steps.

Daniel Webster began leaping up and down enthusiastically, holding his hands clutched over his head in the victor's pose

Chester had taught him.

"I'll kill you yet," the mistress screamed. She took a sideways swipe at his head, this time missing him altogether but losing her balance and falling to the floor in a rustling heap of crinoline.

Halfway down the steps, Granada met Aunt Sylvie coming up. She grabbed the girl by the arm and dragged her back up to the gallery, and before Mistress Amanda could get to her feet for another swing at her husband, Sylvie had wrapped her other beefy arm around the mistress's waist.

"I'll find where you hid my daddy's gun and this time I won't miss!" the mistress shrieked, struggling to break the hold of the brawny cook, who now had Granada by the scruff of the neck.

The master was breathing heavy and had the look of panicked bewilderment. His hand was still trying to soothe his shoulder. Ignoring his wife, he grabbed Granada from Aunt Sylvie and hoisted her under one arm like a cypress log.

On the way down the stairs, over the threats of his wife, the wailing of his human cargo, the crying of his son, and the shrieks of Daniel Webster, he shouted for all of the plantation to hear: "Polly chose Granada and that's the way it's going to be. Go ahead and tell your daddy I took away your play toy. You can always find yourself another Negro girl to shame me with."

When he made it safely into the yard, he turned to glare up at his wife, who was still being restrained by Aunt Sylvie.

"Pick one as black as midnight if you want," he shouted, as Granada furiously paddled the air with her feet, "but this one goes to Polly. And if I ever see her back in this house again, I'll shoot you both."

CHAPTER 12

Violet gaped at Gran Gran in unblinking amazement, still holding tightly to Polly's clay mask.

The old woman laughed. "I ought not be telling you tales about monkeys and witches just before you go to bed. You might never get to sleep." Gran Gran carefully took the mask from Violet and set it on the shelf by the bed. Then she tucked the quilt tightly around the girl.

"The truth of it is, Violet, this is the first time I've been able to tell if you've been listening to my words. Leave it to Polly Shine to raise the hairs on a person's head."

As she did each night, Gran Gran sat with Violet until the girl finally nodded off and the old woman could be certain that the sleep that had taken the girl was a peaceful one.

Gran Gran stood up and then leaned down to kiss Violet on the forehead, careful not to touch the girl's hand that lay open by her pillow. For the first time in ages, Gran Gran felt necessary.

In her own sleep, the velvety fabric of darkness began to part. The current of her dreaming carried her back to the time before remembering. She found herself living the stories she had been told, beginning when she was a newborn in her mother's arms. She reached up for her mother's face and felt the break of that heart when her mother's arms were emptied of her child.

And then she was Violet's age. The kitchen where she had grown up was warm and safe and she was known. The faces around the table returned vivid and distinct. Their voices sounded out once more, each carrying broken strands of memory. Aunt Sylvie and Chester and Little Lord and even the mistress. They whispered into the ear of her memory.

"Granada, want to hear a riddle?"

"The mistress going to be down here any minute with them clothes."

"Granada, let's go outside and play marbles!"

The next day, upon awaking, the past was fresh and moist and as real as the morning dew. She breathed deeply and noticed the unmistakable smell of biscuits in her nostrils.

CHAPTER 13

The raucous laughter from the children down in Shinetown carried sharp and clear through the crisp winter air. Gran Gran was at the water shelf doing the breakfast dishes, trying her best to ignore the commotion. Violet stood no more than an arm's reach away, watching the woman's every move, hands tucked behind her back.

She was done with them, Gran Gran thought to herself, every man, woman, and child of them!

She furiously rubbed the cake of soap between her hands to build a lather in the metal bucket. They preferred the white man's medicine. That's the way it was with this kind. To them the white man's ice is always colder. And because of their meddling she could no longer midwife. Couldn't bring another child into the world, the very thing she was put here on this earth to do, without them turning her in to the sheriff.

They said she was too ignorant and dirty to be touching their babies. Said she needed a license declaring her fit. The thousands of healthy children she had brought safely into this world didn't hold as much water as a piece of paper signed by a white man. Who had the right to tell her she couldn't do the thing that came as natural to her as the winds came to March? Indeed, when they took that away from her, they might as well have taken away her breath.

The sounds seemed to be growing louder, as if on the march to her kitchen. This sent Gran Gran hurrying to her window, wiping the dishwater from her hands on her apron as she went. Violet scurried after Gran Gran, following in her wake like a baby chick.

When the old woman pulled back the curtain, she saw what the commotion was about. "Get back, Violet," the woman said sharply.

It was too late. Violet was already raising herself on her toes to get a look. Gran Gran heard the girl's quick intake of breath. She had seen the wagon — the same wagon and the same black-clad Choctaws who had carted her mother away. Only this time, they were ferrying their tarp-covered burden toward the mansion.

The wagon's approach was achingly slow, traveling in the frozen ruts, while a dozen boys and girls galloped alongside.

Gran Gran reached down and carefully laid her hand on the girl's thin shoulder, to calm whatever memories the buckboard stirred up. The head was already seeking out the secret rhythm.

At some unseen boundary, the chasing children pulled back but the driver continued to urge the mules toward the back of the house and up to the yard gate. One twin held the reins while the other jumped down and strode to the rear and unhitched the endgate, loosened the knot, and whipped off the tarp.

Gran Gran couldn't make out what it was he struggled with until he came around the wagon and headed for the porch. In each hand he carried a suitcase.

Then she remembered. The white man had kept his promise. He said when he returned he would send Lucy's things, and all those pretty dresses she had bought for Violet.

Long after the wagon had departed, Gran Gran and Violet remained standing on the porch, looking down on the two leather suitcases. At last Violet moved. She took a step back.

Gran Gran nodded. "Then that settles it. We'll just put these somewhere we can get to them later, when we both ready."

It must have been the right thing to say, because the rocking of Violet's head diminished.

"For now we'll stick to telling my stories," Gran Gran said, easing into her rocker. "The dishes can wait, too. Let's sit down and have ourselves a chat. We'll cluck away like two old hens with nothing but time and gossip on their hands."

Gran Gran gazed up into the rafters and thought for a moment. Then she looked at the girl, who now sat straight-backed in a kitchen chair, waiting.

"I been meaning to tell you, Violet," Gran Gran began, "after you got me talking about Aunt Sylvie, what do you think? I woke up this morning smelling biscuits! I could have sworn this was Sylvie's kitchen again. You ever have a smell do that to you? I guess at nearly ninety, my smell seems to be waking up again. Just one whiff of biscuits, and there I am, twelve years old and hungry as a hog! Ain't that something?" She chuckled. "No wonder a ninety-year-old stoops so bad. He got a lifetime of memories riding his back! Why, I believe if you give me a smell from any time in my life, I'd be that age again. Such silly things to bind a life together, ain't it? Biscuits and roast lamb and such?

"Why, I can remember like this morning them two biscuits Sylvie give me the day I got tossed out of the kitchen. I sure hated to leave that place. Only family I ever knew. Chester and Sylvie and Lizzie — even Lizzie — and that haughty old Pomp."

Gran Gran closed her eyes and breathed deeply. "And ain't it funny? After all that happened, it's still the biscuits I can bring back the best."

CHAPTER 14

Granada clutched to her chest the only thing she was allowed to take from the great house — a spare dress, the checked gingham of a house slave. Everything else, even the marble as white as Lizzie's blind eye, the one she had won fair and square from Little Lord, she was told to leave behind. Aunt Sylvie said she was sorry, but it didn't belong to Granada. Never had. And she didn't belong there. Not anymore.

Teary-eyed, the cook told Granada never to return unbidden. "Master warned me," Aunt Sylvie said. "You can't never come back to the kitchen no more. He says anybody lets you through that door will end up draining a swamp and fleeing the gators. And, Granada, he says he don't want you around Little Lord, neither."

Sylvie handed the girl two warm biscuits wrapped in a cloth napkin. To Granada's surprise the old cook reached out and grabbed the girl, holding her for so long that Granada could feel the tears rolling down the back of her neck.

"Remember, Granada," Sylvie said, "what is bred in the bones will be in the marrow. You ain't like them out in the swamps that got no behavior. You been brought up around white folks and learned their manners. Don't forget that, you hear? You a proper house-raised girl, and you pretty as a pea, even if you is black as the bottom of a pot. Remember who you become."

She gave Granada another long, smothering embrace, as if she were sending the girl off into wildest Delta forest instead of the other side of the plantation yard.

When she was much younger, Granada had seen a man who had been caught escaping into the swamps dragged across the yard to the stables to get fifty lashes from a fellow slave wielding a finely braided cat-o'-nine-tails. Granada now believed she had some idea of how that poor man must have felt. As she inched her way from the kitchen toward the new sick house, she could think of no worse fate than surrendering herself into the hands of the old woman with the eyes of amber, to be tortured by another slave.

Granada stood outside the new hospital.

She glanced over her shoulder toward the great house, hoping the mistress would step out onto the gallery and call out to her, pleading with her to return.

When no summons came, the girl cautiously pushed back the rough-plank door and was at once accosted by a rush of heat and steam. She gasped loudly and instinctively threw a hand over her nose and mouth. It was like the woman had brought all the forests and fields and swamps inside with her and then loosed the odors to fight it out in the cabin. Granada nearly fell out from the stench of it all.

Once she'd regained her senses, the first thing she spied was the evil woman standing by the hearth, testing something from a pot hanging from an iron hook in the fireplace. The bone-thin creature was singing to herself, apparently unaware of the girl's presence.

Polly Shine had fixed up the hospital and, like the woman herself, it was peculiar in a disturbing kind of way. Gourds and clay pots hung from the rafters in concentric circles. Coiled-grass baskets, their lids securely attached by ropes, were stacked on the floor. Stalks of plants Granada didn't know names for were bound with string and looked to be growing out of the corners of the room. Hanging from the fireplace, pots boiled with vile-colored liquids. In the center of the room was a worktable piled high with cloth scraps, string, and bottles of colored glass. A row of pallet beds ran along the floor.

Collecting her courage, she said from behind her hand, "What you wanting me for?"

Polly said not a word. In fact, she appeared to take no notice of the girl at all. Maybe, Granada thought, the woman was half deaf like Old Silas. The girl raised her voice. "Why I got to be here in this stanky place with you?"

Polly Shine went about her business mixing ingredients from her sacks and gourds in the boiling pots. Granada remembered the picture of the evil witch stirring a big black kettle in one of Little Lord's fairytale books.

This time Granada cupped a hand to her mouth and shouted at the top of her lungs, "How come you ain't talking to me?"

Not looking up from her pots, the woman shouted back, "Because you ain't worth wasting my breath on yet!" She resumed humming her tune.

"Aunt Sylvie say you evil," Granada said defiantly. "And my mistress say you is a madwoman."

"Humph, your mistress says I'm mad?" Polly still had not taken her focus from her work. "I think I done seen your mistress. Ain't she the one who goes around with a monkey shitting down her back?" Polly threw her head back and cackled wildly, setting the shiny disks to jingling.

Granada crossed her arms in protest, but Polly went on about her business with little regard for Granada's bruised feelings.

She decided to become as tight-lipped as the old woman. Granada held her silence until the muscles in her clinched jaw ached, but the woman still refused to tell her why she had asked for her.

The girl could stand it no longer. "If you ain't going to talk to me, why don't you let me go back to the great house where I belong?"

The woman crooked her scrawny neck and looked at Granada with a delighted grin. "Belong?" she repeated. "That sure is a big word, ain't it? It's a mouthful, that word. *Beee-long.*" Her tone was now mocking. "The more you chew on it, the bigger it gets."

Chill bumps rose on Granada's arms as those yellow eyes peeled her back and peered into her again.

"Why you think you *beee-long* up there?" she asked Granada. "You want to sit pretty, perched up on your mistress's other shoulder? So everybody can laugh when you play the monkey for the white folks?"

"I ain't no monkey!"

Polly took her time looking Granada up and down. "No, you ain't no monkey," she agreed at last. "You is a damned sight worse than a monkey! You a house nigger that don't even know it. Them that work the swamps is better off than you is. Least they know they slaves. And y'all say *I'm* the one who is bought!" Polly narrowed those piercing eyes at Granada. "Where's your natural momma at, anyhow?"

Granada stomped her foot, but the woman only smiled. Then Granada spit at Polly Shine.

"I asked you who your momma was."

Wiping her mouth, Granada said, "Why should I care? I was picked out special when I was a baby. Handpicked and hand-raised by the mistress herself."

"That where you was taught to spit on the floor? I said, who's your momma?"

"I don't know," Granada said behind clinched teeth.

"Then you don't know *who* you is, do you? Might be a nigger or a monkey or a

182

pet goose. That's what I'm talking 'bout."

The woman silently studied Granada for what seemed like forever. Polly finally said, "You ain't never seen yourself, have you?"

"I seen myself all the time. In the mistress's gold-framed mirror."

"What you see? You see that skin as black and smooth as God's night sky? Or them eyes so dark they can hold the glittering stars in heaven? Or that hair as rich and full as God's own crown? No, you don't see them things. You see the white man's gleam and sparkle looking back at you. You don't have no idea who you are. And if you don't know *who* you are," Polly continued, "you can't know nothing about where you *beeelong.*"

"I told you I belong in the great house," Granada cried, "looking after the mistress and Little Lord."

"So you thinking you one of them," Polly said. "You thinking one bright morning that white woman going to bring you a satin wedding dress? Marry you off to her pretty little white boy? She probably throw you a great big party because she's so proud!"

Polly snorted loudly, until she began choking on her tobacco. She hawked it up from deep in her throat and then spit a stream

183

that landed exactly between Granada's shoes.

Granada stepped back and looked down with disdain at the mess the old woman had made.

"That's how you spit, missy. Until you can best me, I advise you keep your mouth shut."

"You a evil old witch and ugly, too!"

"Master told me about you," Polly said scornfully. "You think you a big bug, don't you? Because you been wearing a dead girl's clothes. Well, listen to me good. The white man can't tell you where you belong. I can't tell you. Nobody can tell a river where its bed is. You got to remember it for yourself, and girl, you don't remember piddly."

Granada walked up and stomped Polly Shine on the foot.

Polly hauled back and cuffed the girl across the face, on the opposite side the master had hit her. Granada went stumbling backward. When she caught herself, she waited for the pain, but oddly there was little sting to it, like a mother cat slapping with her claws tucked. Regardless, that made twice today, and Granada decided at least for now to keep out of slapping range.

"Girl, you fighting the wrong person," Polly said. "I ain't the one messed with you.

I ain't the one made you forget who you are."

Aunt Sylvie's parting advice to Granada about not forgetting who she was rang in her head. "I ain't forgot nothing," the girl said. "My name is Granada and I'm a house-raised gal."

Polly studied Granada for a moment and then said, "Don't even know your own name."

"It's *Granada,* I said!" The girl stomped her foot harder than ever before.

"That ain't no kind of name. That was made up for you. You got to remember for your own self who you are."

She poked her bony finger into Granada's chest until she had back-stepped the girl to the brick hearth. Granada could feel the heat from the fire on the backs of her legs and heard the thick bubbling of liquids behind her.

"You're soul sick is what you are," Polly said. "And you can stomp your little footsie all you want to, but you ain't going to get well until you remember. And you can't remember until you learn to see."

"See what?" Granada pressed, tempting her fate. "I can see better than you with your eyes all scrunched up." Granada made a face at her, mocking the old woman's squint.

Polly looked at the girl for a brief moment and then grabbed her arm like she was going to toss her in the fire, but instead hauled her over to the table where a giant brass-hinged book lay. With her loose hand Polly flung it open, scattered through the pages, and then pointed at a marked-up verse and read out loud.

" 'But ask now the beasts, and they shall teach thee; and the fowls of the air, and they shall tell thee. Or speak to the earth, and it shall teach thee: and the fishes of the sea shall declare unto thee.' Right there," she said with an air of finality. "Book of Job."

Granada laughed. "What beasts and fowls you meaning? Like a jaybird? You crazy. Birds can't talk. And if that bird could talk, ain't no jaybird got nothing to say that I want to hear."

Polly looked up from the Bible. "It means study with your eyes and ears, not with your mouth. That's how it's going to be twixt you and me. Let your eyes see and your ears hear, but let your mouth be silent. No more chattering on about what it is you *think* you know."

The muscles in Polly Shine's scowling face relaxed. She silently studied Granada for a long while with a quizzical look in her eye. The girl was pleased to think that she had stumped the old woman and beamed proudly.

Then Polly said, "How you learn to read?"

Granada dropped her smile and swallowed hard "I . . . can't read," she stammered and then looked down. "No, ma'am, I can't read a lick. Don't even know what reading is," she said, tracing a crack in the plank floor with the toe of her shoe.

Aunt Sylvie had once told Granada what happened when the mistress caught Lizzie, back when she had two good eyes, looking through one of the master's slave journals. It was just after Rubina went missing, nobody having told Lizzie yet that her girl had been sent to the swamps. Lizzie heard somebody say that Rubina was in one of the master's books. Lizzie couldn't read a lick, but she sneaked into the library and began going through the journals trying to find anything that looked like Rubina. When the mistress saw her, she threw a china vase and hit her so hard up against her head that Aunt Sylvie said Lizzie didn't have another thought about messing in white people's business again. She said that was how Lizzie got her dead-white eye. If the mistress found out about Granada being able to read, she might never get back in the house.

"You lying to me," Polly said. "I seen the way your eyes rode them words on the page. How you learn?"

Granada whimpered. "Don't tell on me, please?"

"I ain't going to carry it to nobody," Polly said, raising her hand, "but I'll plum slap you to Jesus if you don't fess up."

Looking up, Granada whispered, "Mistress got Little Lord some ABC books. He learn, I learn."

Polly now had a smug look on her face. "Uh-huh. See what I mean?"

"No, I don't!"

"That's the way you learn from the beasts and the fowls."

Granada didn't understand. The woman was still talking nonsense about forest animals.

"That boy. He was your jaybird, you see? You kept your mouth shut and he done learned you A from B."

Granada began to argue, but Polly held up her hand again. "Now you do the same with me. Keep that mouth shut and copy on me like you done that white boy. We get along just fine."

"That's all you want me to do?" Granada asked. "Just keep quiet?"

188

"Ain't going to be as easy as it sounds."

"Sounds easy to me."

"Uh-huh," Polly said, laughing, "I can see how good you doing already." She poked her finger in Granada's chest to punctuate her words. "A flapping tongue puts out the light of wisdom."

Granada laid her hand protectively over her chest. It was becoming tender from all the poking.

"That's your first lesson," Polly said. "Can't learn and talk at the same time."

Granada didn't know what that meant, but the one thing she was learning was don't ask. With her chest still smarting, she waited for the explanation.

"The way you learn to see ain't by talking about it. Like the white man, all he do is talk to his own echo. Keeps him deaf and blind to the world he claims to own."

She looked Granada squarely in the eye, and in the same authoritative tone she had used when she read out of the Bible, she said, "The world belongs to them that *sees* it."

Granada shrugged. Nothing would ever belong to her and she didn't care. Of course there were things she would like to have close by and touch anytime she wanted, like Miss Becky's blue satin dress. And the silver comb Sylvie used to fix Granada's hair. And of course she would like to get that marble back.

"Until I say different, there ain't going to be no more talk from you unless you answering my questions. If you keep your mouth shut, least you ain't doing no harm."

She turned and spat out the window. "Flies can't fall in a tight-closed pot," she said, wiping her mouth. "Start by remembering that."

CHAPTER 15

Polly was out front to meet Bridger when he drove in with the first wagonload of the sick and dying. Granada hung back, hoping to disappear into the shadow of the doorway. She figured she could duck out the back if Polly ordered her to touch any of those festering sores she had seen that morning.

"These are the worst," Bridger said, looking at Polly with the same contempt as earlier. "Rest are coming directly."

Granada risked a glance at the bodies that crowded the wagon bed. Lord, she thought! It looked like somebody had gone and dug up a graveyard! The one the master called Big Dante made no movement at all, and it appeared his body was already beginning to lock up.

Those like Big Dante who couldn't walk, limp, or hobble were carried in on wood planks by Bridger and his man. They sorted the diseased as Polly directed, the sickest in the front room, closest to the fire and her remedies. By the time they were all situated, Granada heard the second wagon pull up into the yard. The process began again.

Things continued this way until two rooms and most of a third were filled with filthy bodies, foul smells, and horrible raspy cries. Polly went about her work without offering one word to Granada, not even throwing her a fleeting glimpse. Polly's eyes slid over Granada's face like she was a piece of furniture.

The grisly sights and the heat from the blazing fire in the hearth combined with the chaos boiling around her set Granada's stomach to roiling. When she felt the bile rising up in her throat, she fled right past Polly, out the front door, and into the yard. Kneeling behind the ginhouse she vomited.

"I don't belong in no sick house with no conjure woman," Granada told herself between heaves. "I belong in the great house." When the retching ceased, the tears began to fall.

What was she supposed to do? She had heard about slaves who had run off. The hounds got them if they were lucky, the gators or quicksand if they weren't. Nobody ever got off the master's land dead or alive without his say-so. At least that's what Chester told her.

Chester!

Her spirits lifted at the thought of his name. He was so good with riddles, surely he could puzzle out a solution to her problem.

After wiping her eyes and brushing the dirt from her knees, Granada sneaked around the perimeter of the yard, careful to keep out of sight by ducking behind the outbuildings until she finally made it to the stables without being noticed.

Chester could usually be found around the lot taking care of the horses and riding gear, but now he was nowhere to be seen. There was only the sound of two stableboys laughing in a nearby stall as they curried and combed one of the mares. Deciding to wait, she slipped behind a light buckboard knowing that Chester never went missing from the stables for too long.

Granada had been there for less than ten minutes when she heard the sound of footsteps and hushed voices coming down the stable runway. Peeking between the spokes of a wagon wheel, she spied the hem of Aunt Sylvie's red-checked gingham dress and Chester's shiny stable boots.

Granada opened her mouth to call out but

then stopped herself. Aunt Sylvie would surely send her straight back to the old woman, so she ducked down and decided to remain hidden until she could talk to Chester alone.

"I said stop pranking around and tell me ever thing you heard about this woman."

Aunt Sylvie was impatient and Chester didn't try to make her guess. He said straight-out, "Master Ben has bought himself a *slave doctoress.*"

"A what?"

"A doctor woman," he explained. "Said she studied up under a midwife from Africa and an Indian medicine man in Carolina. Master bought her off a plantation-owning doctor up the country. Supposed to know a heap."

"Don't matter if she studied up under Dr. Jesus Himself," Aunt Sylvie scoffed. "People ain't going to trust nobody doctoring for the white man. She'll be dead in her grave before folks tell her what ails them. And she looks old enough to be dead last week."

"She best not lay down too soon," Chester said. "I heard the master tell it to her face. He said she best teach somebody to take her place real quick. If she up and dies on him before he gets his money's worth, she ain't going to get no funeral. Master

194

told her he'll throw her in a ditch like a dog with nobody but the buzzards to grieve her out."

"Umm-hmm," Aunt Sylvie said. "So that's why she chose Granada. To learn her to doctor." Sylvie's laugh was grim. "Least I know she ain't no quality conjure woman. Nobody who got the sight would put all her eggs in a basket with a busted bottom." Sylvie shook her head sadly and laughed. "Granada? A doctor woman?"

Hurt and angry, Granada had a hard time not leaping out from behind the carriage to tell Sylvie off. Instead she waited until the smart-mouthed cook finally left for her kitchen.

Granada scrambled from her hiding place. Chester took a quick step back and blurted, "What you doing in here? You ain't run away already, have you?"

"Might as well. She don't pay me no mind no way," Granada sulked. "I don't know what she wants me for. She's mean and don't tell me nothing. I want to go back to the kitchen."

Chester sat down on a barrel and motioned for Granada to jump up on his knee. With her arm slung around his neck, she buried her face in his shirt and let her tears flow freely.

When she was all cried out, she wiped her eyes with the back of her hand and asked, "Can I come and stay with you in the stables, Chester?"

"No, Granada. She's put her claim on you and ain't nobody going against her. Folks are right scared of that woman. They can already tell she ain't the common run of midwife."

Chester set Granada on the ground and then stood up. He walked over and peeked around the stable door to scan the yard. "Your conjure woman put the word out. If anybody gets caught talking to you without her say-so, they'll get the cowhide. She told the master it was the only way she could break you to saddle. Said you was too much of a pet to suit her."

"I *told* her I ain't nobody's pet!" Granada snapped, stomping her foot.

He looked back at Granada. "I'm sorry for it, Granada, but you best get on back to that sick house. Master ain't fooling around."

Granada couldn't believe it. Chester was scared of Polly, too!

On her dawdling return to the hospital, she thought about what Chester had told Sylvie, the part about the master throwing Polly in a ditch. Granada sure liked the sound of that. Aunt Sylvie always said that without somebody to grieve you into heaven, you might not be able to find your way.

"Humph," Granada thought. "That woman don't belong in heaven! If God is great, He's going to bar the door." And if there was anything she could do to keep her out, she would gladly do it twice.

That was it!

The solution to all her problems became as clear as day. She would be the basket with the busted bottom Aunt Sylvie claimed she was. When asked, she would refuse to help. If forced, she would deliberately fail. She would stick to her plan no matter how hard Polly poked her in the chest with that bony finger. That would teach the old witch!

Granada grinned for the first time since she had been told to leave the master's house. Polly would surely give up on her and send her back to her mistress where she belonged, or Granada, by being a bad student, would send Polly headlong to hell where *she* belonged.

Granada hurried to the hospital, anxious to work her plan. Maybe she would be back in the kitchen before first dark, eating supper with her friends! She stepped through the doorway and stood there, pretending she had never been gone.

For all Polly seemed to notice, Granada could have stayed gone. When the old woman needed a hand, she walked right past Granada and called out the door to enlist one of the yard slaves. By late afternoon she had a bevy of workers jumping to her commands. They helped her wipe the sick ones down with clean rags and lye soap, carry out buckets of waste, and wash the dirty clothes in a big black pot of boiling water under the live oak.

Polly grabbed a boy and told him to step into the woods and gather some early pokeweed and persimmon bark. When he returned at twilight, she got busy combining the ingredients with mutton tallow, and then by the light of lanterns held by her helpers, she rubbed down the open sores of the diseased bodies herself.

Aunt Sylvie showed up at suppertime at the head of a column of serving girls carrying tubs of roast lamb, steaming side dishes, and tureens of piping-hot broth. Polly poured the wine into tin cups and spoon-fed the sickest.

In all those hours, Polly never once asked for Granada's help, and the only time she spoke to the girl was to tell her to get out of the way, until Granada found herself backed into a corner of the room, nearly hidden by a stack of baskets.

Darkness found the old woman moving much slower, but still she asked nothing of Granada. Sitting cross-legged in her corner, she heard Polly tell her helpers to set the lanterns about the rooms, instructing them to wake her if any of the sick needed tending during the night. Then she fell back into her cane-bottomed rocker and almost at once began snoring.

Not having been told where she should bed down for the night, Granada crept over to the worktable and sneaked a bit of cold lamb, gathered an armload of clean rags, and made a pallet for herself outside on the cold, plank porch, wanting to put as much distance between her and the woman as possible.

This was her first night away from the great house. She positioned her bed of rags to where she could see the lantern in Sylvie's kitchen, where just last night she was lying on her pallet by the fireplace, the coals still warm from supper.

She woke shuddering from the chilled early-April wind. It must be late, she thought, because the lights in the kitchen across the way had gone dark. She had no warm quilt to snuggle under and she shivered so hard she feared she might freeze to death. She had no choice. Granada stole into the hospital and claimed an unoccupied piece of floor next to the hearth.

Granada woke again at dawn, hungry, by a dying fire. The room was thick with the gasping and rasping and snoring and coughing of the sick on their pallets and a failing lantern sputtered on the table where Polly kept her salves and bandages and the platters of leftover lamb. The bluish light of dawn filtered into the room, and Granada could see that Polly still sat in her rocker where she had fallen asleep. The chair was in motion, its creak mimicking the sound of some small animal that could have been trapped in the room.

The girl stole up to the old lady with head bowed. "You want me to tear up some rags, I reckon I can," she said contritely.

Polly did not answer and her breathing remained steady and slow. Granada wondered for a moment if the woman had drifted back to sleep, but dared not look up, lest she find those snapping yellow eyes on her.

"I can gather up some kindling for the fire," she mumbled. "Keep it stoked if you want me to."

The slow rocking resumed once more, but

Polly didn't utter a word, forcing Granada to wait.

When the girl felt herself slipping between the floorboards, Polly finally spoke. "I thought you don't *beee-long* here among all these dirty niggers," the woman said in a raised voice, as if for the benefit of the sick who were waking in their beds. "What you care if they freeze or not?"

Granada's face burned. She dragged the toe of her shoe along the crack between the planks, still avoiding Polly's glare, as well as the curious gazes from those on the pallets.

"Just remember this, girl, the water you hate is the water that's going to drown you." Polly hoisted herself up from her chair with the grunting noises that old people tend to make when they shift their bodies around. She tottered a moment, reaching out for the back of the chair to steady her.

"Nobody here got no use for you," she said, her tone not exactly angry, more matter-of-fact. "Not until you remember who they are."

"Remember," Granada repeated meekly.

"God gave you sight, girl. Look around you."

With her chin still tucked, she tentatively peered out of the top of her eyes and scanned the room. She was first drawn to

Big Dante. At that moment he was also looking up at her, studying her from his pallet. The whites of his eyes were scarlet, his tongue monstrous in his mouth, and his face still so swelled up Granada didn't see what kept his head from busting open.

A man lying next to him had eyes that were swollen shut, but she had the feeling he was focusing all his remaining senses in her direction. From the next room, a woman pleaded for water in a voice so raspy that the words seemed to rip her throat like sharp-edged rocks.

Granada clenched her fists in defiance. She didn't see anything here but dirty swamp slaves! She didn't need to remember where she belonged because she already knew, and it sure wasn't here. Is that what the old woman wanted her to say? Well, she wouldn't. She might have to stay, but she sure wouldn't like it.

Polly shook her head. "Suit yourself," she sighed. "But remember this. When God wants to punish us, he gives us just ourselves to care for." She turned her back on Granada. "Excuse me, I got folks need tending." She dipped a gourd into the water pail and then proceeded in a stiff shuffle into the next room where the woman was crying out.

Granada stood there with the diseased and disfigured all around her. There was no sound except for their breathing, but the silence was potent. It demanded that she answer the question, to tell them where she belonged. For a moment she believed if she did not answer, the ground would open up and swallow her whole.

In a rising panic, Granada found her legs and bolted after Polly.

CHAPTER 16

The days settled into an unbroken routine of watching, listening, and staying out of Polly's way. Granada did what the woman had asked. She studied Polly as she treated the sick using the smelly remedies she had concocted right there in the hospital. From a safe distance Granada looked on as Polly tended to ruptured flesh; wiped mouths and noses that seeped blood; salved eyes that had been blinded from grotesque swelling. But none of this seemed to hold any witch's magic.

The girl noticed that before Polly left the bedside of one person to move on to the next, she leaned over and whispered into the sick person's ear. Without fail this quieted the anxious, brightened the miserable, settled the violent, and gave fight to those who appeared to be on the downslope to death.

Granada suspected the words were some

kind of hoodoo magic or conjure spell. Figuring if she got nothing else from Polly Shine, a few magic tricks might come in handy, she tried her best to overhear. But Granada was never allowed to get close to the person being treated, and strain as she might she failed to make out the words.

Then something unexpected drew her interest.

The real magic appeared to be happening outside the hospital. People were beginning to act oddly. Servants were mysteriously drawn to Polly. The spinners and the stableboys and the milkers and the sawmill workers and everybody else who labored in the yard eagerly took on any task that put them in the vicinity of the old woman. Even the mistress's maid, Lizzie, became a frequent visitor. The boldest stood at Polly's windows and gawked at the goings-on inside, shaking their heads and walking off in muttering amazement.

Polly Shine could have stopped the inquisitive from peeking into her sick house, but instead of shooing them off from the windows, she flung wide the doors to give them an even better look. To assist her, she drafted as many hands as could fit into the cabin. It was like she *wanted* the entire plantation to witness what she was up to.

And the things Granada heard them say! They whispered to each other about how they couldn't get over the spoon-feeding, baby-loving ways of this woman — like she was making herself a mother to every one of them. They were astounded that Master Ben himself came to the hospital to consult with the old woman like she was a big bug herself.

But not everybody was in agreement about the old woman. There seemed to be a storm brewing.

Granada overheard Barnabas, the carpenter, arguing loudly with his woman, one of the weavers. Barnabas told Charity that Polly couldn't be any better than Dr. Barbour, or even Bridger who treated the slaves with a few common curatives from a medicine chest provided by the master.

"She ain't nothing but a used-up nigger woman," he said.

That stopped Charity dead in her tracks. She replied, "That woman sure can't do no worse than the white doctor." She said all Dr. Barbour knew was to dose the ailing with his violent medicines, purging and bleeding and blistering them and making them throw up their insides by forcing salt and mustard down their throats.

She told her husband, "Mr. Bridger is

worse than that! You don't dare tell him you got miseries." Then in an angry undertone she growled, "If you a woman he tells you to get naked in front of God and everybody and then he poke and prods you like a field animal. Yes sir, he especially fond of his doctoring if you got titties." She spat on the ground in disgust. "I shouldn't have to be telling you this, Barnabas."

Stumbling to get out of the way of his wife's stream of spittle, Barnabas was clearly startled by the strength of her feelings.

She hissed, "You know good and well what the truth of it is. White man think he can scare a body out of getting sick and starve a body into getting well. I put my faith in what you call a 'nigger woman' any day."

"Lord, girl." Barnabas flinched. "You taking her side 'cause she's black or 'cause she's a woman?"

"One good and the other better," she shot back and walked off, leaving her husband to scratch his head.

And it wasn't just Barnabas and Charity. It was as if Polly were turning women against men. Chester suggested she might be casting spells on the sick, perhaps stealing their souls or siphoning off their blood to make black-bottle potions. Pomp said she was nothing but a charlatan. Old Silas said, "A big possum was bound to pick a little tree," meaning the woman was nothing but a show-off.

But the women had altogether different ideas. They were struck by the way she anointed the broken flesh of the blackest of Negroes with hot oils and soothing salves. The way she held their hands and whispered secrets into their ears, even the ones who had slipped into comas. It came near to breaking the women's hearts. Some wept.

While Granada's attention was on what was going on outside in the yard, she nearly missed the miracle on the inside. The sick, one by one, left the hospital, exactly like Polly had predicted. Even the big man, who Granada could swear came in on the wagon already dead, Big Dante himself, got up and walked away on his own two feet, like the lame beggar in the Bible. He was the last. Three weeks after Polly arrived, she had delivered every last soul from the black-tongue.

But even a mass healing didn't please some people on the plantation. Polly, who had begun to trust Granada with small tasks like fetching and carrying, needed some supplies from the master's pantry one night

She sent the girl to the great house with a list, but when Granada got to the kitchen, the lanterns were dark. Sylvie was probably asleep. Aunt Sylvie carried the master's pantry key and never took it from around her neck.

As Granada turned to go back to the hospital, she heard Sylvie's voice drifting from the direction of Silas's cabin, and when she glanced that way, she saw the two of them sitting in a soft glow of lantern light out on the porch. Old Silas, pipe clutched in his mouth, appeared to have his feet soaking in a pan of what Granada guessed to be hot water and salts, something Sylvie would fix for him when his dropsy acted up. Their words were solemn and low.

Granada didn't think it would hurt if she lingered a little longer and drew a bit closer into the shadows.

"You got to tell him, Silas," Sylvie was saying in an urgent tone. "Might be your way back in the master's graces. Put the bottom rail back on the top."

Old Silas removed his pipe from his mouth and began shaking his head. "He's not going to listen to me. Thinks I'm too old. Thinks I got mush for brains. And worse, after what I did, telling him the truth about the mistress, he doesn't confide in me any longer."

"But you see the danger!"

"Of course I see it. Been seeing it the minute Polly Shine stepped her meddling foot on the place."

Silas went on to tell how he was growing more concerned every day. When the fragrance of roasted lamb hung over the plantation like a heavenly cloud, he heard that the swamp slaves living miles away in the master's settlements had smelled the aromas and fell under its spell, savoring the sweet odor of something they had never known.

"Sylvie, without a preacher to tell them, some dropped to their knees in the field, risking the driver's whip, to pray for the healing of the sick. They prayed with so much zeal, you'd think they were praying for themselves."

Granada couldn't get over how smart Silas talked, using such fine words. Usually he sat at the table and gummed his food and slurped his coffee from a saucer. She often thought he might be addle-minded. But tonight his words were strong and fine.

"I don't know if the stories from out in the settlements are true, but what little bit I've seen from this rocking chair tells me there is great danger afoot."

"Danger afoot!" Sylvie exclaimed. "That's what I'm saying. You the one who sees it. The *onliest* one!"

"Yes, I've seen them gathering in the shadows, Sylvie, whispering to each other the bits and scraps of what they've seen or thought they've seen, piecing together a tale full of treachery."

Granada had never heard a slave use such big words and she wasn't exactly sure what he meant, but the scary way he said them raised chill bumps on her arms.

"I've managed slave stock long enough to read the signs. I know in my bones what that woman is up to. She's doing more than tending to their bodies. She's meddling with their minds. If the master's not careful, this tale that's being brewed will let loose a plague among his slaves a lot more danger-ous than the cholera or the blacktongue or the yellow fever."

"What's got in the master's head?" Sylvie asked. "Time was he wouldn't go off half-cocked and pay a pot of gold for some broke-down woman who sure as the world is going to turn this whole place on its head. Course back then the master wouldn't buy a cow without my man's say-so. Ain't that right, Silas?"

Granada had heard Sylvie say this before,

how Silas was closer to the master than nineteen was to twenty. Accompanied him when the master went off to college. Some say tutored him. Maybe Silas learned to read like she had, by watching white people learn. Now Granada could understand how he could have run the entire plantation.

"How long Master Ben going to hold it against you? It was your duty to tell him how the mistress was acting. Taking in a baby from the quarter and dressing her up like a play doll."

"He's not holding it against me because I told him. He's holding it against me because I was right. And I get righter every day. Shames him. I should have known better. Never shame a white man."

"But for how long?"

"When his hurt gets bigger than his pride," Silas said. "That's when he'll come to me and I'll tell him what to do. Until then, all I can do is keep watch, bite my tongue, and bide my time."

"It ain't fair," Sylvie said.

"I did my best to teach the master about slaves. Told him a hundred times when he was a boy that it wasn't a black skin that made a man a slave. It's the other skin, the one that grows on the outside, that second hide made of fear and obedience. What a good master does is every once in a while prick that skin, to remind folks that it's still there and always will be. I told him if a slave was to molt that outside skin, you no longer have a slave. 'Mark my words,' I said, 'when a man's not afraid, then he's hoping. And that's when all hell breaks loose.'"

Silas reached over and patted Sylvie's ample thigh. "When the master's hurt outgrows his pride, I'll remind him of these things again."

He lifted his foot from the pan and smiled. "And I can see clear as my big toe, plenty of hurt is on the way."

Sylvie laughed. "That why you say there is danger *afoot?*"

Silas slapped Sylvie on the thigh, laughing so hard he nearly choked on his tobacco.

Granada didn't understand the joke, but what Silas said made her skin creep. She had never heard a declaration of war, but she was certain that Polly had found herself her first enemy.

CHAPTER 17

Gran Gran eased up from her rocker and took hold of the poker to stoke the smoldering embers in the stove. For once, Violet's eyes were not on the old lady. The girl sat in her straight-backed chair, pulled up close to the rocker, looking down in her lap at the snapping eyes of Polly Shine.

"Well," Gran Gran said, turning her backside to a revived fire, "I can't tell how much you understanding of what I'm telling you, but you sure didn't shout for me to hush up! Or run away with your hands over your ears. So I reckon it's fine by you."

Gran Gran laughed. "You know, Violet, the saddest thing about being the only one left to tell a story is everybody who cares to listen is gone. Don't know why God gives some folks longer candles to burn than others, throwing out light when everybody else has gone to sleep. Anyway, when you tell me to shut my mouth, I'll know you wel' enough to tell your own tale. And I promise, I'll listen as good to you as you done to me."

Indeed Gran Gran could tell Violet was taking in the stories, like a body takes to the right potion. The only time during the tale Violet wasn't gazing at Gran Gran with hungry eyes and mouth agape was when she was looking down at the clay mask, tracing the cool lines of the somber face with an index finger.

The storytelling became regular now and when Gran Gran wasn't telling the stories, she was forming the next one. Strands of memory that had long slipped from her grasp, she found again, picking them up like familiar paths through a forest that had grown over. Once she had a stepping-off place, memory cleared the way.

"I guess what Polly said about remembering was about the truest words that ever left her mouth," Gran Gran said one morning as she scooped a spoonful of grits onto Violet's plate. "She said a person has to remember who they are. Ain't that a strange thing to say? Now who would have thought that a person could forget who they were?"

Violet said nothing, but she watched the old woman intently.

"Took me the longest time to understand

that, myself." Gran Gran laughed. "Used to make Polly so mad with me. She said trying to teach me anything was like trying to show red to a blind mule!"

CHAPTER 18

It was a hot day in late spring and a little more than a month had passed since Polly's arrival. An ill-tempered midday sun was breaking from behind a ragged piece of cloud. Polly drove the wagon along a freshly plowed field with Granada hunched by her side, studying a string of women and children, nearly a hundred souls long, stretching from the road ditch all the way out to a distant horizon of cypress. They were stomping down newly scattered cottonseed into the swampy, black muck with their bare feet. The children, wearing only sackcloth shirts down to their knees, looked up at Granada with curious smiles and giggling laughter. Some waved.

The ebony, head-scarfed women, their legs caked in mud up to their tucked skirts, seemed more interested in Polly. They called out to each other excitedly and pointed in wide-eyed amazement like they were looking at somebody who could raise the dead. Then they turned to one another nodding and chattering, as if needing to confirm what they had seen.

Polly looked neither left nor right, keeping her eyes on the rumps of the mules, but Granada thought she noticed an almost imperceptible grin sneak across the woman's face. She probably enjoyed being thought of as some kind of witch.

As for her, Granada still had her doubts about Polly's powers, and the girl had watched closer than most. She studied the woman as she served the meat and poured the port into the tin cups but hadn't seen her do anything that Aunt Sylvie didn't do in the master's kitchen. The miracle certainly couldn't have come from the dirty roots and leaves that grew wild in the woods. No matter what the others said, she could see nothing special in any of it.

She thought for a while the magic might reside in the spells the woman whispered into the ears of the sick ones, thinking maybe they were a charm. But once, when Granada finally got close enough, all she heard the woman saying were Bible words: "In the beginning God created . . ." That was all. Kept repeating it over and over. Didn't even say the whole verse.

As hard as she looked, for the life of her Granada couldn't see where the magic was added.

Wherever her power came from, Polly Shine had definitely proved herself to the master, doing for his slaves what the white doctors could not. When he saw Big Dante rise from his pallet and praise Polly to high heaven, the master put plenty of slack in her rope. She got a traveling pass anytime she wanted to take the wagon to the outlying settlements and look in on the field slaves. She counseled the master on what foods would keep the slaves healthy and working, and prescribed special diets for those women who had not been able to bear new stock. The lists Granada brought to Aunt Sylvie to fill were growing longer and longer.

The master even allowed Polly to leave the plantation to gather ingredients for her remedies from the swamps and woods that surrounded his fields. She would return from her excursions with bulging sacks and overflowing baskets. She stayed up most the night crushing juices from leaves, scraping roots, and boiling down barks, preparing teas and poultices and salves and pine-resin pills.

Once she toted in a heap of yellowish clay

219

from a vein she had discovered near the creek. She commenced to shape little crocks and fired them in the hearth. Then, with the juice of boiled roots and leaves, she painted the pots with strange geometric images and set them up on a shelf, empty and unused, warning Granada to never touch them.

The girl was beginning to believe that she would never be allowed to go along on one of the excursions, when that very morning Polly told Granada to put on her shoes and get in the wagon.

Granada had come in from hanging a washing of laundry. "Where we going?" she asked, but Granada could tell that Polly was done talking on the subject. Another query would only result in her being told to keep her mouth shut lest "flies get in the pot."

Polly yanked hard on the reins, directing the mules onto a track only recently chopped from the towering cane that now walled the wagon on either side. The pulsing drone of insects along with the booming frogs filled the stony silence between Polly and Granada.

The track ended at the edge of a dense Delta forest the master hadn't got around to burning yet. Polly tied off the reins and without a word climbed down from the wagon with her tote sack swinging off her shoulder. Granada watched as the old woman entered what looked to be an impenetrable wall of vegetation by a dim path that evidently only she could see, thrashing at the tangled growth of vines and briars with her snake stick, until she was swallowed up by the forest. Granada had not been asked to follow.

The sun raged from a cloudless sky and sweat trickled down the girl's back. Polly hadn't told her *not* to come, either. Granada jumped from the buckboard and followed the woman's footprints. They had to lead to a place cooler than the open wagon.

As she carefully plucked her way through the stinging briars and pushed back on leafy branches that obscured her vision, Granada wondered if this barely perceptible path had once been traveled by those long-ago Indians, the ones who built the imposing mounds scattered about on the master's land. Chester claimed that they ate their enemies and friends alike. Or perhaps this was the trail of some wild animal that had recently passed through. She knew the woods to be filled with black bear and panthers and so many snakes Adam couldn't name them all. She decided to pick up her pace and scurried across the spongy ground to catch up with the old woman, mindless of the briars biting her arms and legs.

She found Polly in a place where daylight filtered though a lush canopy of honey locust and red maple. From there she watched as Polly bent over and began stabbing at the ground with her little pickax, digging up sundry plants by their roots. She examined them carefully, pinching the leaves, peeling back the bark, breaking open the stems.

Polly tasted everything. After chewing on a leaf or sucking on a piece of bark or bit of root, sampling an early-spring berry, or putting her tongue to gummy resin, she registered her verdict with either a nod or a shake of her head.

At first Granada thought Polly was talking to herself as she worked. But the girl had been wrong. Polly talked to the bits and pieces she was studying, like they were old friends not seen for a long time. Some she was just meeting. She spoke in a steady, rhythmic fashion that after a while sounded to Granada more like music than talk, lulling the girl into a dreamy, half-awake state. Eventually everything the woman said bled together and Granada really couldn't tell if she was speaking words or just made-up sounds. Or perhaps she was singing.

The spell broke when Granada spied Polly doing something that she couldn't keep silent about.

"Why you eating dirt?" Granada blurted. If it had been Little Lord doing such a foolish thing, she would have slapped his hand.

Polly eyed the girl briefly and then spit. She bent over and dug up a burdock plant and began to do the very same thing, scraping the root and putting the dirt in her mouth, squinting her eyes and creasing her forehead like Sylvie did when she was sampling a new batch of soup.

Granada shook her head, disgusted with Polly's manners.

"Miss Prissy think I'm eating dirt," Polly mumbled to herself. "If Miss Prissy was watching like I told her to, she'd see I ain't eating dirt. I'm reading it."

Polly hadn't spoken to her in so long, Granada figured maybe she had misheard the words and laughed at the silliness of the idea. When the old woman scowled at her, she realized Polly had indeed spoken the words, and more than that, she was dead serious.

"What you say?" Granada asked, incredulous. "You reading dirt?"

Polly nodded once and then looked around her, taking in the entire forest with her gaze. "The plants and animals and even the dirt, they got they words, too." Then she looked at Granada. "What makes Miss Prissy think she so special?"

"They talking to you?"

"They talk to anybody got a mind to listen."

"What they saying right this minute?" Granada sassed.

"Don't know why I wasting my breath, but I'll tell Miss Prissy anyhow. They telling me of a place where there ain't no sickness. No aches. No misery."

Granada knew the answer to that riddle. "Heaven!" she blurted.

"What you know about heaven? I'm talking about right here!" Polly stabbed the ground with her stick. "In front of your face! The leaves, the bark, the roots, the berries, the dirt. They all got memory. They hold the memory of how things supposed to be. They all got secrets to tell." Polly held out a pinch of the dirt before Granada. "They tell you how to put things right. All we got to do is listen."

When Granada opened her mouth to argue, Polly slipped a bit of dirt on the girl's tongue. Granada gagged and spat it out.

"You got to hold it in with your mouth shut, Miss Prissy! Open wide and be still."

She put another speck of dirt on Granada's tongue. She held it in her mouth this time.

"What's it say?"

As the girl stood there, the dirt turned to mud.

"Do it taste like salt or sugar or more like rust? Do it bite back? Do it draw up?" she asked, without pause. "Do it act like it want you to swallow? Or do it make you tired? Do it make your stomach rise up and want to heave?"

The only thing Granada knew was she had to get the miserable mess out of her mouth. She spat and then wiped her tongue with the hem of her dress.

Polly cackled at Granada's squeamishness and the girl sassed, "You can't read dirt no more than jaybirds can talk. You a silly old woman." She took a step back, in case her words warranted a slap.

"And you ain't nothing but a pishtail girl who don't know nothing in the world except your own self. And pitiful little about that. You still ain't ready."

"How can I get ready if you don't tell me nothing?"

"I can't tell you how. A head full of 'how' ain't going to do nobody no good. You got to stand back and watch and listen." Polly looked up at the intricate weave of treetops and vines that sheltered them. "Just like all these trees, you got the memory, too."

"How can I remember something I don't even know?" she asked.

"When you start reaching out with something besides your greedy hands," Polly shot back. "That's how you slip into the remembering. You got to be quiet and let it come to you. You can't go hunt it down. And showing off and having a smart mouth don't make it come any quicker."

Granada kicked at the ground. "Remembering. That don't make sense."

Polly turned and began to walk away, still laughing at the girl. She said over her shoulder, "Can't do it in your hand until you see it in your heart. Like going to the river to fetch water without a bucket. No use even trying."

More riddles. Granada used to love the riddles Chester told her. But Polly's were too hard, and Granada was beginning to suspect that Polly's riddles had no answers. It would be too soon if she ever heard another.

Granada waited at a distance, beneath a sheltering sweet gum, and watched until Polly had finally filled her tote sack with an assortment of found things that seemed to satisfy her taste.

Granada remained silent as she followed Polly through the checkered shade of the forest back to the road, feeling more useless than before. "Like tits on a boar hog," she could hear Aunt Sylvie saying. They boarded the wagon and Polly took the reins.

"Giddap!" she cried, and the dozing beasts twitched their ears and began their slow, steady progress down the rough track.

The sun was in their faces, still an hour away from disappearing below the line of cypress off in the distance. Granada now had no problem keeping quiet. For a long time she studied her hands. They looked large and clumsy and Polly said that one day they would become even more grotesque.

Granada was tired of never knowing where to stand or to sit and not being able to say a word without it being wrong. There was no place for her anymore.

CHAPTER 19

It was still light when Polly drove the wagon into the plantation yard and up to the stable lot. Chester winked at Granada as he led the mules off, but she didn't try winking back. She kept her eyes fixed on the ground, lagging behind Polly as they made their way to the hospital cabin.

Polly went to work as soon as she walked through the door, while Granada stood at the table, her arms hanging heavy and useless at her sides. She watched dutifully as the old woman put on a pot of water to boil and then carefully wiped down her stone mortar like it was a favorite child.

When Polly began to peel back the skin on a burdock root, Granada said, "I can do that. Don't look hard at all."

"Miss Prissy's mouth is working fine, but she ain't got no idea what she's saying. She don't know nothing about this."

"It appears mighty easy to me," Granada

said, reaching for a piece of root. "Let me try."

"Leave it be!" Polly ordered. "Like I done said, you can't do it in your hand until you see it in your heart. And your heart is locked tighter than the door to the master's pantry."

Granada picked up the root anyway and Polly slapped the girl's hand. "Put that down. You going to spoil it!" she scolded. "You still trying to show off what's in your head."

Polly turned and cast the root that Granada had defiled out the window. "I ain't got no use for that trash them white folks put in your head. It as dead as you is."

"Why you hate them so bad?"

"I don't hate white folks. They just ain't got nothing I need, is all. You're like a lot of others, thinking everything come from the white man. Long as you believe that, you'll be blind to your own lights. You got to break the lie."

Granada looked at the woman doubtfully. It wasn't a lie. Everything she wanted *did* come from the white man, and from his kitchen and from his wardrobe and from his smokehouse. What could a Negro have that she would ever want?

Polly must have read her thoughts. With

229

heat returning to her voice, Polly said, "You can't get nothing from them because they ain't *got* nothing to give. It ain't theirs to give. Never was." She stared hard at Granada and jabbed a finger to the girl's chest. "*That* is the lie! Every damn thing on this piece of Mississippi dirt they calls the master's plantation," she said, her voice smoldering with a boundless rage, "everything you've known since you was a baby. The great house, the master's big black stallion, them dresses you pine for. Even the sugar cookies from the master's kitchen. All the glitter and the gleam and the gold. Everything you seen and touched and tasted. Everything the mistress holds in her hands. Even you. It all come from one thing and it ain't the white man."

Polly held up her index finger. "Just one place. And you got to give it honor or you be as dead as your mistress."

"You ain't telling me nothing," Granada shot back. "It all come from God."

Polly's laugh was harsh. "And then I reckon God turned it over to the white man for safekeeping? That's sure what they say in the white man's church. You a fool to believe none of their religion. All they got to tell us is that we'll burn in hell for stealing the master's chicken." Then she laughed

230

again. "Ain't even his chicken."

"If you don't think they is no God," Granada argued, "then why you always looking in that big Bible book of yours?"

"Lord, girl! Arguing with you is like trying to show red to a blind mule." Polly took a calming breath and then explained. "I didn't say they weren't no God. But I can read for myself. Most of the mess the white man preaches ain't in the Bible I got. And a lot of things he *don't* say, is. The white man got his own special Bible, plum full of mischief for folks like us."

"So if it all don't come from God, and it don't come from the white man, where ever thing come from?" Granada challenged.

Polly shocked Granada by letting out an earsplitting cackle. "Where do it come from, the little girl asks?" she shouted out to nobody Granada could see.

Polly fell into a fit of frenzied laughter. "Lordy, Lordy!" she hollered. "Lordy, my Lordy! Little Miss Prissy sure be asking a grownup woman's question all right! But little missy ain't going to like the answer I got. No, sir! She liable to spit it out like she spit out dirt."

Her laughter grew wild, scaring Granada. Polly stood and lifted her skirt, swishing it from side to side like a fancy woman, taunting Granada. "Miss Prissy asking me a grown-up woman's question about grown-up woman's things! 'Where it all come from, Polly?' she asks."

She lifted her skirt higher, showing her bony knees and underdrawers. "When I tell her, she'll say, 'How could something good come from such a nasty nappy place?' "

She released her skirt and reached down to thump the girl's ear. "She wants to know woman's things, but she still listens with little-girl ears."

Then Polly began to weave unsteadily on her feet. She reached to brace herself on the table.

Granada held a hand over her throbbing ear. How was she supposed to know about woman's things? Nobody ever told her anything. She watched Polly where she stood panting like a hard-run mare.

"I swear, girl," Polly said, still breathing hard, "you beat all. Argue the horns off a bull."

"How am I supposed to learn?"

"Done told you. Watch and listen to ever thing around you. And when you begin to know it here," she said, lifting her hand to her chest, "make sure you do one thing."

"What?" she asked.

"Keep your damn mouth shut," Polly said

as she turned back to her work. "A flapping tongue puts out the light of wisdom. And that tongue of yours could put out a house fire."

Tears stung Granada's eyes, but she blinked them away, not wanting to give the old woman the satisfaction of seeing her cry. She spun around on her heels and stomped outside, feigning anger instead. Once out the door, she let the dark hide her tears.

Through the twilight she could see the great house across the way. The windows were dark, awaiting Pomp's ritual lighting of the candles. Smoke rose from the great chimney in the kitchen behind the house. Granada breathed deeply. Aunt Sylvie was tending something delicious, pork roast maybe, readying it for the master. Soon she would put it on serving trays and tell a house girl to hurry it down the boardwalk to the master's table while the meat was still steaming.

It had been weeks since she had eaten in the kitchen or stood at the master's table. And longer since that last Preaching Sunday. All those beautiful clothes remained unseen and unworn, locked away in a wardrobe, now more the dead girl's than hers. Polly told Granada she didn't need those clothes, that she was prettier without them. "You got a beauty them people just want to cover up. It scares them," Polly had said. "You got to see it for yourself." Granada didn't believe Polly. The girl knew that without pretty things, she was invisible.

Granada strained to see through the darkened windows, looking for the passing shadow of Mistress Amanda. While she watched the house, Little Lord stepped out onto the gallery.

Upon spying Granada, he ran up to the railing. He cupped his hands around his mouth and called out, "Granada!," his voice barely rising above the whir of insects. "Granada, why don't you play marbles with me no more?"

He was so small and far away. He might have been calling her from some world she had only dreamed once upon a time. She opened her mouth to answer, but tears rose in her throat. She could only wave and watch as Lizzie appeared and, after a wide sweep of her head to take in the entire yard with her good eye, led the boy inside the house.

And the mistress, she wondered, did she dream her up, too? She never came out on the gallery anymore and her heavy burgundy curtains were usually pulled in her room. Did the mistress ever think of her? Was she grieving Granada as much as Granada grieved the mistress? As Granada wiped her eyes with the back of her hand, Polly stepped out of the cabin and stood beside the girl.

"What you crying over?" she asked.

"I ain't crying!"

Polly crossed her arms over her sagging breasts and said softly, "Granada, she ain't got nothing for you."

Granada froze. How did the woman know what goes on in a person's head?

Polly continued. "She's got nothing because she *ain't* nothing but a house of dreams. She's lost to her own self and holding tight to you on her way to hell. She ain't never going to find her way back. Let that woman go. Her time has passed."

Granada began to sob, the words spilling out as freely as her tears. "I can't read no dirt. I can't remember something I ain't seen yet. I don't want to hear no more riddles. Why you ever choose me?"

Granada succeeded in squeezing back her tears, but the unspent sadness quivered through her limbs. She braced for Polly's anger.

The woman bent over and placed her hand firmly on the top of the girl's head, her fingers splayed like she was choosing a

235

melon. "Granada," she said firmly, "this is where learning take place. And you smart, too. I ain't denying it. But that ain't what turned my face to you."

Granada looked up at the woman, whose features had grown soft and, even in the twilight, glowed.

Polly moved her hand from the girl's head to over her heart. The heat from the palm of the old woman's hand penetrated the fabric and warmed Granada's chest. Polly's hand heated up like an oven brick.

"This is where remembering lives," she heard her say. "I seen it in you the first day."

She watched the old woman through a film of tears.

"You got eyes that can see what nobody else can see, if you would only look."

Polly then raised herself up and stood next to the girl. For a long while they remained at the door of the hospital cabin in the cooling nightfall, Polly staring off in the distance, watching the first stars of the evening, and Granada sniffling, the place where Polly's hand had been still radiating an intense heat.

The hounds began bellowing for their supper and Granada heard Chester's laughter drift down through the soft evening air from the kitchen. Granada looked over at the mansion to see the windows lighting up one by one as Pomp passed through the house.

In a low voice, almost tender, Polly said, "There are things you got to know if you going to be of any use to the people. And I can't tell you where you can understand it. My momma used to say, 'I can pour water on your head, but you got to wash yourself.' That's what I been saying. You got to see these things through your own eyes. All I can do is point."

"What are they?" Granada asked, desperate now to know. She was so weary of all the riddles without answers. She wanted something sure and fast to hold on to, a firm place under her feet to stand. "Polly, please tell me."

Polly eyed her carefully and to Granada's surprise, nodded her head in consent. She took a deep breath, as if the things she had to tell were many and weighty.

"The first thing to know is ever thing you *think* you see before you is a lie." Polly said this looking directly at the great house. "A bottom-upward lie. Our people are living, breathing, slaving, birthing, and dying so that lie can keep being told. Like it's something that been handed down from the apostle days. People believe the lie because they forgot how to remember."

Polly's gaze left the mansion and returned to the darkening sky. The moon shone dimly behind a narrow streak of satiny black clouds. Stars were beginning to show themselves.

"My momma was a saltwater girl from Africa. Before the slavers caught her, she was the main weaver in her village. She say all the women in her clan were natural-born watchers of the night sky. So I reckon they knew a thing or two about that moon and them stars up there. We looking at the same sky they seen. The way they told it, all our people — dead, alive, and the un-begat — they all wove up in it, fixed one to the other by threads finer than spiderwebs. A sky of souls, they called it."

Polly smiled sorrowfully, her eyes still searching the heavens. "Our people is like them stars, I reckon. All threaded up together in a bolt of black velvet."

Negroes in the sky, thought Granada. Was that the answer to the riddle?

"When you got a question," Polly said before Granada could ask, "first be silent. Look around you. Let creation speak the truth to you." She raised her arms out before her, like she was letting loose two handfuls of glittering stars.

Granada studied her closely, wondering

238

about Polly's reach, wanting to know.

The girl heard a deep, rich rumbling and at first she thought it came from far off in the distance, beyond the levees, and wondered what kind of amazing animal possessed a call so beautiful, yet so heartbreakingly sad. Then she realized it was the old woman who made the sound. It rose from her throat and began to take on strange rhythms, unlike any music the girl had heard. It reminded her of the wind whistling through the canebrakes and how the raindrops sounded when they trickled through the forest canopy. She thought she could feel the sun on early-morning dew and hear the creek water rushing after a spring downpour. The entire world seemed to be nestled into Polly's sweet utterances.

Polly gently swayed her body side to side, like a streamer of moss caught by the breeze. Her arms extended, weaving the starlit heaven. Her entire body became liquid and flowed like a gentle wave to the rhythm of her voice. She began to make new sounds, and Granada heard what could have been words, foreign to her ears, borne out on the rhythmic cadence.

She didn't understand the meaning of the song in the same way she understood the rhymes that Chester sang, but she found this one comforting, familiar even. The secret part of her, warmed by Polly's touch, was awakening from a lengthy sleep, urged on by the sound, aching to rise from her chest into her throat and fly out into the night.

Granada watched the old woman through the gathering dark. Polly had transformed. She appeared softer and much younger, graceful, as delicate as morning mist. Granada found herself thinking Polly beautiful, in a way that, like the place in her chest, had not been known to her before this moment. She was irresistibly drawn to Polly, wanting to lose herself in the words and the rhythms and the softness of her curving body.

The last of the song flowed gently from Polly's lips and was carried off by the cool evening breeze, and Granada believed she could hear that final, waning note as it traveled to places she had never seen. She ached to go with it.

Polly blew softly through her mouth, as if she were putting out a candle, and then brought her arms down to her sides.

Granada felt many things she had no words to shape, so she remained quiet and let the secret part of her flicker as long as possible until at last it faded to its hiding place.

Polly still peered into the distant night. "Them words come from far off, from my momma."

Was this sadness she heard in the old woman's voice?

"You missing your momma?" Granada asked.

"I do that," Polly answered. "But I don't forget her. I draw memory from my mother's mouth like you draw water from the cistern. Her words are sweeter to my tongue than honey. They come to me from all the way back." Polly crossed her arms and sighed. "From the time before the lie."

"That song sure was pretty," Granada said, edging closer to the woman, craving the warmth that radiated from Polly's body. "Don't know what it says, but I sure would like to learn it. If you was to teach it to me."

Polly nodded. "It's a song the village women used to sing. It says, 'What we see and what we can't see . . . What we know and what we can't know . . . The mighty and the small . . . The Father and the Mother . . . The creatures that prowl the forest and the growing things in the fields . . . The young ones that tread the ground and the old ones that sleep under it . . . The birthing and the dying . . . The laughing and the crying and the bearing up . . . All creation breathes with one breath.' "

She reached up and wiped something from her eye with the back of her hand.

"Anyhow, that's the way my momma told it to me," she said, looking down at Granada. "And that's the way I'm telling it to you. All the people is caught up in this thing together. Like your eyes and ears and heart is one in your body. We all tied by invisible threads, one to another. My momma said nobody can go her own way without breaking them threads that make us one tribe. One breath."

She held both hands out before her. Then she laced her fingers. *"This,"* she said with conviction, "is where you belong, Granada."

Granada studied the woman's hands. Granada looked up at the house lit like a giant chandelier. She then raised her eyes to the stars once more.

"Them stars, Granada. You thinking they need a mistress? They need a master?"

"But they the master's stars, ain't they?" Granada said. "They on his property."

"No. Ain't no white master over them stars. No mistress, neither. Just made-up words. Master. Mistress. Nigger. Slave.

Property. They ain't nothing but bothersome night clouds that keep you from seeing the heavens with a clear eye. Keep you blind to all them stars."

Polly placed an arm gently around Granada's shoulder and drew her close. She pointed a finger to the sky. "Look up, Granada. Look to your people. We as beautiful and as plentiful as them stars knitted together in heaven. We just forgot. Somebody's got to remember for us all."

CHAPTER 20

For the rest of that day, Violet let go of Gran Gran's apron strings for as much as an hour at a time, doing nothing but studying the masks. Already on the table were Sylvie and Silas; Chester, Pomp, and Lizzie; Mistress and Master Satterfield and Little Lord; and Ella, Gran Gran's mother. Violet would carefully lift each up with both hands and move them around, arranging and re-arranging them.

Gran Gran guessed maybe the girl was acting out a story, the way children do with dolls and spools and just about anything else you set in front of them. But she couldn't say for sure. She only knew that it was a relief to see those anxious eyes calm some, and even fire up a bit with what Gran Gran judged as curiosity. Or maybe it was nothing but that age-old game called "play-like." If so, that was fine with Gran Gran. A child's pretending was a much better pastime than remembering all the real-life, grown-up mess this girl had seen. Too much to learn, too quick.

When Gran Gran had been a girl and the time had come for her to leave Sylvie and the kitchen, the only world she had ever known, suddenly nothing made sense. No one had ever told her about the ingredients of life, only of biscuits. No one had readied her for the new things she saw. Birthing and mothering and living and dying. The kitchen had been a pretend place, where life never intruded in its typically messy fashion. Now, remembering, the old woman wished someone had prepared her better.

"Violet?" Gran Gran asked, looking at the girl as she placed Polly's mask between Aunt Sylvie's and Silas's. "I don't know if you old enough for this story or not, but something tells me you are. I know when I was about your age, I sure wish somebody had let me in on the big secret. I reckon Aunt Sylvie and Chester and the grown-up folks who raised me didn't think it was good for my ears."

Gran Gran shook her head and laughed. "Lord were they wrong about that! It was the best news I ever heard!"

CHAPTER 21

Granada was sitting on the porch of a swamp slave's cabin in one of the master's far-flung settlements, wondering what Polly was doing to the woman inside to make her so angry. She had been growling like a gut-shot bear.

Bridger had come with a wagon early that morning, summoning Polly from the hospital. The two exchanged a few words and Polly hurried back into the cabin and grabbed the short cloth sack she kept hanging on a peg behind the door. While she filled it with remedies, she told Granada to fetch one of the clay vessels she had fired and painted the week before.

As soon as they had settled into the wagon, the mules took off at a trot. Polly rode straight-legged in the wagon bed, resting her back against the sideboard. After a while she removed her floppy hat and tied up her hair in the faded flowered scarf with the beaten-brass disks that glittered in the sun.

Granada made the trip sitting in the rear of the wagon, dangling her legs over the rough track. As the overseer persistently cursed the mules and snapped the reins, and the wagon jolted her, Granada hugged the little clay pot close to her chest.

During the four-mile trek to Burnt Tree quarters she had plenty of time to speculate about how long it would be before the woman called Ella would appear on one of these visits. Perhaps she was dead. Or maybe she cared as little for a reunion as Granada did. But still the prospect filled her with an icy dread, and she tried her best to put it out of her mind. She looked back at Polly, who now seemed to be sleeping, her hands clasped in her lap, the little round mirrors catching the rising sun and flashing about her head. There were times now, especially when she slept, the old woman didn't seem so scary.

When they entered the settlement, Granada noticed that Burnt Tree looked nearly identical to Mott's quarter and Hanging Moss — two long rows of small whitewashed cabins with newly built porches facing each other across a well-trod lane. Screening the settlement from the fields was a skirt of woods on one side and a cypress slough on the other.

The quarter lay quiet. It had been light now for several hours and most of the inhabitants were already in the fields. Down at the end of the row she saw an old, shrunken woman sitting on a stump chair under a cottonwood, minding pallets of sleeping babies. Larger children squatted or crawled naked on the hard ground. Bridger pulled the team to a stop in front of a two-room cabin and both Polly and Granada exited through the rear of the wagon.

Bridger called back at them. "Get her done in good time so she can be back in the fields by morning."

Polly didn't reply.

As they walked toward the cabin, Granada spied two women through the open door. They stood on either side of the bed, obstructing from view all but the head of the sick woman, which she threw back and forth on a pillow of straw. Even through the shadows, Granada could see the sweat glistening on the woman's face and hear her pained moans.

Granada dragged her feet as she followed Polly up the two steps and onto the plank porch, bracing herself for the disgusting sights of another sickroom. Polly turned to

248

Granada and brusquely told her to wait outside with the empty crock. Then she entered the cabin and shut the door.

Unexpectedly alone, Granada couldn't decide if she was more relieved or hurt at being excluded, but she felt the need to register her complaint regardless.

"I ain't going to say nothing!" she protested weakly through the cypress door. Then, resigned, she plopped onto a plank bench situated below a burlap-curtained window, the clay pot resting in her lap.

Granada's feelings finally came down hard on the side of relief when the sick woman yelled out like somebody was whipping her with a leather strop. A while later a dark, mud-splattered woman wearing a sweat-stained head rag emerged from the nearby skirt of woods and came running down the track. She hurried up the steps of the cabin, passing by Granada with only the briefest of glances, and then tapped gently on the door.

"It's Pansy," she said.

The door opened to let her in as another woman stepped out and rushed off into the woods.

This odd routine was repeated several times throughout the day with some women collecting a baby to nurse before stepping inside the cabin. It was puzzling, all the comings and goings. The conspiracy seemed to involve every woman in the quarter. By midafternoon, Granada was determined to solve the mystery, even if it meant going into the sickroom.

Polly emerged from the cabin after several hours. When Granada opened her mouth, the old woman shushed her before she could speak. Polly sat down heavily on the bench and unknotted a square of cloth she had packed away in her sack.

Inside was a wedge of corn bread and a bit of salt pork. She nibbled a bird's portion and secured her packet again, never bothering to offer Granada one bite. Then she shut her eyes.

It took only a moment for her chin to drop. She began to snore lightly, leaving Granada to watch the old woman's chest rise and fall with her breathing.

Not more than five minutes could have passed before Polly woke with a snort and scrambled to her feet. She reached down and took the crock from Granada's hands, and then returned inside the cabin. She never said a word.

By late afternoon the cries of Sarie, the sick woman, were raw with exhaustion and her speech more agitated.

"Get the hell out of here and let me die!" the woman screamed. Granada pitied the poor women who attended her, but Sarie's fury only evoked another round of gentle words and soothing tones.

The gray dark of twilight saw the slaves quitting the fields for home. Some of the women stopped off by the cottonwood and picked up a child or two, while the men headed straight for their cabins to sit on their porches and smoke their pipes, or chop weeds in the little garden plots that each family now had, thanks to Polly.

More magic, they claimed. Granada knew different. She had heard Polly tell the master to his face that a patch of greens was a small price to pay to keep out the blacktongue. "Don't worry yourself," she had told Master Ben. "Let them grow it on their own time." Wasn't magic. Sneaky is what it was! Polly also told him they could all use a porch as well. Soon as he started bellyaching about the cost, she explained to him how a porch would get him another hour of work out of them every day. With a porch, they could see to do their house chores like weaving, soapmaking, harness mending, and such after it got too dark inside the cabin. Of course that made folks love Polly Shine even more.

Nope, it sure wasn't magic. It was conniving.

All around Granada rose the shouts of children playing their ring games and mothers singing to their babies and the steady chop-chop-chop of hoes in the gardens. But none of it could disguise the fact that everybody, young and old, was keeping one eye on the sick woman's cabin.

When a weary, barrel-chested man arrived with two somber-faced boys, Polly cracked the door of the darkened cabin. She told the man that he was welcome to come into his own home, but only for a short while. The big man didn't argue. He removed his battered hat and stepped inside, leaving the boys on the porch to stare blankly at Granada like she was nothing more that a porch step.

Granada's belly began to grumble. The smoke from a multitude of chimneys settled over the quarter, bringing with it the suppertime smell of frying meat, reminding her again that she had not eaten all day. As darkness fell, women began to gather around the house. Some brought plates of corn bread and side meat and shared it with Sarie's sons.

At last, one woman with a shy, cringing look, like a dog that had been kicked once too often, held out a plate to Granada. When she took it, the woman startled Granada by breaking into a broad, gapped-toothed smile that lit up her face.

Did the woman recognize her? Granada started and the tin plate nearly fell from her hands.

Terrified, Granada dropped her eyes, trying to make the woman disappear, praying that this was not the woman named Ella. The little woman said nothing and at last Granada heard her limping shuffle down the steps.

Now Granada looked up to see that many more people were milling about the yard. Children had gathered dry wood and pine knots, and a fire blazed in the lane. The men talked quietly while the women carried babies on their hips. But whenever some commotion arose from the direction of the cabin, everyone went still, as if they were awaiting some important pronouncement. Firelight reflected the great anticipation in their eyes.

As Granada sat alone, feeling a stranger to everybody and everything around her, the door creaked opened and out came the sick woman's man. He wiped his hands anxiously on his dirty pants, and then reached into the pocket of a ripped shirt for a clay pipe. He sat down on the bench next to Granada.

"You Polly's apprentice?" the man asked, twisting the pipe stem with his thick, blunt fingers.

Granada shrugged, not knowing what he meant by the word. He smelled of sweat and tobacco. Granada inched away.

"Well," he said, taking her lack of response in the affirmative, "don't reckon you could ask for nobody better to learn under. That's what I hear anyhow." He laughed self-consciously and said, "She make the lame walk and the blind sure enough see. Least that's what they tell me. They right about that?"

He looked at Granada for reassurance. "They say she totes her conjuring herbs in that sack. Some say she do hoodoo on folks."

When she still didn't respond, he muttered softly, "Sure hope she knows what she doing." He tapped the bowl of the pipe against his palm and glanced over at his two sons who stood at the edge of the porch. He lowered his voice and said, "Sarie done lost the three before this one. Last baby nearly took her with him. You ever seer Polly do this before?"

254

"Do what?" Granada asked. "What she doing?"

"Don't you even know why you here?"

"She don't tell me nothing," Granada grumbled.

"Girl, my woman's having a baby!" He laughed. "Thought for sure you knew that. Thought you come to help out."

"She got a baby in her belly?" Granada gasped. She had heard about this happening to women, but had never actually seen it up close. "That why she sick?"

The man laughed. "She ain't sick. She bigged! And that baby trying to get hisself born this very night."

Granada thought about that for a moment. Why didn't Polly want Granada to know anything about babies? she wondered.

Over the next hour, it was Polly's voice that dominated within the cabin, handing out orders left and right. As the hoarse cries from the woman grew more desperate, Polly's instructions became more succinct, sometimes comforting and other times insistent.

"Bear down harder!" she would scold.

Then she would croon softly, "That real good, Sarie. Now breathe in and out real easy, like you blowing in a jug." And in the next moment she would be hollering at the

255

woman again, or commanding the others to get Sarie on her feet and walk her around the room.

Finally, the woman cried out, "Something ain't right! I can't do it no more! It wants to kill me!"

There followed the sounds of the women calling out Sarie's name, telling her she was in God's hands now. "Let it roll with God," they cried. "He'll see you through."

"Yes, Lord," the man next to Granada whispered.

Sarie released a heaving groan that threw a deathly quiet over the yard. The only sounds now were pine knots popping in the fire.

Sarie's man leaned his arms on his knees, clasped his hands together, and mumbled his prayers, while his sons stood wide-eyed against the porch railing, the older boy's arm wrapped protectively around his little brother. Those in the yard began their silent prayers.

God was beseeched with one voice, and in that long moment, there seemed to beat only one heart, growing stronger and louder. Granada's entire body throbbed with it, and when she felt that she couldn't contain the surging force any longer, there came the cry of a newborn baby, breaking over thei heads like a sheet of lightning.

The entire community answered the new arrival with a spontaneous cry of its own. Sarie's man jumped up, flung open the door, and charged into the cabin.

Granada, filled with the wonder of that moment, found her legs and stood to gaze through the door.

The grease lamp on the table cast a golden circle around the group. They were all looking down adoringly at Sarie, whose face radiated light. She held a tiny child close to her, its little arms reaching.

Granada fixed her eyes on Polly as she stood tall and erect, looking down on the mother and child, the disks winking in the lamplight. She neither smiled nor frowned. Her countenance begged no gratitude. Her expression was so complete in itself, nothing was required of those who saw her but to love her, and Granada could not help doing so herself.

Sarie reached out to Polly and, after taking her hand, brought it to her own glistening face. Granada did not know that she herself had begun to weep.

"God bless you, Mother Polly," Sarie said, her voice liquid with tears. And then she did a surprising thing. She lifted the baby in her hands and offered her child to Polly.

Without speaking, Polly gathered the naked child and swaddled it in a piece of snow-white linen. Then she lifted the child to her lips and kissed it on the brow. When she returned it to the mother's arms, she leaned over and spoke very softly what Granada thought must have been a single word, but one that could be heard only by mother and child.

CHAPTER 22

Sarie's man proudly offered his arm to Polly and helped her down the porch steps. Her cloth sack hung from her shoulder, and the clay pot was cradled carefully in the crook of her arm.

Granada followed them into the yard and not until she joined Polly in the track did it dawn upon her that they were going to have to walk the entire distance back to the plantation yard. The overseer and his wagon were nowhere to be seen.

As if reading Granada's thoughts, Polly turned to the girl. "I know you think you too tired to walk, child. But you just think of Sarie in there. After all she done tonight, tomorrow she going to be put back to the fields. Tonight God made Sarie a mother one more time. Tomorrow, white man turn her back into a mule. Remember that anytime your foots get tired, you hear?"

Polly raised her eyes to the night sky.

"Least it'll be easy walking," she said in a frail voice that betrayed her exhaustion. "The woman is sitting tonight."

Granada followed Polly's gaze into the cloudless night sky. The moon was full and heavy, a "sitting woman," as Polly called it. "Means she found her home and is full of joy," she had told Granada once. "She knows where she belongs tonight."

Polly was right. Tonight the woman above was brilliant enough to illuminate the road before them.

A group of chattering women and sleepy-eyed children, still captivated by Polly's performance, accompanied the old woman and the girl down the track to the last cabin, beyond which swamp slaves were not allowed to pass. From there the women bid them farewell with extravagant waves and a chorus of "Blessed be" and " 'Night, Mother Polly" that continued long after the settlement had disappeared from view.

Granada followed at a short distance behind Polly, who trudged on ahead in a world of her own. There were a million questions Granada wanted to ask about the birth, but she could tell from the way the old woman forged her way through the night, her frail body hunched over and both arms around the clay crock, she was in no mood for talk. The sense of magic that Granada felt back in the quarter faded with the voices of the women behind her.

They continued along the narrow road, walled in by a dense canebrake from which emerged the too-real screeching and chirring of the night. Still Polly did not speak nor even glance back to see if Granada was still behind her.

For more than a month now, Polly had forced Granada to stand close by and watch every grisly, bile-raising sight under the sun, but when something that could be fun came along, like watching a woman have a real, live baby, she got the door slammed in her face.

Her thoughts became hot as pokers. "You the meanest, ugliest thing I ever seen," Granada grumbled to herself, not thinking Polly could hear.

"Beauty don't lay on the skin," Polly laughed wearily. "It's the pleasing face you have to look out for, not the ugly one. A pleasing face ain't hardly ever what it appears to be."

"Yes, ma'am," Granada answered, wondering how in the world Polly had heard her from way ahead.

"All right, tell me. What you riled about?" Polly asked, not looking back.

"You never going to learn me nothing about hoodoo or babies or nothing good. You always keep me away."

"Once ain't always. Twice ain't forever," Polly answered. "Coming a time real soon, Granada, when I won't leave you outside no more. Then you can know it all."

"I can get to see the baby being born?" Granada asked. She ran to catch up with Polly. "When soon?"

"When you a woman," Polly said.

"Oh." Granada was disappointed. To Granada that sure sounded like forever.

"Won't be long before you see your flowers." Polly looked down on Granada, squinting the way she did when she studied sick folks. "Most any day now, I figure."

"What do you mean? Is I sick?" Granada asked. "What flowers you talking about?"

Polly exhaled hard. "Didn't those people teach you nothing about being a woman? I'm speaking of blood, the flow of life. It will stream out of you like red blossoms."

"Where's it come out of me?" Granada gasped.

"From betwixt your legs," Polly answered.

"No!" Granada gasped and then swallowed hard.

That was the secret all the women in the yard had been carrying! She had seen those red spots that mysteriously appeared on their dresses. And heard the riddling way they talked about bleeding times, special teas they drank when they were visited by "the wound of Eve," the rags that needed to be washed out secretly. This is what it meant to be a woman?

She reached for Polly's hand and squeezed it. "Can't you stop it, Polly? I don't want to be no woman if I have to bleed to death! You got to make me well."

"Pooh!" Polly said. "Ain't nothing to be scared about. Your eyes will see blood, but it ain't just blood. It's life itself. God flows through a woman like a living river. My momma said that's how the moon gets washed new again, from the woman's river of blood."

"God put a river in me?" Granada asked skeptically.

"In the beginning God created," Polly said. "Them words don't mean nothing without the woman. When you bleed, you'll feel the tug of life from as far away as the moon. From 'In the beginning' time. God ain't got no beginning without the woman. Woman is the way God says yes in this here world. He put the promise on us. The woman carries 'In the beginning' in her body. And every month God will use your blood to wash the moon so the beginning time can begin again. When you get to be a woman you got to carry the promise with respect, and honor all the mothers who passed it down to us."

"Then I get to see the babies born?"

"When the flow comes. Then you can help me with the other women. You won't be a child no more, Granada, and you won't have to stand outside the circle of woman things."

"I can have me some babies, too?" Granada squeezed Polly's hand again, and she noticed how warm it had become. It occurred to the girl that she had never willingly reached out for the old woman before, and this sudden intimacy struck her as curious, but she made no move to break the hold.

"Maybe so," Polly said. "Soon your body will blossom like a fruit tree. And after it blossoms, you'll have the authority to bear life. When that happens, you tell me, you hear?"

"Yes ma'am, I sure will. When I see my flowers. When my blood washes the moon."

This was surely a hoodoo miracle if she had ever heard one. And it was going to happen inside of *her!* Down *there!*

As she walked at Polly's side, holding on

to her hand, Granada knew that what the old woman spoke of must be the biggest riddle of all. One that Chester or Silas or any man could never guess.

"Polly, when —"

"Stop," Polly commanded, like she had heard something.

Granada froze, with one foot still raised, sure she was about to step on a snake that only Polly could see.

"Wait here," Polly said, breaking their handhold. She stepped off the road and disappeared into the pitch-black forest.

The girl waited, figuring Polly had to relieve herself, but after she hadn't come back for quite some time, Granada decided the woman was surely up to something. Determined not to be left out of things again, she slipped into the woods to find Polly.

After tripping over roots and tangling herself in unseen vines, Granada finally entered an open place in the woods where the moonlight filtered through a loosely woven roof of twisted vines and boughs, suffusing everything around her with an otherworldly luminescence. The sight gave Granada the shivers. Though she couldn't name it, she knew something unnatural was happening.

She heard a rustling in the brush and then Granada saw the old woman's silhouette. She had dropped to her knees at the base of a sweet-gum sapling, and with her hands was clearing the leaf mold from a patch of ground. Once she had uncovered the spot she reached into her sack and retrieved a large wooden spoon.

Granada inched up to see.

Polly dug a shallow hole then upended the clay crock, pouring its contents into the ground with a thick, sloshing sound. Then her body began to sway, her head lolling from side to side, moaning low and gentle. Without breaking the rhythm, she took a handful of dirt and held it above her head. Granada heard a cadenced sound being born in her throat and finally an upsurge of words that seemed to be spoken to the sky:

In the beginning God birthed these
    watchful stars and a quickening moon,
In the beginning God laid open this earth
    like a mother's womb,
In the beginning God gave his breath to
    the baby's borning cry.
In the beginning God gave his breath to
    the old one's last gasping sigh.

Polly lowered her hand and sprinkled the

dirt lightly over the hole, then spoke softly
to her handiwork:

> In the beginning is the home we are
>   coming from,
> In the beginning is the home we are
>   going to.

After she uttered those words, everything
went dead quiet, even the night sounds of
the insects had been silenced. It was like
the forest was holding its breath.

What was she waiting for? Granada wondered. Who was she expecting? Ghosts or
witches or maybe the devil himself?

The woods slowly brightened, as if the
filtering canopy had parted and the stars
and the moon had lowered themselves by
invisible threads. Polly's handiwork was now
clearly illuminated. There in the hole was a
bloody mass flecked with dirt. It was veined
and raw, shimmering in the moonlight.
Granada didn't know how loudly she had
gasped and quickly clapped a hand over her
mouth. With her other hand she found a
tree to help steady her wobbly legs.

Polly bent over and filled the hole with
more earth, then broke the pot with a rock
and spread the pieces about the little
mound. When she had arranged it all to suit

her, she rose with great effort and began to make her way back to the road, passing by the tree where Granada stood trembling. She said nothing when Granada fell in behind her on unsteady legs and followed her out of the woods.

They continued their progress down the track, with Granada gradually slackening her pace. When she figured she was at a safe asking distance, she gathered all her courage into the base of her throat and blurted, "What was it you took from them people?" Her voice was all trembles. "What did you put in that pot? Did you hurt that momma and her baby?"

Polly's jagged laugh cracked like ice in the chilled night air. Then the old woman said over her shoulder, "Don't go into no tantrums. I didn't hurt nobody."

Though Polly said no more, Granada found herself believing her, and the girl's heartbeat began to calm. She started walking again but still kept a safe distance.

"But what was it you buried in that hole?" she called, but Polly didn't answer. "Maybe I'll just come back and dig it up and see for myself," Granada said, brave enough now to sass. Then she wondered if she could find her way back to the tree and locate the little grave, even in daylight.

"I'd be proud if you did," Polly answered, and again she laughed. "I'd whop your tail for it, but I'd be proud you were finally seeking some wisdom for your own self."

Polly lapsed into another deep silence, as if distracted by a matter of great weight. In front of them over the tree line was the faint glow from the mansion's observatory where the master would sit late into the night writing in his journals.

Polly stopped walking, allowing Granada to catch up. "Granada, just 'cause you have a woman's body don't mean you have a woman's heart. You like the new moon. There's a heap left to learn."

Granada didn't like the doubtful tone that underlay Polly's estimation of her. "Like what? Just tell me," she said confidently. "I'll learn it."

"God wants more from you than having babies. You got to know your place in the weave of things," she said. "You got to remember where you come from to know where you stand. And you got to know where you stand before you know how to help."

"I know where I stand, Polly." She laughed. "I stand wherever my feet stop walking." And to demonstrate the point, she planted her hands on her hips and came to a dead halt.

But Polly didn't stop. "That's what I mean," the old woman said and walked a little farther before turning around. "See?" she said looking at Granada through the dark. "You're standing by yourself. If you stand by yourself, then you can't do nobody no good."

They stared at each other through the dark, neither taking a step.

The girl panicked. Now Polly was mad again. Why couldn't Granada keep her mouth shut and listen, like Polly told her to? One thing Granada did know for sure, better than her own name, she wanted to see babies being birthed. That was the magic she wanted more than anything. Standing right there, she made a promise to God. She would never say another word if Polly wouldn't give up on her.

Through the dark, as she took a step toward Polly, Granada saw the old woman already had an arm reaching out to her.

CHAPTER 23

As Gran Gran lay in bed that night unable to sleep, she considered taking Violet down to the creek bank when the weather warmed to scrape up a bucket of clay. Then sit with her and show her how to shape and fire the masks, as Polly Shine had done when Gran Gran was a girl.

Of course, that would depend on whether Violet stayed. There could be family who would want her back, a family whose names might be lurking in one of the suitcases under Gran Gran's bed.

With the thought of Violet's departure, for the first time instead of relief, there was a hollow ache in the old woman's chest. Why would God remind a person at the small end of her life how lonely she had been for the biggest part of it? When it was too late to do a damn thing but regret it?

Her mind working too hard to sleep, Gran Gran rose from her mattress, kneeled on

271

the floor, and slid out one of the suitcases from under the bed. She had thought hard about opening them with Violet watching but decided against it. Gran Gran remembered the anxious reaction Violet had to the return of the wagon. There would likely be the smells of her mother, memories of kisses and other comforts. Of picnics and playing with dolls and dressing up, whatever it was they did together. Perhaps the suitcases even contained vestiges from the room where Violet had found her mother that day. No telling what nightmares the luggage held. Not all remembering is a way back. Could be too much hurt, too quick.

Gran Gran recollected what the old heads used to say. That if you woke a person too suddenly out of a dream, his soul would not be able to find its way back. And that girl, Gran Gran reminded herself, is still a house of dreams.

No, she would not take that chance. She decided she would go through the luggage herself. Gran Gran carefully released the latches one at a time, catching them before they could snap back on their springs. She quietly raised the lid.

All at once the room filled with the smell of perfumed silks and satins and lace. Gran Gran inhaled deeply, captured by the effect

It wasn't a feeling for Lucy or even Violet that overwhelmed her. It was another who came to her, so overpowering, the memory brought a catch to her throat.

She inhaled again and then closed her eyes, letting the perfumes carry her to a place she had not been in years. "Oh, Mistress, Mistress!" she laughed sadly. "Don't let anybody ever tell you that you weren't a mess and a half!"

When Gran Gran looked down, it was not the clothing that caught her eye. Whoever had packed the case had emptied dozens of photographs on top before closing the lid. Most were loose, but the one that she noticed was in a silver frame. It showed a man and woman standing in what looked like a church. He was wearing a soldier's uniform. She was holding a bouquet of flowers, smiling big, nothing like the desperate woman who had first come to Gran Gran, painted up and begging for help.

Gran Gran didn't touch the photograph. She had no right. Instead she reached under the frame and removed a yellow silk scarf. She then closed the lid of the case, latched it, and shoved it back under the bed.

"Yes," she said to herself. "We'll unpack this thing slowly, a piece at a time."

That night the current of Gran Gran's

dreams was strong, sometimes even violent, breaking through dammed-up places, searching for its bed. As it surged, images became clear, picking up the light. The silt was settling out to the bottom. She awoke the next morning with the mistress on her mind, the scent of her perfume seemingly in the air.

Over breakfast, she carefully pulled the yellow scarf from her apron pocket and eased it across the table to Violet. The girl stared expressionless at the silk cloth, as if waiting for it to break the silence. Then, as if nothing had happened, she went back to cutting her ham.

She still wasn't ready.

"If I recall," Gran Gran said at last, "Mistress Amanda had a silk scarf like that one."

Violet looked up from her plate, lifting her brows.

"Probably had a trunk full of them. And then there were the ones that belonged to Miss Becky. They mostly got burned up in the fire."

The girl stopped chewing, her eyes intently focused on Gran Gran.

"What, I didn't tell you about the fire? Why I swear, that woman was out to kill us all!"

CHAPTER 24

In Polly's hospital, Granada passed the night fitfully, confusing waking with sleeping, haunted by specters more real than any dream, yet at the same time, more removed. It was as if she were watching herself through a window from another room.

I'm at my place by the kitchen hearth, waiting for the mistress to bring Miss Becky's favorite dress for Preaching Sunday.

Aunt Sylvie is stirring a pot that hangs over the fire, singing a peculiar song in a screeching voice. "Slaves and cotton and cotton and slaves," she repeats each time she tastes from the pot. She smacks her lips with hoggish relish.

Little Lord's prized marble appears on Aunt Sylvie's soup ladle, but then the orb rolls over and stares at me. It's Lizzie's milk-white eye.

Suddenly the mistress appears in the doorway. Her face is hidden by a mourning veil and she carries a bundle of clothes, hugging them closely to her bosom the way Sarie had cradled her newborn baby. She offers the bundle to Aunt Sylvie who dresses me, but when I turn to curtsy the kitchen is crowded with people pointing and laughing. Daniel Webster, holding Lizzie's eye between his teeth, grins crazily and jumps into the arms of a smiling blond girl, the same girl whose pictures hang all over the house.

I feel confused until I look down and see that I'm wearing the rotting rags of those children out in the settlements. The clothes smell like death.

"Stop it!" I scream.

The mistress pulls back her veil, but it's not her at all. It is Polly, cackling louder than the others.

"Watch out for pleasing faces!" Polly taunts.

"Where's my mistress?" I shout. "What you done with my mistress!"

Polly draws a bloodied knife from behind her black satin dress. In the other hand dangles the thing she buried in the woods, purple and veined. "The cord been cut betwixt you and her!" she says. "Her time has passed."

I turn to flee, but barring my way outside the kitchen is a small woman with skin so dark it gives off a purple cast, dressed identically to me. She begins to speak.

276

Granada forced herself awake.

Her chest was clinched in terror and the bed wet to her back. She lay trembling, waiting for the dream shapes to fade with the daylight streaming through the windows.

But something was wrong. The images seemed to be sharpening, becoming more potent in her mind's eye, as if she had borne some vital element from her sleep into her waking life.

"You been dreaming," she heard a voice say. She twisted toward the sound and was startled to see Polly sitting in a chair by the bed, turned full to Granada. The woman was without expression, her eyes deep in their sockets. Her face could have been carved from cypress.

Granada bolted upright. "What have you done to the mistress?"

Polly cocked her head to the side. "Done?"

"Something happened to the mistress and it's your doing. You hoodooed her. I saw it!"

A shadow of recognition crossed Polly's face and she nodded. "Your dreaming is beginning to show you things. That's good."

Nothing about this was good. "I've got to find the mistress. She needs me."

The girl scrambled out of the bed, but Polly snatched her arm and said firmly, "No, first tell me what you seen in the dream."

Granada struggled to free herself, but the woman's clutch was tight and her fingers were bruising her arm.

"You was in it," Granada said, panicky. "You had a knife and you was dressed up like you was the mistress. You made me wear dirty rags."

"What else?" Polly asked.

"I saw Lizzie's white eye, boiling in a pot. Aunt Sylvie was cooking it. It looked right at me."

"Lizzie's eye?" Polly asked and then exclaimed, "Yes, ma'am! Lizzie's eye!" as if she should have known it all the time. "Go on. Tell it all."

"I tried to run to the mistress, but somebody was standing in my way. She wanted to tell me something."

"Who?" Polly pressed. "Who was it standing in your way?"

"A dirty swamp nigger!" she spat. Granada could stand no more of this. They were wasting time. "The mistress needs me!" she cried. "I got to go to her."

"What you got to do is heed the dream, Granada. Your remembering has begun. Who was the woman? You know her."

Granada struggled against Polly's clutch.

"You can't see because you still got th·

white woman in your eyes. The mistress ain't the one who needs you. It's the people calling you. That's the meaning in the dream!"

"Let me go!" Granada screamed.

"Go, then! Go to her," Polly said with contempt. "Go see how she needs you *now*."

The statement seized the girl's heart. "Why you say that? You *have* done something!"

Polly's eyes smoldered. Her voice was barely audible and came from down low in her throat. "The water you despise will be the water that drowns you."

"What?"

"Choose for the people, Granada, and God will be on your side. Choose for yourself and you'll be walking alone."

The words had the sound of a curse. The girl fought harder to get free.

"See for yourself then." Polly released Granada's arm.

The girl fled from the hospital in her shimmy and bare feet. She ran straight to the cookhouse, charged up the steps and through the door. Old Silas sat alone at the table, his cup of coffee before him.

"Where's the mistress at?" she cried, sick with urgency.

Silas didn't look up at once. He sloshed

279

some coffee from his tin cup into a chipped saucer, brought it up to his lips with trembling hands, and cooled it with his breath. He sipped noisily as the girl waited with a choking impatience. Only after he had set the saucer down did he glance up at Granada, calmly. For a moment, she didn't think he had heard.

"Polly send you?" he finally asked.

"No," she wheezed.

He nodded. "Sylvie just now left to take Mistress her breakfast. But you can't just —"

Granada wheeled around. She took off through the door and raced down the covered walkway that led from the kitchen to the great house. Long swords of sunlight sliced through the loosely slatted roof.

Nearly halfway down the walk, she stopped short, her legs refusing to take her another step. Blocking the door at the other end of the boardwalk stood the sad-faced woman with her arms outstretched. Granada squeezed her eyelids shut and then flipped them open again. The dream woman had vanished.

What kind of spell had Polly put on Granada?

Swearing aloud to knock the woman down if she got in her way again, Granada flun

back the door that led into the cooling darkness of the great house and shot up the
grand stairway to the mistress's bedroom.

Aunt Sylvie was rapping lightly at the
door, a silver tray balanced flat on her other
hand. Granada watched unseen from the
top of the stairs.

When Aunt Sylvie got no response, she
called out the mistress's name. Still nothing. Granada saw the cook push the door
open, peek inside, and disappear into the
room.

Granada hurried after Sylvie. The cook
was standing before the bed, still turned
down for the evening. Sylvie called out for
the mistress, then turned toward the door
where she spied Granada.

"What are you doing up here?" Sylvie
stammered. "You want to get us both sent
to the fields?"

"Aunt Sylvie! Where's the mistress at?"

"Lord if I know! She done found her legs
and run off like a swamp slave," she said.
"But I better track her down before the
master comes home from riding the fields
and lets loose on me." She looked at
Granada. "Best you get out of here, before
—"

That's when they both heard it — a child's
hysterical screaming.

Sylvie dropped the tray onto the mistress's teakwood console, the silver coffee pot crashing to the floor and pitching an arc of black liquid across the carpet.

"Let's you and me go see what hell has broke loose this morning." Sylvie's voice was shaking as she ran for the door. She clearly needed Granada's help now.

They followed the screams to Miss Becky's bedroom. Granada could smell the smoke before she made it to the door.

Sylvie turned the brass knob but found it locked. "Little Lord!" she shouted. "Open this door!" Then she muttered to herself, "My merciful God, help that poor child!"

"Get me out, Aunt Sylvie! Get me out!" The boy was hysterical. Next came the shrieking wails of Daniel Webster.

Sylvie turned to Granada. "I got the key hid in the kitchen. You stay right here and . . . Lord, I don't know what. Just stay here." Aunt Sylvie took off down the stairs.

"Mistress Amanda!" Granada called. "You in there, too?"

More panicked screams emerged from child and beast. By the time Granada thought of going out to the gallery and trying a window, Aunt Sylvie came puffing down the hallway with the key and two house servants in tow.

Smoke was now funneling into the hallway from under the door. Sylvie frantically fumbled with the key until the lock finally clicked.

The room was thick with smoke, but Granada could make out Little Lord on the floor cringing under the dressing table, crying out between bouts of strangled coughing.

First out of the room was Daniel Webster, who scurried past them.

"Run, Little Lord," Sylvie shouted as she raced across the room to throw open the window, but the boy stayed put.

When the smoke cleared a bit, Granada saw its source. Mistress stood in the middle of the room, her long graying hair hanging down to her waist. A powder-blue nightgown was tied close to her neck, and folds of the cotton fabric cascaded to the floor, puddling at her feet. On her face was the most desolate expression Granada had ever seen on the woman. She gazed sadly, almost longingly, into the advancing flames, as if she would welcome an end to her grief.

On the floor between her and the tester bed stood a knee-high mountain of Miss Becky's dresses topped by a row of Becky's dolls laid on their backs, their arms reaching toward heaven. The items fueled a good-size blaze.

Aunt Sylvie's shouting brought Granada back to her senses. "Good Lord, Mistress!" the cook cried. "You trying to set the house afire?"

The mistress turned her sorrowful gaze to Sylvie. "No matter, Aunt Sylvie. Only bits and pieces." She coughed and then slowly nodded her head, as if to underscore the insignificance of it all.

When Little Lord's sobs rose again from under the dresser, Aunt Sylvie moved into action. "Lizzie, get the boy out of here."

The maid ran across the room and roughly grabbed Little Lord's arm. She dragged him coughing and crying into the hallway.

"My good Lord in heaven," Pomp exclaimed, still huffing from his run up the stairs. "What happened?"

"Pomp, fetch that pitcher of water on the mistress's washstand," Aunt Sylvie commanded. "And Granada, you give me a hand over here!"

Sylvie and Granada hurried to the other side of the bed. With all their might, they jerked down a panel of heavy damask drapery, ripping the brass hardware from the wall. Sylvie used the material to blanket the fire, smothering most of the flames. All this time the mistress looked on amiably. Sh could have been hosting an afternoon tea.

When Pomp returned with the Haviland pitcher, Granada looked down to see the flames nipping at the hem of the mistress's gown.

"Throw it, Pomp!" the girl yelled as the blaze shot up the folds of soft cotton.

Pomp flung the water on the mistress but not before the flames had blossomed upward, licking at her oily ropes of hair. They lit like fuses.

Lizzie arrived with a leaded vase filled with quince-tree blooms but stopped short when she saw the mistress's hair aflame.

"Throw it, fool!" Sylvie screamed.

Little Lord let go a gurgled shout from the doorway. "Throw the water on momma's head, Lizzie!"

Her son's plea seemed to jolt the mistress awake. She shrieked out in pain and began stumbling around, slapping at her head with the flats of her hands. The stench of burning hair filled the room.

But Lizzie remained stone-still, seemingly paralyzed with fear, until Granada looked into her face and caught the faint remnant of a satisfied grin. Then Granada remembered. The woman on fire was the same woman who had sent Lizzie's daughter to the swamps.

Granada grabbed the vase from Lizzie's grip and hurled the contents, both water and flowers, into her mistress's fire-scorched face.

CHAPTER 25

Two days later Granada and Polly stood on the hospital porch watching the drama unfold at the great house. Moments before the master's carriage had pulled up to the back stairs and halted. Trunks and bags were lashed to the roof. Now Master Ben stood stiffly in the drive, holding open the carriage door.

Slowly the mistress emerged from the house, two housemaids flanking her as they descended the steps. She was wearing a heavy black dress and her face was dark behind a veil.

Granada shuddered.

"You seen all this before, ain't you?" Polly asked.

Granada nodded weakly. "The dream," she answered.

"You know more than you saying," Polly accused.

Yes, Granada could have said more. But

why should she? If she spilled all her secrets, then Polly and Silas would both have her hide. And it wouldn't get Mistress Amanda back.

After the fire, the mistress couldn't be calmed. She paced the room screaming in pain, crying out to both the living and the dead. Aunt Sylvie raced back to the kitchen and returned with a bottle of laudanum, Old Silas following a few steps behind.

Lizzie and Granada held Mistress Amanda down while Aunt Sylvie spooned the medicine carefully past the woman's blistered lips. After a few minutes, she calmed enough for Sylvie to treat her tender spots with a thick coating of lard. It seemed to Granada that the only place on Mistress Amanda's body that had not gotten a blistering were the bottoms of her feet and her backside. But it was her head that gave Granada a fright.

When Sylvie was done, she told the maids to drape all the upstairs mirrors, saving the mistress the additional pain of catching the grisly sight of her frizzled head and swollen, oozing eyes.

All the while they helped tend the mistress, Granada felt Silas's eyes on her. When she stepped away from the bed, he spoke, low enough so that only she could hear,

"You knew."

"I dreamed —" But she stopped, not knowing how to explain. She looked down at her feet.

"Some of these burns look awful bad," Aunt Sylvie called out from the bedside. "I reckon you best go fetch Polly."

Grateful for an errand that would get her away from Silas's questioning, Granada turned toward the door. But Silas grabbed her arm, holding her tight.

"Sylvie, let's not go mixing that woman up in the family's affairs," he said. "Master won't abide a slave woman doctoring on his wife. You know how he is."

"Look at her, Silas!" Sylvie cried. "Eyes swelling shut and her face turning red as an Indian. And her hair, my Lord!" she cried. "Stubble and scalp. We got to do something! Master Ben will kill me."

Silas released Granada to take his wife by the shoulders. "*You* can keep lard on her face as good as Polly Shine," he said firmly, looking hard into her eyes. "And *you* know which flour barrel you hid the laudanum in. Nothing she can do, you can't do better."

Aunt Sylvie nodded, but with little conviction. Granada wasn't so sure, either. She had seen Polly heal all kinds of wounds, including the burns of those clearing the forests. But Silas kept offering his arguments, sounding calm and reasonable and very wise.

"Besides," he continued, "by tomorrow, that prideful woman will have it spread across the countryside how *she* saved Master Ben's wife. Everybody, slave and master, will know how far Mistress Amanda has fallen. How do you think the master will like his business gossiped about that way?"

Aunt Sylvie shook her head. "No, I . . . I reckon not."

"For all we know," he said, looking now at Granada, "that old woman put a hex on the mistress. You ever think of that?"

Granada had wondered the same thing.

Silas put his arm around Sylvie's shoulder and pulled her close. He said in her ear, "Now don't you worry. I'll tell you exactly what to do."

Silas had it all worked out. He told Aunt Sylvie to meet Master Ben at the stables upon his return — before he had a chance to see his wife. "Don't beat the devil around the bush, Sylvie. Tell him everything that happened, straight-out. And don't let him talk to anyone else," Silas said. "Then you tell him something else."

Silas glanced over at Granada, as if surprised she was still there. He studied her fo a moment. "Maybe I ought not be talking in front of the girl," he said. "You going to carry this back to Polly?"

Granada shook her head. Polly wouldn't want to hear anything about the mistress, anyway.

Then Silas asked another question, one she had not expected. "You still wanting back in the house with the mistress?"

"You can get me back in?" Granada asked tentatively.

"Depends," he said. "To get you back where you belong, we need to get rid of Polly first. You ready to go against Polly? You ready to tell me what she's been up to?"

She studied his expression hard, to see the truth in it, wanting to believe. He smiled an all-knowing old man's smile at her. Granada nodded.

"Then tell me something now. Show me I can trust you."

Granada's heart pounded in her ears.

"Well," Granada stammered. "She's always speaking bad about Master Ben. Says one day soon, ain't going to be no more masters. No more slaves. Says one day, we'll all go to a place she calls Freedomland."

It didn't sound like much, but when she finished speaking her face burned hot.

Old Silas seemed satisfied. "Good. From now on you tell me everything she does. Slip off to my cabin when she's looking the other way. I'll get you back in with the mistress where you belong."

Silas had turned back to his wife. "Sylvie, tell the master Old Silas himself saw how bad off the mistress was. Tell him it nearly broke my heart. Then tell him how I got down on my knees asking the Lord's mercy for him and his mistress. Tell him just like that. You understand?" he asked. "Tell him I'm in my cabin, all broke up over it."

"I do like you say, Old Silas."

"And one more thing. Most important of all. Make sure he knows Little Lord was in the room. That the mistress tried to kill his only child."

"But I don't think she —" Sylvie caught herself and then nodded.

"Good. Don't let anybody get to him before me. If you do like I say, then everything will be all right."

He smiled at Sylvie now and winked. "It's as plain as my big toe, Sylvie. Remember?" he said, chuckling. "Master Ben's pain's about to overtake his pride. He's got no one else to turn to. He'll be needing me now."

An hour later found Granada sitting outside Mistress Amanda's window on the gallery, one eye watching the levee road and the other on the mistress, drugged and resting uneasily in her bed. Aunt Sylvie sat at the bedside. Her lips were in constant motion, rehearsing what Old Silas had told her to say.

When the dust cloud rose on the horizon, Granada signaled Aunt Sylvie, who shot out of her chair and made haste for the stables.

Granada watched as Sylvie walked hesitantly up to the master while Chester led the stallion to the barn. Master Ben stood stone-still, letting her speak without interruption. When she had finished, he didn't open his mouth.

He finally took several heavy steps over to the stable gate. From there he looked up at the house, staring in Granada's direction. Little Lord had stepped out onto the gallery. The boy and the father were watching each other, neither making a motion or even a gesture of recognition.

The master nodded to himself, and then walked through the stable gate, passed under the sprawling limbs of the oak, his shoulders slumped, and before even going to see his wife, he headed straight to Silas's cabin. He stayed there for well over two hours.

Granada didn't understand everything

that had transpired, especially the complexities of Silas's plan, but she could see with her own eyes the results. As Polly and Granada stood watching on the hospital porch, the master helped his unsteady wife into the carriage.

Granada heard a child's scream and looked up at the top of the stairs. There Little Lord struggled to free himself from Lizzie's grasp, trying to get to his mother. But even when he bit into Lizzie's arm, she would not release the boy.

Lizzie was gazing unflinchingly at the carriage with her one good eye, and then she grinned. It was the same gratified smirk she wore the day of the fire.

Granada's heart sank. All she had wanted was to be back with Little Lord and the mistress. That was the bargain she thought she had struck. But somehow it all got turned upside down. Everybody got what they wanted but her. Lizzie, Polly, Silas — they got rid of the mistress. And it was Granada who helped them do it.

As she watched the carriage retreat into the distance, trailing a cloud of dust, Granada remembered Polly's words from the dream: "The cord been cut betwixt you and her!"

Polly had been right. A thread had been

broken, the one that linked Granada to the mistress and to the only place where the girl had ever felt she belonged.

CHAPTER 26

Granada fought to stay awake, determined to have no more dreams.

Before blowing out the lantern, Polly had instructed once more, as she had each of the previous three nights since the mistress had gone away, "The remembering has begun. Don't be scared of your dreaming. Go where it wants to take you."

"I don't want to dream no more," Granada whimpered. "Make them go away."

She was accustomed to dreams that were vague and fuzzy, vanishing like morning dew after she woke. But the remembering dreams were like the one she had the morning of the fire. They seared themselves into her memory like a hot iron and instead of fading away with daylight, grew in strength and vividness, until the dream felt so real she knew one of two things had to be true: that the events in the dream had already happened or that they were about to happen.

Polly said there really was no difference. "When you stand in the river, downstream or upstream, it's all the same water."

For three nights now Granada had dreamed of floods bringing great snakes that devoured the master's house and everyone in it. She dreamed of getting lost in dark, endless tunnels that had no exit. She dreamed of the mistress falling into a bottomless well, her shouts growing fainter. Each morning Granada's own screaming woke her. And each morning Polly was sitting by the bed, asking what it was the girl had seen.

Polly assured her the dreams were a gift of sight, but how did she know that envisioning bad things didn't *make* them come true? Maybe the mistress would still be here if she hadn't dreamed about her.

"I didn't ask for no gift," Granada had argued. "I don't want it."

Polly's amber eyes flashed. "You don't *want* it?" she snapped. "Wanting ain't got nothing to do with it. The sight ain't no gift to *you*. It's *your* gift to the people."

Despite Polly's scolding, Granada battled against sleep in every way she could imagine. She pinched her arm, and threw her legs off the side of the bed, and softly sang the words to a silly song Chester had taught her. She counted the croaks of a rainfrog hiding nearby. But she couldn't win. Tonight, as all the other nights, sleep eventually took the girl, and as Polly had predicted, the strange dreaming returned.

I'm naked, standing before a dense growth of trees, thick with interlacing limbs and woody vines. A narrow, cave-like opening offers the only way in. As I step toward it I hear terrible voices, moaning, and sobbing, the grinding of teeth, the raspy whispering of mysterious words.

Polly comes up behind me and tries to push me forward, but I kick and scream. Something reaches out and prickles my cheek, like the legs of a giant spider.

I swat at my face, trying to rid myself of the hideous creature.

She woke herself up. Blood was surging in her ears. Her body was coated with a thin film of sweat and the darkness seemed to quiver before her eyes.

But this time waking did not stop the sounds. Again she heard a voice, but now it spoke her name and she felt the spidery legs once more on her face. She grabbed at it. In her fist was a switch from the althea bush that grew by her window.

"Granada," she heard the voice say, "wake up."

She glanced up and saw a face like a pale moon gazing down on her. "Little Lord!" she gasped. "What you doing?"

The boy shushed her. "I'm going to find Momma," he said. "You got to go with me!"

At the mention of the mistress, Granada was at once up on her knees in her cot, face-to-face with the boy in the window. "You know where she is?" So far no one seemed to have any idea where the master had taken her.

"I heard Daddy say he was going to keep her in Port Gayoso until they could catch a steamboat to New Orleans," Little Lord whispered. "If we hurry, you and me can catch her."

The boy's rascally grin reminded Granada of her homesickness for him. He hadn't been down to see her in months. "Why you want me to come?"

"There ain't nobody else."

Granada could hear the panic rising in his voice.

"Daniel Webster run off after Momma last night and Lizzie said she's glad Momma's gone and hopes a gator gets Daniel Webster!"

"Lizzie's probably looking for you right

this minute."

"She's drunk on Daddy's brandy," he said. "She told me, 'First your momma, and now the monkey. You the only one left!' That's when she passed out. I think she's going to kill me if I stay."

Granada nodded and looked over in the dark to where Polly lay snoring in her bed. "I got me the same problem."

"Aunt Sylvie said Polly put a spell on Momma and made her start that fire."

Granada again nodded. "She say she don't do hoodoo. I reckon that makes her a witch and a liar both."

He leaned in closer and in a whisper so low she could barely hear him, he asked, "You learned enough yet to take a spell off somebody?"

Granada figured on the question for a moment. If she said no, would he still want her to go with him? "I been studying her close," she said. "I seen her doing some things I might can copy." It wasn't exactly a lie.

"You're smart. You're the quickest person I ever seen at learning. I bet you can make Momma well in a minute. Look," he said lifting his leather game pouch, "I took some stuff for us to eat."

"How we going to get there? It'll be first light before long. Somebody bound to see us on the road." The thought of the fierce slave-catching hounds popped into her head. But surely Mr. Bridger wouldn't sic those flesh-ripping animals on the master's boy, would he?

"We'll take my canoe down the creek."

"No!" she gasped, remembering her dreams. Snakes lived in that creek. "We can't, Little Lord."

"Sure we can. Barnabas taught me. I'll show you how. It'll be easy. The water's still high enough to take us right up into town."

"We'll get bit for sure!" she said. "Mocs swimming in the water and coppers crawling on the banks. Rattlers up under every log and leaf. Snakes everywhere. They even dangling from the trees."

He reached into his pocket and pulled out his mother's derringer. "I'll protect us," he said in a way that sounded uncharacteristically manlike.

Granada was so touched by the thought of Little Lord wanting to watch over her that without thinking, she reached out and patted his arm. She quickly caught herself and drew her hand back like she had touched fire. Aunt Sylvie would have slapped her face.

But Little Lord didn't seem to notice. "Granada, please," he begged, boylike again.

"If we can get to Momma, you don't never have to come back here. We can stay with her until we grow up and then you can be my slave and we can live wherever we want to."

Granada knew there were a lot of things out there his momma's little gun couldn't protect her from. She hadn't even mentioned the gators and whirlpools and quicksand and bears and panthers and buffalo gnats. But she decided against arguing. She didn't want to scare Little Lord out of going.

Besides, she thought, as long as he was taking her, it wasn't like she was running away. She was doing her master's son's bidding. She really had no choice.

"You got to promise me, Little Lord. If we get caught, you got to swear you made me go."

"I promise, Granada," he said, crossing his heart and then laughing. "I'll tell them I was going to whip you good if you didn't."

Granada felt around on the floor for her brogans and slipped the freshly laundered calico dress over her shift. She listened for a moment to the light, steady snores across the room and then crawled out the window.

CHAPTER 27

They soon found themselves paddling easily down the creek on a beautiful May morning, savoring the stolen sweetness of their escape. Every once in a while a nesting crane rose from the banks and took flight. Turtles basked in the sun, lined up on fallen limbs that reached out into the creek. As the canoe neared, a line of four or five plunked themselves into the water one after the other like ticks of a clock.

Granada had never been on the water before and she marveled at how the creek was a living thing with a will of its own, like an untamed horse challenging her to ride upon its back. At first she was unsure and jumpy and nearly made them spill, but Little Lord had proved a good teacher. Barnabas had constructed the craft out of a hollow log and made it small and light, easier for a child to handle, and the oars were made to fit Little Lord's boy-size strokes. Within an hour, he had Granada paddling like a fur trapper.

At times the creek narrowed so that branches from the locusts and sycamores arched over the entire width of the creek, and when that happened, Granada dropped her paddle to the bottom of the canoe and wrapped her arms over her head, certain that moccasins were about to rain from the limbs and bed down in her hair.

Otherwise things couldn't be better.

Granada looked back over her shoulder to check on Little Lord. His fair skin was already beginning to pink up in the intense morning sun. His pale blue eyes were bright. The boy grinned at her.

"You studying hard to be a witch like Polly?" he asked. "My book says witches use graveyard dirt and bat wings and salamander eyeballs and such to cast spells and turn princes into frogs. You know how to do any of that yet?"

It was true. Granada had read the book before he had. "Never seen her do nothing like that," she admitted. "I figure it's the way she looks at folks. Like she can open them up with her eyes and count their bones."

"The evil eye!" he exclaimed. Granada could tell he had been listening to Aunt

Sylvie as well as reading books.

"And the way she touches folks all over their bodies with them hot hands of hers," she said. "And she whispers things in their ear."

"Incantations," he said.

"I reckon," she said noncommittally. She thought of the night in the forest when Polly dug the hole. And the time outside the hospital when Polly sang the song and her body seemed to become young again. She remembered the warming in her own chest when Polly touched her. Was that magic? Was that the hoodoo Aunt Sylvie talked about?

"What else she do?"

"She crazy," Granada said. "She say varmints, jaybirds, and such talk to her. She say they always telling her what to do."

Little Lord laughed with delight, encouraging Granada to say more.

"And, Little Lord!" she exclaimed, forgetting her paddling and swiveling her body to look him in the face. "She goes around naming things! Up and down creation, she puts a new name on everything she sees. Things I never knew had no name. She showed me something she calls a headache tree. And toothache bark. Rattlesnake weed. A fever bush. Polly say folks don't really see something until somebody names it. But soon as it got a name on it, they say, 'Sure, I know what that is! I seen it all my life!' She says to name something is to remember it down deep, where the roots go."

She turned back around, shifted her paddle to the other side of the canoe, and dug deep into the water. "Yep," she sighed, feeling old and wise, "she says a long time ago, her people used to be the namers of the world. I reckon she figures Adam who named all them critters was the first of her people. She says for the people to be free, they need to lay a claim to naming things again. And a person ought to start with his own self."

Granada surprised herself at how effortlessly Polly's words were flowing out of her mouth, almost like she believed them herself. She couldn't help but continue. "And she says that God ain't the one give the white man everything he got a hold of."

"Where it come from then?"

"She says it comes from the slave woman's bagina."

"Bagina? What's that?"

Granada shrugged. "I don't know. Every time I ask she hoots and hollers at me and pops up her skirts real high. Laughs her fool head off. I told you she was crazy."

Little Lord giggled again. It made Granada giddy to tell him everything. He was the only one who acted like he didn't much mind what it was she came out with, whether he understood it or not. He just liked listening to her.

She had no sooner had these thoughts than Little Lord asked, "So how will you make my momma well?"

Granada had clean forgotten! There was something that Little Lord was listening for after all. She said the only thing she could think of that for sure wouldn't do any harm. "I reckon I'll feed her some mutton and port wine and whisper in her ear."

"You reckon that works on a white person?"

"Course it does!" she snapped. Granada pulled hard on her paddle. Did he think their insides were so different?

The sun had begun its afternoon descent when the creek opened up into an immense bayou where the water stood dark and still and bottomless. Giant cypress and tupelo gum rose imposingly out of the depths, dropping curtains of moss from their branches. The children paddled without speaking into this gloomy maze of trees and water.

The long hush was broken when a sudden

and terrible roar rose up. Granada's heart seized in her chest. The sound had been as fierce as the bellowing of a bull.

"That was a gator," Little Lord said in a dry whisper. "A big one."

What frightened Granada the most was that Little Lord felt the need to whisper. Was it that close?

"Smell that?" he asked.

A slight breeze wafted through the swamp and she caught a sweet and sickly scent.

"Gator wallow," Little Lord said before Granada could answer. "Barnabas says it's the only thing smells like that."

"What if he chunks us in the creek?" Granada gasped. "Nobody learned me how to swim."

"Just hold on to the canoe," he said. "Hey! Maybe we get a gator that got no more teeth than Silas." He made an attempt at laughing, but it sounded more like a strangled cough.

At last they found an outlet from the bayou, a small stream flowing between two overgrown banks. For a while the channel coiled snakelike but then it started to unravel, branching off into a confusion of choices. They wound around so much that the sun was never in the same place. In their faces, behind them, first to their left and then to their right.

"Little Lord, you reckon you know where we are?"

Little Lord didn't answer.

There was no current at all now and the water stood shallow and stagnant. They had to work their oars mightily. At times the creek was so narrowed by grass and cane and overhung with trees, it looked to Granada like they were moving atop solid land. Sometimes the channel gave out completely and they had to backtrack.

The late-afternoon sun was blazing hot, and Granada shook sweat off her face like she had stepped from a rain shower. The salt stung her eyes and blurred her vision. While she was lifting her shoulder to wipe her face, she thought she saw some creature scamper beyond the reeds along the shore, but by the time she looked, it had disappeared into the overgrowth.

It was while she strained to detect any movement at all that she heard the shriek. Both Little Lord and Granada recognized the sound.

"Daniel Webster!" the children shouted simultaneously.

Sure enough he emerged from a patch of mutton cane and began leaping up and down near the water, chittering wildly.

Little Lord nosed the boat toward the bank, guiding them under a dense overreach of branches. As they neared the shore where Daniel Webster waited, Little Lord reached up to sweep aside a screen of moss. What appeared to be a broken limb fell to the bottom of the canoe.

Little Lord screamed when he saw the moccasin slithering toward Granada. The panicked girl threw one leg over the side and then another, upsetting the canoe and throwing the two of them, along with the snake, into the murky creek.

Granada splashed furiously, sure that she would drown. Then her feet touched the muddy bottom. The creek was only knee deep.

She wiped the water from her eyes and saw the canoe floating empty down the channel. Little Lord was a few feet upstream wading through the cane toward Daniel Webster. And then she saw the snake swimming toward Little Lord.

Before she could scream, Daniel Webster leaped into the water, brandishing some kind of cudgel in his paw. Granada couldn't believe her eyes. He was charging the snake with a heavy stick. After he landed two blows, the snake glided away.

Granada joined with Little Lord in cheering the monkey, laughing with relief. She had totally misjudged Daniel Webster and now wanted to hug his neck.

She started toward the shore only to have the deep mud of the creek suck a shoe right off her foot. As she felt around for the lost brogan, she heard the pitiful whine of a child. Granada looked up to see that now it was Little Lord who held Daniel Webster's stick, furiously pounding the ground around his feet. And then the scream again. Little Lord dropped the stick and the wailing monkey jumped into his arms.

"Hurry up, Granada!" he shouted, red-faced, cradling the monkey in his arms. "Daniel Webster's been bit. You got to save him."

His words seemed to turn the water into molasses and the mud to quicksand. How could she tell Little Lord she didn't know the first thing about snakebites? That she had never healed anybody of anything?

Granada slogged up on the shore, her dress heavy and clinging to her legs. She began to tremble, not sure if it was from the chill breeze off the water or the expression of frightened expectation on Little Lord's face. In his eyes was such a look of awful wanting Granada decided that if she didn't know what to do, she would have to make it

311

up. She began like she had seen Polly begin, by taking charge.

"Let's find a place to lay him down," she said, trying to control the quiver in her voice.

Granada led Little Lord to an open place under a locust tree. She knelt and raked up a soft mound of leaf mold. "Now put his head down here like it was a pillow and I'll take a good look at him."

As Little Lord began to lower Daniel Webster to the ground, Granada tried to think of what Polly would do. She decided to begin by looking into his eyes and then whispering into his ear.

But the monkey never made it to his bed. Shaking violently, he lurched from Little Lord's embrace onto the ground, where he staggered drunkenly on all fours.

Daniel Webster's left leg was impossibly swollen. Halfway down from his knee was the double-fang mark, red and raw.

"Do something, Granada!" the boy cried.

Granada could no longer look at him. "Polly ain't learned me nothing, Little Lord," she confessed, her voice small. She threw a hand to her face, not wanting Little Lord to see. "Ain't nothing I know to do."

Daniel Webster was stumbling erratically, veering from side to side for a short distance. Then he would stop, weave a few moments on his feet, and begin again.

Granada knew what the monkey was doing. He was trying to make his way into the deepest woods, like animals do when they are ready to die. She had never thought of Daniel Webster as an animal before. He had always been so humanlike. Unlike her, he even had a last name and ate at the master's table. He was allowed to touch the mistress anytime he wanted. But now he was dragging himself off to die like the poor beast he was.

Granada turned to Little Lord, wondering how badly he hated her now. Though his face was wet with tears, his fists were clenched and his jaw locked. She had the sense he was readying himself to do something required of a man.

Granada watched as he reached into his pocket and retrieved his grandfather's derringer. He held it in his little-boy palm, gazing at it for a moment like he was disappointed to have found it. Then he gripped the gun firmly, his finger on the trigger.

Several yards away Daniel Webster moved slowly, pulling himself along by his arms. His legs dragged uselessly behind him.

Without speaking, Little Lord walked toward the dying pet, his steps weighty.

"Little Lord!" Granada gasped.

He stood over the animal, his arm stiff by his side, the gun pointing at the ground. Daniel Webster moved forward a few inches, and Little Lord took another step. Finally Little Lord reached down to stroke the monkey's head. Daniel Webster turned his eyes toward the boy to see who had touched him, and, as if knowing what was about to happen, raised his eyebrows in expectation, a forgiving grin on his face.

Little Lord raised the silver barrel to the suffering animal's head. The boy's sobs were so intense they lodged in Granada's own chest, but she kept her eyes open for him. She would bear the memory for Little Lord.

When he pulled the trigger on the old derringer, the dead dry click echoed through the woods. The gun's age or perhaps the creek water had saved Daniel Webster from a quick, easy death. The boy flung the pistol into the bramble and then stood there with his arms useless at his sides, lost and alone.

"Little Lord," Granada said.

The boy's frail body seemed to collapse in on itself. His shoulders caved and his back slumped.

"Little Lord," she said again, her voice breaking.

This time he heard. He ran to her and

threw his arms around the girl, nearly unbalancing her. He continued to clutch her in a ferocious embrace, sobbing violently into her chest.

They remained locked in each other's arms for a long while, until Daniel Webster had dragged himself from sight and his cries died out in the deep Delta woods. In the leftover glow of the setting sun, as they fiercely held on to one another, Granada thought back to the day Mistress Amanda had gripped her hand so tightly, and recalled how at that moment she understood, in the deepest parts of her, the place where she belonged. She felt that way now.

The children sat shivering under the locust tree as a light breeze from the creek carried the lush scent of wild blooms. They were wet and hungry. Little Lord's hunting pouch was empty of all the food stolen from Aunt Sylvie's kitchen, and they had not even been able to build a fire to warm their clothes or to keep the wild animals away.

In the distance they heard the scream of a panther, and they moved even closer. Granada could tell that Little Lord was thinking of Daniel Webster somewhere out there alone. Soon, she imagined, there would be wolf packs prowling through the woods. She had often heard their howls from the plantation. Once during broad daylight she had seen a bear snatch up a squealing hog and tuck it up under his arm and carry it off like a sack of feed. Maybe the bears would not be hungry for children tonight, not with all the spring berries.

She sighed wearily. "Little Lord, I ain't getting back in that boat, even if we can find it. I'll take the roving beasts of the woods over them tree snakes and rumbling gators."

Little Lord said it didn't matter really. He was so turned around he didn't know the way anymore. He'd got them good and lost. Walking was as good as paddling, which was as good as sitting, he reckoned. He was farther away from his mother than ever.

Dark was coming fast to the forest, and the air already vibrated with the shrilling of night insects. In the dimming light, they walked deeper into the woods, hand in hand, looking for a place to sleep. They found a giant oak with thick mounds of moss spread between its sprawling roots and, without speaking, settled together onto a soft green bed. Neither resisted the sleep that beckoned.

Granada's dreaming seemed to take up where it had left off that morning. She was standing again at the entrance to the forest tunnel. Polly was there, but she was no longer shoving the girl and Granada felt no fear. The voices calling her into the darkness were not as menacing. Tonight they were chanting, and Granada recognized the words as the same Polly had sung outside the hospital cabin. It was the song Polly's mother had taught her. As she had that night, Granada was both lifted and drawn by the words.

After a time, the words blended into a single sound and Granada knew it was her name they were calling, but one she had never heard before. She strained to make it out, but the voices grew faint.

Granada woke and from where she lay she could see the night sky through a break in the bowering branches. For a moment she thought she might still be in the dream.

Again she tried to recall the name the voices had intoned, but could not. She remembered only the beautiful music. No longer tired, her mind hummed and her heart ached with a knowing she could not name. The dreaming had aroused within her a far-flung sadness that would not form itself into pictures or words. She found herself wanting to wake Little Lord and tell him about the dream, but what would she say?

She raised herself on her elbow and studied the boy. He was lying on his side facing away from her. A small square of pale moonlight framed him, and she could detect the soft rising and falling of his shoulder.

Granada had never once seen the mistress embrace Little Lord, but she had often watched the child of a field worker or yard servant as he slept serenely in his mother's arms, the two, mother and child, forming one. What it must be like to hold and be held so tightly, to belong so completely to another, that one could never be hurt or lost.

The hollow place below her throat filled with the distant longing once more, a vague memory of touch and caress.

She conformed her shape to his, like a spoon, and carefully draped her arm over his chest. As she drifted off to sleep, she could feel his heart beat secretly into her palm, as if she had been entrusted with the most fragile of things.

The next morning Granada was startled awake by a sharp poke at her back. Looking up into the gray-lit sky she saw a dark, scowling face peering down at her. Granada didn't move at once, her mind not willing to accept what she saw. But there was no denying it, there she was, as big as life, standing bright against the early dimness. For a moment she forgot to be ashamed of her closeness to the boy.

"Polly! How you find us?" Granada asked, scrambling to her feet and waking Little Lord.

"Weren't hard. Monkey whispered in my ear." Then Polly laughed scornfully. She pointed her snake stick toward the rising sun. "The house is just over thataway. Took y'all all day to get out of spitting distance."

They had been going around in circles! Granada didn't know whether to feel shamed or relieved, but when the hunger suddenly gripped her belly, relief won out.

Little Lord was lying on the ground, gazing up at Polly like she had stepped out of one of his fairy tales. His dirty, sunburned face was still streaked with tears, and again Granada felt a consuming tenderness for him.

"What you staring at, boy?" Polly fussed, and then studied him for a moment. "Looks like you done lost your best friend."

Granada was about to tell her that he didn't need reminding of what he had lost, when she heard a familiar screech followed by a burst of excited chattering.

Limping around a clump of sweet gums

319

came Daniel Webster, bandaged and frail but alive, hurrying the best he could toward Little Lord's extended arms.

CHAPTER 28

Out on the porch off the kitchen, Gran Gran was in her chair gathering the last warmth of a setting sun, her rocking as unbroken and deliberate as her thoughts.

Below her on the steps sat Violet, her attention silently and unyieldingly focused on the rough track that led into Shinetown. While the girl watched the hill, the old lady watched the girl. They now spent a good piece of each day this way.

Violet still never let Gran Gran out of reaching distance, but never touched her, those anxious eyes forever darting about into the dark corners of the house. The girl wore the scarf constantly, even to bed, but she refused to go near the suitcases, acting like they might bite. Gran Gran couldn't blame her. She was afraid of them as well.

The old lady noticed Violet seemed most at peace outside on the porch, so Gran Gran sat with her, even on cooler days, taking the opportunity to spend long moments considering the girl as the two kept their separate vigils.

If there was talking, Gran Gran still did it all. She hadn't heard herself go on this much since she was a chattering little girl in the kitchen. Gran Gran smiled. Violet was the only one who had never told her to shut up!

This girl was surely starving for words. Couldn't seem to get enough. The more words Gran Gran spoke, the more the muscles in the girl's face relaxed.

And yet, even now on the porch, Gran Gran could detect the nearly imperceptible tick of the child's head, left to right to left, steady, like the pendulum of a clock. The old woman couldn't say for sure, but she wouldn't be surprised if Violet was keeping the same time she brought with her the very first night. Perhaps that rhythm is the last living piece she holds of her mother.

"I can't swear to it," Gran Gran said, as casually as she could, "but it could be you're expecting somebody to come down off that hill."

Violet remained silent and facing away, but the ropes in her neck tightened. Gran Gran didn't need the sight to tell her what desperate hope Violet was holding out for.

Gran Gran judged it close to suppertime now. A trickle of white-uniformed maids were making their return trek from the top of the hill, where their white ladies dropped them off each day after working in the big houses up in Delphi. "All them people living in a place called Shinetown," Gran Gran said, "you might think they would know something about who the woman was. But I expect just because you live on Oak Street don't make you no expert on acorns. Of course back in my day, Violet, everybody knew about Polly Shine."

The girl turned back to Gran Gran with upraised brows.

"There was a time when you called that name, Polly Shine, and folks thought you were speaking of God. Now some of what they said about Polly weren't true. But she did do some mighty fine things. She didn't fly to heaven in a fiery chariot or bring the sun to a dead stop in the sky. But still, folks today ought to know what she did for them. She is sure a big part of who they are."

CHAPTER 29

Polly's reputation rose up and spread like winter floodwater after she came back with the master's lost boy and the snakebit monkey.

When Master Ben returned from New Orleans, he gathered all the house and yard servants together for a special ceremony on the gallery and gave Polly a ten-dollar gold piece for saving Little Lord. The master was more certain of his purchase than ever before.

Neighboring plantation owners were less impressed. They had heard about Polly traipsing all over the county in the buggy, flaunting her passes to the patrollers, and they feared such license might be giving their own slaves dangerous ideas. But Master Ben placated them by offering his hospital to their sick stock for one day a month, at a negotiated fee.

As Polly's fame spread, the debate between the men and women yard slaves heated up. Old Silas, more distressed than anyone at Polly's ascent, whispered to whomever would listen that she was up to no good. She was a conjurer, a hoodoo witch, a false prophet, or maybe even Lucifer himself. Pomp told Granada she could settle it once and for all by snatching off Polly's bedsheets at the stroke of midnight. If she was a witch, she would have scales on her feet.

Chester even made up a song about Polly:

Everybody say the woman is wise.
   Hoodoo!
She can make a body well before his
   eyes. Hoodoo!
But she got two hands in her bag of
   tricks,
One to lift the spell, the other to make
   you sick. Hoodoo!

But the women on the grounds argued that it did them proud to see one of their own getting so much respect. Whether she was evil or good, it made no difference.

"Same to me if she doing it by foul or by fair," Charity, the weaver, said. "She's one slave the white folks can't own. Always one step ahead, she is."

Lizzie, who hardly ever said two words on the same day, agreed. She was convinced Polly had set the mistress on fire. "And I don't give a fig if it was Jesus or the devil who lit her torch. I just wished my poor Rubina could have seen that woman blaze up."

Even Aunt Sylvie was heard to say behind Old Silas's back, "Just because the devil brung her, don't mean God didn't send her. She saved my Granada and Little Lord from the wolves and raised a monkey from the dead. That got to count for something in heaven."

Only one group of folks saw eye to eye on the question of Polly Shine. The field slaves — those laboring far away from the great house, working the cotton, clearing the swamps, building the levees, driving the mules, breeding new stock, always the first to be struck down by sickness and disease — had come to a common conclusion: Polly Shine had indeed been sent by God on a holy mission.

The first who had been carried from the swamps to the old woman's hospital, doomed to die with the blacktongue, only to walk out whole after being touched by Polly Shine, were revered by their people. They called them the Blessed Ones.

Others came now late at night, after

Granada and Polly had put out the lanterns and gone to bed. They walked the miles from the fields, under the cover of darkness. Granada saw how they looked at Polly with misty-eyed reverence and called her "Mother Polly," like children calling to Jesus in their prayers.

The first to come were the mothers, carrying children who suffered from ailments they had hidden from the overseers, afraid their remedies would kill the child along with the disease. Not long after, the women began bringing their men and soon all sorts of folks were visiting the cabin, complaining of stomach pains or achy teeth or boils. Some came with pneumonia or the croup or bilious fever or a sprained back. Some hurt in places they could not point to.

Granada would feign sleep but watched through the slit between her lids as Polly rose up to light a lantern and put on her special head scarf before she walked through the cabin to the door. She turned no one away.

Whether the people who came were sick or not, Polly always gave them a remedy. But before prescribing anything, she asked all manner of questions about their loved ones and about their fears and their dreams. She listened intently, sometimes with her eyes closed and other times moving her gaze very carefully over their entire bodies, studying the color of their eyes and skin and fingernails. Pretty soon she had the person talking about a lot more than stomach pains. Other pains, too.

Pains in here, Granada thought, reaching her hand to her chest where weeks ago she had felt the penetrating burn of Polly's palm. Soul-sick pains. Grudges they held. Losses they had known. Hopes that had died. Old wounds they had suffered.

They laid themselves bare and then Polly told them what to do. Sometimes she gave them a poultice or a tea to prepare back at their cabins. Sometimes she put dried roots in a pouch and told them to wear it around their necks. Sometimes they went to the big Bible together and Polly found words for them to repeat while they labored. And before they left, she whispered something into their ear and they nodded and smiled gratefully. They all seemed to leave feeling better than when they had come.

That's when Granada knew.

Polly was doing the same thing to these callers as she did in the forest to the roots and the herbs and the bark. She was peeling back the skin and tasting their insides and learning their nature. Once she divined their nature, that's when she did her hoodoo. That was her power!

One night, after Polly shut the door and the last visitor had stolen away, Granada decided it was time. If she was ever going to get the mistress back, she needed to learn the spells that Polly was casting. Granada never wanted to disappoint Little Lord again.

She sprung up in her bed and announced, "I want to learn me some hoodoo, too."

"What you mean, hoodoo?" Polly answered, turning from the door. "I don't truck with no hoodoo!"

"I been watching you like you told me to," Granada said, propping herself up on her elbow. "You been putting hoodoo on all them sick people. I seen it."

"That what you seen?" Polly answered. "You been watching me all this time and that be the smartest thing you and Silas come up with?"

"Huh . . . ?" Granada stammered. "What you mean?" It had been weeks since she had agreed to help Silas.

The old woman shook her head. "Girl, you can't fool me. I got eyes in the back of my head." She gave Granada a look that was dead serious and held the lantern up and turned her head. "See?"

Granada gasped.

Polly squealed with laughter and then reached down and lifted her dress, showing her bare ankles. "Surely! I got them backward eyes the same place I got these scales on my feet. Bought them at the Devil's Dry Goods Store!" Polly laughed again. "I know what lies that fool Silas been spreading about me. And I know he wanted you to help him."

Granada opened her mouth to deny it, but thought better of it. "I told him some bad things about you," she admitted.

"Was they true?"

"Yes, ma'am."

"Well, I reckon I can live with that," Polly said. "Can you?"

"Yes, ma'am."

"I guess mostly I'm just proud y'all been talking about me," Polly chuckled, setting the lantern on the table. She began putting away roots and herbs, remnants from the evening's work.

"Hoodoo," she said, getting back to Granada's question. "Girl, you like a cork on the water, bobbing up and down with every ripple that comes along. You got to learn to reach down deep beneath the surface to get the truth of things."

Granada thought carefully about this for a

moment. "But everybody saying it's got to be hoodoo," she finally insisted. "Like what you done with them that had the black-tongue. Them white doctors couldn't do nothing with them. Everybody saying you made them well because you got the hoo-doo."

Polly scowled at Granada. "If a nigger did it, got to be hoodoo. That right?"

"Then how else you make them well?"

Polly dragged her rocker over to Grana-da's bed, bringing her spit cup with her. She leaned back in the chair and closed her eyes. She began breathing so deeply, Granada thought Polly might have fallen asleep. Finally she opened her eyes. "Child, weren't magic to see a body starving for more than cornmeal and fatback." She shrugged her shoulders at the obvious truth of her words. "I fed them so they could make themselves fit. I didn't do nothing but see what was in front of my face."

Granada was skeptical. "But the doctors —"

"What did them doctors see when they studied those poor creatures?" Polly said with disgust. "They seen field animals. So they dose them like animals. White man see a mule so he feed him like a mule." She cast her eyes upon Granada again, her stare

331

intense. "But I seen people, Granada. Don't you understand yet? I looked at them poor sick folks from here," she said, putting her hand over her chest. "Soon as I remember them, then my hand knows what to do."

Polly's eyes narrowed. "Look to him that suffers. He'll tell you what to do," she said. "The person that wears the shoe knows where it pinches. They was just starving people is all. I fed them. Talked to them. Listened. That ain't hoodoo. Just plain sense. The magic weren't in the food. It was in the seeing."

"But you found me and Little Lord out in the woods. And Daniel Webster —"

"Animals know how to heal themselves," she said, studying a callus on her dog finger. "They the best doctors they is. He knew; I listened. All there was to it."

That was not the answer Granada had wanted. "You saying they ain't no hoodoo?"

"I suppose plain ol' life is the biggest hoodoo they is. When you got the sight, you know life ain't never still. Creation is always birthing itself. *That's* what the sight is."

"That why you always putting them 'In the beginning' words in their ears?" Granada asked, wondering again if that truly might be a magical charm.

"That's right."

Granada yawned. Through the window, she could see the dark outline of the trees. Dawn was not that far off and she could feel sleep trying to take her, but she needed to learn.

"It be the very first thing that got writ down in the Bible," Polly said. "So it got to be powerful. 'In the beginning God created the heavens and the earth . . .' It does seem to give a body comfort."

"That ain't nothing magic," Granada said. She had heard Old Silas quoting the Bible a lot lately, gathering up folks in the barn and telling them how Jesus had warned about devils like Polly.

"It ain't nothing magic in how the white man preaches it. In the white man's Bible, it means God's done finished His work. Put out the lights and gone to bed. They think it means God is good and happy with the way things is. White one up and the black one down. White man's Bible don't got nothing to say to you and me but 'No!' But in my Bible it mean something different."

Granada looked up at Polly through bleary eyes. "What's it mean?"

"My Bible say them words ain't finished leaving the Lord's mouth. And He ain't going to be finished saying them words tomorrow. Nor the day after tomorrow. It's always

'In the beginning' with God. Our God is sure enough a starting-over God."

Granada asked, barely able to keep her eyes open, "How you know?"

"It's the promise a woman carries in her body," Polly whispered.

"Oh," Granada said sleepily, "the river."

Polly nodded. "That's right, Granada. The river."

For a moment Granada forgot about the mistress. There was something else she needed to know, but she couldn't name it. The river. Something about the river.

"God always creating something," Polly said, her voice carried away by a strengthening current. "Always something trying to be born, Granada. That's what I whisper in they ears."

Granada's eyes were closed now and she was drifting on the waters between waking and sleeping, between what was and what would be, between childhood and womanhood.

Granada could sense Polly hovering over her, studying her closely through the dark. Then she felt the breath against her ear.

"In the beginning God created. That's all anybody need to know about God, Granada. It ain't never over with God."

CHAPTER 30

Granada pulled the corncob through her knots and tangles, trying to get her hair smoothed out before preaching started. Already hundreds of slaves had streamed into the big yard, cleaned up and dressed in their Sunday clothing. Most were barefooted, but some carried shoes freshly polished with fireplace ashes, and they stooped to put them on as they neared the yard. This was the first Preaching Sunday the master had held since Polly had arrived and the mistress had departed.

Polly stood at the window, her brows furrowed and eyes squinting, carefully scrutinizing the passing crowd. Granada knew exactly what the woman was doing. She was tasting the people, peeling back their skin and looking underneath. "Remembering them," as she would say. It still didn't make much sense to Granada. Remembering things you've never even seen. Remembering things that hadn't even happened yet.

Listening to Polly you'd think time was a sack full of days you could shake up anyway you wanted. Granada sighed. Just more riddles without answers.

She went to the window and stood with Polly. There was nothing that she hadn't seen before. Many of the women wore colorful head rags. The younger ones had sprigs of flowers and berries in their hair. Some were sashaying proudly in calico dresses awarded by the overseers for good work or plentiful breeding. Even those wearing crude homespun had washed and stiffened their dresses with homemade starch. Some women had even sewn onto their dresses patches of cloth dyed with random splashes of color — red from pokeberry and light browns from walnut and rusty orange from elm. A few wore the master's or mistress's broken buttons as brooches.

Awhile back many had tried emulating the mistress and made hoops for their skirts out of grapevines, much to her distress. She interpreted their actions as ridicule and told Master Ben to put an immediate stop to it. But today a few had revisited the practice — having heard of the mistress's recent misfortune — and their skirts billowed out around them like toadstools. Back when

Granada lived in the great house, the servants would point and snicker at all the preposterous getups the swamp slaves fashioned for themselves.

"Used to," Granada said wistfully, as she tugged on the cob, "Aunt Sylvie greased my hair and combed it out with the prettiest silver comb. And I had me real dresses. Not pretend ones like them out there. And I didn't have to wear no nandina berries in my hair. Mistress gave me store-bought satin bows. Red ones even."

"You know what the white folks say," Polly laughed. " 'Dog begs for bread, nigger begs for red.' That's what they say anyway. Even my momma said she lost her Freedom for a scrap of fine red cloth. First white man she ever seen waved a hank of red in her face. Said that sure cured her from wanting no more red." Polly looked down at Granada and asked, "Reckon what it'll take to cure you?"

Granada ignored Polly's question and kept her eyes on a woman passing by the window. She was tall and had very light skin, nearly as white as the keys on the mistress's piano. The woman's hair was curly yet fine, and her eyes were an emerald green, her nose smallish and sharp. She walked with a kind of aloof dignity, holding her head high and keeping her eyes straight ahead, like she was warding off unwanted attention. Granada had never seen her on their visits out to the settlements and wondered why somebody as pretty as she wasn't working in the great house.

The thought pricked her memory. That had to be Lizzie's girl! The one they called Rubina. They said she used to be a house servant, a playmate to Miss Becky, a long time ago before the mistress sent the girl to the swamps. At least she was pretty, Granada thought. At least she had that. Granada wondered how she herself would bear up under such a sentence in the swamps. She caught her breath at the dreadful prospect.

"What you studying her for?" Polly asked, startling Granada.

"Who?" Granada asked. How could Polly tell who she was looking at? There were more than three hundred people out there. Granada glanced up at Polly and saw that her jaw was set and in no mood to play any guessing games.

"Just was," Granada answered, wondering what she had done wrong now.

"No such thing as 'just was.' Tell me what you see. Why did you settle on her?"

"I reckon 'cause she's pretty," Granada said.

"Uh-huh. Because she ain't black like you, I reckon. And her eyes is colored like bottle glass. Her hair ain't nappy, neither. Remember what I said about pleasing faces. They ain't what they appear to be. To me, you prettier than she ever be. But you won't see it 'cause you blind to your own good looks."

The old woman spit out the window. "Now, this time look at *her*, not what strikes you as pretty. What you see?"

Granada shrugged and then answered the best she could. "She walks all by her lonesome. Ain't talking to nobody. Don't look at nobody. Maybe she think she better than everybody else."

"That what you see in your head, Granada. What you see in there?" Polly pointed to her chest. "What is your *understanding* of that woman?"

Granada shrugged her shoulders. "I don't know." She didn't like being tested. Polly was being a bully, bound and determined to ruin the day before it even got started.

"No such thing as 'don't know,' neither. Study her from here." She put her hand flat against Granada's chest. "Remember her. Like you done with her momma, Lizzie, way back."

339

But Granada resisted, stepping away from the old woman's touch. "How I going to *remember* her if I ain't never *seen* her before?"

"Just 'cause you ain't seen, don't mean you don't know. Close your eyes. Bring her inside here," she said, again placing her hand on Granada's chest. "Let her melt like butter next to your heart."

Granada did as she was told. Polly's hand grew warm, and soon, without willing it, Granada was filled with an overwhelming compassion. Tears welled up in her eyes and she spoke the first thing that came to her. "She's so sad, Polly. Like she carrying a secret she can't tell nobody. I think she lost something. Something she loves more than anything."

"What?" Polly asked.

"I don't know," Granada answered. "But she can't tell nobody about it. Somebody might hurt her."

Granada suddenly felt foolish, like she had been making up a silly story, but Polly sighed. "Um-hum. Yes, Lord, yes. Your sight getting stronger every day."

She had got a riddle right! Granada flipped her eyes open, surprised she hadn't been scolded for lying. "Why can't she tell nobody, Polly?" she asked, now excited to know how the story ended.

"See there!" Polly fussed. "Now your mouth took over again. What I tell you about a flapping tongue? It done blew out your pitiful little flicker of wisdom."

Granada scuffed her shoe against the floor.

Polly reached down and put her hand against Granada's chest once more. "Just keep the woman here, Granada. There is a reason why you studying her. Why your sight searched her out. Like it did with her momma, Lizzie. It's trying to tell you. Be quiet about it and you get your answer when it's time. Maybe you dream it. Maybe you hear it through your hair or your skin. All kinds of ways to listen."

"My hair going to talk to me?" Granada muttered under her breath. "My skin going to tell me a secret?"

The old woman draped a ratty fur around her neck. Today she was without the scarf and wore her braids loose, those immense eagle feathers placed randomly in her hair.

Granada laughed to herself. My skin telling me something right now, she thought. It's telling me that woman is addled in the head!

By now the entire dirt yard was carpeted with quilts, blankets, and burlap sacks,

341

anything families could bring from their cabins to sit on during the service and keep their Sunday clothes clean. Across the grounds, up on the gallery of the great house, the master's guests were also being seated. That's when Polly announced it was time for her and Granada to step out into the yard.

As they waded into the crowd, Granada kept her eyes fixed on the gallery. There were at least twenty guests up there, more than Granada had ever seen in the days of the mistress. Master Ben stepped out with Little Lord following close behind, dressed in his little-man suit. A wave of longing washed over her as he took the chair next to his father, the one formerly reserved for his mother. That was where Granada used to stand, clad in one of Miss Becky's frocks.

Polly pushed deeper into the throng, stirring up a new ripple of commotion with every step. As they made their way, folks got to their feet and greeted Polly with joyful and adoring looks, men holding their hats, women reaching for her hand to touch or even bringing it to their lips to kiss, everybody God-blessing her and calling her "Mother Polly."

Granada had planned on choosing a spot on the outer edges so as to avoid the woman

Chester claimed to be her mother. The girl was still convinced that one day, without the mistress to protect her, the woman would reach out and grab Granada and drag her off to the swamps. But Polly didn't slow. At last she decided on a place to light. While Granada ducked down out of view, two men, both as big as oxen, rose to their feet and offered to help the old woman to the ground, one taking her hand, the other gently supporting her at the elbow. They lowered her as if she were as fragile as a china teacup, and as they did, half a dozen freshly laundered scarves were unfurled from around women's necks and smoothed out on the ground before Polly's dress touched her resting place.

With all the attention on Polly, Granada felt invisible enough to venture a glance at the second-floor gallery once more. Standing next to Little Lord, in her old place, was Silas, dressed up in a swallowtail coat, boiled white shirt, and string tie.

What in the world! Granada thought.

His face was set in an angry frown, and he was glaring right at Polly. The old woman must have felt his eyes because she looked up at him and shrugged, like she couldn't help how the people felt about her. A sheepish half grin spread across her face.

Just then the fat, red-faced bishop who always smelled of rum heaved himself out of his chair and, after a little elegant bow to Master Ben, walked up to the lectern. He wiped his face with a gleaming white handkerchief. "Slaves," he began, "be submissive to your masters and give satisfaction in every respect; do not talk back . . ."

The bishop rarely preached on anything that Granada cared about and she began to steal looks into the crowd, furtively searching for Lizzie's daughter. Granada had almost guessed the woman's riddle and she wondered if she could bring her back to the "remembering place" and let her melt like butter. As she scoured the heads in front of her, she caught sight of a sad-faced woman in a blue-checked head rag standing on the edge of the yard. She seemed to be looking Granada's way, searching her face.

Granada dropped her eyes and tucked her chin. The girl dared not look her way again. The stare had been too intense, the wanting eyes too desperate. But even when Granada shut her eyes, she could see the woman distinctly. Her skin was black, so black it shimmered with a purple sheen. She hadn't even bothered to fix herself up. Her head rag was sweat-stained and her clothes filthy from field work. She held the hand of a dirty-faced little boy as dark-skinned as she. Her face was so very sad.

The more the face burned into Granada's memory, the more familiar the woman seemed. Yes, the girl reasoned, she had probably seen the woman before, that's all. Perhaps she had been one of the sick ones? Maybe Granada had seen the woman at one of the settlements. Or maybe she had found her way to the hospital late at night. There was probably a good reason why the woman stared at her. Plenty of good reasons, other than the one that filled her with dread.

After the bishop said his last amen, he toddled over to his chair, fell back, and mopped his face with a handkerchief now limp with perspiration.

Next the master stood up and looked out over the yard. "I hope y'all heard every word the good bishop said," he boomed. "I want y'all to meditate on it when you go back to your cabins today."

"Meditate?" someone chuckled.

"It don't mean a damned thing except to ponder," someone else replied.

"Sounds like white man's work," observed another.

The master cleared his throat and smiled warmly. "Now there is somebody else I want y'all to hear from today. He told me the

Lord has called him forward to deliver the Word, so he's asked me to let him be a preacher right here on the plantation. A lot of y'all already know him. Him and me cleared most of this land together. We made the very first crop."

Granada peeked up at the gallery. Master Ben was looking over to where Old Silas stood. "Come on over here, Preacher Silas."

Old Silas began his slow, proud walk to the podium while the master continued. "I know Old Silas is going to be a fine preacher so y'all heed his words."

Silas, his face radiant and looking elegant in his new clothes, bowed to the master and his guests and finally turned toward the gathering of slaves.

He grinned at the crowd. "Now I know most of y'all," he said in a quivering voice. "Some of y'all might think you on up there in years, but I suspect nobody is old as I done been blessed to be. So I reckon the master figured since I done trod so far down life's ways and byways, he hoped maybe a few cockleburs of wisdom might of clinged onto me in passing."

The laughter he evoked was warm, from white folks and black. From everybody, that is, except Polly.

"Why's he talking that way?" Granada

whispered to the old woman. This was the first time she had heard him speak more like the other slaves instead of like the master.

"I jest here to testify," he continued, "to what a blessing it been being up under Master Ben and his daddy afore him and his daddy afore him."

Old Silas turned to the crowd again and then lay both hands on the lectern, his face solemn. "So we blessed to have found us a home with such a Christian man. Lot of slaves don't get no church. Don't get no half days on Saturdays and all day Sunday to praise the Lord and spend with they families."

There was nodding in agreement, and a few affirming moans from the women.

"Old fool," Polly said under her breath. Polly stiffened her back and her breathing was short and quick.

"And they is a terrible disease on the foot worser than the cholera or the yellow fever or the blacktongue," Old Silas called out, now beating the air with a clenched fist. "They call it Freedom. They a place called Freedomland and it be chunked full of the half starved and the homeless. Scrounging in the dirt with the dogs for a crumb of bread. No loving shepherd to look out after them. To go looking for them if they was to get theyselves lost."

He looked over at the master to show him his face beaming with joy.

Master Ben smiled and then dropped his eyes, brushing his nose with the top of his finger.

He wasn't the only one appreciating Old Silas's sermon. Granada might not understand what Old Silas was talking about, but she was struck by how he hitched the cadence of his words to the beat of her heart and took her for an exciting turn around the yard. Granada was about to tell Polly how she much preferred Old Silas's kind of preaching to the bishop's, but when she turned to the old woman, she saw fire in her eyes. It looked like she wanted to kill Silas where he stood.

"Liar!" she grumbled. "Judas goat!"

A few heads turned in the crowd and nodded approvingly at Polly's accusations.

Silas's eyes went upward. "As for me, when I goes to heaven and the good Lord asks if I been a good and faithful servant, I wants to say, 'Yes sir, Lord!' "

Then Old Silas dropped his voice to a violent whisper. "I want to see the smile on the good Lord's face when He says to me, 'Old Silas!' " Every head in the crowd was leaning forward to catch each emotion-drenched word. " 'Welcome into my kingdom thou good and faithful servant.' "

Tears glistened on Old Silas's wrinkled cheeks, and all around him the master's friends had produced a flurry of snow-white handkerchiefs and were presently dabbing their eyes and blowing their noses. Even Granada got teary. She still didn't understand what exactly he had said, but she sure liked the way he said it. She could listen to that kind of preaching all day.

But Polly wasn't crying. After the master dismissed the slaves, she sprang to her feet and looked as threatening as a thundercloud. Without waiting for any assistance, she took off through the crowd at a furious trot, looking like she was about to spit lightning bolts. "Fool talking 'bout how he going to die and go off to Glory with the master," Polly fussed aloud to herself, weaving this way and that through the crowd. "I guess the master going to need him a nigger to shine his boots and feed his chickens when he gets to heaven."

Granada had to hurry to keep up with Polly, who continued her march to the hospital, waving her stick at those in the way. "He ain't no preacher," she said, almost shouting now. "His biggest job is to keep our people *Freedom-stupid.*"

Polly had already stepped into the hospital door when Granada heard the voice.

"Yewande!"

The word stopped Granada like a lightning strike to the heart. "Yewande," she whispered to herself. Saying the word set off a liquid pounding in her throat and sent shivers shooting down her arms.

"Yewande," she said again and her head swam with the pure music of the word.

She turned. Coming toward her, with the little boy in tow, was the same woman she had spotted earlier in the crowd, the one with the dark, sorrowful eyes. Granada was seized by an uncontrollable trembling.

"Your name is Yewande, ain't it?" asked the woman.

Now she knew why the woman looked so familiar! She was from the dream about the mistress. She was the one who tried to grab Granada before she could step through the door of the great house.

Polly came out from the cabin. She looked first at the girl and then into the yard. "What's the matter with you? What you seen?"

Granada couldn't say a word nor move a muscle. Her ears roared like a rushing river Sweat had broken through her dress, dark

350

ening the gingham that clung wet to her shoulders. As she kept her gaze fixed on Polly, afraid to look anywhere else, Granada became aware of the slow dawning in the old woman's straining eyes.

Before Polly could say it, and make it true, Granada blurted "No!" and then found her legs. She stumbled off in a panicked run, fleeing from the women who summoned her by two different names.

Across the yard the open kitchen door loomed like a threshold to another world, the last safe place. She tore across the ground so quickly she was hardly aware of the tree root that threw her flat-faced onto the hard, bare soil. Without brushing off her skinned-up knee she scrambled to her feet and took off again, limping.

"I don't want your gift," she called aloud. "Take them all away. The dreams. The remembering. That little room next to my heart. I ain't going to remember nothing no more," she promised God. "I'm going to forget how she gaped at me and called me Yewande."

"No!" she shouted again, trying to submerge the memory. She's dirty and ugly and she wanted to touch me, she told herself. And if I let her, it won't never come off. That's all anybody ever going to see on me.

CHAPTER 31

Granada stumbled breathless up the steps to find the kitchen swarming with servants stirring pots, loading steaming mounds of food onto silver platters, scurrying through the passageway to the great house. Aunt Sylvie was in the middle of it all, sniffing, tasting, and shouting orders, a great sweat draining off her.

The cook glanced up from her work to where Granada stood at the door. She instinctively took hold of her apron and began flapping it like the girl might be a chicken that had got loose in the kitchen.

Sylvie's frown melted when Granada's trembling turned to tears. "Girl, what's done put the fright in you so?"

Granada refused to answer.

"You shaking like a kitten," Sylvie soothed. "It's all right now. Nothing going to get you here in my kitchen."

The cook's kindness made Granada cry

even harder. Sylvie stowed Granada in the little bedroom off the kitchen and told her she could stay as long as she wanted. Before sending her off hours later, Sylvie poked her finger into two cold biscuits and filled them with molasses.

Granada eased through the door of the hospital, hoping to escape the old woman's notice. Polly was nowhere to be seen, but before she could take comfort, the sound of hushed voices drifted in from the next room.

"You swear you ain't going tell nobody I come to see you," someone pleaded.

"Nobody else's business," she heard Polly say.

"Old Silas been telling it around that every child you touch will carry the mark of Satan," the voice whispered.

Polly laughed. "Most preachers I come across appear to know the devil's business better than God's."

The visitor giggled.

"My momma was a weaver just like you, girl," Polly said. "You got to keep your eye on the thread, not on the devilment all around you."

Granada heard the shuffle of the women rising from their chairs, and she quickly plopped down at the table with her two biscuits, pretending she hadn't been eaves-dropping. Granada glanced up when they came into the room and she saw that it was Charity, Barnabas's wife.

Ignoring Granada, Polly went to the shelf where she kept her bottles and reached for one Granada recognized to be an extract of black-haw-root bark. Then the old woman dipped her hand into a gourd suspended by twine from the rafters and pulled out a fist-ful of sassafras root, which she placed on a scrap of burlap, folded it over twice, and tied it off at the neck with a length of broom straw.

"Now you brew you some sugared sas-safras and mix it with a teaspoon of this here root bark to make it go down good," she said. "Take a dose every evening, start-ing two nights after the moon has stood up again."

Charity took the packet, her eyes misting over. "God bless you, Mother Polly."

Polly reached out and laid the flat of her hand on Charity's belly. "This one going to make it, you hear?"

Granada swung her gaze toward the women, forgetting she was pretending not to care. Was Charity asking Polly to give her a baby? Could Polly do that?

"Now you be sure to come tell me when

you begin to feel the quickening," Polly was saying. "Then we start getting you ready for birthing."

That had to be it! Charity was childless and everybody knew she wanted a baby more than anything, but she kept losing them. Aunt Sylvie said in Charity's case "the apple kept falling green from the tree."

"This leopard cub going to stay safe in her cave for nine months."

"Her? My baby going to be a girl?" Charity asked.

Polly grinned. "She will grow to be a strong, healthy woman, proud like a leopard cat. Though your baby is still but a stone in the river," she whispered, as if she were reciting a heartfelt prayer, "she's already a blessing to our people."

"Who's *our* people?" Charity asked curtly. "Satterfield slaves, you mean?"

Polly laid her palm gently against Charity's reddening cheek. "I mean the people who always was," Polly said. "The people who will be forever. Your child and her children and her children's children. The remembered and the remembering. Keep your eye on the thread."

Charity looked at Polly, amazed at her words. "*Our* people," Charity whispered, trying hard to fathom the sense of it. "My baby will be a blessing to *our* people."

"Your sons and daughters, your blood will lead the people home."

"Home," Granada repeated to herself, scowling. Home was wherever the master said it was. Was Polly talking about stealing folks away from Satterfield Plantation to live with some other master?

"Granada," Polly called out. "Come here and put your hand on Charity's belly."

Granada's mood instantly lightened and she jumped up from the table.

"Lay it right here," Polly instructed.

Granada did as she was told. "I don't feel nothing."

"No, not yet. I'm asking you to remember this baby under your hand, Granada. This is why I ask you to learn everything else. What lies under your hand is all of us, Granada. It's where we are going. This child comes from the place where the river is born."

Granada dropped her hand from Charity's belly, still thinking about this home Polly had mentioned.

"Now go sit down, girl. I need to say something to Charity."

Granada did as she was told, but she studied them over her shoulder.

"You got to protect this child," Polly said.

"She's going to be a blessing to all of us."

"I will."

"Don't go eating nothing you ain't made with your own hand. You mighty light-skinned and some folks don't think slaves ought to be getting any lighter, especially living this close to white folks. You understand?"

Charity thought for a moment and then her mouth dropped. "You mean Aunt Sylvie . . . ?

"She only does what she's told. When they bring you food from the kitchen, you just say, 'Thank you kindly,' and then go feed it to the hounds. Throw it over the fence when nobody's looking. We don't need no more of *them* rascals multiplying!" Polly laughed. "Besides, them dogs will love you for it. Best friend a slave can make on a plantation is with a bloodhound."

The old woman laid her cheek against Charity's and whispered into her ear. This time Granada heard the words clearly: "In the beginning God created."

Charity's hands quivered so, Granada thought the woman was going to drop her parcel. Polly put her arm around Charity and led her through the back room to the door at the rear of the hospital. Charity's astonished gaze never left Polly's face.

CHAPTER 32

Polly closed the door and finally joined Granada in the front room. For a long while she stood there with her arms crossed over her chest and watched the girl as she sat at the table. Granada did her best to avoid those searching eyes, having no doubt she was being opened up and read like a book.

"They turn you away at the great house again?" Polly said at last.

Granada didn't deny it. "Told me I had to come back here."

Polly walked over to Granada where she sat on the stool. "Maybe you ain't begging hard enough," she said, snatching up the girl's dress, revealing her scraped legs. "You get down on your knees this time?" Her stare was hard. "Was your pride worth them two biscuits?"

Granada shielded her prize with both hands. "They're mine," she said. "Don't matter how I got them."

"You ain't no better off than that Silas fool. Traded his pride for a biscuit, too, I reckon."

Granada took a careful bite from her biscuit, catching the crumbs with the other hand, determined to make them last.

"You know," Polly said, her tone turning casual, "you ain't the only one been having dreams. I been having me some fearsome dreams, too."

Granada swung her gaze to Polly. "You?" she exclaimed. Was it possible that the old woman could be scared as well? "What you been dreaming?" she asked.

"Me, I been dreaming about a snake."

"Snakes!" Granada gasped. "I've been dreaming about snakes, too."

"No, not snakes. Snake. One particular snake. The very one that bit that monkey. Rascal been coming to worry me ever night."

"What's it mean?" Granada asked in a low, hushed voice, excited to be working on someone else's riddle for a change.

"I'm still pondering it," Polly answered, "but maybe he's telling me y'all Satterfield slaves won't see Freedom if it comes up on you like a snake. That's what I'm thinking. Freedom will bite y'all bigger than a moccasin." She shook her head sadly and looked at Granada. "Don't any of y'all got no self-respecting notions about Freedom?"

Granada shrugged. All she knew was she got two biscuits and they tasted good. Freedom couldn't be any better than that. She heard folks talk about Freedom, but nobody ever explained it to her. Nobody ever laid it out on a map and said, "Here, follow this road and you get to Freedomland."

"Where this Freedom place you always talking about anyway?" she asked.

Polly gazed at her in disbelief. "What you mean *where?*"

Granada told Polly she figured Freedom must be some other plantation. Maybe one with more to eat and softer beds.

"Freedom ain't no plantation!" Polly said, amazed. "And it sure ain't no place the white man holds the deed to."

"Then what is it?" Granada asked, retrieving the crumbs from her palm with little flicks of her tongue.

That stirred Polly up again. "Granada, Freedom means not having any white man laying claim to your body. Putting you to work in his fields. Stealing your labor and sticking the money in his own pocket. Making you hand your babies over to him like melons. And telling you to feel blessed because he takes the notion to feed you."

"They ain't never made me work in the fields like the others," Granada said.

"Humph," Polly snorted as she watched Granada take a nibble off her second biscuit.

"I don't want to go to no Freedomland," the girl muttered. "I want to go back to the kitchen. I want to eat what they eat —"

Polly reached out and gripped Granada's arm, tight as a vise.

"Ow!" she fussed. "Why you grappling at me?"

"Because I ain't done explaining yet and you already telling me what your greedy self wants," she said. "You always asking what remembering is." She lifted the girl's arm higher.

"Well, see this? Freedom mean remembering a time when *this* arm and *this* body didn't belong to no white man, to punish nor to pamper. It means remembering your people, even if you ain't never seen them before. Like a river never forgets its old bed. You got to *remember* Freedom before you can grab at it."

Then Polly narrowed her eyes and said in a hushed, fearsome voice, "And don't you think I ain't figured why you want to go back to the kitchen and hide. I know who

361

you running from."

Granada dropped her head, ready to push the old woman out of her mind. She wouldn't listen to this.

"You know who I mean."

Granada shook her head. "No."

"God touched you through that woman. And through her momma, all the way back to 'In the beginning' time. One day you'll have to follow that thread to save your self- ish soul. *That's* how you get to heaven. Ain't no *white* woman going to get you there. You turn your back on her, you won't never be free."

Polly lifted the girl's chin and gazed into her face. "I told you once. You got a passel of things to fight in this world but I ain't one of them." A deep sadness now filled the woman's eyes, as scary to Granada as the rage. There was so much sorrow there.

"I ain't got much longer here, Granada. Soon, it's all going to be on you. One day the people will be needing so much from you. But . . ." Polly reached over and stroked Granada gently on the head.

"Listen to me. I'll tell you what Freedom is," she said. "All Freedom is two words: 'Yes' and 'No.' Two words a slave ain't got no right to 'cause the white man done took them away. The only way the white man can

362

keep them is to make sure we forget where we come from. Granada, the white man didn't birth us."

Granada sniffled and rubbed her nose with the back of her hand, but said nothing. Polly took her apron and wiped the tears from Granada's eyes and the crumbs from her face.

Polly smiled sadly and touched Granada gently on her head. "Girl, I know the remembering is coming on you fast. You got to stop splashing and flailing around, trying to make things suit yourself. Just stand firm and let the river flow to you. Let it take you where you need to be."

Granada looked blank-faced at Polly, her arm still smarting.

Polly shook her head, and trudged over to her chair. She seemed overcome with both tiredness and sadness.

Granada knew Polly was done with her, at least for now.

"So much to do," Polly sighed. "Y'all are all Freedom-stupid, and that snake I been dreaming about say he's on his way."

She rested her head back against her rocker and closed her eyes. "Don't seem you all know how to fight nothing but the devil and the skeeters," she said, and then laughed, "and me."

She shifted the wad of tobacco to the other side of her mouth. "Up the country, the mommas bury their babies with little canoes and a paddle so they can get back to Africa. They minds stayed on Freedom. I knowed of folks who walked off into the sea, trying to get back home, drowned themselves traveling to Freedom. But y'all? Look like here it been bred out of folks. You all soul sick as can be. Ain't got no history. Ain't got no memory to lift you up. No threads to weave you all together. Lord, how these people going to even know Freedom when it gets here?"

Polly's eyes flipped open. "That's the nub of it," she said, nodding to herself. "They ain't going to know how to *be* one until they *see* one."

Then, staring off at one of her tightly woven baskets she had brought with her from up the country, she smiled an all-knowing smile, as if she had hit upon the exact remedy for every slave on the plantation.

Chapter 33

Over the next few months, Granada had plenty of occasions to remember that mysterious smile and wonder what Polly had set in motion. The season was filled with unsettling dreams, and not just Granada's. Signs prophesying endings and beginnings appeared across the plantation.

While the cotton bloomed pink and yellow in May, the men came to Polly disturbed by fevered visions and stirring passions, whispering about Freedom. Even the biggest of them shook when they uttered the word. The women began to notice their days of blood coinciding with one another, and there was a great increase in fertility. Barren women, and those thought too old, found themselves with child.

In August the fields turned snowy white with cotton, signifying a good crop for the master, who would get on his horse and disappear for days at a time. Everyone whispered that with the absence of his wife, he could most always be found in the fine cabin he had furnished for himself and Rubina.

In September the first of the crop — picked, ginned, baled, hauled to Port Gayoso on wagons, and loaded on barges — made its way down the river to New Orleans, where Granada knew the mistress was kept, being prayed over by nuns and treated by European doctors.

Each Sunday morning, Granada watched Silas, dressed in his preaching suit and toting a black leather Bible, climb up on his mule and head out to one of the master's settlements to honor God and curse Polly.

As for Polly, each month during that succession of nights she called the dead moon, the old woman had visions of the snake. She said it had grown in her dreams into a monstrous double-headed creature without a tail, but with gaping jaws at either end, devouring slave and master alike.

"It's going bite us either way," Polly would call out mournfully in her sleep, "coming and going, going and coming," until she woke herself. Then she would rise in the dark and go out to the snaky places, where she sat under a moonless sky, listening to what the no-legged beasts had to say.

Though Granada's seeing was still tentative, like the uncertain light cast by a flickering candle, Polly promised that with time it would blaze up like hickory logs burning on the hearth and show Granada things that she could never imagine.

Throughout this season of signs, Granada learned to watch and to listen. She waited for the sight to burn bright, to light the way for her, to reveal her place in that river of souls.

CHAPTER 34

It was a late afternoon in October when Polly and Granada sat down to a feast of sweet potatoes, corn bread, turnip greens, pork chops, and fried chicken — all leftovers from the master's Sunday dinner, compliments of Aunt Sylvie.

The cook was struck with a bad case of bloody flux the previous week and, without Silas knowing about it, sneaked down to Polly for a healing. Granada had taken her usual place, standing beside Polly's rocker to watch and learn. Before she even got started, Polly pushed herself up from her chair.

"Nature calling me," she said, "and I might be a spell. Granada, sit here and see what's ailing Sylvie."

Sylvie's eyes grew big and she made the motion of getting off her stool. Polly laid her palm on the woman's shoulder and pushed her back down.

"You in good hands, Sylvie. This is something Granada knows better than anybody."

Granada's cheeks burned hot as she waited for Polly to bust out laughing at her cruel joke, but Polly didn't crack a smile. She winked at Granada and then walked straight out the door.

"So," Aunt Sylvie stammered. "You seen this before? You sure you know what you doing, Granada? Why don't we wait for Polly to get back? I ain't in no big hurry."

Granada remembered well how Aunt Sylvie told Chester that Granada was a basket with a busted bottom that couldn't hold any learning.

"You want to get healed or not?" she asked.

"Well, of course I do, but I —"

"Then stop talking and show me your tongue."

Though Granada knew what the remedy was right off, she put Sylvie through the entire routine of poking and prodding — and then some. She finally presented the cook with an infusion of green persimmon and red oak.

The next day Aunt Sylvie could be heard singing Granada's praises to anyone who would listen, telling them that she always knew Granada was something special and bragging that she herself had wet-nursed the girl. "Granada's got Dr. Jesus on her side," she said more than once. From then on, Aunt Sylvie made sure that Granada got the choicest bits from the kitchen.

"How you enjoying your doctoring fee, Granada?" Polly laughed, reaching for a pork chop. "Folks think you a big bug now, I reckon. Start asking for you by name. I guess I've had my day!"

Granada beamed. Throughout the summer Polly had taken her to gather medicinal plants and taught her what soils they favored, the right season in which they should be taken, what their uses were, and with what other herbs they worked best. Granada learned quickly, and sometimes Polly even let her work alone.

There was a single piece of chicken remaining, but Granada was full as a tick. She slid the platter across the table to Polly, who reached for the buttermilk-crusted drumstick, then froze, her head tilted.

Granada stopped chewing. When Polly had that look, something was about to happen.

Polly lifted herself up from the table and stepped over to the doorway. Only then did Granada detect the sound of a man running, his footsteps growing louder.

"It's Barnabas," Polly said. "Must be Charity's time."

For months everybody had been studying Charity with worried looks as she grew bigger, sure that she was doomed. But as Polly had promised, this apple held fast and now it was ripe, ready to drop to the ground. Lately everyone was calling this the miracle baby, blessed by Polly Shine.

The old woman and Granada left the hospital and hurried down the hill to the servants' quarters.

It was still light out, and the lane was filled with people awaiting them. The crowd wordlessly parted, allowing Polly to cross the yard to the cabin and climb the two porch steps. Granada followed close behind, stopping, as always, at the door.

That's when she felt it — the warm dampness between her legs. It was happening! She was going to see her flowers! Even though there was a cramping like a hot knife twisting in her gut, Granada told herself not to be afraid. Polly had told her what was going to happen, and she claimed it was a glorious thing, a miracle. But the girl couldn't calm herself. It was as if her body now had a mind of its own. "It will be your body remembering, Granada," Polly had said. "Remembering God's 'In the

371

beginning' promise."

Shaking, the girl set the crock on the bench and fled the cabin on unsteady legs.

Back at the hospital, she removed the bloodstained dress and retrieved the twine-and-rag contrivance Polly had created for Granada when her time came. She then lay on her bed waiting for Polly.

After tonight she would no longer be left out of women's things. Her body, her new body, was the private doorway she had been waiting for. It would admit her into that circle of women where she would know and be known. She would at long last belong. There was no dread, only longing in the thought.

It's the river, Granada thought. The river never forgets its old bed, Polly had said. It was true. Part of Granada had not forgotten.

As Granada lay there listening for the old woman's footsteps, she rehearsed how she would tell Polly that it had finally happened.

But when she believed she had the words right, she was swept up in an immense sadness. "Why am I going on so?" she asked herself. "Being silly is all. Polly probably already knows."

That's when Granada understood why she was crying. It wasn't Polly whom Granada wanted to tell. Granada needed to whisper it to her mother first.

CHAPTER 35

Granada awoke with Polly standing over her, grinning to beat the devil. She felt the blood rush to her cheeks, knowing the old woman was reading her thoughts.

Without speaking, Granada looked away and then rose to her feet. The cramping had calmed, but her heart raced.

"You back early," Granada stammered.

"Um-hum. Charity did just fine. Easy birthing. She got herself a healthy leopard cub." Polly added sheepishly, "I heard you had to leave all of a sudden. Something get into you?"

Granada was sure Polly already suspected. Could probably smell the blood. But that didn't matter. Granada knew it was her mother she wanted to tell first. She was determined to stay quiet until then.

While Granada cleared their meal from the table, the sound of muffled hoofbeats rose up from the yard. Polly stepped over t the doorway and gazed into the darkening night.

"Old fool," Polly sighed, shaking her head.

Granada knew instantly whom she meant. Of all the people Polly had taken a dislike to, only Silas rated the title of "old fool."

"What's he done now?" Granada asked, scraping the leftovers into the bucket by the door.

"Nothing to my face. Don't you know a cat never howls where he's been kicked?" Polly turned back to Granada. "It's me Old Silas is riled at, but he don't rear up and fight me face-to-face. He has to go off a mighty far piece to stir up his trouble. I suspect his throat is sore from all the yowling he's done today, calling me every name but a child of God."

Polly's gaze returned to the yard. "I'm going to have to do something about that man," she muttered. "Tonight is as good a time as any, I reckon." Then she looked back at Granada. "I got something I want you to take to him."

"What you going to do to Old Silas?" Granada gasped. Though Polly denied trucking with hoodoo, Granada wasn't completely convinced. The woman certainly had some spooky ways, going out into the night and talking to snakes and all. And

Lizzie still swore to everybody who would listen that it was Polly who conjured the mistress into setting herself on fire.

Granada watched warily as Polly went to one of the leather trunks she had hauled with her from Carolina. After rifling around in a nest of unginned cotton, she retrieved a stoppered bottle of tinted glass.

By now Granada recognized all the remedies that Polly used on a regular basis, both the patent medicines the master got for her as well as those she prepared herself. But this one she had never seen before.

"What's that you got there?" Granada asked. Perhaps the trunk was where Polly kept her hoodoo magic.

Polly gently shook the bottle. The glass was the same amber color of her eyes. "Can't find this around here. Grows up the country. Don't look like it, but it comes from a plant that's got the prettiest purple flower you ever seen."

"What's it called?" Granada asked.

Polly grinned. "Called a lot of things. Bloody fingers. Deadmen's bells. Witches' gloves."

It certainly sounded like hoodoo, Granada thought.

"You take the leaf after blooming, dry it, and then grind it up real fine."

"What's it for?"

Polly smiled but didn't answer. Granada could see the devil in the old woman's eyes.

"What?" Granada blurted.

Polly only laughed.

"How come you want me to do it?"

"Because that old cur will come nearer to eating out of your hand than mine."

"I ain't going be the one to poison Old Silas!"

Polly threw her head back. "Yes, Lord!" she hooted, slapping her thigh. "I suspect that'll be exactly what he thinks if I give it to him!" Polly laughed again. "That's why you got to take it to him. Maybe he trust you enough to swallow it."

Polly still hadn't answered her question. "That bottle got poison in it?" Granada asked.

"Sure do. Two pinch kill. One pinch heal. What you think we ought to do?" She chuckled. "Give the old fool an extra pinch?" She laughed again at Granada's befuddlement.

Polly took a smaller bottle from the shelf and half filled it from the whiskey jug. Then she added a small dose of the powder.

"Let's just give him one pinch this time," she said, securing a stopper into the bottle's mouth with a quick twist of her wrist. "If he's grateful, we'll let him live."

Then, in an instant, Polly's manner changed. The girlish mischief was gone from her eyes. She fixed a serious gaze on Granada and spoke in a tone that was both solemn and measured. "You tell Old Silas this is a lot more powerful than the mullein tea Sylvie been giving him. This will take the swelling out of his feet and give him his breath back. But he's got to be careful with it. You understand? Take half now and half in the morning."

Granada nodded. "But you know good as me he's just going to throw it out the window."

"No, you wrong. He'll take it all right. He just won't tell nobody." Polly chuckled softly, shaking her head at the old man's ways. "You see, Silas can't let nobody know, but he has it figured out. He's caught on to the biggest secret about healing there is. And it scares him spitless."

"What secret?"

Polly looked down at Granada and smiled. "Can't you figure out that riddle? You been looking for magic all this time and you still ain't seen enough to know?"

Granada shook her head. "What riddle you talking about?"

"This," Polly said, her yellow eyes gathering up all the light in the room. "Once you been healed by a nigger, you can't be a slave no more."

Stepping up to Silas's open door, Granada heard the quick, jagged gasps of strangled breathing.

"Old Silas!" Granada called out.

She hurried into the cabin, and in the night shadows saw Silas lying on his bed with his forearm resting over his eyes. He still wore his preaching suit and though no lamp had been lit, the fabric glowed white from a day's worth of road dust. He hadn't even taken time to brush himself off.

Granada stood at the side of his bed. "Old Silas, you taken sick?"

The old man shifted his arm from his eyes and looked up at her. "Granada," he said, more to himself than to her.

He carefully dropped his legs over the side of the bed and then raised himself to a sitting position, his bare feet flat on the floor. His chin was down and his eyes closed as he labored to get his breath.

"Old Silas —" Granada said.

"I'll be fine," he said in a thin, dry voice. "Just need to get up on my feet. Need to walk a bit. Helps me to get my breath."

Granada put the bottle on the table and

took Silas's arm at the elbow. And indeed once he was upright, his breathing became easier, but she could tell his feet were bothering him terribly. He balanced himself against the table, leaning on it with both hands.

"What's that?" Silas asked, spying the bottle on his tabletop.

"For your dropsy," Granada said. "Polly mixed it for you."

He reached for the bottle with an unsteady hand, removed the stopper and waved it once under his nose. "Smells like whiskey."

"She says it will soothe your heart better than mullein. It's stronger. Take half tonight and half in the morning."

"You try some of it?" he asked, squinting at her through the dim light.

She shook her head.

"No, I reckon not." He smelled it again. "Soothe my heart, she say. Stop it stone-dead cold more likely."

He set it on the table and then weaved a bit on his feet. Granada stepped closer, ready to catch him.

"Old Silas," she ventured, "maybe you ought to try you some."

"That's right," he said. "I hear you a regular hoodoo woman yourself now."

"No, I ain't," she said flatly. "Polly and

me don't work hoodoo. She says hoodoo is taking over from God. She says healing is helping God do what He trying to do anyhow. Like mending a bone or curing a fever or . . . or . . ." She dropped her eyes again.

Silas cocked his head. "Or what?"

"You know," she said, scuffing the floor with the toe of her shoe.

"Humph. Birthing babies," he guessed. "Might of known you still stuck on that." He waited until she looked up again and said, "But she don't let you, does she?"

"Soon," Granada said.

"You better off not getting into that mess. Let me tell you, there's nothing special 'bout dropping babies," Silas said emphatically. "Just go out to the sheds and barns and you can see critters being pushed out all day long. Sheep and cows and horses and hounds." He drew up his face into a disgusted scowl. "Cats and rats. Folks aren't any different."

"That ain't the way it is," she said.

"I've seen it and it's not pretty to watch. You don't want any of that, do you? Hauling a dishpan full of blood and guts and burying it in the woods? Dirty work."

"It ain't dirty!" she blurted, unable to hold her tongue any longer. "And it ain't blood

381

and guts. It's named a placenta. And you bury it so you can root the baby in the world."

His lips tightened. "She got you spouting nonsense."

"You got to bury it so his soul don't go off wandering," she insisted.

Gripping both arms of his rocker, Silas lowered himself into the chair. He looked up at her and even in the dim light, Granada could see the disappointment that lay heavy on his face, deepening the lines in his brow.

He let out a heavy breath. "Seem to me like you've forgotten all about your mistress. Taking sides against her."

"No, I ain't forgot her," she said, looking down at her feet. "You lied to me, Silas. You said you was going to . . ." Granada decided not to finish. It didn't matter anymore. She no longer wanted to be back in the great house.

"I didn't lie to you," Silas snapped. "She's coming back. I'm in good with the master and soon I can still get you in good with her."

For weeks now Granada could summon no feelings for the mistress at all. Granada recalled well enough Mistress Amanda's touch that magical Sunday in the parlor. She remembered the beautiful dresses, the times she sat by the mistress's bed, watching her sleep. How when no one was looking, she reached over and gently stroked the long, dark hair that draped the pillows and covered her milky-white shoulders. Granada had once been able to cry at even the mere mention of Mistress Amanda's name, but lately she couldn't squeeze out a single tear.

Polly Shine had dangled another life before her eyes, one that promised healings and birthings and her own babies, and all that was left for Granada to do was to find Ella and say the words.

Silas was still watching her. His brows were raised, the concern still in his face.

"You haven't forgotten about what the mistress did for you?" he asked, shaking his head sadly. "Taking you out of the quarters and putting you up in the great house. Mistress saved you from being a *swamp nigger,* Granada. You owe her plenty. You even owe her your name."

A darkness crossed over Granada's mind like a shadow over water. "Mistress was the one who named me?"

"That's the gospel truth," he said solemnly. "I was there the night she gave it to you."

Granada became quiet, and after a long pause, asked carefully, "What's my other name?" Her breath began to quicken.

"What do you mean?" he asked, squinting his eye at her.

"The first one. The one my mother give me."

Silas drew back in his chair. "I don't recollect," he said, his manner short, like he was ready for her to leave. "That was a long time ago."

Granada's forehead beaded with sweat. She was getting closer and closer to her mother, only a few steps farther. "Was it Yewande?"

It was the first time she had said the name since the day she had heard it.

Silas opened his mouth to speak, but his lips seemed to stall. It was like he was offering Granada a chance to pretend she hadn't asked the question. Then everything could be right between them once more.

Her heart throbbed as fast and hard as the hoofbeats of the master's horse in full gallop.

"That the name my momma give me?" she asked.

Silas cleared his throat. "Could of been Yewande," he said. "Sylvie tell you that?"

"No, Old Silas. Somebody else," she said. "My momma told me."

"Ella?" He looked up at her now, his

expression confused.

She nodded. "Where did she get that name?"

"Named you after her grandmother," he said, his words terse. "Old Bessie's mother."

"Yewande," Granada said again.

"She was a saltwater slave. Brought over on the boat. Yewande was the heathen name she came with." Silas then angled his head suspiciously. "When did you say you talked to Ella?"

"Preaching Sunday," she answered. "Last time."

Silas shook his head. "No, can't be."

"I did," Granada argued. "My mother came after me, calling me 'Yewande.' "

"Weren't Ella. Not that day," he said confidently. "Ella was the first to be took by the blacktongue. Along with her boy. The both of them been up in the burying ground since last winter. You were still in the kitchen."

"Dead?" she said. "No, she ain't dead. I seen her. My brother, too!"

"What's this?" Silas asked, suddenly angry. "You and Polly playing some kind of trick on me? That it? Trying to make me believe she can raise up ghosts from the dead?"

Granada's legs began to go wobbly and

her head spun. Outside, gin wagons were still rumbling into the yard. The drivers yelled their howdys to one another as they drove the mules into the lot. Down in the quarter mothers were calling their children in for supper. It all bled together into a terrible deafening roar that threatened to sweep her up on a mighty wave if she did not leave this place at once.

Granada turned quickly, thinking of running, but she could only stumble on shaky legs out the door and into the yard. When she got to the hospital, she bolted up the steps, but went no farther than the dark of the open doorway. She stood there breathless and finally gasped the only words she could manage: "Silas said she dead!"

Polly stood next to the table with the lantern, her shadow looming large on the wall behind her.

Granada searched the old woman's face for a trace of understanding, hoping she wouldn't be forced to say more, because that was all she understood.

Polly eyed her carefully but offered nothing and made no effort to come closer.

"But that ain't true, is it?" Granada asked finally. "I seen her and you seen her. And my little brother," she said, her voice cracking with panic. "Silas said he's dead, too."

"Your brother," Polly said.

"My brother. My momma. But I seen them," she repeated. "And you seen them."

Polly shook her head carefully. "I seen you, Granada," she said softly. "I ain't seen them."

"You did!" Granada shouted, frantic now. "In the yard. You seen her!"

"No, baby," Polly said gently. "What I seen was what was in *your* face. I seen how scared you was. Your face told me what you seen."

"Ghosts?" she cried. "That what you saying? All I seen was ghosts?"

"No, ma'am!" Polly insisted. "You seen your momma and your brother."

Polly turned her back to Granada and walked with a heavy stride over to the rocker next to the hearth.

Granada had not moved from the doorway, still not wanting to come closer. From across the room she studied the old woman sitting in her rocker, her serene eyes lit softly by the lantern light. When Polly looked upon her, at once Granada's panic turned to a deathly weariness. Her body went liquid and her legs felt as if they might crumple beneath her.

Just then Polly beckoned Granada with a slight gesture of her hand. The girl crossed over to the woman and then collapsed at her feet. Polly drew the girl's head to her, resting it against her knee, and gently stroked Granada's hair.

"Dreams you and me have don't go away just because the sun comes out. They abide in our hair and skin and in our bones. They get to be part of us." Polly drew a deep breath and held it in her bosom, as if to underscore her meaning.

Granada turned her head from the light and hid her eyes in the skirt of Polly's dress. "I want to forget her now. It hurts too bad."

"No, baby, no," Polly said softly, "you don't. Your heart has been hurting for that woman all your life. You've been holding out for her. Waiting on her. Scared to move on without her." In a whispering voice, Polly said, "And she knows it. She is telling you she ain't forgot you. She remembers you."

Now that her mother was no longer, Granada was flooded with needs, never before spoken. She wanted her mother to explain to her this crumbling wall between dreaming and waking. The foreign feelings that arose from a forbidden thought or an unintentional touch. The pulsing and surging of new sensations, so pleasant they scared her. How tenderness could hurt so and how delight could be so terrifying.

She needed to tell her mother how scared

she was all the time now. How each new discovery was tinged with a sense of shame and loss. What would happen, she wanted to ask, if she did take that step as a woman? Would she be swallowed up by the gaping darkness she felt inside?

Would becoming a woman mean more shame, even more loss? Who else would she be forced to give up? Granada began to weep into the folds of Polly's dress. She could not bear to lose anyone else.

"Right this minute," Polly whispered, "you as close to your momma as knuckle to nail. As blood to bowel. She ain't lost to you. And you ain't lost to her."

Polly leaned over and lifted Granada's chin with a slender finger. "What you been wanting to tell her, child?" the old woman whispered tenderly. "What you been holding on to for your momma? Let her hear it now."

CHAPTER 36

I stand before the darkened forest again. Polly is by my side. I hear a chorus of women's voices, surging and tugging at me like a river current. But the name they say is not Granada. It is Yewande and it is the word that gives strength to my legs.

I look up at Polly and say, "I'm a woman now," and then step alone into the dark.

I can see nothing and stand in place, not knowing where to go. A hand takes mine, and I am not sure who it is that is leading me forward through the darkness, but I follow without fear.

We emerge from the dense growth and walk for what seems like a long distance on a floor of cool, soft grass. A gentle breeze carries the sound of rushing water. The air is clean and sharp.

The guiding presence has departed and I walk alone in the dark toward the sound of the river. I see dimly a mist rising from the water's surface. The rush of the river is as comforting as a womb and there is no part of me that does not thirst for the water that now flows at my feet.

From a short distance ahead, Polly calls out. "To know a woman," she sings, her voice very young, "is to know a thing underwater! Come and remember who you are."

But the mist is like a curtain. "I can't see you, Polly."

"Don't trust your eyes. Close them and come to me."

Behind my eyelids, the world is brilliantly lit. I see Polly ahead of me, standing midway across the river. She is a young woman again, as she was the evening she sang her mother's song. She wears a large turban, a regal coronet, made from many folds of a fabric that is rich with purples and with golds. Her body is draped in the same shimmering cloth and it appears to melt into the water that surrounds her.

I look down. I, too, am clothed in a garment of delicately woven cloth, shimmering white, embroidered with elaborate patterns. They are the drawings of the moon from the clay pots.

It is not the sun that glows overhead but many moons. They shine like beaten brass, like the disks that dangled from Polly's head scarf.

Everything I see is new, but nothing I see is new. It has been before my eyes all along, unnamed.

"Come," Polly says again.

I step into the warm, rushing water, my internal eye still on Polly. The river is dark, quietly surging with a potent force, but my feet are sure. I reach out and Polly takes my hand. When we touch, I hear the rumbling of thunder. The wind picks up, rustling in the trees onshore, taking their leaves. The current strengthens and I lose my footing.

Polly grips me tighter and I feel the fierce pulsing of a single heart in my hand. I can't tell if it is mine or Polly's or another's.

I hear the terrible whoosh of giant wings beating overhead. Tremendous birds are circling, throwing shadows across the water. The creatures finally roost in the now leaf-bare trees on the far bank. Their weeping is unearthly, terrible and sad.

"You hear them now, don't you?" Polly asks. "Oh Lord, so many need comforting tonight."

"Who is it, Polly?"

"The ones who give the people life."

"Why are they sad? What are they crying for?"

"To be known again. When the Old Ones are forgotten, they cry for their children."

"What do they want from me?" I ask.

"These are the ones who sent you the gift. They are calling you to heal."

And with that, Polly places one hand firmly against my chest and the other on my back. Completely trusting, I allow myself to be lowered gently into the water.

As the water courses over me, my body, my flesh and bone, seem to dissolve and flow with the current, and I finally understand that there was never a part of me that was unknown. No part unclaimed. The rushing of my blood, the pulsing in my heart, every breath I take is reaching back to long before. I have been thirsty for the water, and the water has thirsted for me.

I rise up from the river and the water rains down my face and breasts like gentle kisses. Polly takes me by the shoulders and faces me upstream. We are not alone anymore. I am now looking into the glistening eyes of the woman from whom I have been running. Her face glows like a dark sun, her hair woven into intricate plaits. The woman called Ella reaches out to me and puts her hand on my breast.

"They are touching you and you are touching them," Polly says. "The water never forgets. It never dies. It rushes and whirls from the very mouth of God. Women are things of the river, creatures poured out onto the earth."

And then my gaze is drawn to another woman, who has risen from the river upstream from Ella. I know her to be Bessie, my grandmother. And behind her, Yewande, Bessie's mother, the one out of Africa, whose name I bear.

"God spoke the Old Ones into this world, and he still must be speaking because we keep coming," Polly says. "Look!"

Polly points, her arm strong and straight above the water, the silken sleeve draping down to the river surface like the shimmering wing of a bird. "All the way back to Creation, you are being touched."

When I look up, there are women as far as I can see, standing in the river one behind the other, generations going back to the beginning time, from the very womb of God.

When Granada awoke at dawn, there was an unreal shimmer to the light gathering around her bed. The unrelenting heartbeat still throbbed in her hand. She was still being borne by the river, its current propelled by the abiding pulse of that unseen heart.

She looked up to see the cane-bottomed rocker next to the bedside and in it slumped the old woman, her chin on her chest, holding tightly to Granada's hand.

CHAPTER 37

There was barely room anymore for both Violet and Gran Gran at the kitchen table with all the masks. It was a peculiar thing for Gran Gran to witness. Here they all were at the same table where she had seen them as a girl. Aunt Sylvie, Old Silas, Pomp, Chester, Lizzie. All of them. She reached out to touch Little Lord as she remembered the child. On the mask she had used corn silk for his hair. That had long fallen away. Sweet, sweet boy, she thought.

Gran Gran looked around in the back room and on the porch, but didn't see the girl. Violet was getting stronger. She hadn't said a word yet, but she was venturing farther away from Gran Gran's reach. Yesterday she had found Violet standing by herself on the porch, looking off into the distance toward where the wagon had disappeared with her mother. Gran Gran noticed that she wore the silk scarf around her shoulders, an odd complement to the flour-sack shift the old lady had made for the girl. Violet was still between two worlds, but she was slowly finding her way back.

"Violet! Where you at, girl? It's time for supper! Come on out, wherever you are!"

After a few anxious moments, Gran Gran heard footsteps coming down the hallway from the big house. The old lady held her breath until Violet emerged at last.

"Violet, that house ain't safe! You go roaming around in there and you might fall right through the floor!"

Violet didn't look up at Gran Gran. Her attention was on the mask she held in her hands.

Gran Gran smiled to see it. "So you done decided to take over storytelling, have you? You found somebody you want to hear about? Let's see who it is."

The face came at her like the swoop of a hawk. The two pieces of broken glass, wet, brilliant green, unsettling, like mossy pebbles in sparkling creek water, fixed her soul. Years ago, unable to bear the accusing look of this face of clay, she had shoved it into an upstairs closet.

"No, Violet," the old woman said. "Let's do another story. Let me tell you about how Polly found me sneaking sugar from her medicine trunk. How that be?"

Violet shook her head. "I want this one, please, ma'am."

Gran Gran stared, silent. The girl's words were serious as death. Why would she save her words for now, to ask about this particular face?

"Violet," Gran Gran said carefully, still distracted by the mask in the girl's hands, "I'm happy to hear you say some words. And glad to hear you talk so mannerly. But . . ." The old woman smiled uneasily, shifting her gaze between the girl and the mask. "But . . ." she said again, unable to find the words. She finally reached out to take the mask from Violet.

"I want her," Violet said, resisting but then releasing the earthen face to Gran Gran.

"Yes, I know," Gran Gran said, suddenly worn out, remembering how Violet had come to her to begin with.

Gran Gran looked down into Rubina's eyes. "I guess she would be the one you'd want to hear about."

The old woman took Rubina to the rocker and lay the mask in her lap. She began speaking, unsure, as if starting down a path that had become disused over time and had grown unfamiliar, so that each step had to be carefully placed.

CHAPTER 38

Polly and Granada were working together in the hospital, the girl preparing a batch of rattlesnake root for one of the gin hands, Polly mixing another tincture for Silas's dropsy. He had not asked for it, but Polly knew he was taking it. He had to be, from the way his breathing had eased and his walk had become as spry as a pullet's. He was even wearing shoes again.

Of course he probably wouldn't give Polly a "thank you" or a "go to hell," either one, but now at least he took the cure directly from her hand. Polly said that was as close to working a miracle as she had ever come. In fact, Granada had noticed that Polly and Silas's visits were becoming longer and longer, their nods more intimate in passing, as they caught and held each other's eye.

The late-afternoon heat of the cloudless October day, along with the fire that blazed in the hearth, made the room unbearable.

When Polly left to see about Silas, Granada got the root to boiling and then stepped outside the hospital to catch an early-evening breeze. The days had been hot and dry without the hint of rain, but now on the horizon, the sun was setting behind a slate-gray thunderhead. Down by the cabins the light fluff from the creek-side trees rode a gentle wind like snow flurries.

As she stood outside the door fanning herself with the hem of her apron, the dogs started whining. Charity strolled with her baby over by the hound yard. The woman was so proud of her daughter she walked the miracle baby around the grounds each morning and afternoon, showing off Jolydia to everybody she came across. Even the dogs, instead of growling ferociously like they did with everyone elsc, whimpered when she approached. Maybe Polly was right. Maybe this child was blessed.

Granada glanced over at the ginhouse to see Master Ben reaching deep into a wagon heaped with cotton and retrieve a fistful of the fleecy white stuff. He pulled at the fibers like they were threads of gold, then scribbled a few notes in his leather-bound journal. Shutting the book, he gazed at the rain-threatening horizon and did a quick survey of the loaded wagons lined up in the yard.

As if hearing his name, he abruptly shifted his gaze to the great house.

There she stood, the mistress, board-straight, fingers gripping the wrought-iron railing of the gallery. Just as Silas had predicted, the master had fetched his wife and brought her back. But she had not returned grateful. Even in the shadow of her bonnet, the mistress's stare was fixed hard on her husband.

When the mistress first arrived, Granada had been surprised to see that the woman's eyes were no longer clouded over, aimlessly wandering. The muddled expression had vanished. The watery bluish tint of her irises had intensified into a piercing violet and her face had darkened to a lustrous vinegar brown. Her look was focused but patient, like a panther waiting to pounce.

Granada held her hand to her heart, trying to remember, to see what distressed the mistress so. She still wished there was something she could do to mend her grief.

But nothing came. Polly would say Granada's own needs of the mistress were still too recent. "It's only when you don't want nothing from a body that you can see who they are," Polly had said. "It's strange, but when you don't want nothing, seems like you can give everything you got."

400

It was true. Sometimes she thought about the dresses and the sheen and shine of the fine things that surrounded the family. The embrace from Little Lord still found its way into her daydreaming. But less each day.

Granada heard a rumbling in the distance. A fast-moving wagon was hurtling up the levee road. It swung past the house, throwing up a storm of dust over the yard, before finally coming to stop a few feet from where she stood on the porch.

"Get out here, Polly!" said Bridger. Granada was about to tell him Polly wasn't back yet when she came scurrying around the corner.

"Give me a hand with this wench!" he ordered.

Polly and Granada stepped up to the wagon and looked over the sideboard. A woman was stretched out in the wagon bed, holding on to her belly with one hand and the sideboard of the wagon with the other.

She was lean but muscled, in a dirty tatter of a dress, her hair hidden beneath a head rag. The overseer was tugging at her dirt-encrusted legs, trying to drag her out from the endgate, but she held fiercely to the wagon, kicking at the white man.

"Goddamn you!" he shouted. Then he checked himself, casting a glance over at the ginhouse where the master seemed otherwise occupied. Under his breath Bridger spat, "Don't matter whose bastard you carrying. I can still lash your back. Let go that wagon."

"Ain't nothing wrong with me!" she shouted. "Take me back to the field, Mr. Bridger. Please, sir."

"You sure sounded like something was wrong with you when I found you fell out between the rows and crying out to good God Almighty. I swear if you shirking, I'll sure enough cut you with my whip. Now get out the wagon." He jerked again on her legs.

"Please, Mr. Bridger! Don't leave me with no hoodoo woman. Let me be!" She kicked hard at the overseer.

Only when her greenish eyes flashed like a jewel in the dying sun did Granada recognize her. What had happened to the high-stepping, proud woman she had seen at Preaching Sunday? Then Granada understood. This is what she had seen beneath the pleasing face: fear and suffering.

"Leave her to me, Mr. Bridger," Polly said firmly.

The overseer scowled but released his grip on Rubina's ankles. "Just hurry it up and get her inside before the master's wife sees her."

"Get on up now, gal," Polly said evenly. "I suspect you can use your legs a lot easier than us grappling over you like a buffalo cat. Just as well come on in under your own steam. Either way, you going to end up in the same place."

The woman reluctantly lifted herself and then eased down from the wagon. Polly walked her to the cabin, the overseer following behind. Though her face was streaked with dirt and tears, and the shift she wore was raggedy, Granada couldn't help notice once more how beautiful she was.

"What happened to this child?" Polly asked.

"Said the plow jumped up and hit her in the belly." He spat on the ground. "She better not lose this one," he said. "She been a good breeder, but she ain't no natural mother."

"What's your meaning?" Polly asked.

"Good God!" he said with a disgusted snarl. "Last time she birthed, instead of taking the hour I give her to leave the fields and go home to nurse the child, she stole off to the woods and slept. Had to threaten the lazy wench with the whip to feed her own baby. Then, by God, she rolled over and mashed the child in her sleep. Already had it sold for a hundred dollars when we found it dead underneath her. Mr. Satterfield is liable to take it out on both me and you if she loses another. Probably sell her to boot."

Killing your own baby! Granada thought. How could a woman ever survive that? No wonder Rubina was the very first person Granada had been able to read. Her pain must be unbearable.

As Polly carefully led the woman toward the open door, Granada caught the reckless look in the woman's eye. It was then that Rubina broke loose, sidestepped Bridger, jumped the porch, and staggered as fast as she could in the direction of the great house.

"Momma!" she screamed out, just before Bridger's whip caught her at the ankle and yanked her to the ground.

The overseer reached down and picked her up, roughly hoisting Rubina onto his shoulder, and then rushed her through the cabin door before either Lizzie or the mistress could check on the commotion.

When he dumped her onto the floor, Rubina lay there not looking any the more submissive, and Granada could tell the woman didn't care what the next words out of her mouth were going to be. But before she could utter them, Polly quickly thanked the man and then turned her back on him, half pulling and half pushing Rubina to get her across the room and onto the corn-shuck tick.

While Bridger eyed them closely from the doorway, Polly bent down and whispered fiercely into the woman's ear, "Be still and shut your fool mouth!" and then looked up sweetly to tell Granada to kindly close the door behind the overseer. That everything was just fine now.

Bridger's footsteps pounded the porch after being dismissed by a Negro.

Polly stood over Rubina for a long time but didn't touch her. The woman's face was glistening with sweat, contorted by pain and rage. Polly studied her like one would an animal of questionable temperament.

"Leave me be," Rubina finally said, her voice hoarse from screaming. "Just let me lay here for a spell."

Polly rested her hand on Rubina's belly, but she fiercely slapped it away. "Don't you put your devil hooves on me," she spat. "I already told you I don't need nothing from you, old woman."

Granada watched with growing unease.

She had never seen anyone take on Polly with such ferocity.

"The devil ain't nowhere in this here room," Polly said calmly. "Just us gals. Now you let us do our work. I'd sure hate to get somebody in here to bind you."

Polly did not relent under Rubina's scalding gaze. The young woman removed her hand from her belly.

"Now let me have a look-see." Polly lifted up the woman's filthy shift by the hem and pulled it back, revealing smooth cinnamon legs. Granada spied the dark nest between her thighs. Rubina made a motion to snatch her dress back down, but thought better of it.

Granada stood entranced. She watched as Polly laid the flat of her hand on the woman's rounded belly. It was not long ago that Granada believed the stories Chester told her about finding babies in stumps. Now she realized he told those more for the fun of the house servants than to satisfy her questions. Granada had seen her flowers. She was a woman now, and women knew the secrets of such things. Today she would learn more.

She shoved her hands into her apron pocket and fingered each item, wanting to be quick if Polly should need anything.

"Plowing under cornstalks, was you?" Polly said. "Where that plow get you at?"

Trembling, the woman touched low on her belly.

Polly nodded and gently probed the spot where the woman had indicated. Next she laid her ear against the woman's belly and listened to her insides.

"Ain't so keen with a plow, is you?" Polly laughed, rising up. "You must be just a quarter hand."

The woman's thin nostrils flared. "I can carry a row better than any man!"

"And you let the plow get you? How could that happen if you so keen?"

The woman became sullen and looked away. "Plow just jumped up on its own. Must of grabbed a root."

"Well," Polly said after a few moments, "I don't know, but maybe we can save your baby."

Granada giggled at the news. She wanted to join Polly at the bedside and smooth the woman's hair and hold her hand, to share her happiness. Perhaps even risk Bridger's whip and run up to the great house to bring Lizzie down to be with her daughter.

But Rubina's reaction made Granada stop short. Her stare was hard and straight, her face as unflinching as stone.

Polly pulled the dress back down and then eased herself over to her rocker. She fell back with a groan. "Granada, get Rubina a cup of sassafras tea. Stir in a spoon of sugar." She smiled at Rubina. "Will you like that, child?"

"It ain't got no potion in it, do it?"

Polly laughed. "I ain't no conjure woman. And Granada, get this gal some corn bread with a little molasses poured on it. I know you like that, don't you, gal?"

Rubina's eyes widened. Then she lifted up on the mattress, placing the flat of her back against the wall.

From where she sat, Polly quietly studied the woman as she drank the tea and devoured the bread, and then carefully wiped the crumbs from her mouth with the back of her hand. She finished those off with hungry flicks of her tongue.

"Now weren't that good?" Polly asked. "Ol' Polly ain't so bad now, is she?"

For the first time the woman smiled a bit.

"I reckon we just got off to a rough start, but we're doing fine now, ain't we? You want more bread?"

The woman nodded slightly, and Granada brought it to her.

"Bridger called you a good breeder, Rubina," Polly said. "How many children you birthed?"

"Three," Rubina said, lifting the cup to her lips.

"Hmm. Where they at? I ain't never seen them."

Rubina lay a palm on her belly. For the first time her face showed a hint of softness. "I ain't seen 'em, neither," she said quietly.

"Master put your babies on the block?"

She shook her head sharply. "Never made it to no block. Bridger said my babies so pretty and white, like me, the master had them sold before they left my belly."

"Never heard of selling no baby before it even been birthed."

"They *his* babies," Rubina hissed angrily.

When Polly didn't respond, Rubina laid it out clear. "*He* been laying with me since I was little as that girl there," she said, motioning her head toward Granada. "You understanding now? My babies is *his* babies."

Polly nodded calmly, but Granada could see the clench in the old woman's jaw. Granada sensed that whatever was going on between Polly and Rubina had something to do with all the whispering and eye-cutting that arose every time one of the house servants mentioned the green-eyed girl.

"It's the mistress," Rubina continued. "She say she don't want to never lay eyes on none of my children. She make the master get my babies off the place as soon as the cord been cut. Mr. Bridger come down with a wet nurse and take my babies out my arms. Done that first two times I was a momma."

For a moment neither woman spoke. Then the old woman asked, "But they couldn't sell off the last one, could they, Rubina?"

Polly had taken on such a tenderness, a moment passed before Granada flinched at the cruelty of the words.

If the woman was hurt, she didn't show it. She smiled that reckless, crooked smile again. "No, ma'am! My baby girl never left her momma's side. And she went to Jesus with the name *her momma* give her."

"And this one. Mistress ain't going to get this one, neither, is she?"

The woman didn't answer. No one spoke for several moments, and no eyes met.

Finally Polly laid a hand on Rubina's arm. "You be still for a spell, now. It might be best if you stay here the night."

Polly went to the hearth to fix another cup of tea, but Granada noticed that she drew from a different batch. She had poured a strong potion of sweet gum and jimsonweed.

The woman would soon be very drowsy.

She handed Rubina the cup. "Drink this down. It helps you rest."

Rubina did as she was told.

"Now lay back down and close your eyes," Polly whispered. "Nobody going to do you bad while you're in my hospital."

As the woman lay there, her breathing evened and the muscles of her face relaxed. Again, Polly went to the hearth, which constantly had a pot of water heating, and dipped a gourd full into a tin basin. She reached for a cake of soap and then returned to the woman.

"Granada, come help Rubina out her dress so I can give her a warm soap bath." Knowing she was not to say a word now, Granada did exactly as she was asked. Nor did the woman resist. The room took on a peculiar sense of inevitability. There would be no more arguing with Polly Shine.

The sun had set and pulled in its last rays. Lantern light flickered across Rubina's naked body. Polly began speaking to her softly, in a soothing cadence, as she wiped her down with a warm rag.

Next Polly took tallow fat and began applying it to Rubina, massaging it into her skin.

Granada watched things unfold before her

411

like a wondrous vision. There was a magnificence about Polly. Her old hands seemed reborn, lithe and limber, moving gracefully over Rubina's body. Polly began with the woman's face, moved down to her neck and shoulders, lifting each arm.

Rubina's skin glistened and became fluid like the surface of a dark river. Beautiful expanses of rich, silky skin, more beautiful than any of the mistress's satins, stretching forever in Granada's mind. In that vast, never-ending river, beneath the shimmering surface, beneath that little mound, was a child. No, Granada thought, not one but multitudes of children. Granada's own child was there.

Rubina moaned sadly. "What will happen to my baby?"

"I told you. Your baby will be fine. I don't believe you hurt her."

"Her?" The woman smiled sadly. Then she shook her head and tears streamed down her cheeks. "Ain't going to be my baby. Going to be his to sell. Not my baby."

Granada could not understand the woman's sadness. Shouldn't she be happy? Her baby was safe. It wasn't right. Granada wanted Rubina to be quiet, to stop ruining the magic.

"I can't," Rubina cried. "No more. He

ain't going to do it again."

"Do what, child?"

"I kept hearing the steps, coming to take my baby. God forgive me, I prayed for the last one to die. When I was told to leave the field to go to nurse her, I went to the woods and prayed God to take her. But she wouldn't die. And I heard them coming. I just couldn't . . ."

Rubina was sobbing now. "I give her a name but they was going to give her another. Send her away from me. Going to make her lay up under white men because she's so fair. Work her until she dies, she never knowing nothing but the name they call her to bed with." She took Polly's hand. "Don't you see? It was a blessing for her to die. It was the only thing I could give her except her chains." Rubina placed Polly's hand over her heart. "Kill me, too!" she sobbed.

Polly stroked Rubina's dampened hair. "You go on to sleep now, Rubina," the old woman said. "Rest yourself. I understand now."

For a while Polly continued to work the woman's body, kneading the fleshy parts of her arms. Then she laid both hands on the woman's belly, where the baby lay sleeping. She closed her eyes and whispered softly.

"In the beginning God created."

"Polly," Granada whispered, as not to awaken Rubina. "Want me to go get Lizzie?"

"No," Polly said. Her countenance had hardened. "Take your blanket and sleep outside on the porch tonight."

"But Polly," Granada gasped, not understanding what she had done wrong. "I want to stay. I want to see how you tend to the woman. You said I was ready. You said —"

"I know, Granada. I'm sorry. But I need you outside. If anybody comes up, you call out. You understand?"

Granada glared at her.

"And don't be coming back in here."

The scald of anger rushed to Granada's face. Polly had promised! *Granada, you are a woman now and you no longer have to stay outside of women's things.*

Granada yanked the blanket from her bed and stomped outside. She took up the place where she had slept her first night with Polly, many months ago. But on this night Granada lay wide awake, her fists clenched and her thoughts dark.

After all the promises! After all the learning! Nothing had changed. Nothing at all.

CHAPTER 39

Gran Gran stopped her story. She looked over at Violet, and when she saw the rising horror in the girl's eyes, the old woman noticed the cold terror that had formed in her own chest.

No, she shouldn't tell the girl any more. It wouldn't be right to say it aloud. There was no way Violet could be ready. For a while Gran Gran said nothing. There was only the sound of wood knots popping in the stove.

"What happened to Rubina's baby?" Violet finally asked, breathless.

Gran Gran could not look the girl in the eye now. Since Violet had found her voice, her presence was becoming more real to Gran Gran. The girl wasn't deaf and dumb. She was understanding exactly, taking the story inside of her and stitching it together with her own thoughts. Those stitches can last forever.

Gran Gran finally found the girl's eyes. "She had her a beautiful little girl, Violet."

"But what happened to —"

"It's time to get you and me both to bed," Gran Gran said, her tone final. She could not bear to be around the girl now, not with the memory so near. She heaved herself up from her rocker. "I'm wore out and I bet you are, too."

After she turned the lantern in the girl's room down low, Gran Gran stood for a moment and studied her through the dim light. Violet smiled at her and again Gran Gran found herself unable to keep her eyes rested on the girl's. She had lied to Violet. But it wasn't just to Violet. That one lie shone a light on so many others.

The old lady said good night and pulled the door behind her, only to return to her rocker by the stove.

Gran Gran sat wide awake, her heart still beating fast from the undammed rush of memory. For so long it had been a distant recollection with no more weight than a story heard in passing — a terrible thing, yes, but something that had happened to someone else. Only tonight did Gran Gran feel its pulse again.

There was no shoving it back into the closet to let the lie sleep another century.

The memory was alive tonight, demanding that she look it in the face. There was no choice but to let it take her.

CHAPTER 40

The dawn broke with little help from the sun. Clouds hung low over the plantation yard, heavy with the rain the skies had threatened all night. The wagon rumbled up to the hospital, waking Granada from a fitful slumber punctuated by the growl of distant thunder. Through her sleep-bleary eyes, she saw that it was Bridger coming to see about Rubina.

Granada leaped to her feet and scurried into the house to wake the two women, but Polly and Rubina were already sitting at the table as if they had been waiting. Rubina's head was cast downward. Polly had the woman's hands in hers.

Bridger entered the room and swaggered up to the table. "You save the child?" he barked.

"Weren't no child," Polly said.

"There sure as hell was when I left her here. What did you do?"

"I told you there weren't no baby. Happens. Woman thinks she got a baby growing inside of her, but her body fools her. Swell up just like she bigged. But Rubina didn't have no baby growing inside her. I know you seen that before, ain't you, Mr. Bridger?"

Bridger glared at her, his steel-gray eyes straining in their sockets. He worried the stock of the whip he toted at his hip.

Polly half smiled. "Least now you don't have to tell Master Ben no hundred-dollar child died under your watch."

Bridger opened his mouth to speak, but then shut it quickly, scowling in resignation. He stepped back from the doorway and nodded brusquely at Rubina, who got up to leave with him. He snatched her arm, not letting go this time until he had her legs chained to the iron ring on the sideboard of the wagon.

Rubina never spoke a word, but Granada knew. There had been a baby.

After the wagon had pulled away, Granada asked, "What you do with that baby? Did you hide it? Where is she?"

Polly raised her chin and cast her eyes over to the corner. Granada spied the large clay urn with a bloodied rag lying across its mouth. She stepped over to look, but Polly reached for the girl's arm, pulling her back.

"The baby died?" Granada asked.

Polly was stonily quiet, staring into Granada's eyes, signaling her the best she could without saying the words. While they stood there frozen in each other's gaze, a flurry of brittle oak leaves blew into the room on a short gust of wind through the open door. They skittered about them on the floor. The rumbling thunder from the approaching storm was becoming more intense.

It dawned upon the girl what Polly had done. "You killed it!" Granada gasped. She clenched her jaws against the outrage that surged from her belly. She waited for Polly to answer, needing her to deny it all.

Still Polly didn't speak. She looked haggard, her face ashen, the familiar light having deserted her eyes.

"You're a liar!" Granada screamed. "You don't care about the people. That baby was the people. Weren't it?"

Again there was only Polly's awful silence.

It was *all* a lie! Granada had lost everything because of this woman and her evil lies.

She slowly backed away, still watching the old woman's stooped figure, giving her one last chance to rise up and set things right.

Granada turned away, released at last from Polly's web. "There ain't no magic," she spat. "Never was!"

Granada took off in a fevered run across the yard. Raindrops as big as bullets splattered the dust around her.

CHAPTER 41

The mistress was sitting in a parlor chair, sipping tea from a china cup. She acted as if Granada had not entered the room and was not standing before her on the carpet, trembling and soaked.

The girl had not known she was coming here, only that she had had to run hard and keep running through the driving rain. Without thinking, she had returned to a place where she had once belonged.

But as Granada stood waiting for Mistress Amanda to notice her, the girl felt the old wavering in her legs. She didn't know whether to step closer, sit, curtsy, leave, or just run. The fine woods and delicate fabrics and gleaming crystal made her feel as uncertain as she had been the day Polly arrived.

A flash of lightning lit up the room, followed by a quick thunderclap that shook the floor, sending a shudder through Granada's body.

The mistress finally set her teacup on the silver service tray and lifted her gaze. "Why are you here? I didn't send for you."

Daniel Webster, perched on the back of her chair, chittered.

"I want to come back," Granada said, her voice trembling. "I want to be here with you and Little Lord."

The mistress dabbed the corner of her mouth with a snowy napkin. "You shouldn't be in here," she said. "Go back to the old woman." She rang the little silver bell and Granada knew Pomp would arrive at any moment to drag her away, maybe banish her to the swamps.

Granada blurted, "Polly did a real bad thing, Mistress Amanda. She killed Rubina's baby."

At the mention of Rubina's name, the light seemed to shift in the room and the air vibrated. The mistress's eyes flared at Granada like blue flames. She saw the woman's hand grip the rosewood arm of her chair, whitening her knuckles.

"Ah, yes, Rubina," the mistress said coolly.

Pomp entered through the parlor double doors, swinging them back with a confident flourish. But his face went slack when he saw the girl there. She had slipped into the house right under his eyes. Pomp reached for Granada and began to drag her across the floor, but the mistress spoke evenly. "Pomp, let her go, and wait outside. I need to speak with Granada. And pull the doors to."

He snapped his head back, his face darkening, but then he quickly recovered his stiff-shouldered posture. "Yes, Mistress Amanda," he said. He aimed another daggered look at the girl and left the room.

The mistress and Granada were alone once more.

"Go on," the mistress said, looking directly at the girl. "You were saying?"

Granada was held in place by the mistress's expectant stare.

"Mistress," she began, "Mr. Bridger come with Rubina and said she had hurt herself and was scared she was going to lose her baby."

Granada realized she wasn't breathing and when she inhaled, it felt as if her heart might explode from her chest.

She gasped a lungful of air and quickly continued. "Then Rubina told Polly she didn't want that baby. She said you was going to take that baby girl away from her. Like you done her others."

Granada waited for the mistress to say

something, to at least nod in agreement, to acknowledge that this was true. There was nothing forthcoming but the icy half smile.

Granada, less sure of herself, continued without prompting, stumbling over her words. "And then Polly told me to sleep outside and the next morning she say there wasn't never no baby. But I know there was, Mistress. A baby. There was a baby and they killed it!"

Again Granada waited for the mistress to respond, to show her gratitude for Granada's loyalty, to take the sting out of the betrayal. But the mistress did not speak, or even move, and for a moment Granada wondered if the mistress thought the entire story a lie.

Finally the woman rose and noiselessly crossed the rich carpet on beaded silk slippers. She offered Granada a piece of fig toast from the china plate before proceeding to the door and turning the gleaming brass handle. She told Pomp to fetch her coachman at once.

Granada remained standing for a long while, holding the uneaten toast in her hand, waiting silently with the mistress, but not sure at all what she was waiting for. The trees beyond the yard swayed hard on the wind, and sudden gusts rattled the windows in their frames. All around them the storm sighed and gasped, like a woman giving birth.

Granada's head swam with a woozy sunstruck feeling. It had been so much easier than she had ever imagined, like kicking a pebble. But the pebble, once kicked, kept moving, like it had a plan of its own.

Chester rushed into the room wearing his brass-buttoned jacket, the woolen shoulders darkened by the rain. When he saw Granada, he gave a grin and then seemed to remember himself. He solemnly strode up to the mistress and half bowed.

Very sweetly, very politely, she said, "Be so kind as to ride out to Hanging Moss and find a Negro called Rubina. Do you know her?"

"Rubina," Chester repeated, warily. "Yes, ma'am, I know her. Lizzie's girl."

"I have a message I want you to relate. Are you ready?"

Chester answered with a bow, but he seemed somehow off-balance now.

"Tell her I'm so sorry to hear about the loss of her child," she instructed. "Say those exact words. Do you understand?"

"Her child? Rubina lost —"

"There's nothing you need to know but the words. To recite them, not interpret

426

them. Now repeat my message."

Chester's face darkened. "Mistress is sorry about the loss of your child."

"No, say 'daughter' instead. And tell her this," the mistress added, her voice tightening, "tell her I promise to let the master know all about it over supper. I'm sure he shall consider it his loss, as well. And not a word more, do you understand?"

After being made to repeat that as well, he walked toward the door, his shoulders heavy. His face was beaded with sweat. Before leaving the room, he looked directly at Granada, his expression confused.

"Mistress," Granada said in a voice that sounded so small she was not sure it carried. "Can I stay in the kitchen tonight?"

"No," the woman answered, looking almost surprised to see the girl still standing there. "Not tonight. You are to go back to the old woman and not breathe one word of what you have seen or heard. Do you understand? She'll find out soon enough. Then we'll see about moving you back into the kitchen."

Granada stole away to the spinning house, empty now of workers, and spent the long day there, hugging her knees in the corner behind a loom, listening for any sounds that would incriminate her. The thunder rolled again overhead and Granada watched through the gaps between the shutter boards as the rain curtained the plantation, turning the yard into a lake, raising the creek dangerously close to the tops of the levees. Tomorrow there would be snakes swimming on porches.

When night finally came Granada braved the deluge and ran splashing through darkness and ankle-high water to the hospital. She was soaked through to the skin when she stepped into the cold, dark room. The fireplace was dead and Polly stood at the open window, peering out into the storm. For a moment, Granada remained where she was, shivering, the water puddling on the plank floor around her feet.

The wind blew hard through the window, and water trickled down Polly's face, drenching her ginghamed chest, but she stood rooted, her arms crossed, unspeaking, peering into the heart of the storm.

She didn't ask Granada where she had been. Polly had frequently been mean and angry, but even in her punishing silence, she had never for a minute been distant. Polly Shine's presence always loomed large. But Granada sensed tonight, if she were to lay her hand on Polly, it would pass through her like a specter.

"What you looking at?" Granada asked, shattering the quiet like a rock through glass.

Polly turned toward Granada and studied her, the old eyes straining at the dark. Then she turned back to the window and stared vaguely into the night. "Something is bad wrong, but I can't see it. Won't come to me." She turned back to Granada. "You feel it?"

Granada's chest seized up. She was unable to speak.

Polly's gaze returned to the window. "They come and got the hounds awhile back. Master went with them. Out on this kind of night. Something evil is afoot. I know it in my bones, but Lord help me, I can't see."

Polly heaved a sigh and then closed the shutters to the storm. She wiped her face on her apron and lifted the globe to light the lantern that sat on the table. When she turned the metal knob and the flame flared, Polly's and Granada's shadows were cast colossal on opposite walls.

"Granada, come here to me."

Granada wrapped her arms around her body, trying to stop her shivering, unable to move her legs. Could Polly now, in the lit room, see what she had done? Granada could only stand where she was, afraid even to raise her eyes.

"You need to know something about today," Polly began.

Granada sucked in her breath and held it. Her teeth clenched.

The old woman crossed over to her. "When I speak of the people," she said barely above a whisper, her voice all weariness and grief, "I ain't just talking about the flesh, the blood. It's their voices. Their yes's and no's. That's what holds muscle to bone. The biggest thing the white man takes from us ain't our bodies. He takes our voices, too. He swallows up our yes's and no's like biscuits. But one day our yes's and no's will be so loud and strong they will lodge in his throat. He will have to spit them out to keep from choking. He will starve. There won't be nothing left of him except the shadows he casts on the deadest night."

Polly lifted Granada's chin with her finger.

"Every slave here got to tell the master 'yes sir' and 'no sir' just to stay alive. There ain't no shame in that, as long as we don't let him kill the voice inside. Sometimes you got to lie on the outside to keep your voice loud on the inside. We don't owe the master the truth. He owes us. Nothing comes from the master. He is the thief in the night. He steals it all. And every time we have to say 'yes sir' and 'no sir,' he steals some more. But we can survive it, if we stay loud in here," she said, throwing a fist hard against her breast.

There were tears in Polly's voice. Granada wanted to hold the old woman in her arms, but knew she had given up the right.

"Baby, I'm telling you all this for a reason," Polly said, hush-breathed. "Rubina said *no.* In ever which away she could, she say *no!* With all her woman's voice. She weren't lukewarm about it. As much as a person could, she said *no.* That's got to count for something. At lease once, it's got to count for something. A momma got to say yes to her baby or she ain't no momma. She ain't nothing but a field animal."

A fear as potent as the storm outside swallowed up Granada. She wanted to reach out to Polly and have the old woman hold her and tell her she was just a little girl and couldn't be blamed for the careless thing she had done. But Granada remained frozen.

Once Silas had talked about how he could straighten out a winding river by pinching off the place where it began to meander and tangle back on itself. You would be left with what he called a false river, a body of water with no inlet or outlet, just sitting off by itself while the old river passed on by in a new bed, more direct to the sea. That's how it was with Granada now. She no longer belonged to the river of life. She was no longer just downstream from God.

So Granada did not reach out, and her arms hung useless by her sides. The distance was now too great to be bridged by a reach as diminished as hers.

CHAPTER 42

Granada was wrenched from her sleep by a frightful scream, and her first thought was that a panther had got into the yard again. After the second scream, she knew it was human. She didn't dare move or breathe, not wanting to discover its source, afraid it was Polly.

The rain had slacked some and a weak, watery dawn was breaking. The girl peered through the shadows of the room and saw that Polly's bed was empty. The next scream was louder still.

Granada bolted from her cot and reached for her dress. While she was bringing the shift over her head, she heard the creak of the door hinge. At the sight of Polly her heart gave a leap. The woman was wet and muddy, but she was safe. She was toting her herb sack and the bottom sagged from whatever it was she had gathered during the night.

Granada's relief yielded to a sharp stab of loneliness. She knew they would never go gathering in the woods again.

The wailing outside was constant now. Whoever it was was scraping her throat raw, unleashing a torrent of outrage and loss. Polly stepped up to the window that opened to the yard. She unhooked the board shutter and flung it back. After a moment she turned to Granada, her face grim. "Come see."

Granada walked to Polly's side and looked out across the muddy expanse. A woman was kneeling in the mud, her arms thrown up to the gray morning sky still heavy with rain. Aunt Sylvie hovered over the woman, trying to pull her up from the mire. Then Granada made out the figure.

"Somebody must told Lizzie about her girl," Polly said, her tone flat. "Don't you reckon?"

When Granada didn't speak, Polly, whose gaze was still fixed on the stricken woman, continued. "Listen good to that voice, Granada. Take it deep down in your belly. That's how a momma feels when her child been stole away."

Granada stilled her breathing, praying Polly would stop. She didn't want to know any more about Rubina.

"Hounds found Rubina after she run off last night," Polly continued. "Course it weren't too hard for them dogs to tree that poor girl. Rubina saved them heap of trouble by hanging herself from the low limb of a cottonwood. Today Lizzie lost her girl for the second time over."

Granada reached out and put a steadying hand on the windowsill. She shut her eyes and began shaking her head, refusing to believe any of it.

Polly whipped her head toward the girl. "Look at me!" she commanded.

Granada saw the old woman's anger flaring like a torch in the dark room.

"What have you done?"

"You killed her baby," Granada whimpered, with no conviction to her complaint, but still she continued. "That baby was the people, too. Weren't it?"

Polly's jaw clenched. "You think you know all about it because you had some dreams. Well, you don't know nothing. You and your pretty dresses. Eating scraps from the master's table." Polly pointed to the yard. "Was it worth the trade?"

Granada's cheeks burned hot. She shook her head sharply, trying to deny it.

"You're lying!" Polly spat. "Ain't nothin' inside the yam that the knife don't know. I know everything there is about you."

Granada took a step back.

"You some kind of woman, ain't you?" Polly continued to rage. "Don't you understand yet? Ain't you figured it out yet? Where all *that* come from? That house. The fields. The crops. The gold. The mistress and the white boy you love so? Them fancy clothes you miss so bad. Down to the corn bread and molasses and that damned monkey. They all come from the same place. And it ain't the white man's God. It ain't Him that do the groaning and the heaving and the grieving. It's all been stole. It's been stole from the same place. That place I'm talking about ain't nothing but a bloody slit in this world of His. But everybody wants to rule over it. It ain't for the white man to rule. Ain't for any man to rule."

And then Granada knew.

"Yes ma'am, that's right. And until you can pay it the honor and respect it deserve, weep for it and pray for it. Until you can do that, you best get out of my sight. Go back to the great house. Go back to them that kill what little remembering you got. Give them your yes's and no's to swallow down and get fat on. Give them your own children to feed off of."

Granada began stepping back toward the

door, expecting Polly to jump on her at any minute and strangle her.

"That's right. Walk out the door. You thinking you got what you wanted. You thinking, 'I'm free of Polly Shine at last.' " Her laugh was vicious. "Free! What you know about free?"

From behind her Granada heard the old woman shouting, "For all your born days, until you get to be a crooked old woman, you ain't never going to be free of Polly Shine."

What was once given as a blessing had now been hurled as a curse.

Granada stumbled through the mud, making a wide panicked sweep through the yard, staying as far away as she could from the place where Aunt Sylvie still struggled to lift Lizzie to her feet.

Granada had no idea where to run. She belonged nowhere now. She looked up at the house, wishing that Little Lord would come out and save her like he had promised. She wished he would scoop her up and take her far away on his father's stallion.

She began crying again. Polly had been so angry. She had never treated her like this before. But of all the things that Polly had said to her, the cut that sliced deepest was her saying that she knew Granada. That she knew everything about her.

No one, ever, had considered Granada important enough to study, to know inside and out. No one would ever again. She would not let them because she herself had learned what they would find, and it revolted her.

Maybe she could hide in one of the stalls on a pile of dry hay. Chester might even tell her what to do, where to go. But when she turned and looked in the direction of the stables, she stopped, not daring to take another step.

Bridger was driving a mud-spattered wagon into the lot, trailed by a troop of hounds. The beasts were growling low in their throats, leaping, furiously trying to get at whatever was wrapped in the tarp.

Another wail rose up from Lizzie, and Granada saw Aunt Sylvie struggling to keep the woman from taking off toward the stable. That's when Granada knew what cargo the wagon carried.

Bridger stood by the wagon, cursing the dogs. Master Ben rode up wearing his rain slick and dismounted, motioning to one of Chester's stableboys to lead the steed away. Master Ben then took off in a fast stride with Bridger following close behind, a rope in his hand.

"No," Granada gasped, when she understood where they were heading.

They didn't slow until they got to the hospital and then Master Ben busted the door off its hinges with his boot. The sound of wood splintering cracked across the yard.

He stepped aside and let Bridger enter alone. Granada's heart beat furiously against her rib cage.

"No!" she cried, louder.

A moment later Bridger backed out the door, pulling a taut rope. He gave it a furious yank and Polly came stumbling out, her wrists bound together. She landed facedown in the muck. She tried to stand, but as she was about to regain her balance, Bridger yanked the rope again, sending her lurching another few feet before collapsing once more on the muddy ground.

A sickening chill gripped Granada's insides as the two men, their prisoner in tow, made their halting progress back to the stable.

CHAPTER 43

The low black clouds brought night early and the rain was unyielding. Granada didn't dare go back to the hospital, so she found herself sitting at the big pine table in the kitchen, watching the faces that had once been so familiar. Now she wondered who these people were after all.

Aunt Sylvie sulked about the kitchen grumbling to herself, every once in a while wiping a fugitive tear from her eye. Chester, who had made up clever songs about Polly before, now wore a hangdog look that said he hated himself for every mean rhyme.

Except for Bridger, nobody seemed to take any satisfaction in Polly's fate. Even the master was foul. When he saw Granada standing in the yard after they had dragged Polly to the stable, he had shouted, "You goddamned better have been a fast learner and picked up some remedies. Five thousand dollars' worth to be exact."

The prospect of taking Polly's place put Granada's head into such a sickening swim she wasn't able to offer a response, other than to lean against the big oak and retch into the black mud.

Lizzie had seen her there, walked out of the barn straight from Rubina's cold body and, when Granada raised up her head to wipe her mouth, slapped Granada's face. "You killed my girl," she spat.

Silas hadn't been seen since he finally abandoned his chair on the porch, where he had been rocking relentlessly for hours, shaking his head, and every now and then muttering Rubina's name. Eventually he rose up from his chair and walked directly across the muddy yard through the pouring rain and disappeared into the stables where they were keeping Polly. As far as Granada knew, he still hadn't come out.

When she thought things couldn't get worse, Granada overheard Pomp saying the master was going to take Polly into Delphi when the court came in session and have her tried for destroying his property and hanged as an example to anyone with similar ideas. Pomp said Granada was going to be hauled to court and be the main witness against Polly.

At that moment in the kitchen, Chester

was hunched over in his chair, a far-off expression on his face, his brass buttons tarnished.

Aunt Sylvie was now telling Granada not to get her hopes up for a new fancy dress anytime soon. The mistress had found a better way to geld the master and seemed to be enjoying every minute of it.

Pomp was quiet, keeping his eyes on his untouched coffee, cold in the cup. He never had any particular fondness for Polly, but tonight they all knew it could be any of them out there in the stable, tied up like a veal calf. It didn't matter how light-skinned you happened to be, tonight there was only one shade of black and one shade of white.

"Wonder who it was that told," Pomp muttered every so often. No one answered, but Granada could feel the creep of eyes.

But worse than their suspicions was Lizzie's relentless sobbing from Aunt Sylvie's room across the kitchen. The mistress had not allowed her near-hysterical maid to return to the stables to tend Rubina's body, which still lay in one of the stalls where Bridger had pitched her. When it got to be too much for Lizzie, she went off to the kitchen to cry, curse, and mourn. Each outburst was like another condemning slap to Granada's face.

Chester shifted in his seat and looked toward the room where Lizzie lay. "I heard that cottonwood where Rubina hung herself got struck by lightning," he said in his lowest voice. "Split that tree through the middle. But didn't take it down."

The words had no sooner left Chester's mouth than the door flung open and the howling wind rushed across the room. Old Silas, his preaching coat buttoned, stood with his back to the gale. The storm sounded like a mighty river roaring toward them.

Then it was quiet. Even the wind seemed to have subsided.

Silas began to speak. "I tell you in that night there shall be two men in one bed; and one shall be taken, and the other shall be left. Two women shall be grinding grain together; the one shall be taken, and the other left. Two men shall be in the field; the one shall be taken, and the other left. But of that day and hour knoweth no man, no, not the angels of heaven, but the Father only."

Aunt Sylvie was the first to move. She poured her man a cup of coffee and sat it down at his eating place closest to the hearth. She closed the door behind him and retrieved a towel from a nail in the doorframe. She held it out to him, but he didn't take it. She tried to unbutton his wet coat, but he only shrugged her away.

"Silas," Aunt Sylvie said finally, "you all right? Why you so peculiar? Your dropsy acting up?"

Sylvie's words seemed to have broken the spell. "Polly needs to be fed," Silas said, his tone now gruff. "Fix her a plate of something hot." Then Granada thought she saw the trace of a smile on his lips. "And pour her a cup of port wine."

Sylvie laughed, but then seemed to realize he might be serious. "The master's wine? He'll —"

"To hell with the master," Silas muttered. "He's got plenty. Ain't even his."

Silas's words again knocked the breath out of the room.

Only Aunt Sylvie dared move, nodding warily. "I'll take it to Polly directly," she said, "but you're sopping wet —"

"It's not you she's wanting to see, Sylvie," he said. "She's asking for Granada. Just Granada."

Every head in the room whipped to where the girl sat, trying her best to disappear, the dread pulling her lower and lower into the chair.

Silas never even addressed her directly.

After he had delivered his message, he walked past his wife and up to her bedroom door. He knocked softly. "Lizzie, I got a message for you from Polly."

When the door opened, there stood Lizzie, her good eye raw from grief, glaring hot at Granada, the white one as dead as her daughter.

"Sylvie, pour a cup for me and Lizzie, while you are at it. We'll be in here talking."

With that, the two disappeared into Sylvie's room.

Granada tried to get to her feet but couldn't manage it the first time, falling back into the chair. No one moved to help her. No one seemed to notice her at all.

When Granada entered the barn, there was no light. "Polly, I . . . I brung you something . . ." she managed, her throat choking off her words. "Aunt Sylvie sent me . . . something to eat, Polly."

"Back here, girl," the woman answered, her voice barely a whisper. "Best if you don't light no lantern. Just follow my words."

Thankful to be spared the sight of Rubina's body, Granada stepped into the darkness on trembling legs.

"That's right. Just keep coming. About

halfway back. I'm in here. On your right hand."

By the time Granada had come to the stall where they had tied Polly, the girl's eyes had begun to adjust, but still Polly was only a shadow among darker shadows.

"I'm afraid you going to have to feed me like a baby, Granada. I ain't got no hands to work with."

"Yes, ma'am," Granada mumbled. She could make out Polly's head, but there was still too much dark between them to read her face. Granada lifted a wedge of corn bread to where she supposed the mouth to be, but her hand trembled so, she dropped the bread onto the loose straw floor.

"I'm sorry," Granada stammered, setting the plate and cup down. "I'm sorry," she said again, now frantically pawing the ground with both hands to retrieve the corn bread from the dark. "I'm sorry, Polly. It's here . . . I'm sorry," she said once more, her voice filling with tears. "Polly, I'm . . . I didn't mean . . . I'm . . ."

Something inside gave loose. The girl threw her arms around Polly and wept, pressing her face against the cold iron collar that ringed the woman's neck.

Polly said nothing, and when Granada at last pulled away, wiping her face with the back of her hand, her head light from crying so completely, Polly asked, and not harshly, "Granada, what is it you sorry for? Tell me."

"I . . . Polly, I was bad to you. All you done for me and I hurt you."

"Say it, Granada, what you done."

"I told the mistress on you. I told about Rubina."

"Was it the truth?"

The girl was silent for a moment. She knew what Polly was going to say, but Granada could not bear to hear it. "Yes, Polly, but —"

"Then I can live with that, Granada," the old woman said. "Can you?"

"Polly, no!" the girl cried out. "It's all my fault. I'm the one to blame!"

Polly took a rasping breath. From somewhere in the stable, the master's stallion whinnied. Pigeons fluttered in the rafters.

"Granada, remember I told you my momma was a weaver?"

The girl nodded, sniffling. "Yes, ma'am. In Africa."

"That's right. All her people, the women, were weavers. The finest anywhere." Polly paused for a moment to catch her breath. She was weaker than Granada had thought.

When Polly began again, her words were

447

too low to be heard. Granada leaned in closer.

"She told me the secret . . . what made them so fine, mother after daughter after granddaughter, all the way down the line."

"What was it, Polly?"

"She say, the difference in weavers is, some see the tangle and others see the weave. The ones that can't take their eyes off the tangle, they never rise above it."

"Yes, ma'am," Granada said, knowing this was important, trying to understand.

"Granada, this here . . . what happened to me, to you, to Rubina . . . ain't nothing but a tangle. It's the *weave* you got to remember, Granada. It's bigger than you and me. It went on before you and me got here. It'll go on after you and me leave this place and go to wherever it is Rubina is waiting. Just a tangle, Granada."

Her whisper became so small, the girl had to put an ear to Polly's mouth. Granada felt the parched lips brush against skin.

"Yewande, lift your eyes and see!"

CHAPTER 44

Granada had gone to sleep thinking about the weave of things. Trying to recall all Polly had said about the threads that stitch folks together. About a heaven of stars being like the people. About daughters and mothers and mothers' mothers touching through time. She tried to find the room next to her heart where the sight for things outside herself was first born. But when she slept, her dreams were black and sightless.

Granada woke to the blunted toe of a shoe nudging her back.

"Polly!" she called out from her pallet.

A familiar voice splintered the darkness. "Get up, quick! Satan is treating Creation like his own tonight."

Finally able to focus, Granada made out the short, wide silhouette of the cook hovering over her. Aunt Sylvie poked the girl in the leg, harder.

"What happened?" Granada cried, bounding to her feet. "Somebody do something to Polly? She ain't . . . is she . . . ?"

Aunt Sylvie grabbed the girl's hand and began dragging her barefoot across the kitchen.

Granada wore only her shimmy. "Wait," she protested, reaching for the rain-soaked calico shift that hung over the chair.

"Ain't got time to dress," Aunt Sylvie said, gasping for breath. "Got to hurry. Might be too late now."

When Sylvie headed for the door that led to the great house instead of the one opening into the yard, Granada's heart gave a leap. Maybe this wasn't about Polly after all!

They raced through the darkened dining room and to the foot of the winding double staircase. From there Granada could see the lamplit upstairs. Shadows flitted about on the landing.

Aunt Sylvie pulled Granada, stumbling, up the stairs and didn't let go of her hand until the cook had deposited the girl in Little Lord's room.

"About time!" Master Ben bellowed.

Panicky, Granada took in the room with a quick glance. Master Ben, in stocking feet and wearing a nightshirt tucked into his riding trousers, stood glaring at her on one side of Little Lord's tester bed. Glaring at her husband from the other side of the bed was Mistress Amanda in her sleeping cap, arms crossed over her dressing gown in a kind of protest. Granada assumed Little Lord was in the bed, but the footboard obstructed her view. Over in the corner, her face beyond the light of the lamp, stood Lizzie's darkened figure, cringing like she was about to be hit.

Then Lizzie turned her face to Granada. "Ain't my fault! He was ailing when I come up to see about him," the maid whined pathetically.

Granada now saw the red print of a hand on the maid's face. The mistress had already struck.

"Maybe it was something he ate," Lizzie whimpered.

Aunt Sylvie stiffened. "Weren't nothing I fed him," she declared too forcefully. She quickly changed her tone and added, "But now that Granada's here, Little Lord will be healed in no time."

"What are you waiting for, fool!" Master Ben commanded. "Get over here."

Granada at last found her legs and moved through the fog of her stunned stupidity toward the bed. She couldn't remember a longer walk, not even the slog to the creek bank to heal Daniel Webster.

Her little friend's eyes were closed, his pillowcase darkened with sweat. On the floor, she saw a chamber pot. He had been vomiting. Maybe Lizzie was right. He could have been poisoned.

With her thumb, she lifted his eyelid and saw that the pupil was barely a dot in the field of pale blue. The pulse in his neck was so faint it took a moment for Granada to find it.

"Well, what is it?" the master snapped. "What's wrong with my son?"

Granada bit into her lip to stem her growing panic. The idea of her trying to doctor somebody was madness. And Little Lord himself!

She bit deeper into her lip, seeking the pain, for all her other senses were shutting down. There was no sound but the loud roar of her blood in her ears and her vision was dimming to a quivering dark.

But then she smelled it, and the noxious odor brought her back. It was like rotten fish. Her eyes followed the smell, searching for the source of such a stench. That's when she saw the thing lowering its stubbed nose from under Little Lord's bedding toward the carpet. The unhinged mouth was as white and shiny-slick as a fish's belly. And now it was in striking distance of Granada's leg.

She sprang back and yelped. "Snake!"

Master Ben had also seen it. He was already gripping the poker from the fireplace and was on the moccasin like a flash of powder. After several fierce blows, he had mashed the creature's head into a red pulp. The snake continued to undulate, coiling and uncoiling on the carpet until the master raised it up from its middle with his weapon, carried it through the open door to the gallery, and flung it over the railing into the mud for the dogs.

"He been snakebit," Aunt Sylvie said in a low, hushed voice. She quickly lifted her skirt and scoured the floor. "That the only one?"

The shock served to clear Granada's head. She took hold of the coverlet and yanked it off Little Lord.

And there it was. Little Lord's thin, pale legs were lying in a mushrooming puddle of blood. One leg had ballooned beyond recognition. A few inches above the ankle it was wine-colored and raw, looking more like meat to be hung in the smokehouse than a little boy's leg.

Granada spied a pair of purpling puncture marks. At least one fang had found a vein, and blood still pumped to the rhythm of the slowing heartbeat.

"How did a snake get up here?" Master Ben stammered. "In his bed? How could it have happened?"

The mistress exploded. "It happened because we live in hell!" she shouted. "How many children do you need to kill before you finally cede that point?"

The master fell back like he had taken a blow. He seemed unable to respond in any way other than stunned silence.

However, Granada now knew exactly what needed to be done and shouted above the fray. "Get Polly! She's got a remedy."

"Polly!" Master Ben cried. "She's half dead. Last I looked she wasn't even conscious. She's no use to anybody."

The words cut like jagged steel. Granada tried to imagine he was talking about somebody else being half dead. "No," she finally managed, "you got to get Polly."

"Don't you dare bring that witch near my boy," the mistress hissed. "She'd kill Little Lord just to spite me. Besides, you're bound to know the remedy."

"Amanda's right," the master chimed in. "You've got to. I can't let Polly around the boy, her knowing she's going to be hung anyhow."

Granada agreed with the master. She *should* know the remedy. But it was the only one Polly had kept quiet about. When she asked Polly how she had healed Daniel Webster, Polly had gone hush-mouthed. All she would say was that Daniel Webster had healed himself. Perhaps Polly didn't have a cure after all. But still . . .

"Little Lord's going to die for sure if you don't get Polly. He might die if you do. Might sounds better than will to my ears." She pressed her fingers to the boy's impossibly pale throat. "I can't hardly find his heartbeat now."

Master Ben heaved out a furious breath and then took to the stairs, still in his stocking feet.

While they waited, Granada put pressure on the vein below the oozing wound to keep Little Lord from losing any more blood.

To keep from falling apart, Granada focused on a riddle. The one the master had posed. How had the snake got into Little Lord's bed? The levee above the house had breached during the storm and brought snakes into the yard, and she knew from experience snakes could find their way up trees. But up the stairs to the gallery, across the hallway, up the staircase, into Little Lord's room, finally nestling in his sheets?

She lifted her finger from the vein and there was only a slight seepage now. What did it matter how he got bit? He was almost gone.

Mistress Amanda perched on the bed next to her son. She leaned over him and tousled his hair. Granada noticed how wooden and tentative the mistress's gesture was, sadly absent something essential. Granada remembered holding the mistress's hand and tried to recall her touch. Had it been so empty after all?

Several minutes later, Master Ben strode back into the room, sopping wet, his feet encased in mud. He was followed closely by Chester, who carried the dying woman in his arms like precious cargo.

"What took you so long!" cried the mistress from the bedside. "My God, this is just like Becky . . . the waiting on you . . . if you . . ."

"No!" Master Ben snapped. "It's not just like Becky. I had to throw a bucket of water on Polly to bring her to. Then she had to go to the hospital. But she's got the potion, all right. I seen it."

Chester gently set Polly down next to Little Lord's bed. She stood for a moment, but then her legs crumpled beneath her. The coachman caught Polly under her arms before her head bashed against the floor.

When he lifted her, Granada gasped. From the light of the lamp by Little Lord's bed, the rope burns around Polly's wrists were clearly visible, bloody and raw. The iron collar had bitten so hard into her neck that the skin around her throat was an open wound. Her face was bruised, her lip bloodied.

The mistress stood up from the bed and took a step back, putting her hand to her throat. "My God, Benjamin, is she still breathing?"

Granada feared the same, but then she heard her name spoken in a barely audible voice.

"Granada, you come hold me up."

The girl rushed to Polly and carefully took her from Chester. Granada had a hand around the tiny waist and draped a skeletal arm over her shoulder. Polly's legs were bent at the knees. Her muscles had to be cramping from all her time kneeling in the stall.

Polly tried to laugh. "I guess I'm needing more than a walking stick today, Granada. Now step me close to the boy's wound." Polly craned her neck a bit, but even that movement seemed to exhaust her. Her weight fell back on Granada.

"Yes, snakebit," she said wearily. "That's the sad truth of it."

"What can you do, Polly?" It was the master. His tone had softened like a man who knew his dictates went only so far.

"He's nearly dead now," Polly said, shaking her head. "The poison already squeezed most the life out your boy."

"You got that remedy!" Master Ben cried. "Aren't you even going to try it?"

Polly again shook her head. "No, Master, I'm sorry. Your poor boy can't be saved."

"You can't just let him die!" Master Ben was frantic now.

"For God's sake, Benjamin," the mistress snapped, "don't stand there arguing with a slave. Cut out her tongue if she won't obey."

Polly grew heavier on Granada's arm by the minute. The old head fell against the girl's chest. The breathing was shallower, raspy.

"She's hurting bad, Master Ben," Granada cried. "Let me tend to her, please, Master." Both Polly and Little Lord were slipping away from her, and she could do nothing!

Polly took a sharp intake of breath. "I'm all right." She managed to lift her head. "Just my legs, mostly. I'll get them to working directly."

Master Ben was pleading now. "Polly, if

you know to try anything, anything at all, there's nothing to lose. Granada said something about the way you healed Daniel Webster."

Granada saw the mistress stiffen, scalding her husband with her stare. The girl wondered if the woman was more upset at her husband for begging a slave for her son's life or for suggesting Polly use monkey medicine to save him.

"Master," Polly said, "I only tried it that one time. I just can't take that chance with a flesh-and-blood boy this far gone." Polly looked up into Master Ben's face. "I'm not going to kill your son."

"You'll be killing him if you don't try!" Master Ben blurted. "Why . . . I'll kill you myself if you don't try. I'll hang you before you ever get to Delphi."

She went quiet again. Granada was afraid Polly was losing consciousness. Her body was going limp.

Her voice seemed to come from the grave. "All right, then. If I try," she said, her speech halting, as she rationed her breath, "and if the boy dies, you have to hang me. You got to promise it. I can't have it on my head that I killed your son."

For a moment Master Ben was at a loss for words. "Have you gone mad?" he finally blurted.

Granada was in agreement. This was not like Polly at all. She was delirious. The girl looked into Polly's face. Then she saw it. The old woman's expression might have been one of near-death exhaustion, but the devil was in her eyes.

"Promise it!" she rasped.

"Promise her!" the mistress implored. "For God's sake, Benjamin! I'll promise her if you won't."

"My God, yes! I promise," Master Ben sputtered. "We're wasting time with this foolishness."

But Polly gave no indication that she was ready to lift a hand to heal the boy. Granada could tell the woman was gathering her strength. Her breath was becoming deeper, more regular.

"And by the same turn," she said at last, life seeping back into her voice, "if he was to live . . ."

"Yes, go on," the master urged. "If he was to live . . . what?"

"If he was to live," she said, her voice reclaiming some of its old vinegar, "I can't let it be said that your precious *white* child owes his life to no nigger slave."

"Goddamn, you are mad!" the master

snapped. "I don't care who he owes his life to."

Polly held her tongue now. Granada couldn't help but grin, amazed at the old woman's gumption.

The mistress grasped the meaning before her husband. "Fool!" Mistress Amanda cried. "She wants her freedom. Promise it to her."

Master Ben clenched his fist and his eyes flared. "I won't be blackmailed!"

"I swear, if you let your pride kill another child —"

"Enough, Amanda!" The forked vein in the master's forehead throbbed. Granada could tell he was still considering his options, but there was no other move to make.

"Fine!" he said, glaring at the woman. "You have my word. You go free if Little Lord lives. Is that what you want? *Now* can you see to my boy?"

"You swear it on your boy's life," Polly said, making things plain. The old woman began to straighten, shifting more weight to her own legs.

"I swear it on my boy's life," the master said, speaking the words like they were acid in his mouth.

Almost as an afterthought, Polly said, "And the girl, too." She turned her face to

Granada and gave her the faintest of grins.

Master Ben nodded his promise. "Now, will you do something before it's too late?"

"All right, then," Polly pronounced, standing on her own two feet now, still a little wobbly. "We understand each other. Now both of you get out of my way so I can save your boy. Go stand in that corner."

Granada was astounded. Red-faced, both the master and the mistress followed Polly's pointing finger.

Polly limped over to an armchair and fell back into the deep cushion with a groan. She reached into her apron pocket and retrieved a small vial and began rolling it between her palms, warming the liquid.

"Granada," she said, "you should have already had that boy's leg cleaned. First, get him laid so his heart is higher up than that bite. Chester, you lift him to where Granada says. Sylvie, rip me three long strips of the mistress's fine linen to bind the boy's leg. Long enough to tie a good knot. Lizzie, you get ready to help me to my feet when I tell you."

The room came alive with activity, everybody following their orders. Granada began by looking for more pillows to prop under Little Lord. She knelt to retrieve one off the floor that had somehow been kicked partway under the bed. She was in such a hurry she didn't give what she saw there, lying wadded under the bed, a second thought. The sight registered only a vague unease, but it was something that could be attended to later when the immediate crisis had passed

In a short time Lizzie had Polly standing over Little Lord, forcing some kind of potion down his throat. The boy gagged, managing to swallow only a tiny amount of the dark liquid.

Master Ben jumped to his feet. "He's choking! What are you giving him?"

"Something that works better when I ain't got nobody standing over my shoulder."

The master took two steps back. It was obvious that no one was up to arguing with even a severely weakened Polly.

The old woman kept at it, giving Little Lord a small dose at a time, and then massaging it down his throat. After several repetitions, the boy swallowed without resistance. It was only then she bothered answering the master's question.

"It got some skullcap and some snakeroot and some black sampson. Some other things Daniel Webster whispered in my ear. I'll show you how and you can write it in one of your books. I reckon you done paid for it." She looked at his wife and chuckled. "It even got a drop or two of monkey blood. I calls it my monkey potion. Course you can name it what you want to."

Granada had never heard of such a remedy. And how strange Polly would have it freshly made, ready to go. That's when the nagging discovery from before forced itself into the forefront of her mind. She knelt down to look once more.

Her eyes had not been playing tricks. There it was. But it made no sense. How did Polly's herb sack get under Little Lord's bed?

Granada was certain Polly hadn't brought it into the room with her. In fact, the sack should still be in the hospital, where it was when Bridger had dragged Polly to the stables. It should be where she had left it when she came in that last morning, tied at the neck and dropped in an iron washpot by the hearth. Granada had thought it strange at the time. The early hour. Polly being out in the weather. And why had she tied it off? She had never done that before.

Granada shivered when she remembered how the muddy bottom of the sack had sagged with the weight of its contents.

But how? she thought as she reached for the sack.

"Silly me!" a voice from behind announced as a hand snatched the sack from Granada's fingers. "That's where my mop rag got off to."

Granada swiveled around to see Lizzie stooped behind her, grinning and clutching the muddy sack close to her chest. In the light of the lamp it was clear that her good eye shone as brightly as a brand-new day.

CHAPTER 45

Granada watched hard and silent as Polly packed her tote sack. The girl was corralling her courage for the moment she would be forced to make her stand.

"We got to travel light," Polly said as she retrieved a jar from her trunk, "so make sure you got a knife and some twine handy in your pocket. Fetch two small bowls and a few stoppered bottles and pack them in that nice hunting pouch Little Lord give you for going away. Maybe some scraps of burlap would be good to have. Such things as that. And don't forget your pick and digging spoon. Everything else the road will give us."

Granada didn't move. Since the day Polly got that moccasin to bite Little Lord, Granada suspected there were more secrets crawling around than snakes in the yard.

The girl held her sulking stare until Polly at last glanced up at her. Granada set her jaw.

"Granada," she asked, "why ain't you doing like I say? Best to leave while we can." She laughed. "You know how the pharaoh changed his mind that time he let Moses go!"

"I might not want to go." Her voice did not tremble as much as she had feared.

"What do you mean you don't want to go? You're free now. You can go anywhere you please. Nobody can make you stay here."

Granada crossed her arms over her chest. "I don't know the first thing about no Freedomland."

"I *told* you Freedom ain't no place you go to!" Polly said. "You free if you stay. You free if you go. You free to be a slave, if you got a mind to. From now on, Freedom is anywhere you stand." Polly sighed heavily. "You still mad at me because of what I did to Little Lord?"

"How could you do that?" Granada blurted. "It was you made that snake bite him."

"You hurting for Little Lord or you mad at me because I didn't tell you about the snake potion?"

"Everybody knew! I had to figure it out myself, but now I know what you done. Silas come in the kitchen out of the storm with your sack of snakes under his coat, didn't he? And then he give it to Lizzie. And then Lizzie took it up to Little Lord's room and put a snake in his bed, didn't she? That about right?"

"Yes, that's about right," Polly admitted.

"You told everybody but me!"

"You might have tried to save Little Lord from getting bit. I didn't know for sure."

"Did you know *for sure* Little Lord wouldn't die?" Granada asked.

"No, not for sure."

"But you didn't care. Like he was just a tangle in your weave?" Granada looked at the floor. "And Rubina's baby. Was she just a tangle? She was one of the people, weren't she, Polly? And . . . me? I reckon you thinking I'm a tangle, too."

"No, baby." Polly walked over and stroked her hair. "Them things ain't got nothing to do with you. This is bigger than you. Bigger than me. Them things is about all of us."

"You talking about the weave of things," Granada said, sniffing. "But Sylvie and Chester is in my weave. And Little Lord and the mistress. They all here. And my momma, she's here. And her momma. This is the place I know. And I can heal folks now. They need me here."

"Yes, they do."

468

"But what if nobody needs me where you going? What if you die? You almost did already. And then there won't be nobody to look out for me. Whoever owns that Freedomland might up and send me to the fields." Surely they had fields and swamps in this new land. Maybe worse.

"That why you so scared? Because you thinking you don't have a say in things? You thinking I'm making you go?"

"Ain't you?"

"No, ma'am."

Granada swallowed hard. "You letting me stay?"

"I ain't *letting* you do nothing." Polly laughed, but then her voice turned serious. "Granada, you got so much to learn about Freedom. You got to make up your own mind now. You are a free woman. If you come with me, you got to come as a free woman, not a slave and not a child that's dragged this place and that, being told what to do. But either way, going with me or staying put, it's going to be your first step as a free woman. You the one got to take it." Polly smiled. "I can chew your food but you the one got to swallow."

"I don't *have* to go?" Granada asked.

"Going with me or staying put," Polly repeated, "neither one right, neither one wrong. It all hangs on the woman what does the choosing. You the one got to make it right. But I'll warn you now. Getting free is easy. Staying free ain't."

Polly nodded once, the way she did when she was through with arguing. The old woman reached into her ginghamed bosom and retrieved the leather pouch that hung around her neck by a string. She carefully removed a folded piece of parchment and held it out to Granada.

"These your Freedom papers. Mail rider brought them in from Jackson this morning. Signed by the white men who claim to have say-so about Freedom and such."

Granada didn't reach for the packet at once. Instead she shoved her hands into her apron pockets, still not sure what Polly was up to. A warm November breeze wafted through the trees outside the window. She heard a gentle sprinkling as the wind loosed a thousand droplets of water that had held tight to the leaves since the last downpour.

Polly waved the paper in the girl's face. The draft of air made her blink.

"Go on ahead. They yours."

Granada refused to touch them, not knowing what touching Freedom even meant, what it bound her to.

Polly unfolded the paper and pointed with

her bony finger. "See here? What's that name say?"

"Granada Satterfield," the girl read, amazed her name was known in someplace called Jackson, beyond her world of levees and swamps.

"That's your slave name," Polly said. "That's going to be the second thing you do as a free woman. You got a right to call yourself what you want to. Granada, from now on you get to hear what you want to. See what you want to. Think what you want to. And you can stand where you damn well please. It's not my place or nobody else's to tell you these things no more."

Granada took hold of a corner of the document, but Polly didn't let go at once.

"You can change your mind right now and still go with me . . . if you want to. After I walk away from here and you can't see the back of my head no more, you can change your mind and come after me. Just holler my name. That's the other thing about Freedom. You can change your mind this way and that way until it feels right. You understand?"

Granada nodded, but her head still grappled with the notion. This is not what she expected at all. She thought she would argue awhile with Polly, and then Polly would tell her to shut her mouth and to come on quick.

"Just in case you don't change your mind, Granada, I got to speak some words to you before I leave this place. I'm going to say them now, but you probably ain't going to hear them until later. So hold still and look at me when I talk so you don't forget."

Granada raised her head and looked up at the old woman's face, into those amber eyes that could fix you like a stickpin through a beetle. The notion of forgetting anything about Polly Shine seemed unthinkable.

"Just remember," Polly said carefully, "these pretty words on this scrap of paper ain't going to make you free. The master can't give you your Freedom. The Yankees when they come can't. I can't. If you think any somebody can, then you always going to be their slave."

She grinned a tight little smile. "Truth is, ain't a soul wants you to have it. You wait and see. One fine day, you go to acting like you got Freedom, then watch how they fight you for it. You got to take your Freedom, and then you got to be ready to take it back the next morning and the next morning after that."

She released her hold on the papers and gently laid her palm against the girl's cheek.

"Bless you, girl," she said tenderly. "Walk through life listening for your name, the name that remembers you. Until then, go ahead and be Granada if you want to."

Her face grew feverishly hot under the old woman's hand.

"You still got the gift," Polly said. "Tend to your people the best way you know how. You don't have to love them to claim them, so claim as many as you can. You'll love them the second you start to take care of them. Don't seem right, but that's the way that works. And you right when you say they need you. They do." Polly removed her hand and straightened up. "And I promise," she said in a forbidding tone that chilled Granada's insides, "one day, you going to need them. Never forget that."

Polly picked up her sack and hung it off her shoulder. She reached for her snake stick where it leaned against the doorframe. Then she looked back and chuckled. "Like I told you, girl, you ain't never going to be free of Polly Shine." Polly's face warmed to deep affection and a slight tremor came to her voice. "Wherever you be, however old and crooked you get, I promise, you will be remembered."

The girl's insides trembled and her throat clenched so tight it hurt. Was this Freedom?

she wondered. Why did it hurt so bad?

Polly turned and with the familiar water-jointed gait walked through the door. Granada went to the window to watch her departure.

I could still go, she told herself. I get to change my mind. The papers burned her hand. The thought was foreign and frightening. Her legs went weak, like they wanted to make the decision for her. She gripped the windowsill.

Polly shunned the road and headed for the woods, stepping onto a path that probably only she could see. Granada prayed for the old woman to turn, only once, to look back at her. Then Granada would know for sure. If Polly would do that, Granada promised herself she would go.

But Polly never turned and the sky began to dim as the sun found the clouds.

Granada held her breath and watched as the old woman headed out, her stick feeling the way before her. Only when she had vanished into the dense, rain-washed foliage did Granada dare to breathe.

She knew me before anyone, Granada thought.

"I'll remember you, Polly!" she shouted from the window, but there came no response.

Granada ran out the cabin door and up to the edge of the wood. "I'll remember about listening to the beasts and the fowls!" she called out. "About digging holes and breaking pots and rooting babies in the world. About those threads that stitch everybody together. Do you hear me, Polly?" She waited, but there came no answer, only the light rustle of leaves in the wind.

"I'm going to listen, Polly," Granada said softly now, cradling herself with her arms. "I'll always be listening for you."

CHAPTER 46

For years to come the puzzling events following Little Lord's miraculous recovery would be hotly debated by the inhabitants of the Mississippi Delta, both white and black. In fact, most could only agree upon a few things.

First, Master Ben, being a gentleman of his word, gave Polly her Freedom as promised. Of course there were those who insisted nobody gave Polly Shine a thing. She took it.

Second, as soon as her Freedom papers arrived, Polly struck out on foot, alone, carrying only her snake stick and a tote sack swinging from her shoulder.

Third, two nights following her departure, during a rain so heavy it breached the levees in four locations and flooded the great house and all the cabins, sixty-four of the master's slaves, including his most loyal servant, Silas, went missing, the largest single incident of runaways in the history of the state of Mississippi.

And finally, it was common knowledge that when Master Ben was alerted to the mass escape, he immediately sent for the dogs, and it was Bridger who had the unpleasant task of telling his boss that every one of those ferocious slave-catching hounds was too violently ill to join the hunt, forcing the men to wander the rain-swollen swamps with benefit of neither track nor scent. They spent three miserable days in the swamps only to come back empty-handed.

Other than that, nothing could be said for certain, but that didn't stop the speculating. Granada discovered everyone had his theory. And each of them put Polly Shine at the center.

Some swore that the band of runaways were biding their time, trapping and fishing on some secret bayou, waiting for the abolitionists to find them and escort them to Freedom.

Those with religion believed that Polly, after bartering for her Freedom with the life of the pharaoh's son, had led the escaped Negroes right up to the banks of the Mississippi River and commanded it to split wide open like the Red Sea. Some went as far as to say that Polly and her followers carved out their own Promised Land out West, some milk-and-honey Canaan for Negroes only.

A favorite theory held by the master and his fellow plantation owners was that the runaways never got out of the swamps alive.

Granada wasn't sure where Polly ended up, but the girl was good enough at riddles to figure how she got away. Granada knew that the best riddle is the one whose solution is obvious. You think, "Why didn't I see that before! The answer was in front of me all the time!"

Indeed, after repeatedly sifting through the facts, Granada decided Polly's planned escape had been right in front of her. Silas didn't have some miracle conversion. He had been working with Polly ever since she began taking him his medicine. His access to the settlements through holding preaching meetings was in no doubt beneficial in planning such a large-scale operation. She remembered the stormy night he came into the kitchen out of the rain, quoting Bible verses about the two men working in the field, one being taken up and the other left behind. He had told anybody with ears to hear what was coming. How many times had he preached that same message to his three hundred congregants? Freedom was coming like a thief in the night. Only the Father knew the day. But get ready if you were going.

Charity, who walked her baby out in the open, always chose to circle by the hound pen until the dogs grew accustomed to her presence. Granada had even heard Polly tell Charity to feed the dogs when she passed. Quietly slipping them the same purgatives the white doctors were so fond of could be done easily, with little fuss.

Charity's husband, Barnabas, who had hollowed Little Lord's canoe out of a log and then showed him how to use it, was also one of the runaways. He could certainly be counted on to build a cypress-log armada, keep it hidden in the swamps, and then teach the group what to do with a paddle.

Silas, who had first settled the swamps with the master, mapping every river, stream, tributary, and alligator slough, would know how to captain a fleeing army of canoeing slaves.

Polly had been warning Granada about the snake called Freedom for months, trying her best to get the girl ready without risking the entire scheme. And maybe if things hadn't happened so suddenly, Granada could have been ready.

The only person to blame was Granada herself. Polly had to speed up her timetable when Granada told the mistress about Rubina. Granada had forced her hand.

With the riddle solved, there was just one lingering question, and it meant more to Granada than any other: Would Polly Shine do as she promised?

Granada could recite aloud the exact words, the last thing she heard Polly say: "Wherever you be, however old and crooked you get, I promise, you will be remembered."

"Will you really remember me?" Granada asked the night sky from her window. "Years from now, when you cast your eyes at these very stars, wherever you are standing, will you see me in the weave? Will you remember that you loved me?"

If the answer was yes, if Polly, who knew Granada before anyone, remembered her, then Granada believed she could bear anything.

CHAPTER 47

When Violet arose the next morning, she found Gran Gran in her chair before a cold stove, Rubina's mask in her lap. Her head had dropped to her chest.

"Gran Gran!" Violet cried out. "Are you dead?"

The girl's outburst startled Gran Gran awake. When she looked up at the girl, she could see the forehead smoothe out and the eyes calm. "I'm all right, Violet. Just resting my eyes."

"You been talking to Rubina?"

Gran Gran glanced down into her lap. "Rubina. Yes, I guess you can say that's what I been doing most of the night."

"Want me to put some kindling in the stove, Gran Gran? You going to be wanting your coffee soon, ain't you?"

Gran Gran laughed. "Girl, I'm liking this new talking Violet. No sooner she putting words together than she's asking what she can do for me. I might can get used to that kind of talk!"

Violet got the fire going all by herself. Gran Gran watched the efficiency of the girl's movements, the confidence she showed in filling the pot with water from the pump and then setting it on the front eye of the stove.

At first Gran Gran guessed the girl had done these things before, but then noticed that each movement — the way she held her head and leaned one hand on the water shelf as she waited for the water to spill out; how she laid the kindling three sticks on the bottom and two across on top, and how she lit the match to a small splinter and then held it in the stove until the fire caught; the way she tapped the spoon on the table before she put the coffee in the pot; how she retied the coffee sack with a double-loop knot — were all mannerisms Gran Gran recognized as her own. The girl had been studying her close, memorizing her movements. Violet had been watching and listening in a way that would make Polly Shine proud.

Violet managed to pour Gran Gran a cup of coffee without spilling and then got herself a glass of milk from the crock. She pulled a chair up close to Gran Gran and waited.

After taking a sip of coffee and complimenting its strength, Gran Gran said, "Now you got me all pampered, I got the feeling there is something you going to ask me."

"Gran Gran," Violet asked, her voice solemn, "did you ever see you a real live baby being born?"

Gran Gran recognized the wonder that shone in the girl's face. It had to be the same look she had given Polly on their walk back from Sarie's delivery.

Gran Gran smiled. This was a much better story to tell.

CHAPTER 48

The master had his own interpretation of Freedom. Now that Granada was free of him, he claimed he was free of her as well. If she wanted food to eat and clothes to wear and a roof over her head, she would have to hoe Polly's piece of the field, doing everything she had been brought to the plantation to do.

So at thirteen years old, and with great doubt and trepidation, Granada became the doctoress for Satterfield Plantation. But that wasn't the only change.

After Polly left, the fabric of Granada's life began to unravel. Just like Polly said, the two-headed snake of Freedom was threatening from the North. Little Lord was hastily packed up and sent off to a military school in Charleston. Not long after, the mistress went to live in New Orleans while the master rode off on his stallion to fight the Yankees.

"I'll be back as soon as we whip the Yankees," he shouted across the yard on the drizzly morning he left, "so keep my supper warm, Sylvie!" Sitting ramrod straight in his saddle, he flourished his preposterous-looking hat with the ostrich feather, already frizzling in the rain.

Granada could tell he was only putting on a show for those slaves thinking that now would be a good time to run. When he gave Bridger final instructions on how to run the plantation, he wore the worried look of a man going to his own funeral.

Life went on, knitting itself in a new way, without the master and his family. Granada dutifully attended to the sick and dying at all hours of the day and night. On occasion she traveled by mule out to the settlements, Little Lord's leather hunting pouch slung around her shoulder and packed with everything she had seen Polly put in her tote sack.

Polly always seemed to be present, watching and listening. While Granada worked at setting a broken leg or diagnosing an ugly rash, she felt Polly's hands guiding hers. In times of crisis, Granada came to depend on that old cocksure voice in her head, lecturing and laying out an uncompromising set of instructions.

Polly's presence was especially strong on

the days Granada spent studying the brass-hinged Bible in which the old woman had recorded her cures and practices in the margins beside pertinent verses. Granada would often look up from the book, expecting to see Polly across the room in the cane-bottom rocker, muttering to herself. Sometimes Granada would close her eyes, trying to catch the words.

Yet there was one thing Polly had not taught her, and it was the thing she wanted to know the most. Sooner or later, she was going to have to come face-to-face with the birthing bed. It was the thing she feared the most, and the thing she loved the best.

But for months, no one bothered to alert her when a woman went into labor, and Granada figured they probably had as many doubts about her ability as she did herself.

When the call finally came on a cold night in February, she had been sitting by the fire in the hospital studying Polly's crimped handwriting. One of Bridger's overseers summoned her out to the porch.

"Gal at Burnt Creek about ready to drop," he announced from astride his mare. "Must be some trouble, because the women down there are shouting up a storm for you to hasten to them."

"They calling for me?" Granada gasped.

There had to be a mistake. The terror cut through her stomach like a razor.

"You best get your things," he answered over his shoulder, riding his horse to the stable. "Going to take you best part of two hours to get there."

Stunned by fear, she staggered about the cabin as if in a dream, mechanically filling her bag.

She rode alone in the moonless night, trusting the mule to find the way along the rutted track. The wind was bitter and stung her face and hands, but Granada didn't want the journey to end. Or perhaps it could last long enough for the trouble to pass.

When she arrived at Burnt Tree, a woman in a ragged shawl pulled tight to her throat met Granada before she had dismounted the mule. The girl could feel the eyes of the quarter watching warily through the chilled dark. Could they see how unsure she was? How she was bound to fail them?

Granada's steps were leaden as she walked toward the cabin. Again, she remembered the day when she had fallen into the creek from the canoe and waded through the sluggish water. She could see Little Lord waiting on the bank holding his dying pet in his arms, watching Granada with pleading eyes.

He had believed in her and she had let him down. But this was no boy and his pet. This was a mother and child. And there was no Polly to save the day.

The night was freezing, but when Granada entered the cabin, she was hit by a wall of sweating heat from the fire in the hearth. The flames lit up the room and in a flash of terror, she saw everything at once. Four women crowded around a cot where the mother lay naked and glistening with tallow and sweat. She had completely soaked the quilt on which she lay.

All eyes were on Granada now. Her face burned with shame and her arms hung useless by her sides, her hands so empty. At least with Polly she had been allowed to carry the little crock to the birthings.

Granada's lip began to quiver. She had forgotten the clay pot! She wanted to tell them how sorry she was, that Polly had never let her enter the birthing room before. That she was not ready for this.

But then, as she was about to speak, she noticed the women's expressions. They were not at all like Little Lord's had been, desperate and expectant. In the faces that looked upon her, there was a serenity that calmed the pounding in Granada's chest. Even in the haggard face of the mother, Granada saw a composed acceptance. It was clear that these women didn't want anything from her. Nor was there any "trouble" she was supposed to save them from. On the contrary, she got the strange feeling they were there to save *her*.

The oldest woman, as gnarly as a hundred-year oak, beckoned Granada with stiffened fingers to a place next to her in the circle. Granada now recognized her. Too old to be useful in the fields, she was one who minded the children while their mothers worked.

Granada went to the far side of the bed where she had been summoned. The old childminder beamed her toothless smile and took Granada's hands. She placed them on the mother's stomach and revealed to Granada the feel of an unborn child.

Granada had never touched anything that thrilled her so, not even the finest satins and silks. At once she knew that her hands belonged on this woman. They belonged *to* this woman. And like a wandering soul who catches sight of home, Granada's heart began to beat with anticipation and delight.

For the next few minutes ancient hands guided Granada's, showing her how to knead the loins and abdomen, how to decipher the position of the baby, how to raise up the contractions of the mother.

Granada looked into the mother's face. The velvety dark skin was soaked with the sweat of birthing. The eyes were closed, the hurting visible in her wrinkled brow and clenched jaw. She groaned loudly, throwing her head from side to side. All at once she bucked violently against the pain.

Startled, Granada quickly withdrew her hands and stepped back, afraid she was hurting the woman, but the others stayed with the mother, urging her in calm voices not to bear down too hard, counseling her to breathe instead.

"Let it roll with God," they soothed.

A bottle was placed in Granada's hand and she was shown how to hold it to the mother's mouth.

Someone murmured, "Hassle, Celia. You doing real good, girl. Just pant your breath in that bottle." And Celia did as she was told, blowing rapid puffs of air into the mouth of the bottle until the seizure passed.

During the next contraction, not five minutes later, the mother grew even more irate, now fervently cursing those around her. Remembering Rubina, Granada began to fear for the baby. Was the mother refusing her child? Did she want her baby dead?

Granada looked to the circle of women

once more and was struck to see how graciously they received the outburst. The mother wasn't angry with the women, or with her baby, or with God for putting her in this fix. It wasn't anger at all.

This was the woman's way of saying yes. It was life stretching beyond itself, forcing its way into a cold, unwelcoming winter. This mother, in all her fury, was boldly claiming a place for her child, demanding its due. It wasn't anger. It was a fierce love.

Soon Celia was flailing again. The women managed to get her up on her feet to walk off some of the pain, and for a while she squatted on the floor, stretching her aching muscles. Finally she was helped to her feet and guided once more to the bed, where the shouting and the thrashing began anew.

Everything Granada had understood about birthing was wrong. This was no sentimental wish uttered on a plaintive whimper, some softhearted hope. This was a mother's readiness to weep or to fight or maybe just to endure and outlast, no matter what it took. Perhaps this was how a mother scratched out a place in the cold, hard ground for a child to take root.

Now the chorus of women was calling for Celia to push. It was time for the baby to come. She spread her legs wide, groaning.

Again the old childminder took Granada's hands and this time guided them between the woman's thighs.

At first Granada resisted, but then her uneasiness gave way to elation. "I'm touching the baby!" she exclaimed, as her fingers found its crowning head. The women's laughter was warm.

Together, Granada and the old woman guided the baby from the birth canal, the head and then the shoulders. At first the baby faced downward, but as it steadily emerged its body began to turn and soon Granada was looking upon its face. Next came the buttocks and finally two legs freed themselves from the womb.

Granada had come so close to giving up on magic completely. But there she was, standing at the mother's bedside, cradling a newborn baby boy. Granada could not speak. She was spellbound by this miracle that could fit in her own two hands, this entity last touched by God.

The slick coating on the child's skin glistened in the firelight. Even as Granada held him, he was threaded to his mother by the thick, veined rope, still pulsing with her heartbeat. Moments passed as Granada breathlessly waited for the baby to cry out, to declare the beginning of both their lives.

But the child did not move, nor did his eyes open. The baby lay lifeless in her hands. She looked up in terror searching for the old woman's face.

"I want my baby," the mother called out. "Let me hold my baby." She heaved herself forward, reaching out for her child, but the women held her back.

All eyes were on the unmoving child in Granada's hands. She felt her legs wanting to give beneath her. The old childminder reached out and took the boy from Granada.

The old woman slapped the baby sharply on his buttocks but there was no response. She laid him down on the bed. With her finger she cleared his mouth and nose, but the baby still did not breathe. She looked up at Granada.

"You do it" was all she said.

"What?" Granada gasped.

The old woman said simply, "Give the child your breath."

Trembling, Granada bent down and put her mouth over the baby's. She exhaled, like the woman told her, filling his lungs with quick puffs of air.

Granada's feet nearly left the floor when the baby sneezed, and then sneezed again. When he cried out at last, it was with Granada's very own breath.

The cord was tied off and cut. Granada carefully lifted the child and handed him to his mother and watched as she nuzzled her baby close, the two forming one. Neither could ever be lost from the other, she thought. One breath, Polly had said. We all breathe with one breath.

She ached to run to Polly, to tell her that she understood now.

At that moment Granada noticed that the old childminder was holding out some object, offering it to Granada. The girl couldn't make out what it was through the glistening blur of her tears, yet she reached for it anyway. Upon first touch, she knew what it was she held, and she clutched it close to her breast, as if she had been handed her own child.

It was one of Polly's clay pots. Polly had known Granada would be here. It had been waiting for her all along.

CHAPTER 49

By the time Freedom arrived, people all over the county had come to depend on Granada's doctoring. She traveled in her own buggy and on the back of her own mule, crisscrossing the swamps and the fields, making a good life for herself as a midwife, delivering more babies than anybody in the history of Hopalachie County, white or black. Her love for catching babies only grew.

The children she had delivered, when they were old enough to speak, called her Gran Gran. By the time she was twenty, everybody in three counties had heard of Gran Gran Satterfield, the big-boned woman with hands large enough to span a good-size watermelon and strong enough to slap a bull cross-eyed, but gentle enough to nestle a sleeping baby in her palm.

They said nobody was better with a difficult delivery. Her hands always knew exactly what to do. "But don't expect to find out nothing else about her," they said. "That woman is all business."

She grew to be a large, dark-skinned, stern-faced woman, appealing at first sight, but the men she came across didn't know what to make of a woman like her, a woman who acted like she had no need of them.

Granada did go on to marry a man named Luster Canary. Besides a pretty name, he had skin the color of parlor-room mahogany and a penchant for roaming — and was in need of a steady source of funds to do so. She didn't care. What she wanted was to bear a child, a little girl to raise around the very same hearth that had illuminated her earliest memories. Granada would teach her daughter everything she had learned. The girl would take her mother's place when she became too old to mount a mule at midnight. But after years of hoping and trying, she finally gave up on Luster ever giving her a baby. She was more relieved than pained when one day her pretty husband didn't come home. The only thing she kept was his name.

After Luster there were other men, but she was never able to birth a baby of her own. The woman who knew every lullaby there ever was never got to sing one to her own child.

There were plenty of people who needed her and that's what mattered. Their pains and miseries, spoken and unspoken, filled her days, and her days filled her years. She was as happy as a person had a right to be. The sights and sounds of birthing occupied her senses and the busyness kept a certain nagging uneasiness at bay, a vague memory of something she had once let go of, dismissed before she had even learned to say its name. The remembering was as fine as a silken thread and as faint as a word whispered upon a breeze. It was as sure as the turning of a face to its beloved.

CHAPTER 50

For a long time after the story, Gran Gran said nothing, while Violet studied the old woman's face.

Finally the girl asked, "What happened then?"

"Nothing much," Gran Gran answered too quickly. "No," she laughed to herself, "you come along. That's what happened."

The girl still looked at Gran Gran, waiting. She could tell Violet was confused, but this was where it had to stop. Gran Gran had decided to give the girl a happy ending. She deserved at least that. Sometimes, in spite of what Polly said, a person needs to be protected from memory.

"I didn't work as many miracles as they say Polly Shine did. But I did all right. Polly trained me real good."

"But you still missing her," Violet said.

"Missing who?"

"Polly Shine. Is that why you crying?"

Gran Gran reached up and touched her face. She had found herself doing this quite often since Violet's arrival, crying without realizing it, as if something inside was trying to free itself, like when Polly would place the flat of her hand against Gran Gran's chest.

But this had to stop, as well.

The girl was getting better and she would soon be moving on. One day they would open a suitcase. They would begin to pull out the girl's stories, one by one. She would remember an uncle she loved. Then they would come across an address and that would be that. Gran Gran would go back to days of nothing. Being needed would just be a thing to miss. The girl would be another.

"I plum run out of stories, Violet."

"Ain't no more faces?" Violet asked, clearly disappointed.

"We done took ever last one off the wall." Then Gran Gran said carefully, "Maybe it's time we heard some of your stories. You got a story to tell?"

Violet smiled and nodded. "But first you got to show me how," Violet said.

"Show you what?"

"How to make the faces, so I can tell you a story."

"You mean you want to copy a mask after somebody?" Gran Gran asked.

"But I can't tell who. It's a surprise. For you."

At first Gran Gran resisted. It would mean hiking down to the clay bank where she and Polly used to go together, then Gran Gran alone.

She told Violet she was too old and tired.

Of course there was a time she wouldn't think a thing of walking twenty miles or getting on her mule and riding all over the county on the road and off, delivering and tending. She owned the countryside back then. But nowadays, the old woman hardly ever left her kitchen. The Choctaw twins with their mules and wagon called on her regular and took her lists of dwindling needs.

And besides, a trip to that stretch of the creek would mean going near Shinetown.

"Maybe you can draw it for me," Gran Gran suggested.

But the girl insisted. It had to be like Gran Gran's. "You told me you'd teach me how, Gran Gran," she begged. "Like Mother Polly did you."

Yes, Polly would go. The girl had found a thread, a way back, and in the end, Polly would never refuse the journey.

As they made their way across the damp field, the girl carried the empty molasses can and Gran Gran stabbed the ground with her cane, ever wary of snakes and strangers. The old woman resisted the urge to grasp Violet by the hand and place palm against palm, beating heart against beating heart. The gesture might be a comfort to Gran Gran, but it would greatly disturb Violet. She wasn't ready yet. At least Gran Gran had been right about that much. It would be the last thing to heal. Violet's hands were where her darkness had finally settled. It would empty soon enough.

The walk was longer than it had to be. Cutting through Shinetown would have been quicker, but that was a place the old woman swore she would never set foot again. What used to be the old slave quarters had been fixed up, several of the cabins now occupied by descendants of house slaves who had never left the plantation. As far as Gran Gran was concerned, the place was haunted. Ghosts of the Old Ones, trapped in the eyes of strangers, inhabited the settlement now.

Gran Gran would circle through hell and back to avoid those folks. It was their soul-sick eyes she dreaded.

Of course there once was a time when she

was recognized and loved by everyone who lived there. They all needed her. Said they couldn't do without her. They said she had the sight. A few old heads compared her to somebody called Polly Shine, a long-ago miracle-working woman they swore had really lived, once upon a time.

The younger ones listened respectfully but didn't believe in all that old-time foolishness. Gran Gran didn't notice the contempt in their eyes, didn't notice how embarrassed they were by anything that reminded them that they came from slaves.

When they grew up and had families of their own, they fell out of the habit of sending for the old woman. They bought the new patent medicines and listened to the educated folks who warned of the old woman's unsanitary ways. Mothers became wary of her slave-time birthing methods. Preachers called her out from the pulpit, claiming she was using root magic on people. She was not defended. Everybody had heard of her, but there was no one who knew her.

Her days eventually became as empty as her massive hands, as if time had been nothing but a fistful of sand. There was seldom any sleep, and when there was, there were no dreams. She would walk the old plantation yard day and night, down past the stump of the ancient live oak where she had once played marbles, along the footpath that ran by the ruins of Polly's old hospital, and then off into the woods, searching for something that had gone missing but whose name she could not remember.

Once, while trudging down the track, she had been startled by something she saw in a child's face: eyes belonging to an ancient time. Some grandfather or great-grandmother of the child looked right into her, but she couldn't name who it was. She had fled back to her hearth, out of breath, her panicked heart racing in her chest, trying to remember who it was peering at her across the ages. She recited the old names like a chant — "Lizzie, Sylvie, Silas, Chester, Pomp . . ." — trying to picture each one in her mind, asking them, "Is it you?" Those eyes stalked her for days.

She had returned to the place by the creek where she and Polly had scooped clay, and hauled basketfuls back to the kitchen. She spent weeks molding the clay, recalling the old faces with her fingers. She fired them and painted the eyes and skin and replicated the hair with moss and string and cotton, coaxing the dead to reveal their secrets.

What was it they wanted? What was it she was supposed to remember? But the answer never came. Gran Gran refused to tell Violet a story with such an ending.

The old woman and the girl arrived at the clay bank without coming across a soul from Shinetown. Tired from the walk, Gran Gran found a log on which to sit and issue directions while Violet did the back-work, stooping and digging, filling the bucket with wet clay.

"Did Aunt Sylvie miss Father Silas?" she asked, as she labored with the big soup-spoon.

"Who?"

"Father Silas."

"I never called him that. You must be thinking of Mother Polly. I told you how everybody picked up on saying that. But they called Silas 'Old Silas.' "

"But he didn't like it," Violet said expertly as she tapped a spoonful of yellow clay into the bucket. "He wanted to be called Father."

Gran Gran laughed. "I reckon you getting healthy enough to make up your own story, then."

"How come Aunt Sylvie didn't go with him?" Violet asked.

"Sylvie said he tried to talk her into going, spent two days begging, but she wouldn't leave the kitchen. Funny, she hated the mistress, but she sure loved her kitchen."

Gran Gran smiled, understanding now. "I guess Sylvie thought that's where she *beee-longed,* like Polly would say. After Freedom, everybody all of a sudden had to decide where they belonged. Nobody to tell them no more. Wasn't easy for some of us." She smiled sadly. "Some of us picked wrong, I reckon."

As the morning passed and the easy back-and-forth between Violet and Gran Gran continued, the woman found herself unaccountably content. The rhythm was familiar, an old woman overseeing a young girl's work, the fluid intimacy earned between teacher and student. It was comforting, she thought, like the unconscious ticking of the head to the cadence of a secret verse.

So when Violet asked Gran Gran if they could walk through Shinetown on the way back, for the first time in years the idea did not bring up the dread that had kept the old woman away.

"Why do you want to see Shinetown?" she asked Violet.

"We can see if Chester is home," she said.

Gran Gran laughed. "Violet, Chester is long dead."

"Oh," the girl said, like she was sad to hear

the news. Violet considered this and then ran her hand over her yellow head scarf. She turned toward the rise where the slave graveyard lay hidden in overgrowth, frowned, and then scraped another spoonful of clay. Gran Gran could tell the girl was still struggling with the idea.

"Chester up in that graveyard?" Violet asked after a short while.

"Yes, I put him there myself. Aunt Sylvie, too. She was the last."

"All those people . . . up there," she said, casting her gaze in the direction of the old burying ground again, "they in boxes like my momma, ain't they?"

"Some of them got boxes." Gran Gran fought hard not to take the reins, letting the girl take this at her own pace.

"Some ain't?"

"No, some ain't," Gran Gran answered truthfully, now thinking of how Master Ben had tossed Rubina in a hole like a dog. "Don't even know if my momma got one or not. But your momma does for sure."

Violet nodded and looked up to catch Gran Gran's eye. "I know," the girl said. "I reckon I seen it. My daddy's, too."

Not a minute later the girl was chattering away again, as if they had not just had their first conversation about her mother. Gran

Gran was once more struck by how a person goes about healing themselves, if you let them. Polly had preached it over and over, but when it happened, it always struck Gran Gran as curious that more magic wasn't involved.

When the bucket was full and they were ready to depart, Gran Gran was surprised to find herself looking forward to walking through the settlement. She would not be alone this time. She would be with Violet.

The first houses came into view, but still the old dread did not raise its head. Gran Gran kept right on walking and talking with the girl, lulled by the ease she was feeling with Violet, bound by the stories they now shared.

For the first time in many years, Gran Gran stepped onto the lane. She knew that people were beginning to notice, coming out to their porches to watch, but being with the girl, the old woman didn't feel their stares.

The girl became more animated. She began asking questions about who lived in each house, pointing this way and that, looking shamelessly into the perplexed faces surrounding them. She asked how each one was kin to the characters in the old lady's stories. She made Gran Gran recite entire family trees.

As they cut between two cabins to return to the mansion, a pinch-faced boy standing on the porch, watching them pass, called out, "Look, Momma. It's that old witch."

From behind her, Gran Gran heard the sharp slap of the woman's hand against the child's face, and then words of indignation hurled at the wailing boy. "You leave her alone, you hear? She's crazy!"

Gran Gran stopped walking and turned back to look. The woman and her pinch-faced son had disappeared into their house.

"Who they meaning, Gran Gran?" Violet asked. "Who's crazy?"

"Me," the old woman answered flatly. "They meaning me. I'm the one they calling crazy."

The blood rushed to Gran Gran's face and she picked up her pace, not answering any more of the girl's questions.

"Hush now," Gran Gran said, no longer understanding Violet's words. "We got to get back. We been out too long already."

Maybe she wasn't crazy, but she had been an old fool. Tricking herself into thinking for a moment that Violet was hers to raise up, to train in the old ways, as Polly had done her. She wasn't Polly, and Violet wasn't her apprentice. Polly was dead and gone and Gran Gran would soon follow. All of it would be forgotten. She would be the last.

Ahead Gran Gran gazed at the mansion. The master said it had taken six years, a hundred and fifty slaves, a Philadelphia architect, and a genius of a water-shifter to build it high and dry.

But now it appeared to Gran Gran like one of those monstrous beasts out of Revelations, lowering itself for its last drink of fetid water. For a century the creek had eaten its way up to the doorstep, long ago swallowing the front gardens and washing out the winding drive where those wealthy planters and their well-bred ladies had stepped from fancy carriages onto the graveled surface.

She knew the creek would never stop searching for its old bed, gnawing its way farther and farther into the rotting mansion, until it finally reclaimed the entire foundation.

Even now, as she neared the house, it seemed to tilt a little more toward the hungry current.

CHAPTER 51

Back in the kitchen, Violet sat quietly at the eating table working her clay while Gran Gran watched from her rocker by the stove. She could tell the girl was vigorously pushing her way back into the world. When she had healed, she would leave.

Tired beyond relief, Gran Gran headed out of the house and into the brush, driven in the direction of an old half-standing shack.

She found herself beside the broken chimney, in the same place she had stood so many years ago when she had last glimpsed Polly's loose-limbed body before it disappeared into the dense, wet growth.

The sun had dropped well behind the tree line and for a moment the curtain of twilight that separated present from past was flung back.

She was a girl again, not much older than Violet. The choice had yet to be made.

There was still time to call out, to rush through the door, crash into the bramble on nimble, youthful legs, and catch up to Polly, grabbing hold of her leathery hand, taking in the heat and her strength, feeling again that solitary pulse where their palms embraced.

Yes, there had been that one moment when she stood there watching, her breath locked in her lungs, the muscles in her legs tensed to run. There had still been time, even as the sounds of Polly's steps and the sweep of her body against the leaves grew fainter.

If Polly had but turned and looked at her. The girl had waited in that spot, listening, watching, long after Polly disappeared through trees. Then as now there was only the sound of water dripping from clean wet leaves as a slight breeze stirred the branches.

"You said you would remember me. But you forgot like the others. Everybody done forgot. There ain't no threads stitching us together. You left me here by myself. You should have told me! I would have gone."

The old woman watched the sky grow dark. Then finally answered Violet's question. "Yes," she said barely louder than a breath, "I miss you bad, Polly. I want you to turn your face to me." She closed her eyes and imagined her words being taken by the breeze.

CHAPTER 52

When Gran Gran at last returned to the kitchen, the room had gone dark. "Violet?" she called, but there was no response. She shouldn't have left her for so long. "Violet," she called, her voice panicked, "where are you?"

Gran Gran reached for the lantern next to the door and almost tripped on the suitcase at her feet. It was lying open. Violet must have pulled it out.

The fear notched tighter around her chest. She raised the lantern and saw that the girl was still at the table. Her head was down, resting on the tabletop.

Gran Gran began to breathe again, her heart still racing.

The yellow scarf was hung carefully on the back of a kitchen chair. In front of the girl was a molded face, but nobody Gran Gran recognized. Tomorrow she would show the girl how to do the eyes and shape the features with the flat of a knife and trowel.

Spread about Violet's head on the table were dozens of photographs. That's what she had taken from the suitcase, probably looking for faces to copy.

Gran Gran reached for the framed photograph she had already seen, the one taken at Lucy's wedding. She tried to remember the day Lucy came seeking her help.

She was so beautiful and again Gran Gran noticed the resemblance to Violet. The almond-shaped eyes. The small mouth. If the man in uniform was Violet's father, it made sense. He was much darker than Lucy. Again, she wondered, who is it Lucy favors? It wouldn't come to her.

As she looked at the photograph, for the first time she drew her eyes to the background, what appeared to be the front of a church. There was a pulpit behind the couple, and on the wall hung three paintings in elaborate frames. It took a moment, but holding the picture up real close, she recognized the middle one as Jesus praying in Gethsemane.

"They got him painted as a colored man!" Gran Gran gasped. She had never seen such before and began to chuckle to herself, wishing to visit a church like that.

Her eyes strained at the portrait on the left, wondering who else they might have claimed as one of their own. But this man was very dark, and very, very old. A black beardless Moses, maybe?

"Hmm," she mused. "If I didn't know any better, I'd say that looks like Old Silas!" She shook her head. "I reckon I've lived long enough to say most of us old folks look pretty much alike."

Violet yawned and then lifted her head from the table. Rubbing her eyes, she said, "You seen what I done?" Then she pointed to the face. "Want to guess who it is?"

Gran Gran studied the face, but couldn't say it looked like anyone in particular.

"I'll tell you. It's Charity. You didn't have her up on your wall. I'm making her for you."

"Charity?" Gran Gran asked. "Charity who?"

"You know! Charity and Barnabas, who went off with Mother Polly."

"Charity," Gran Gran said again. "How you know what Charity looks like?"

Violet picked up a tintype from where her head had been resting earlier. "See?" she said holding it up. It was of an old woman sitting in a chair with a man standing beside her, one hand placed firmly on her shoulder.

She was old, yes, but merciful heavens, it very well could be Charity! And the man standing over her, was that Barnabas, the carpenter?

She looked at the unfinished piece of clay but saw no resemblance. The resemblance was in the girl herself.

Gran Gran grew unsteady on her feet, not knowing if she wanted to stay, sit, or run.

She held the lantern over the table and il-luminated the photographs. Families gathered in the churchyard at dinners on the ground. A brick bank building. In front were rich-looking colored men wearing suits and high-collar shirts. A photograph of a few dozen youngsters sitting on schoolhouse steps flanked by several prim-looking women — everyone colored. A city hall, and lined up in two rows for the photographer, elegant-looking colored men and women. She had heard of towns like these. Colored towns. Out West.

"But I know these people," she said. "I see somebody in every face."

She looked back at the wedding portrait she still held in her hand. When she went to examine the third portrait, on the far right, the old woman's hand began to shake.

"No," she gasped. "That can't be."

The portrait was partially obscured by the

shadow of the couple, but Gran Gran could distinctly make out the round disks that fell from the woman's wrapped scarf onto her forehead.

"No," she said again, and shook her head, refusing to believe. "My Lord, Polly, is that really you?"

"Mother Polly," Violet said. "And Father Silas."

"These pictures . . ." Gran Gran stammered. "All these pictures. This town and all these colored —"

"Where my momma come from. I ain't never been. She showed me the pictures at night and told me the stories. Like you done with the faces." She laughed. "Y'all tell some of the same stories."

"Who are you?" Gran Gran asked, dazed now.

"I'm Violet," the girl answered, suddenly concerned. "You know who I am. Don't you remember?"

"What game you pulling on me?" Gran Gran now hovered over the girl, her voice frantic. "You taking me for a fool?"

"No, ma'am. I . . . don't know."

Gran Gran held the lantern to the girl's face. The light flickered in her moistening eyes. "You lying!"

But her eyes weren't lying. The mournful

hazel eyes. Those were Charity's eyes. The small troubled mouth. It was Charity, and with her name came snatches of memory . . . Charity, the weaver . . . never able to have a child . . . the apple fell green from the tree . . . until Polly . . .

"I ain't lying!" Violet cried. She pulled away from Gran Gran's panicked anger, and then shielded her hands behind her back. "Why you so mad with me?" she whimpered. "I wanted to surprise you is all!"

Gran Gran struggled to catch her breath. She could see as clear as crystal that day in the hospital. She remembered the words Polly had spoken to Charity. "Your sons and daughters, your blood will lead the people home." And then Polly asking Granada to put her hand on Charity's belly. "What lies under your hand is all of us, Granada. It's where we are going. This child comes from the place where the river is born."

"You're Charity's blood," the old woman said in barely a whisper.

The kitchen had become as close as a coffin. From the masks and photographs on the table, one face broke through the darkness like a bubble rising in water, glowing in its own light, the disks gleaming, like the first day she had seen her.

"No," Gran Gran muttered, shaking her

head against the thought. It couldn't be.

Gran Gran stepped back from the host of faces. She eyed the girl again.

"Polly send you?" Gran Gran asked, her voice raspy. "What she want from me?"

The girl looked at the woman. "I don't know Mother Polly. She's dead and buried . . . next to that church." Violet motioned with her head to the framed photograph the old woman still held.

Gran Gran shut her eyes. "No! This ain't nothing but lies."

The old woman was terrifying the girl and she knew it. She had to get away from Violet. She fled to the porch, stumbling, not wanting to see or hear. Tears brimmed behind her lids, and her breath was short, strangled, like a steel band was tightening around her chest.

A vision of Polly's little town blazed in her inner eye. Neat white cottages with roses and sunflowers and vegetable gardens out back. Neighbors calling to one another over fences. Children in the streets. So much life! In a great sweep of vision she saw them laughing and crying in each other's arms; and marrying and bearing children and comforting one another and growing old together; grieving and burying one another and then beginning again.

519

She let go a great shuddering sob. "Why did you leave me?" Gran Gran covered her eyes with a trembling hand.

The chill night wind carried the sounds of her plea over the empty yard and across the quarter, but no one lit their lanterns to see what ancient heart was breaking. Her ragged cry drifted over the graveyards that hugged tight their silent dead and fluttered through a primeval forest, taking the last leaves of the hardwoods and scattering them over the souls that once had been rooted there. It rippled the surface of the yellow-mud creek, below which lay drowned a secret name that had not been called in seventy years.

The old woman at last opened her eyes and dared to look across the darkened yard. Staring back at her were hundreds of faces, women, men, children, and at once she knew each one of them, their names and their fears and their hopes. The night was full of shining eyes, unblinking, looking up at her, wanting.

There was a great uprushing in her throat and she cried aloud, "You were my people!"

Gran Gran began to quake. It was not just skin and muscle, but something had set her bones to trembling, as if the earth had shuddered. Her cane went rattling down the steps and Gran Gran, unable to bear the weight any longer, crumpled to the porch floor.

She was not aware of how much time had passed before she lifted her head to the velvet star-filled sky. Behind her she heard the careful footsteps, and then felt a hand, small and chilled, take her own. The grasp was tentative but then gathered strength as it warmed like an oven brick, until the girl's grip was as sure and strong as any the old woman could remember, the heat soothing her ancient sorrow like a salve.

The revelation was neither blinding nor thunderous.

Polly Shine had remembered.

CHAPTER 53

A winter's twilight found them skirting the puddles and then stepping carefully down a disused path that cut into the overgrowth beyond the house. Picking their way through briars and creeper vines, they passed the falling-down chimney of the old hospital, destroyed at the turn of the century by fire during a lightning storm, and from there proceeded deep into a dark skirt of woods.

It was a path seldom used because it led only to the old slave cemetery, forgotten by most and unrecognized by anyone else who happened to stumble upon it. It was sheltered by hardwoods and carpeted by bramble, underneath which lay the old rotting wooden crosses, rough-hewn stones with scrawl long faded, toppled by the relentless spread of roots.

By the time they arrived, the old woman's breathing was labored and her step halting. She stood silent for a moment among the graves to catch her breath. In one hand she gripped her cane, in the other she held a lantern, as yet unlit. Over her shoulder hung the leather hunting pouch given to her by a pretty, blue-eyed boy, never grown, and now long dead, buried with his mother over the rise. While Gran Gran waited for her strength to return, she listened to the graves, as if they might remember her. The girl, who toted the cross, listened, too.

But all the graves were silent. Gran Gran heard only the rush of her own breath. It was coming easier now, calmed by the soothing night sounds of the forest. "You and me gone have to get out here one day and clean this mess up. First warm day in spring maybe."

The girl nodded. "They's a lot of them."

"It's a sight," Gran Gran said, "but we got time."

It would have to be later. Today Gran Gran and Violet had other business in the cemetery.

The old woman and the girl found their way to the far side of the ridge to a muddy gash of earth that had not had time to heal over. Gran Gran searched the bramble for signs of another grave, dug before Freedom. Somewhere under the creeping vines was a rusted cast-iron plowshare that Lizzie had cradled through the woods and placed where Rubina's head rested, disobeying the master's decree to leave her grave unmarked. It must have been the last thing she did before taking off through the woods to catch up with Polly and Silas.

Gran Gran set the lantern by the more recent grave and then nodded to Violet, who positioned the cross at the head of her mother's grave. As the girl steadied the cross, Gran Gran pounded it into the ground with a hammer retrieved from her pouch.

The two stood silent over Lucy's newly marked grave mound for quite a while, Gran Gran remembering the woman as best she could.

"Polly said a soul needed to be grieved out of the world proper to make sure they joined the Old Ones," Gran Gran said. "If you don't give them their respect, they might wander until the Second Coming. That means a string of generous words, a grave song, and some praying."

She had told all this earlier to Violet as they planned the ceremony, but it bore repeating.

Gran Gran spoke serious and slow. "Lucy, me and your girl here, Violet, are standing for you today. We are here to give you a marker for your grave, so you can be re-membered. And we come to do what we can to grieve you into heaven."

She paused for a moment as the chirring sounds of dusk rose around her and then looked down at the girl, who stared pensively at the grave. "Any words you want to say to your momma?"

Violet breathed in deep and then said what she had rehearsed. "Momma, I'm sorry I didn't hold your hand when you was dying. I love you. I hope you are happy in heaven with Jesus."

Gran Gran nodded. "Those are some fine words," she said.

Speaking to the grave once more, the old woman said, "I ain't much for singing these days, but I'll sure give you what I got left."

In a weak voice, quaking with age, she sang what she could remember of the words she had overheard Polly sing so long ago over Rubina's grave:

In the beginning is the home where I
    come from.
In the beginning is the home where I'm
    going.
In the beginning, oh Lord, You created
    Your children
And told them to come home by and by.

She sang low and gentle, swaying to the rhythm.

The girl held the woman's arm, steadying her as she knelt down to the grave. Gran Gran opened her pouch and placed some of Lucy's personal possessions on the grave dirt. A tube of lipstick, a compact mirror, a sewing needle and thread, a necklace of glass beads, a butterfly brooch of rhinestones, all things Violet had chosen.

Next she took the bottle from which the woman had drunk the potion, placed it on the grave, and shattered it with the hammer. She buried the pieces in the dirt.

She sang again, her voice stronger this time:

In the beginning is the home we all are
    coming from.
In the beginning is the home we all are
    going to.
Oh, Lord, take this child by the hand,
Yes, Lord, see Your children home by and
    by.

The last word rose toward the bare branches and seemed to hover for a moment in the chill air, before finally fading away into a darkening sky.

Gran Gran dropped her head and prayed.

"Lord, we all done left this poor girl alone and I'm sorry for it. She was Your precious daughter and she must have been about as alone as a person can be to do what she done. I don't know why she done it. But I reckon only You and her know the business of it. Please forgive her if she's needing forgiveness and let her join You in Glory."

With Violet's help, Gran Gran raised herself to her feet and brushed the dirt off her hands. She looked down upon the grave.

"And Lucy," she continued, "I want you to forgive me for any way I let you down. For not seeing what I should have seen. And this girl Violet sure loves you and she's going do right by you in the world and ain't never going to forget you. You going to be remembered, I promise you that. We both going to see to it."

Violet was weeping now. She held the lantern while the old woman lifted the globe and lit it. The girl placed the lantern on the head of her mother's grave, so that the shadow of the crossed boards loomed large over the mound.

"Now, by the light of our remembering," Gran Gran pronounced, "find your way home, Lucy."

The old woman began singing the grave song again, and now the words were infused

527

with the wistful gladness of crossing over rather than the grief of dying.

Gran Gran reached down and opened her hand. The girl laid hers across the old leathery palm. Gran Gran could feel the warming pulse in the place where they touched, the single beat of a heart.

The woods were dark and the path disappeared beyond the light cast by the lantern. But Gran Gran knew the way home. With her memory and the girl's sight, they would do fine.

They departed the grave, both of them singing. The lantern still burned, throwing its light in their path. With Gran Gran stabbing the ground before them with her cane, they led each other out of the woods.

EPILOGUE

Today the living will surely outpopulate the dead. It is sociable weather, the kind that naturally draws people together. The dawn broke with the threat of rain, but it cleared off nicely. Now a procession of low billowy clouds wafts through the mid-August sky, mercifully capturing and holding the sun long enough to provide a steady succession of shady reprieves.

Folks are still climbing the ridge to the old burying grounds, leaving behind their mules and wagons and the occasional automobile strewn about the old plantation yard below. Women in their Sunday-best dresses kneel at gravesides pulling weeds, while their men carefully situate newly chiseled slabs of concrete or brush on new coats of whitewash to wooden crosses, sweat darkening the shoulders of their freshly boiled white shirts.

On the back side of the ridge a chorus of

cheers rises up as two men set the last section of the low border fence. After a century, the burying place is now completely ringed in iron. The biggest portion of the fence is made up of the elaborate grillwork that had once adorned the mansion's galleries, but the supply ran out and the back side was left unfinished. Earlier in the day, the great-grandson of Big Dante showed up with a truckload of rusted bedsteads. The fence will be so heavily swathed with honeysuckle by next Cemetery Day no one will be able to detect the slightest inconsistency in style.

As the day progresses, the grounds begin to take on the look of an overplanted garden. Syrup buckets, rusted enamel dishpans, and coffee cans brimming with plants and flowers of every imaginable color and fragrance are still being placed on the grave mounds. Overpowering the senses is the smell of lemon lilies mingling with fried chicken.

The old pine table was hauled up from the mansion's kitchen and positioned in a shady grove of oaks and sweet gum. It is already laden with tubs of greens and ham hocks and potato salad, platters of every kind of meat, plates of corn bread and biscuits, pies and cakes and cobblers and puddings, everything covered with dish towels. Makeshift tables built by laying planks across stumps await the overflow. Women stand guard, shooing off the gathering storm of flies and hungry children with sharp flicks of their starched aprons.

Beyond the tables and deeper in the shade, the old ones sit in straight-backed chairs and favorite rockers toted up from the quarter, or hauled halfway across the county in the back of a mule-drawn wagon or pickup truck. The ground before them is a field of patterned quilts on which lie a small army of babies either drowsing or hypnotized by the pretty bits of silk and satin hanging from the branches of the shade tree, their gauzy edges tinged by fire, fluttering in the breeze like candied cobwebs.

A flock of giggling children race by, chased by a boy with a handful of ice stolen from beneath the burlap sacks. As they pass, a flurry of shushes and stern warnings not to trample across the graves "lest the devil burn your feet!" rise from among the grownups. The oldest voice breaks above the rest.

"Violet!" she fusses from her rocker. "Gather up all these little chicks, you hear? Get them to mind you."

The slight girl with color-shifting eyes commences to corral the host of children.

When she gets them quiet, she herds them about the graveyard like a master shepherd.

Her voice is as solemn as any preacher's. "Now this is where Aunt Sylvie is buried. She made biscuits and dressed up Gran Gran when she was only a little girl."

The children's heads turn in unison to the old woman. With open mouths and wide eyes, they study the crooked lady in the rocking chair, as if trying to imagine such an ancient creature ever being a girl.

"Father Silas was her husband," Violet continued, "but she stayed behind because she didn't want to leave her kitchen. He's the one who led the people to Kansas and was their first preacher and mayor both. He lived to be a hundred and three!"

Violet draws their attention with the wave of her hand to the silk tatters in the tree. "Them is the *very* dresses Gran Gran wore!" she exclaims in a voice that says she is as astonished as anybody to find them there, as if she hadn't hung the scraps with her own two hands, somehow knowing that the sight would not only quiet the babies but charm the children. "That's all that was left after the mistress set that terrible fire."

A young woman big with child pauses at Gran Gran's rocker. "Your girl sure got a way with the young ones. I reckon she could dose them with castor oil and they would say, 'Thank you for the candy.' "

Gran Gran nods, but she knows Violet has a way with more than just children. Everyone here sees something in Violet, though they can't name it yet. Even now as the girl leads the reverential procession from grave to grave, all eyes follow her, ears cock in her direction. The old ones raise up their chins and the chaws of tobacco are momentarily stilled in their cheeks.

It has been this way since that day Violet first stole off from Gran Gran and wandered down into Shinetown, bubbling with the stories she collected from her mother and from Gran Gran, quilting together the history of a scattered people.

She showed up at the doors of complete strangers, unembarrassed, twining threads of memory into rope, drawing folks one by one to the burying ground to see the graves of those long dead yet somehow familiar. Soon word of the stories spread across the county. Folk took trips to Kansas to visit. Today there is not a grave that goes unclaimed on Cemetery Day.

Violet's voice seems to ride the cooling breeze as she travels from grave to grave, counting down ancestors. "This is my mother," the girl says, stopping at Lucy's grave. "Her momma was my Granny Cindy and her momma was Jolydia." She pauses, letting that sink in. "And Jolydia was Charity the weaver's *miracle* baby, saved by Polly Shine herself."

The children murmur their amazement, whispering Polly Shine's name like a charm, as if the old woman might appear before them at any moment.

"Don't need me to tell any history," Gran Gran laughs. "The girl's doing fine."

After Gran Gran rocks herself up from her chair, a sudden wooziness sets her to tottering. The pregnant woman reaches out, offering to steady the old woman. At first she waves off the assistance, but then reconsiders, taking hold of the woman's arm.

Upon seeing Gran Gran being guided to the head of the old kitchen table, folks begin to draw near from all parts of the graveyard, calling out to one another, "It's time! Gran Gran getting ready to do the history!"

As they gather to hear the old woman tell once more the story of Polly Shine, Gran Gran casts her gaze over the spectacle. Hundreds of faces, descended from a time and a place that only she could remember. She finds their eyes and whispers the names of those who have come before, and the multitude seems to grow, coursing toward her like a great flood.

She watches as the children elbow their way confidently through the crowd, surging up to the very front. The proud pretty girls: hair greased and plaited, twirling their starched skirts washed bright in rainwater, their eyes fresh and eager, expecting magic around every corner.

The bold-blooded boys: every shade of God under the sun, self-assured yet with faces fixed in innocent wonder. The Lord could show Himself at any second and they would see Him first, for He was already in their eyes.

They all press closer, each trying to stand near enough to touch the old woman, to feel her leathery hands, to know firsthand the tough-skinned fabric of eternity.

And then she begins. "They tell me my momma's name was Ella."

ACKNOWLEDGMENTS

Writing is not, as I once believed, a solitary effort. I relied on a community of experts to write this book. The collaborators who came to my aid as *The Healing* took shape were gracious, generous, and patient; and there are several I'd like to acknowledge by name.

Victoria E. Bynum, Ph.D., Professor Distinguished Emerita at Texas State University, author of *The Long Shadow of the Civil War: Southern Dissent and Its Legacies,* offered rare insight into the role gender played in the antebellum South.

Joanne Jones-Rizzi, a developer of the highly acclaimed "Race: Are We So Different?," a national traveling exhibit sponsored by the American Anthropological Association, helped me to understand the artificiality of race and to see it as a social rather than a biological or genetic construct.

Dawn L. Martin, M.D., a pediatrician at the Hennepin County Medical Center, and her husband, Dr. Gregory T. Lehman, an internist at the Park Nicollet Medical Center, made themselves available to put into layman's terms the medical science behind the conundrums that stalled my narrative.

Katherine E. Murray, M.D., at the University of Minnesota, is a developmental-behavioral pediatrician who taught me about the psychological impact of trauma on young children. Elise Sanders, a psychoanalyst and president of the Minnesota Psychoanalytic Society, was invaluable in validating for me the psychological and spiritual roles a healer can play.

Alice Swan, dean of the Department of Nursing at the College of St. Catherine, St. Paul, Minnesota, made available her nurse teacher/practitioners, including specialists in midwifery, to read and respond to a draft of the book.

My dear friend Margaret Block from Cleveland, Mississippi, is a veteran civil rights worker who as a teenager in the sixties escaped the Klan by hiding in a coffin and being carried across the county line in a hearse. Her brother was the well-known activist Sam Block. Margaret drove me down dirt tracks, levee roads, and through cypress swamps to show me old sharecropper cabins and ancient slave quarters, and she introduced me to Mound Bayou, a Mississippi town built, occupied, and run by the ex-slaves of Jefferson Davis, all while teaching me the Freedom songs she sang with Fannie Lou Hamer during the "Movement." She gave me a view of the Mississippi Delta that I could not have imagined on my own.

The late Mrs. Willie Turner, midwife of Midnight, Mississippi, served as a living, breathing, and exemplary model of a healer. After spending two hours with her one summer afternoon in 2002, I often drew from Mrs. Turner's spirit, her compassion, and the fierce love and pride she had for her calling. She obviously adored "her babies," all 2,063 of them, and they all adored her, still calling her "Mother" until her death at ninety-nine in 2010.

Two of my teachers were researchers whom I have never met but whose work I referred to so often that I feel they are old friends.

One is Sharla Fett, who wrote the paradigm-shifting book *Working Cures: Healing, Health, and Power on Southern Slave Plantations* and who introduced me to the subversive role midwives and healers played during slavery.

The other is Todd Savitt. His two works, *Medicine and Slavery: The Diseases and Health Care of Blacks in Antebellum Virginia* and *Race & Medicine in Nineteenth- and Early-Twentieth-Century America* provided a lens through which to compare and contrast the way whites and blacks understood, responded to, and treated disease.

The treasure trove of documents and recordings made available by the folks at the University of Southern Mississippi's Center for Oral History and Cultural Heritage and by the Delta State University's Capps Archives was indispensable, as was their enthusiasm for my project.

I relied extensively on the words of former slaves themselves, as recorded in the WPA Slave Narratives, the Fisk Collection of Slave Narratives, and oral histories of midwives from the twentieth century, including Onnie Lee Logan in her book *Motherwit, An Alabama Midwife's Story* and Margaret Charles Smith, whose life is recounted in *Listen to Me Good: The Story of an Alabama Midwife.*

I'm blessed to know a number of very fine authors who also excel at editing. I am greatly indebted to the time they invested as well as to the tact they displayed in giving feedback to a writer with a very thin skin. They include my partner, Jim Kuether, C.M. Harris, Mary Gardner, Lindsay Nielsen, Pam Joern, Lee Galda, and Christopher Davis. (Oh, yes, at the moment I am writing these words, my eighty-three-year-old mom is in the next room checking the final draft for typos, just as she did when I was in the third grade. Luckily, some things never change.)

I also want to acknowledge my African American readers who had the task of letting me know whenever they could tell a white man was writing the book. They were patient with my naivety. Thanks to Maye Brooks and her book club and to Joanne Jones-Rizzi of the Minnesota Science Museum, and to my friend Merthlyn Collins.

I'm a committed introvert who needs to immerse himself in the story, with no distraction for extended periods of time, in order to be productive. Over the course of writing this book I have been fortunate to have several "cabin fairies" in my life. Thank you to the Martin-Lehmans, the McGray-Forsyths, and to Rickie and John Ressler for loaning out your lovely vacation homes so that I could spend extended periods writing in the woods and on the seashore, listening to "the beasts and the fowls of the air."

My agent, Marly Rusoff, and her partner, Michael Radulescu, are a pair of angels dropped to earth. For years I had admired their successes from afar but never believed that I could be fortunate enough to have them champion my work. When they said yes the route was short, quick, and painless to publisher Nan A. Talese and her editor, Ronit Feldman. These four have transformed my life.

And, finally, I want to thank all the Mississippi folks, black and white, who trusted me with your stories. For letting me onto your porches, into your kitchens, yards, and parlors; for showing me the old photographs, genealogies, and family Bibles; but, most of all, for letting me into your lives.

A NOTE TO THE READER

While my mother was giving birth to me in the little town of Laurel, Mississippi, Willie McGee, a black man, was being legally lynched only a few blocks away at the courthouse to the cheers of over a thousand white citizens. If you walked a bit north, you could spy the mansion a young Leontyne Price regularly helped her aunt clean, until the white lady of the house heard her sing and got her into Juilliard. And if you kept on walking to the other side of town, you might spy a respected businessman, Sam Bowers, the owner of Sambo's Amusement Company, closing up shop. He was only a few years away from becoming the Imperial Wizard of the KKK of *Mississippi Burning* fame and charged with planning one of the bloodiest atrocities of the civil rights era.

Home sweet home.

But I knew none of these things until I

was well into adulthood. Like most white citizens, I was isolated from the events and assumed they had nothing to do with me.

It shames me to admit that in the white-defined society in which I was raised, blacks were considered merely background. This was worse than physical segregation. This was psychological segregation. It wasn't that we were taught not to associate with blacks: close association was unavoidable. Instead, we were taught to see half the population not as individuals but as functionaries — maids, yardmen, etc.

I distinctly remember the first time I was taught a lesson in bigotry. I was about eight and sitting under a tree in our backyard on a hot summer day. Over in the next yard I spotted an elderly black man in a flannel shirt, raking straw.

"Why are you wearing that hot shirt?" I asked. "Ain't you burning up?"

He looked down at me and smiled. He explained that he wore the shirt because it made him sweat and when a breeze came up, it was like air conditioning.

As I mulled over the wisdom of his reply, his employer, an older white lady, approached us. Her name was Helen Callahan. I called her Miss Helen, not because she was unmarried, which she wasn't, but because older white women were not addressed using either Mrs. or their last names. When they advanced past some unspoken age you just knew to address them using Miss and their given name. It's part of the complex nomenclature of titling in the South.

As was typical of older southern women, Miss Helen felt obligated to shape every rough-edged boy within her purview into a southern gentleman. So besides teaching me various titles of respect, she told me to always say "yes, sir" and "no, ma'am," never to talk with my mouth full, and to keep my elbows off the table. I loved Miss Helen dearly. She was one of the gentlest and most refined women I ever came across. To make her proud was my most noble ambition.

"What y'all doing out here?" she asked sweetly, joining her yardman and me.

Minding my manners and wanting to make her proud, I said, "I'm just talking to Mister Joe."

Miss Helen knitted her brows and pursed her lips in a way that indicated I had been "unmannerly."

"No, Johnny," she said, "Joe's not a mister. Joe's a nigger."

You may be shocked when you read this. After all, the vernacular is distasteful, if not abhorrent, nowadays. But this was 1959 Mississippi. And when it happened, I felt somehow relieved. Suddenly so much in my world made sense. In that moment I understood why there were certain water fountains that I was not supposed to drink out of. Why blacks had to eat their food from the café out in the alley. Why the shacks in the colored town had no paint and the roads had no pavement. It all made perfect sense. No longer did these conditions seem arbitrary. I finally understood that it was about color, and Joe's color was "wrong" and mine was somehow "right."

"Now, one day, Joe will call *you* mister," Miss Helen went on, "but never the other way around."

She was gazing sweetly at Joe. Her words had not been harsh nor her tone unkind. There was no villainy in what she believed, only the Christian truth. It was obvious she cared for Joe.

And Joe was also smiling pleasantly, nodding his head in agreement.

This was the way it was supposed to be, I thought, and it was just fine with everybody. It was indeed a fine thing to be a white boy in Mississippi! The silence of an entire race was evidence of your superiority.

Fast-forward a few decades to an April

evening in 1988. I was living in Minnesota, on the more tolerant end of the Mississippi River. I had created a comfortable existence as a business consultant. I had come out as a gay man, a liberal, and an agnostic. I believed I had overcome all my prejudices and left my past behind.

That night PBS was running film clips from the civil rights movement in commemoration of the twentieth anniversary of Martin Luther King's assassination. I had watched these scenes on the evening news when I was growing up in Mississippi — blacks marching down the middle of Main Street in some hot and dusty nearby town. I could smell the thick, humid air, the sweat. The dust prickled my nose.

But this time, as an adult, I saw something I had not noticed before. Instead of focusing on the marchers, I noticed the white people who lined the streets, throwing rocks, jeering, waving Confederate flags. *My* people. And again I studied the marchers.

For the first time I saw the whole picture. This is not black history, I thought. This is *my* history! And I know nothing about it. These people, white *and* black, and especially the unspoken space between us, made me who I am. Every day as a white man I shape and am shaped by race.

I remembered Joe and his silence and it was clear to me that I owed Joe a tremendous debt. I still can't begin to fathom what his mandatory silence cost him that day, but I am beginning to understand how his invisibility was used to underwrite my sense of privilege and entitlement, to embellish my history. His dignity was the price extracted so that an eight-year-old child could feel superior.

I also became certain that I would never understand my own story until I discovered Joe's. He and I held the missing pieces to each other's narrative, and for our stories to be complete, one would need to include the other.

When I decided to write novels focusing on the racial divide, I got some good advice from a black friend. "Don't you dare write another *To Kill a Mockingbird*," he cautioned.

I was taken aback. I told him every "evolved" white person I knew loved that book.

"Exactly," he said. "Self-respecting black folks hate it. Whites get to feel sorry for the poor, ignorant, and powerless black man. And conveniently put the blame on the white southern cracker. I'd rather your book be about a black scoundrel, just as long as he's a full-blooded and complex human being. We don't need any more victims for you white folks to feel sorry for. I don't want my children to have to read one more book about a pitiful black man who needs saving by the white man."

I went back home to Mississippi. I sought out African Americans who could introduce me anew to myself through their stories. I did countless interviews. I read books, listened to oral histories, pored over slave narratives, spent hours in the cellars of county courthouses. I collected all the broken pieces, all the missing links that I could find.

When *The View from Delphi,* my first novel, was published by a small press, *Kirkus Reviews* wrote, "Odell, *an African American,* is the rare writer on race who allows for a range of responses — and for the possibility of change." (Italics mine.) I really hated to alert them to their mistake. To assume that I was a black man was the greatest compliment they could have paid me.

In this, my second novel, I wanted to delve even deeper into the shadowy world uneasily inhabited by both the black and white psyches. I specifically wanted to look at the black midwife. During my research I had interviewed several elderly ladies who had "caught" thousands of children in their communities. I learned that midwifing served spiritual and communal functions as much as a physical one. Midwives could trace their practices back through Jim Crow, through slavery, and all the way to Sierra Leone and Temne tribal practices.

Their occupational demise began in the 1950s when the white medical establishment orchestrated a campaign to discredit midwives in order to make way for government-funded public health services. In other words, when it became once again profitable for white men to touch black flesh, the midwives had to go. They were portrayed in medical journals and state legislatures as dirty, ignorant, and superstitious abortionists. When the medical establishment required that they be licensed, many were forced to "turn in their bags" because they could not read. A category of "nurse midwives" was created to work under the direct supervision of a doctor.

The midwives I spoke with were gracious, proud, and spiritual, saddened to have been barred from their calling and eager to have someone listen to *their* story — not the official white story that vilified them. After I discovered that the live-birth rates among these "uneducated" black women were higher than those of the white doctors who replaced them, I knew I needed to write their story.

Serendipitously, I discovered something about my own family history that fueled my desire to write.

My grandfather lived to be ninety-seven, but just before he died he called his estranged son, my father, to his bedside. "I think it's time I told you about your mother," Papa Johnson said. My dad was then in his seventies.

We had all been told that my dad's mother died of pneumonia in 1927, when my father was only an infant. But that wasn't the truth.

In the nursing home that morning Papa explained that when my father was six months old, his mother, Bessie, planned to take her child and run away with him. But then she found out she was pregnant again. She had sworn she would never have another child by my abusive grandfather, whom she had come to despise, and so she went to her stepmother, my great-grandmother, who happened to be a midwife. Big Sal performed an abortion on her daughter, from which Bessie contracted blood poisoning and died. My father was left motherless.

Big Sal went on to help raise my father, whose mother she had had a hand in killing. My father loved her dearly and never learned the truth until seventy years had passed.

I began to wonder, what could it have been like for my great-grandmother to have that child reach out for her, the same woman who was responsible for his mother's death?

And then there was a third element that intrigued me. Can stories about which we are not consciously aware still serve to shape our lives?

The fear of betrayal by the ones you love most, whether by death or deceit, was never talked about in my family, but it affected at least three generations of men. It is the genesis of our common unwillingness to be truly vulnerable before one another, especially those we love. It explains the high premium my family places on self-sufficiency, on never relying on others for help.

The repression of story can scar the soul.

But knowing our common story can heal. My father, my brothers, and I have learned to connect with an understanding and compassion that was not available to us before. We recognize ourselves in one another.

Through writing *The Healing* and by stitching together my own family history, I have discovered the truth in the old saying "Facts can explain us, but only story will save us."

If you want to destroy a people, destroy their story. If you want to empower a people, give them a story to share.

ABOUT THE AUTHOR

Jonathan Odell is the author of the acclaimed novel *The View from Delphi,* which deals with the struggle for equality in pre-civil rights Mississippi, his home state. His short stories and essays have appeared in numerous collections. He spent his business career as a leadership coach to Fortune 500 companies and currently resides in Minnesota.